Moonlight Man

Richard O. Benton

John,
Enjoy the adventure!

[signature]

STORYCRAFT PUBLISHING

Storycraft Publishing
P. O. Box 1647
Litchfield CT 06759

For information:
storycraft.publishing@gmail.com

Disclaimer
This is a work of fiction. Names, characters, places and
incidents are the products of the author's imagination or are
used fictitiously. Any resemblance to actual events, locales,
persons or groups, living or dead, is entirely coincidental.

ISBN: 978-0-9822424-0-7

This book is printed on acid free paper.
Printed in the United States of America

Acknowledgements

I would like to thank the following people for helping to move Moonlight Man forward. For being a critic extraordinaire not only for what was right, but also best, my friend Barclay Johnson, retired English teacher from the Taft School of Connecticut, whose abundant knowledge and owlish wisdom has been the cause of many edits and more than one rewrite.

For encouragement, Barb Francis, Dora Cox, Rob Pizzella, Louis Jacaruso, Amy Nicholson, Adrienne Barbe, Barbara Fincken, Wilma Hubbard, and Maletta Pfeiffer, all members of The Litchfield Writers Guild, which has been my sounding board for six wonderful years. I want to mention two others who offered encouragement, Blanche Geshwind and Bob Curtis, also members of the group until health issues intervened. I would also like to thank a fan of mine, Lorraine Stillman of Vancouver, Washington, once a childhood friend, and after we reconnected fifty years later via the Internet, a staunch supporter.

For reading the manuscript and commenting upon it to its betterment, Ann Moler, Eileen Mehr and Joseph Keeney. For constantly reminding me that there is life beyond these written pages and for striking a balance between my fiction and our reality, my vote goes to my wife Holly.

Preface

I began writing this book three months before 9-11. The terrorist group al-Qaeda, certainly best known, but only one of many, is still responsible for much of the world's unease, and if anything, today we are closer to the premise of this book than we were then. In other words, this dangerous world has become more dangerous.

Terrorism doesn't happen for no reason. It is the end product of repression and failed systems, which lead to rebellion. When rebellion goes underground and takes on a paramilitary character and lashes out surreptitiously to damage the thing that has caused its perceived damage and hurt, one outlet for revenge and redress is through terror. Terror bleeds away the confidence of a people and creates only two choices for those affected, flight or fight.

The people who run governments are interested in the status quo. Anything beyond that is downward. They hold the power. They must fight to preserve their positions. Its people are given two choices, accept the rightness of the government's position, or join the rebels. The middle ground is also the battleground; the place where complacency disappears and sides are chosen.

Rogue states sponsor terrorism, provide safe haven and allow insurgents to train and recruit within their national boundaries in their quest to infuse others with their ideology or simply to exercise power over others. So long as there are people, terrorism will be a feature of human existence. I have not yet seen a plan that will eliminate it and so we must live with it. Perhaps the human race will eventually grow beyond the need to inflict horror upon itself, but my guess is, we and our needs and desires are too diverse for that.

1

Out of sight below the top landing, Amber Pierce shed her spike-heeled evening shoes and nylons. Winding each stocking around a forefinger she stuffed them in the toe of each shoe. Barefoot now, she moved more quickly. The bright lights and blaring music became indistinct, a wall of meaningless sound at her back. Every fiber tense, she stole downward, casting furtive looks back. Could she make it to her sailboat unobserved?

Once on the dock she moved even more carefully. Dock hands? She saw none, but there could be. She couldn't smell cigarette smoke or hear mumbled conversation. Evidently nobody home, but still she hid behind a piling and searched deep into the shadows! Now close enough to see the Lucky Lady in the moonlight, she noted with a jolt that it lay fifteen feet off in the water. Someone had moved it. Her breath caught.

The five-eighths nylon mooring line attached to the pier pulled taut as the incoming tide angled off to her right. The line looked tight enough. She reached down and strummed it. Good enough. She checked up the hill. No pursuit. Not yet. She mounted the piling. With her experienced and almost prehensile large and second toes, she reached out and began to tightrope the line. Five feet out, arms outstretched, evening shoes in her left hand, she heard a voice.

"Hey, grab onto this!" A tenor voice just above a hard whisper came out of the darkness. It came from *her* boat!

Her breath caught and she almost lost her balance! Her eyes quickly turned toward the disembodied sound. A little shiver crawled up her back. No one should be on her boat.

A smell of diesel fuel came from the slick below. Mentally she kicked herself for coming.

When she'd arrived for the party, her host had directed her in. In smooth baritone he'd welcomed her with a smile. A couple of dock-hands in jersey-shirts had jumped on, smiled at her, quickly made her boat fast, and laid out the ramp. Tom had graciously helped her off and offered her his arm. As they walked the dock toward the stairs to the mansion above, she noticed a brilliant red Donzi to her right and thought, what a nice, fast, money boat!

She hesitated for only a second, but in that second, Amber became aware of the toes wrapped around the mooring line. It had begun to sag. Her weight...the line had become unstable. She gauged a leap for the side rail. Too far! She could see the outline of the hull and spars in the moonlight. Her hushed contralto reached out into blackness. It had a lilt that set it apart from the average womanly sound.

"Who are you?"

She heard a swishing sound and her eye caught movement. The sailboat's boom moved quickly over the water toward her. Her left foot slipped! Just as she lost it, Amber reached wildly up and out with a muffled gasp. Her right hand grabbed the boom end, held. Releasing the mooring line with her toes, she swung out over black, disgusting water, dropping her shoes at the same time. With a tiny splash they disappeared. Reaching with her free hand, Amber seized the round, polished wood surface. Now the weight of her body started pulling them both toward the water.

God, I'm going to get gucked, she thought. Her mind shuddered at the thought of having to go back to the party smelling like diesel oil and harbor slime. She didn't want to; she wouldn't!

An incoming swell rocked the boat upward just enough to put off the final insult. She licked her lips and effortlessly hand over handed her muscular, five-foot six, hundred and thirty pound body toward the starboard rail.

Wonder how her "date" felt now, she idled as she moved. She'd left him in a room off the mansion's main hall. He wanted to play.

She didn't. Bet that knee in the nuts cooled him off. Evidently—for him—understanding must come with pain. Too bad! Life is full of pain. Until he showed his internal ugliness—he'd no doubt call it ardor—he was a handsome man with nice manners and a quirky smile that went with a pleasant, low-key sense of humor. His low, earnest voice pleased her ear.

Hanging precariously from the Lucky Lady's boom, Amber's thoughts suddenly raced back to the day she'd met the guy.

She had few days off between jobs. She'd ferried her rental car to Long Island from Bridgeport on that hot mid-summer afternoon. She'd missed lunch but only felt thirsty. At Port Jefferson she dropped into the Four Leaf Clover for a quick beer on her way to Patchoque Marina where her baby, a thirty-foot sailboat she named Lucky Lady floated patiently. She couldn't wait to get her into Great South Bay.

The bar's dark, somber inside had made her pause. She waited until her eyes adjusted to the low light and when she could make out the heavy furniture and deep-hued walls, she moved to a stool at the bar. In her mind it was a perfect setting for the dark Irish humor that pervaded the place. The Four Leaf Clover had a tired look, but it also had ambience that whispered of comfort and friendship.

Stepping on the brass rail to gain the high, dark wooden seat, she looked around the nearly empty place.

A sandy-haired, freckle-faced bartender stood polishing glasses at the end of the bar, getting ready for the usual end of day surge. He put down a newly polished glass.

"What'll ye have?" He didn't smile, but Amber loved his distinctly Irish flavor. She pictured a man who'd probably fallen into bartending right out of high school in Ireland, had come to America and discovered years later that he had no place else to go.

"Sam Adams, please." The bartender had reached into a cooler and brought up a cold one. With a deft move he popped the cap and set it in front of her. With no wasted motion he'd upended a beer glass and set it out.

"Thanks." She dropped a ten-dollar bill on the bar. Ignoring it, the bartender returned to his polishing.

She'd sat quietly, staring straight ahead. The first few thirst-quenching "glugs" were the best. Then she leaned her tanned arms on the wooden apron and nursed the rest.

A man came in alone not five minutes later. She'd just picked up her glass, held it to the light and made a small connection with the amber fluid and thought about how it was really her namesake. My job is fluid, too. The stranger took a seat beside her. Amber paid no attention. She was used to being hit on. He ordered a Sam, too, and sat minding his own business for a minute or so. Then he gave her a quick look and started a conversation.

He'd seemed pleasant and this bar with the bartender close by didn't raise any flags. Except for her date with the marina, she had no plans, so she talked to him. He was a good-looking Italian man with a fine boned patrician face; she'd found him serious and funny and articulate and she'd unexpectedly developed an interest in him. Somewhere deep inside she got a message. It said, "You really need this time off, girl." So she listened and smiled at his jokes.

He'd mentioned he had a small business involving industrial supplies. He told her he was single, that he found it hard to get away from the business, but that he'd been invited to a big party at the home of Nick Trafalgar, a very wealthy industrialist he'd met through his connections.

"Ever hear of him?" he persisted.

"No."

"Tom Geacali." He'd put out a hand and she shook it half-heartedly. It was a warm hand with slightly feminine fingers, well cared for and well tanned. He'd painted a pleasant picture of the mansion and surrounding estate. He'd asked her if she would consider going with him. After she first said no, he told her the party was to be held in southeastern Long Island at the end of a private bay. She could sail there. She mulled it over silently for a few while staring straight-ahead, taking an occasional sip. He left her alone and that impressed her. Eventually she changed her mind. What could be wrong with putting direction and destination to her sailing lark? She wrote his directions down. He offered to make the trip with her.

She'd said, "I don't know you. I'll meet you there."

"How do I know you'll come?"

"I say what I mean," she said simply.

Geacali sensed he'd better not push it, so he smiled and said, "Okay, I'll meet you at the dock on Tuesday, around six."

"Sounds good to me." They'd shaken hands again and it felt like a contract. He left. Amber had sat and wondered why she had uncharacteristically agreed. She decided she *really* needed this time off! She'd left the Four Leaf Clover and headed south.

Now, everything had changed. She suppressed the unbidden thoughts.

Amber…focus!

Whose voice came from the Lucky Lady? The uninvited guest on board could be an enemy. The fact that he had saved her from a dunking in the fetid water meant nothing.

In the stark silver moonlight a hand reached for hers, a strong hand, fine, light, doubtless blond hairs marching across the back of it, not a youthful hand. Amber made a quick decision.

"Back off!" She hung five feet away, just out of reach.

The silhouette of an athletic looking man of average height in a bathing suit moved respectfully away. Bathed in shadow and moonlight, he was a caricature in black and silver.

"No problem, Amber, come aboard. I'll get way back so you will know I mean you no harm." Another shock! She didn't know him.

The man stepped into the cabin well near the stern, giving her a much wider berth than necessary. Amber swung once, twice, and vaulted over the rail, landing catlike on the mahogany deck. She spun and faced the mystery man, her body and hands easily moving into defensive posture.

"Okay," she said reasonably. "Who the hell are you and what are you doing on my boat?"

The man had blond or white hair, thinning a little at the widow's peak. She judged him around fifty, but in fine shape. He had northern European features and a strong jaw. In the moonlight his eyes were black pools under blond, hairy brows. There was a soft glint in the center of that darkness. He carried himself well. English, maybe.

His black trunks loosely fitted his well-kept body, the tie cinched up in a tight bow that hung over the front. No attacker here, no body need. He obviously exercised a lot, and she was convinced in the first moments that he had plenty of muscle if he chose to use it. She took this in as his face moved from the shadow of the mast.

"Amber, I'm a member of your organization." He hooked a hand over the edge of the cabin end, probably trying to look non-threatening.

He began. "Forget the party. After you hear what I have to say, you won't want to go back. I may have ten minutes to convince you to leave the harbor with a total stranger, and ten minutes to get underway—very quietly!"

Amber involuntarily glanced at the raging party high up in the bright lights of Nick Trafalgar's patio. Modern hedonistic delights above but no one was paying attention to the dock area...yet.

She'd been having a good time until Tom tried his dumb move and jumped her. Up to then he'd been a gentleman. She hadn't failed to note that the guy had some high-powered friends. Regardless, she had begun to have doubts about the crowd before Tom made his move. Nothing felt in sync, so when she left, she did so carefully.

"I'll give you five minutes to convince me I shouldn't start screaming and bring the whole party down to the dock. Don't move from that spot!"

"I won't move and you won't scream." He paused. "Yes! Time is short."

The man leaned away from the cabin wall he rested on and his face turned further into the moonlight. She could see his smile, kind of off-handed, most disarming. He didn't look like the kind who would smile at you and stab you in the back. She had a sense about people, but she'd had plenty of experience with her own species and remained wary. That tonight she'd tried to enjoy a rare time away had nothing to do with her instincts or her occupation. And, she didn't get her to-die-for body gorging on chocolates.

The man had presence about him though, a kind of command that made you listen and weigh his words carefully. He spoke again in his interesting tenor. She detected the faintest trace of an accent, but couldn't identify it.

"You are connected to International Fabrications. You are a covert operative. The organization behind InFab fights elements of third world terrorist groups and other crime."

Who is this guy?

"You have no connection with Nick Trafalgar. I'm sure you don't have a clue about your date tonight, or why Tom Geacali brought you to *this* party."

Amber Pierce hesitated. The guy had a lot of information, the kind an operative would have.

"But you do?"

The stranger went on. "Trafalgar lives in that fortress above us. He is an exceedingly dangerous underworld thug with many Mob connections. Nick has occasionally been useful to the nearby New York families, so they leave him alone.

"Geacali is a hit man for Nick's organization. He's a throwaway from one of the same New York families and he's made a home with Trafalgar. He isn't that good, but Nick allowed him in for some of his light dirty work. Taking Geacali helped Nick with a family who didn't want him dead, so they owe him.

"I'm a wild card Nick would like to know about. Actually, I wanted to get to you before this and prevent you're being here, but you were being followed on land and I couldn't find a place to intercede, so I got here early and nosed around."

Amber waited.

"Tonight you are to be killed. Geacali doesn't know, so he couldn't act out of character. Like always, Nick gets things done without his pawns knowing anything. Nick's guy Bernie Homenio's got the hit. He's a good deal more dangerous than Geacali, but he's still a punk."

There were a lot of guests. She could have missed someone, especially someone who didn't want to be seen. And, she *had* let her guard down for the evening. An operative shouldn't do that, not ever. She mentally slammed her forehead.

The man smiled again. "I don't think he suspects anything, but Nick's got him on a leash and he'll be getting antsy soon."

Amber stayed wary, but relaxed a little. The mystery man looked very capable, and Amber believed he'd be dangerous if it came to that. But he *did* inspire confidence. Why?

"Where do you fit in?"

"I'm your guardian angel. There are two aspects to me. You will learn one now. The other will be revealed at the appropriate time."

"Why should I believe you?"

"The organization has a keyword. It's *Stoic.*" He said it softly, as if aware that someone could hear it, even though he had taken extreme precautions.

Momentary shock! She regained control instantly, but the man had seen it. She still didn't know who he was, but only five people, maybe six, knew that code word. She *had* to trust him, but she'd keep an eye on him. Matter of fact, she should play along; find out what this was about.

"Shouldn't we de-berth and get the hell out of here, Amber?"

2

"You know sailboats?"

The man smiled again, bigger than before.

"Oh, yes!" he said. "For now, call me Ted."

"My draft is four feet. There is a sandbar about a quarter mile out. It's low tide. I have a retractable keel, amidships. I can maintain steerage under power. Might need the seventh swell to clear."

"I'll cast her adrift. Steerage power only."

"Okay."

He looked up. Large, spotty clouds drifted shoreward at about two thousand feet. A cloud had just begun to cover the moon. At the moment it had a silver lining, but in a minute or two the moon would slide behind it and nobody who happened to look out over the bay would see the sailboat's trail. Ted gauged the cloud and guessed it would hide their departure for about fifteen minutes. The two flashed through their preparations.

"Don't start the engine yet."

She waited.

"Now." With a deep rumble and the faintest vibration the engine caught.

The light above went out and the harbor became totally black. The sailboat slid out of the slip with only the faintest thrumming sound.

As they moved into the harbor, Ted threw out details. He figured Geacali would suddenly get too drunk to walk and Bernie would take her back to her boat. That's why she'd found Ted here.

"I know you to be a dangerous woman." He smiled thinly.

"Why do you say that?"

"Been following your career. Your contact worked for me. I know a lot about you."

The responses seemed right, but she kept the jury out.

Ted expected Nick's man to shoot her on board her boat, take her body out a few miles beyond the bay and dump her. Bernie conveyed arrogance found in many underworld characters. He'd be alone for the job.

It wasn't accidental her sailboat had been moved away from the pier. Nick's people figured she'd be stymied in any attempt to get to it and have to ask for help, which would alert them. There were no watchers at the dock. How supremely confidant they were.

The sailboat headed due south, straight out of the narrow bay.

They could make about three knots without sail, but soon enough her depth finding equipment sounded the presence of the sandbar. Amber unlocked and raised the deep keel. She pulled binoculars from an insulated cupboard right of the wheel. Behind them on the now distant shore she saw lights make their way down the long stairway toward the dock. She'd been missed.

"Trouble in River City," Ted said.

"Pay attention!"

"Right."

They slowed to a crawl and took careful readings. The sailboat began to lightly scrape bottom in time with the incoming swells. Ted gauged the water from the bow and began looking for the more robust seventh swell.

He squinted. The blackness didn't make it easy. He had it! He called back to Amber. "Give it all the juice when I say the word."

"You got it."

A thousand years passed.

"Now!"

She gunned the little engine and the vessel picked up speed again. A heavier, grating sound at the bow made Amber cross her fingers.

She felt the sailboat lift. The sound stopped as the heavier swell picked Lucky Lady up and carried her over the sandbar.

"Good!"

Amber looked nervously at the shore. A lot of activity at the dock now! The lights came on in Nick's fast cruiser.

"Won't be long," said Ted, "but, I'll bet that hull won't clear the sandbar. We may have a chance. Glad they didn't decide on the Donzi."

They looked worriedly at the shore and gauged their chances.

"My guess is that he thinks you are alone. You came in on high tide. How *did* you know about the sandbar?"

Amber shrugged. "I like to know what's under me when I'm running an unknown harbor. Tommy met me at the dock."

"Leave nothing to chance."

"Would you?"

"No. We aren't trained that way."

Facetiously she fluttered her hands, revival fashion. "I see the light!"

The man laughed. It took away some tension. That funny lilting laugh pealed from her lips.

Ted became serious again, his mind working. He spoke musingly to Amber.

"Rather than leave the party, he'd probably send Malfo. Alonzo Malfo's his first lieutenant. That would be good. Malfo isn't as expert with the cruiser as Nick. Donzi's are noisy. I don't think he wants noise or gunshots over the water tonight. Something sensitive. Maybe one of his guests..."

He took the glasses gently out of Amber's hands and surveyed the secluded scene for a long moment. On the bright spot at the top of the hill sat the mansion. From the monster party patio in the rear, distance-altered tinny sounds of music could still be heard. At the dock the cruiser had started to move. He caught a glint of wake as the fifty-foot boat swung around.

"Could be one of his guests is an important person. Hmm." He changed the subject. "If Nick is driving, he'll be thinking to ram us. That cruiser has a special steel "L" plate fitted to the bow, and the hull is reinforced. It's strong enough to plow up to ten inches of ice, and that means it could cut through the center hull of this sweet thing like so much butter.

Amber asked, "Would he do that? The harbor's only three fathoms deep."

"If he's intent on your not leaving his control, it wouldn't be a problem, not for Nick Trafalgar. Did you do soundings the whole way?"

"From about a mile out. It's thirty fathoms out there. I'm sure you know the seafloor shelf is gradual for quite a few miles."

"Yes."

He looked the lovely, bright young woman over and smiled. He handed her binoculars back and she returned them to the cabinet.

Ted checked the sounding device. Already the seafloor had started to drop off steadily. Thirty fathoms a mile out, plenty of water to drown in. Plenty of water to sink a sailboat. They cleared the tight harbor lines and the muting effect of out-jutting land and scrub trees.

"He's got to get over the sandbar first. Ah, a breeze! Let's get out some sail."

They worked together like they'd been doing it for years. In short order the beautiful Lucky Lady began to show the lady she was. Five, seven, eight knots. They moved away from the deadly harbor, the only sound the swish of water parted by the sleek bow.

3

Bernie got to Nick as soon as he knew the girl had fled. He tapped the boss on his left shoulder.

"Message from Liverpool," he said.

Nick Trafalgar looked at Bernie and back at his guest, Senator Robert Hartfield.

"Excuse me, Senator, I have an important call. May take awhile. I'm interested in our subject. I'll get back to you as soon as I can."

"Fine, Nick. Take all the time you need." The Senator waved at a waiter approaching with a tray of champagne.

Nick nodded and turned to leave. Bernie followed discretely. When they got to the library and shut the door, Nick turned on Bernie Homenio.

"*What?*"

"The girl's gone."

"Quick!"

"I was keepin' track of her and Tommie, when Tommie takes her behind the drapes in the sitting room off the main hall. I figures, no problem, Tommie's got her and tryin' one of his moves. I goes to get a drink. When I gets back, I peeks behind the curtain and he's doin' okay, so I leaves them alone for maybe, like ten minutes. Didn't figure anything was goin' down, except maybe the lady and it was safe enough. I goes to the main hall and keeps an eye out. Figures she'd be happy. You know the rep Tommie has with the ladies.

Nick gave him a hard stare. Bernie didn't like that stare.

"Well, after ten or twelve, I checks back and finds Tommie on the floor, groanin', holdin' his cojones.

"Where's the bitch?" I asks Tommie.

"Mother fucker!" he says to me, "That little cunt kneed my balls up inside me! Oh, Jesus God, it fuckin' hurts."

Where's the bitch?' I asks again.

"I dunno," an' he groans an' says, "all's I can see is white. Jesus, it hurts!"

"C'mon Tommie, how long you been down?" I asks him."

Nick's look of annoyance deepened, but he only stared harder at his soldier.

Bernie didn't miss the look. "He says, 'I don't know, Bernie. Look for her. She's got to be around. Where can she go?' Nick, I looks around both floors, even downstairs. Then I goes out the end of the patio and looks down the dock. I don't see nothin', there's this cloud over the moon.

"I take the stairs down toward the dock, gets about half way, and that's when I notices her sailboat's missin'."

Nick's right hand came around on his hit man's face and knocked Bernie off his feet. Bernie got up looking big scared!

"What, I got two assholes in the organization? Geacali can't think of anything but getting his wick wet, and you can't keep track of one little bitch? That doesn't make me happy!"

"Nick, I ran back and got your attention soon's I knew!"

"Ahh...fucking incompetents! What you think we should do now, *Bernie boy*?" Nick glared at him.

Bernie didn't like the way Nick said that. Wrong side of Nick. He had to pull it out.

"Nick, she can't be far. It just came down. How about the Donzi?"

"Too noisy."

"Cruiser?"

Nick raised his hand again, but did not strike. He thought for a second. "Try it! Get Malfo. Move!"

Bernie moved like Nick held a torch to his ass. He knew better than to cause ripples amongst the guests, so he walked carefully enough, but moved like his life was on the line—very likely.

He found Alonzo Malfo in a little knot of people near the white marble Virgin's Fountain. Bernie pulled him aside and in a whisper told Malfo what Nick said. Malfo gave him his "you're a dead man" look, but excused himself properly and left more or less casually with Homenio. They walked out the portico and down the wide marble steps. To a spectator, it looked like the two were just checking things out, making sure their guests were secure and having a good time.

They got to the cruiser in silence. Malfo told Homenio to cast off the lines, and he busied himself getting power up. This took three minutes, not enough time, but a record for Malfo.

"Bernie, grab a sub and make ready."

"It's okay, Alonzo. I got my piece."

"Grab a fuckin' sub, Homenio." Without another word, Bernie headed to the gun locker.

Malfo backed the cruiser out of its berth without taking time to warm the engine. It coughed and sputtered, but smoothed out quickly. The expensive piece grabbed the ocean and backed up. Malfo spun the wheel hard and slued the big boat around, clearing a big two-masted sailboat in the next berth by inches. As he realized it, sweat broke out on his forehead.

They moved out as fast as they dared until Malfo decided the sound wouldn't carry back to the still blazing party. A few hundred yards out, still under the umbrella of darkness from the cloud, he opened it up. Malfo knew about the sandbar, but he only had one chance, and he had to take it. If he could overtake the bitch's sailboat, he'd get her. Otherwise…

The two thugs headed straight out into the bay. Once moving the cruiser could make fourteen knots. Malfo had it up to ten by the time they came on the sandbar. Bernie stood out on the fore deck, feet splayed wide to handle the rolling deck, glasses at his eyes, searching the ocean ahead.

"I see 'em!" he shouted back, "Two degrees to port."

Alonzo moved the wheel a miniscule amount to correct and just at that moment, Bernie, with a yell, plunged over the bow of the boat. The cruiser rose out of the water and hung on the sandbar.

Malfo hit the wheel like a racecar ramming a cement wall. The boat sat in the shallow water and churned sand a few seconds until the engines stalled.

21

Bernie left the bow so suddenly he had no time to think about it, except for that very proper yell, and he slid under the port side of the boat. The cruiser crunched alongside and the wake pushed him away from the props, lucky Bernie. He sputtered to the surface, got his feet under him, caught a hanging line and pulled himself aboard. Malfo lay out cold on the deck, blood leaking in several places from his face where he'd hit the wheel housing.

Bernie listened to Nick's lieutenant's labored breath for a few moments, then worked to loosen Malfo's collar, all the time thinking he ought to let the little son of a bitch choke on himself, but he got to thinking that if Malfo died and he was the cause of it, losing the woman like that, that his ass would be grass. It seemed a less attractive option.

Malfo had stayed in his tux, only shedding the coat. Bernie had removed his own coat and tie and unbuttoned his shirt after they got underway. Tuxes aren't easy to swim in.

Soon Malfo breathed easier and Bernie decided to slap him awake. He went at it with a vengeance. He didn't like the guy.

"Hey, Malfo, you okay? Talk to me. C'mon you bastard, wake the fuck up!"

Malfo's head lolled, but after a half a minute he began to respond. Bernie changed his tune. "Hey, Alonzo, thought you was dead meat, man. You okay?"

Malfo came to gradually. Finally his eyes focused and he struggled to get up. Homenio moved back and sat on his haunches.

"Thought you bought the big one, Alonzo. Welcome home."

Malfo got shakily to his feet, the meanness in him becoming a glint in his eyes.

"What...?"

"Hit the sandbar, is all. You okay, me okay! Ain't no fuckin' way we goin' to catch that bitch tonight. I was you, I'd call in for a tow."

"Shit, shit, shit..." Malfo didn't like this.

"It was a shot, Alonzo, no worry."

"Yeah." He went to the cell phone in the wheelhouse and called in. He got Mitch. He told him what happened and Mitch said he would get to Nick as soon as he could. A very long pause ensued, made longer because the two men on the boat were sweating what the boss would say. Finally Mitch came back and told them they'd have to wait awhile until certain guests were put up for the night and tucked in, then Nick would send a crew out to pull them off the sandbar, if the tide didn't do it first.

"Right," Alonzo said and disconnected.

He sat back against the bulkhead, not bothering to find a comfortable seat, though there were many aboard the *Nicosia*.

"Go over it again, Bernie."

"Sure, Alonzo. That bitch Nick wanted wiped, well, she flew. That's the size of it. I was it, and I got shit. What else can I say?"

"You're fuckin' incompetent!"

"Alonzo, I already took a hit from Nick, and he's got a bigger hand than you do. Do I look happy?"

"Fuck it! We just start fresh. But how did it happen? I thought we figured all the angles. Somethin's missin' and I want to know what."

"I'm a soldier, Alonzo. You and Nick tell me what and when, and I do it. You can't want somethin' from me you didn't give me."

Malfo looked him over. Homenio was being straight.

"Ah, fuck it!" he said.

They sat and waited. The bright lights on the hill cast a nebulous, ever-moving glitter on the low swells that rolled monotonously by. Malfo lit a cigarette. Homenio watched silently, thinking surface thoughts about the way the smoke curled, and how for all the shit he lived with, at least he never took up smoking.

Almost as an afterthought, he got up and put his gun away.

RICHARD O. BENTON

4

"I scoped out a safe harbor," Ted said. He took the binoculars from the cabinet beside Amber and scanned the shore—blackness punctuated by an occasional light.

"Where?"

"Stay lee of the point light." He indicated the approaching lighthouse. Its search beam washed gently over them, highlighting the white sail for only a second, then repeating it thirty seconds later as the secondary beam moved over them. On. Off. On. Off.

Amber turned the wheel slightly to correct for drift. The lighthouse sat on a rock surrounded by an ever-changing ocean. It made her suddenly melancholy and she spoke her thought. "There is the meaning of lonely." She always got a catch in her throat when she thought that. Quick, hardnosed and capable she might be, but deep inside, it reminded her of her. It reminded her that she couldn't afford any relationship one could draw lasting comfort from. To drop her guard was to miss the elusive thing that would bring her down. Ruefully, she thought, like tonight. Without Ted...

Ted heard her. He removed the glasses from his eyes and looked at her. Amber Pierce, a beautiful, truly fine featured blond, lithe and well muscled, highly trained in the martial arts, a dangerous catch, he thought, except to the right man. She'd have a lot for the right man. Amber stood statuesque at the helm. Ted liked very much what he saw.

He spoke to her in an almost fatherly voice. "We don't get to submerge, to forget—people like us. We believe in what we do. It means we can never fall off the edge. Maybe someday it will be right to change our names, our lifestyle. Maybe we could live like the vast majority who don't know we exist, or care. But we keep the wave from washing over them. We keep the Devil at bay. And we can't tell them."

He looked away from Amber and again at the lighthouse. "There is the meaning of lonely, all right."

He showed sensitivity. It gave Amber a glimpse of the man under the hard exterior. She felt a brief connection to this mysterious moonlit man.

They had been on the water for twenty-five minutes now. The salt sea air had a calming effect on the two sailors. No sign of pursuit. Looked like the sandbar had done the job. The two had just met, but clearly their training had been similar, another item that convinced her he was on her side. They both took advantage of any natural defense. Amber thought they were a matched pair.

"Tell me more. Tell me what you can," she said to Ted.

"If we were captured, I would have to break this capsule I keep under my tongue during all delicate operations. In fifteen seconds I would be dead. When I feel we are as safe as we'll ever be, I will tell you things you need to know. Until then, your guardian angel is still on duty."

They stood silent with their thoughts.

That was the accent she couldn't identify, a death pill under his tongue. Except for her training and her very perceptive nature, she probably wouldn't have picked up the slight alteration the pill caused in his speech pattern. This was a top-notch agent.

He had not made any moves other than to help and to protect. Wariness is trained in us, she thought. But this man was so disarming. She, without more than the barest information, had come to believe in Ted. Believe in what they do, not what they say. She believed her instincts had not let her down, and yet she'd turned them off to have a good time and she couldn't *do* that. She had been a fool about that idiot Tommy Boy—that's how she thought of him now.

The forces they were up against were the meanest on the planet.

They had been gliding through blackness for nearly an hour. The moon had come out and the clouds began to evaporate as night temperatures equalized. The moon sank steadily toward the western horizon. They were quite far out. Ted told Amber he felt confident that from shore Nick's boys probably couldn't track the boat visually. He believed the cruiser had the only radar equipment capable of tracking them now. That, he guessed, would be hung up another three hours at least.

Amber opined that Nick probably wasn't having as good a time as he had earlier.

Ted smiled that lopsided smile.

Although he said he thought Nick might be having some fun with Amber's date right about now, he didn't feel sorry for him. Live by the knife…

Amber loved to listen to that soft spoken, thoroughly assured voice.

"Good. Okay, we headed straight out of the bay. When we were out of visual range, we came left, parallel to shore. Getting a fix shouldn't be hard. It's nice and choppy now. We'll be hard to see and he doesn't have anything else in the harbor big enough to handle this chop."

He went aft, standing, knees against the backstop, handling the pitching deck as any sailor would, and laboriously worked his binoculars to find their little spot on the ocean.

He called forward to Amber. "Okay, got my points."

He took measurements. "Come about to two-four-seven degrees."

That turned them back toward shore. The sail, running moderately slack, filled, became taut and the Lucky Lady picked up speed. Distant in the lowering moonlight she could just begin to make out the wet sheen of cliffs at the water line.

They were in the Atlantic south of Long Island. Amber searched her mind. Where were they now? Little light shone from the sparsely populated shoreline. Ted headed them right for the cliffs. Below them to the water line blackness was total, but as they maintained their heading and the minutes ticked on, the cliffs rose from the ocean and she began to see a white line at their base.

Beautiful line of death! Why do so many things of beauty have such a deadly side, she wondered? It occurred to her that many men thought that way about women. It wasn't a bum rap either, she knew.

They sped swiftly toward land. She caught herself feeling pride in the Lucky Lady's awesome speed, now ten knots in a strong, following breeze, a record, Amber thought, with her at the helm. The wind whipped her blond hair around both sides of her face

Finally she recognized the cliffs. They were called Spicer's Rocks. Her nautical map said the bay was unusually dangerous. Shipping and pleasure boats were warned well away because underwater rocks created a special hazard. There were so many that buoys marking the area were placed a mile offshore.

"You do know where we're going, don't you?" Amber asked with only a trace of nervousness. She didn't intend for the Lucky Lady to become so much salvage. Floating face down dead didn't seem attractive, either.

"Yes. We're okay here. When we get opposite the Head to port, we'll have to slow and pick our way in, but I can get us there. I did it twice before at night. Practice runs."

"You know a lot more than you are letting on," she said.

"For your protection. Once we're in safe harbor, you will know much more."

"There's no harbor in those cliffs…is there?"

Ted smiled. "Officially, no."

Catchy, a wealth of non-information.

"This evening hasn't turned out much like I imagined."

"That's fair." Ted kept his seaman's stance, legs spread, moving with the roll. "We are entering dangerous water from the proper angle. Now I have to pick up on a few landmarks to guide us. I'll call course changes."

"Okay."

He made his way forward. Before sitting, Ted made a long, careful three-sixty sweep with the glasses. Nothing showed in the glass. He focused on the sweep of the distant lighthouse beam seaward, trying to pick up any low glint near the water. A couple of times he stopped and searched a small area for a minute or so. Finally satisfied, he eased into position, legs dangling on either side of the prow, arms on the low rail.

"Seems clear seaside," he called back.

"Good," Amber acknowledged.

They were in luck with the clouds. Just enough to give cover; the clouds didn't stay long. They needed moonlight now like they needed the cover of darkness before. In a few minutes they would need the light desperately. Ted took a long look at the sky. It was tricky, but he finally decided to go for it.

"Okay."

They were silent for a little while. Amber kept the Lucky Lady on the course her companion had set and she'd keep it there until told to change it. Unlike her to be so trusting, yet her instincts told her not to worry about danger from Ted.

She stayed alone in her thoughts until Ted called back, "Amber, steer five degrees starboard. After that, we have to take in all sail. It's going to get dicey soon."

"Okay, Ted."

Amber spun the wheel. Once on the new course she locked it and Ted joined her. They got sail in with dispatch. She fired up the steerage motor. Ted returned to his place on the prow. Another period of silence, followed by an occasional order from forward, fine-tuning. It implied the whole scenario had been thought out long before this, so what's happening tonight is a very big deal. Why couldn't she smell something bad coming her way before this?

Obviously one reason only. She'd been deliberately kept out of the loop.

The cliffs loomed huge and frightening now. The stark gray granite at night provided sheen but little reflected light. Amber thought the cliffs had shone up better when they were farther away. Much closer, the glint had washed out of them.

She paid attention but channeled her thinking toward the thunderous glory in front of her. Amber loved geology. Plate tectonics and mountain building flitted through her mind as they approached. Eons of pounding surf, wind, wave and an ice age or two thrown in had created the scene ahead; all part of a changing and glorious world. Her job, she reflected, was to save it from the destructors, the uncaring and the vicious.

I wish we weren't needed, she thought. But only a few could qualify for the training and the psychological downsides of living on a razor's edge. She knew how high the stakes, and she knew that someday it would get her, somewhere, somehow. She had to be ready.

"Starboard, three degrees…"

A minute went by, then, "Port, fourteen degrees, quick!"

A light staccato grinding, like perforation lines on a page told her how close they'd come. Have to check for damage sooner, she thought. She said nothing.

Ted concentrated on the ocean like she had on the tightrope she'd walked…when? It seemed so long ago.

More silence. Perfect time to think.

"Starboard, ten degrees."

She came about. The cliffs were very close now, and the thunder of surf made it difficult to hear Ted. He raised his voice almost to a shout.

"Starboard four." He hand motioned in the dimming light.

Directly ahead of the sailboat, she swung into a run of smooth water.

Ted called back. "Keep it steady. Head for the cliff dead ahead. Stay in the middle of that smooth run. Don't be faint of heart!"

When had she been faint of heart? She almost laughed. Amber trusted this man completely, knowing they were too close to the cliffs. Unless something happened in the next half minute, they were going to crash right into it. She planted her feet and awaited impact.

5

After sending Bernie to get his lieutenant, Nick returned to the party. On the way he picked up a double martini from the bar. Matthew Goggins, his personal secretary and accountant, was doing bar chores. Everyone knew him as "Stone" because he never smiled. Nick raised his voice above the din, "Want somebody to spell you?"

Stone, had been working for three hours. He said, "No prob, Nick. I'm running on all cylinders. When it slows, I'll grab a nip-o-joy."

Stone didn't drink. He'd find a corner somewhere, where the wind would carry the smoke away from the building, sit quietly, and bring himself up. Some of the guys thought his name should be "Stoned" and they laughed about it, but they seldom found him that way.

"Okay." Nick went off, chuckling. He had a knack for keeping the right people happy and the rest unhappy.

He spied Senator Hartfield off in the distance and headed toward him, stopping every so often to touch the arm of a lady and say something, or to put his massive arm across the shoulders of one of the male guests. Nick made himself very likeable at parties.

He reached the Senator. The man stood alone, looking out into the blackness on the momentarily cloud covered sea. He seemed introspective. There were knots of people not far off who weren't paying attention to anything but their drinks and their partners, and by this time they were all pretty wasted.

"Ah, Nick, back again?" The Senator spoke first.

"Yes, Senator, a bit of business."

"Didn't I see your cruiser out-berth and take off like a bat out of hell? Not on its way to Liverpool, was it?"

Nick smiled, looked at his guest and answered smoothly, "No, Senator, that was just a thing I ask my employees to say when something important is happening. Makes it easier than just busting in with who knows what and maybe upsetting some of the guests.

"It's a minor deception. In this case one of my people heard a distress call, a small fishing craft just off the bay from my place on its way home from a long run, if I heard right. Evidently some net fell over the side and got tangled in the prop and they needed a little assistance. I sent my friend Alonzo out with one of my guys to give them a hand. He is a good pilot. If they haven't cleared the problem, we'll help 'em out."

The Senator looked long at Nick before answering. "Very noble. I assume the Coast Guard is off for the night?"

Nick noted the Senator's delay in answering. Hartfield was smart and perceptive. He'd have to make sure his boys backed up the story he'd made up. He'd also call a friend in the Coast Guard and find out where the cutter out of Southampton patrolled tonight, just to be sure. He didn't want the Senator to get any more curious about it and do some checking on his own. His friend would see to it that a cryptic note made its way into the USCG log, if necessary.

"Not at all Senator. I'll find out what went on when my cruiser gets back. You interested in hearing about it?"

"No, Nick, I don't think so. Now, where were we?"

"Something about the Appropriations Bill."

"That's right. It's going to have a hard row to hoe. Not enough votes to ensure passage yet, but I have a few chits up my sleeve. It's not over yet."

"That's good to hear. I'm sure you'll do your best. By the way, I think I can arrange for my company to up my "campaign contribution" some."

"Really? Now isn't that good news!"

"Well now, we wouldn't want you to lose the next election, would we?"

"No, we wouldn't."

Just then the Senator's wife arrived, a glass of champagne in each of her tiny white hands. A pretty woman, dark-haired and well made up, she had a regal bearing. She obviously came from some well-to-do family, the kind that sent their daughters to Miss Porter's School or the like, one of the silver spoon crowd, Nick thought.

"Hello, Sally," the Senator said brightly, "having a good time?"

"Oh, yes," she replied, sipping champagne from first one and then the other of the glasses in her hands, and she looked at Nick with a bright smile. "Nick, you throw just the best parties!"

"Well, thank you, Mrs. Hartfield. It's a pleasure to have you and your husband here tonight."

"Shally." Her words were a little slurred.

"Sally," he corrected with a smile.

She was having a good time all right. The Senator didn't look as pleased as she did, but he covered it up.

Senator Hartfield looked at his watch and then at his wife. "You about ready to retire, my dear?"

"Shertainly not!" she said with emphasis.

Hartfield looked at Nick and said, "Let's talk some more in the morning on our subject, okay, Nick?"

"Sure, Senator. Why don't you take your beautiful lady over to the hors d'oeuvres bar? I think I saw another platter come out?"

The Senator smiled gratefully, excused himself and his wife and headed in the direction of the food bar.

Nick decided he wouldn't have to follow up on tonight's incident with the Coast Guard, just with the house staff. Then he slowly went back through the crowd, entertaining constant interruptions from the reveling guests with savoir-faire.

6

Just as she thought they were going to hit the cliff, a darker blackness opened up in front of the sailboat. A gash in the rock face she couldn't see until they were right on it swallowed them and they slowed measurably.

"Don't ease up on it yet, Amber," she heard over the roar around them.

She kept the power on full and her hands tight on the wheel. The roar of the surf became a noise behind them and they moved into utter blackness. A wing and a prayer, she thought, and she smiled.

"Beautiful job, girl! Stay with it. Not a bad first try."

Amber lived her life all over again. Where were they? It's perfect! Just as she felt the sailboat begin to speed up, she heard Ted at her elbow.

"Okay. You can cut power to minimum, enough for steerage. We're past the outflow region. Pretty nice, huh?"

"You scared me silly! I used plenty of adrenaline in the last few minutes. And to your credit, I can't remember when I have trusted anyone like I just trusted you."

Ted laughed in his rich tenor. "A thousand thanks, Milady."

Middle English. How gallant!

"Let's berth up and we'll light a candle and show you around."

He reached into the weather chest and grabbed a five-cell flashlight. He knew every inch of her sailboat. No surprise. The beam that sprang out blinded them. They quickly accommodated. Ted directed the beam in a slow, full circle so Amber could see around their safe harbor.

Amber caught her breath. They were on a small lake deep under Spicer's Rocks. The vaulted granite ceiling was so high that the light beam became large and defuse at the top. She saw no stalactites.

"Geologic fault?" she asked.

"Actually, it's both. This part is a recent geologic feature. Head for the landing area up ahead." He pointed with his flashlight.

Ted resumed. "There are caves that go back for miles. I explored some when Stoic decided I should handle this alone. It's about perfect as a hideout. Almost a mile west of here the river submerges for quite a long way, maybe a couple hundred feet, maybe more. Unlikely any spelunker would try to bridge that, scuba gear or not. The current is fast and I'm told it doesn't open up even in dry season.

"From the entrance you simply can't see the gash that lets the river flow directly into the ocean except in one place. That rocky spit about a half mile out covers the entrance, so ships can't see it from the ocean side. Once discovered, our crew helped to keep it hidden by placing the 'Dangerous Rocks' buoys farther out than they need to be, thus assuring privacy."

He went on.

"Before the feature that is now a lake appeared, probably only a few thousand years ago, the river did indeed empty into the ocean, but then it was forty feet below the surface. That's about sea level for this area a hundred and fifty million years ago, our experts tell me. When the quake or whatever happened caused this," he gestured, "the granite ceiling fell and blocked the old waterway, allowing the lake to form. You noticed how Lucky Lady slowed when we entered the channel."

"Yes."

"The water leaves this lake with quite a bit of force."

"So locals wouldn't likely try to get in here with the boats they use."

Ted nodded. "We passed a rumor around that there was a high concentration of radon in the region, that it wouldn't be healthy to get too near the area."

"Clever!" Amber thought the organization had sewed this place up tight enough.

"Steer along that ledge." He shined the light on it.

"Okay."

"I'll attach some lines. Couple more surprises, and then we can get comfortable."

"And then you'll tell me something?"

"Yes." Ted pulled out four bumpers from the scuppers and ran them casually on the port side. They pulled alongside, and Ted made a practiced leap onto the flat rock. Amber noted steel pegs driven into the rock in a couple of places. He looped the lines over the pegs and made fast. Then he jumped easily back aboard, pulled out the gangway and laid it down. Ted handed her a flashlight and Amber walked off.

"Well, thank you, sir," she said.

Ted came back, "We aim to please."

They both laughed. Amber's suspicions were gone; she felt comfortable now.

"Cold in here," Amber said.

"We'll get you warm in a few."

They walked fifty yards along the ledge and entered another crevasse. It wound like a serpent for fifty feet, very tall but very narrow. It opened into another room, not so large as the cavern they had left, but of good size. The floor slanted a little, but to Amber's real surprise a prefab building filled the center of it. It had a flat roof and sides built from modern materials. It had the outward appearance of T-111, the plywood stuff you get at a lumberyard.

A door faced them. Ted opened it using a three-digit combination on a hidden panel. It swung easily, but seemed quite thick. Her glimpse to the left showed two bedrooms and a large enough living room. To the right she noted a self-contained kitchen that had cupboards and a sink. It looked well planned. There were no windows. Between them she saw a closed door.

"I'll be!" Amber put her hands on her hips. "No windows, I see. I imagine the travel agent isn't promoting the view."

Ted laughed again. "No, but the place has its points."

Before they left the doorway, Ted stepped back and showed his light around. There were barrels of fuel, barrels of water, crates of food, and an arsenal she found it hard to believe, all locked behind some capable looking chain link fence that ran to the cave ceiling.

"Are you planning a war?" She asked.

"No, this is our east-coast depot. And now that I've told you that, it's time to let you in on a few other tidbits." He gestured again with the light.

"The cabin, as I will refer to it, to all appearances, is made of wood. Actually, the exterior five-eighths is indeed wood. Inside, you will encounter three quarter inch boilerplate, procured from a local shipyard the front organization owns. One of InFab's businesses is shipbuilding. Our engineers calculate that it would stop just about anything small enough to be moved into position in this cavern. Getting that stuff in here required serious work. Inside, well, let me show you."

He took Amber to the door and pushed it open. It swung freely, although a bit sluggishly. It was very heavy. From some source, lights came on automatically. She glanced over the interior appointments and nodded at Ted.

"Nice!"

"More coming."

Amber smiled. She could see that Ted felt safe now. He led them to the interior door. He knocked. The door opened. Beyond the entranceway the bewildered young woman saw a plethora of electronic equipment, some of which she recognized as the latest technology, and some she didn't recognize at all.

She didn't quite gasp.

A young man she had never seen before stood up and nodded to her. He had been sitting in the dark under a hood in front of an advanced communications screen.

"Hi, Rolph," Ted said, "This is Amber."

The young man's eyes lighted up. "Hi, Amber. Pleased to meet you! Watched you come in. Nice job."

He held out his hand, which she took and they shook. She put him at no more than twenty-eight to thirty. He was a handsome specimen, with a lively gleam in his gray-green eyes. Like Ted, he seemed in prime condition. No, more than prime! He was a hunk!

He looked at Ted. "Does she know?"

"Not yet. We'll retire to the War Room and I'll give her the scoop."

Amber thought it sounded cloak and dagger and she laughed.

The two men looked at her.

She got control and said, "Sorry. I'm not laughing at you. All this..."

She'd had surprise upon surprise thrust upon her in the last—what was it—three hours, and she rapidly approached overload. She knew she stood in a top-secret base filled with expensive stuff and that emphatically believed wasn't for sale on the open market. She offhandedly conversed with two men she didn't know, a handsome, virile young man and one in whom she had placed complete trust under circumstances that would have daunted a less self-assured person.

"Ted," she said, her voice rising, "take me somewhere and give me the scoop. I need it!"

Ted looked at her sharply, but relaxed immediately and gave her that off-handed smile again. "Yeah. Come on; let's go into the ready room. Rolph, we'll talk later. All okay?"

"Yeah, Ted, copasetic."

Ted led Amber to a comfortable room with a long table and cozy chairs.

"Sit. You'll be glad you did." He waited for her to pick a chair and moved it under her. Amber said nothing, but felt unaccountably pleased.

Ted moved around the table and sat opposite her, all serious.

"Amber, you have been promoted."

The woman sat perfectly still.

"Of necessity, you have been drawn into the inner circle. I am your contact. Your immediate superior has been deliberately trans-ferred to break the chain of contact. As before, you will not know who the others are except for associative names."

Amber gave him a wry smile.

He smiled, too. "I know you know this. But I want to go through the steps, so that my perspective of the organization will come through and specifically what it will mean to you."

Amber thought, we're about as covert as it gets, why not? It's easy to see why Ted mentioned scoping out a safe harbor and had left it at that. If either of them had been caught, any information they had would be dragged out of them by any and all exotic means. It's how an organization kept its secrets.

"Amber, your last assignment was handled with tact and sensitivity. Although you did what was called for, Stoic was more than impressed. The fact that you had been made by Rathmanizzar just after you freed yourself up from the Gringelli affair made it necessary for you to disappear and become someone else. Stoic's operative, Balkan, is missing and presumed dead. He's another part of the big picture. It's a sorry loss, but each of us is expendable."

Amber thought, Rathmanizzar I've heard of, but who is Balkan, and how does it affect me?

Ted watched her, read her expressions, noted the slight widening of the eyes at the mention of Stoic, the wizard who ran the operation, a brilliant, totally nondescript appearing man capable of unusually effective disguise. His genius formulated unusual solutions to apparently insurmountable problems. He'd put a dent in the dark side and had stayed alive to the chagrin of his many enemies.

Ted discussed Rathmanizzar at length as an extremely capable religious and political leader of the Lorida Liberation Faction, the LLF. The nation of Lorida, if it could legitimately be considered a country, existed in the Sahara desert of Africa, a camouflaged place consisting of several villages and one tent city of size. Ted told Amber that in reality; it was not much more than a terrorist organization led by Rathmanizzar, a fanatic. As Muslim cleric and political leader, he'd reinterpreted the Koran to fit his jaded view of the harsh world he lived in. His soldier/disciples thought him near divine, and would give their lives unquestioningly to him, whatever direction he took.

His organization had laid claim to some pretty awful dirty work. Stoic had been trying to bring down its leader and crush the organization for years without success. He'd had to tread lightly, with serious finesse. Too many other covert organizations from more than one side made it difficult. Rathmanizzar seemed to anticipate Stoic's every move and disappear just before his operative could make a probable hit. Stoic finally decided he had a traitor in his own organization.

"What did Rathmanizzar want with me? He wasn't connected to Gringelli, was he? I thought I closed that chapter."

"Rathmanizzar has his fingers in so many pies that we don't know them all. Apparently you hurt him a lot when you neutralized Gringelli. We *think* Gringelli had made a connection inside the U.S. Atomics Lab that Rath wanted badly and it probably involved enriched uranium. You evidently severed that connection, and many months of hard, slow work. That story isn't over."

"Is this why you brought me here?"

"In part. You have always had more value to the organization than you have thought, but keeping you in the dark was necessary. We've actually gotten much more mileage out of you than we could have by focusing your efforts in one area. You are far less expendable than you think you are.

"We are certain Rathmanizzar got to Nick's organization and asked them to make you disappear. We think it was a mistake, one of very few Rath has made, to order your killing as a vengeful act. We're going to try to turn that mistake into a big advantage for us."

Ted shifted position in his chair and grasped a nearby remote.

"Simply stated, they want to win. We'd prefer we did."

"World chess," she said.

He pushed a button. A screen at the far end of the room came down from the ceiling. He pushed another and that half of the room lights dimmed. A third and a still picture showed an old man wearing a turban. He seemed to be looking straight into the camera. He didn't look happy. Seams in his dark face belied an easy life. His eyes were those of a soldier.

"Rathmanizzar," he said simply.

"I'm surprised he sat for the picture."

"He didn't. That was taken by Balkan. It's the last picture Balkan smuggled out to us before he disappeared."

"Oh."

"Human chess, Amber, nothing more. But you're a knight, not a pawn, our knight-errant, so to speak. You have played your part so well that soon we hope to checkmate that old bastard, maybe take him out for good."

Ted's next words showed some of his strain. "And we can't afford to lose you. Into every ointment there seems to be a fly. In our scenario there are two. I'll run Nick Trafalgar by you first."

"I don't understand." Amber looked puzzled.

"Think of an organization like Nicks' as a cancer. It metastasizes through a body. In Nick's case, pieces of him don't break off to form new colonies. Rather, he forms them and flings them off into fertile areas of his choosing. It's the reality. When we discovered he was a major player in the Rathmanizzar scenario, like Rath's, his organization was so far flung and dug in that we may never find all of it."

"But that's similar to many covert organizations in the world. The Russians have done that for eighty years. It's not new." Amber said.

"True."

"So what…"

"The CIA and other groups spawned by various governments throughout the world have been at their jobs for so many years that it's like employment for both sides. Their agents are serious about it, but in essence they share information. The effect of it is to keep the playing field even. Once in a while, a rich piece of information gets stolen and they go to work, but for the most part those groups are unofficially directed to keep the status quo."

"Okay. I get it."

"I mean *directed*."

"Right."

"All this is not lost on the underworld."

"Ah!" Real understanding crossed Amber's face.

"Rathmanizzar is old, but very bright. He is a political animal. He sees potential where no one else does. To a lesser extent, but don't underestimate him, so does Nick Trafalgar."

"So why am I here?"

Ted went on. "They have formed an alliance of convenience. Several months ago they met at a Black Sea resort, the Budkovka in Varna, Bulgaria. We got Balkan close enough to make a tape and to get that picture with a lapel camera. Last week several other operatives have sent coded messages to the Head. Certain materials including highly sophisticated electronic equipment are disappearing from inventories we've been watching. It seems haphazard, but Nick isn't haphazard. Something is up."

He pushed the remote button again. Rathmanizzar disappeared and a spider chart with too many legs appeared. At the ends of the "legs" were boxes with names.

"This represents what we know to date."

Amber studied the chart for a long minute. It made immediate sense to her. Nick sat in the center with his lieutenant. Within the upper echelon were name boxes surrounding the center. They represented specialists in Nick's organization with capabilities that would make the FBI envious.

"The specialists made sure every 't' is crossed and 'i' dotted in each of Nick's seemingly unconnected businesses. They are good, with little turnover in that rank. They are in for life and Nick makes sure they know it. Otherwise he treats them very well and they have no complaints. They are his chess-masters."

"So why am I here?" Amber asked again.

Ted looked at her intently. "One of Stoic's top people is a double agent. Rathmanizzar always seems to know our every move, and Nick set this date up so cleverly that Tom Geacali didn't know it was anything more than a chance meeting. It points up how dealing with Nick can be fatal."

Amber remained silent.

"You're getting a new identity. You and a partner are going to invade InFab and find the traitor. Your new name will be Audrey Penwarton. Except for the Head, your former supervisor, Rolph and me, no one in the organization has ever seen your face. The top operative files are inaccessible to any but 'thee and me', as they say."

He stopped for a moment.

"Partner?" Amber coaxed.

"Your new cover will be a shaped identity and you will have a partner. Your mission will be to identify the double agent and his or her sources and contacts. You will have to infiltrate from the outside. Stoic will put you in the way of a situation that will get the notice of each of our top people individually without alerting the others. He's the only one who can do that. I will be in the loop only through Stoic."

Amber listened intently, but focused on something Ted said that stunned her.

"A woman at top?" Amber asked, unbelieving.

"Two. Don't underestimate the Head's desire to get the best people into the organization. This is war."

Amber was shocked. She assumed an organization run by men. Never assume!

"I see that surprises you. Add it to the list. You have quite a string of them tonight."

"Yes, I do!"

"Not over yet." He pressed a contact on the table. Rolph came in immediately. Ted looked at Amber.

"Meet your new husband. His name is now Richard Penwarton. "Rolph" doesn't make it with a last name like Penwarton."

He looked at them and smiled again, that old, quirky smile that had so captivated Amber, now Audrey, from the beginning of this dream...or perhaps *nightmare*?

"You two are the most likely to succeed, based on your profiles and training. This is likely the most dangerous assignment you will ever handle. Our traitor is at the highest level. It can only be one of five people. Whoever it is will be watchful and always dangerous. Don't turn your back on anyone. You won't have to worry about me or the Head, but regardless, so that your focus on turning up the traitor never waivers, consider everyone, that means *everyone*."

"Got it," said Audrey.

"Got it," said Richard.

"Amber?" Ted threw off casually.

Without missing a beat, Amber said, "No, I'm sorry, you must be mistaken, I am Audrey."

"Excellent! You are both to acclimate to your new roles starting immediately. Study the character sketches I have created for each of you, and when you can both move into the part, destroy the sketches. If you're going to work together and live together, you might as well have what fun you can with it. I like you both. I suspect you will enjoy each other, too."

Ted got up, nodded to the two and left the room. They heard him comment about being very tired and needing some sleep. Audrey thought that likely. She smiled after him.

7

To a visitor it would seem that the desert tent city had a sprawling, unordered appearance. In fact, its tents and other structures were positioned in such a way that prevailing winds carried up and over the top of the staggered line. Desert men became engineers of the first order when it came to survival. Near the center of the grouping rose the largest tent, providing a focal point for the community.

All tents were of durable white canvas made in factories in the northern Loridian villages. Although the desert grudgingly provided, hemp, originally transplanted from Asia grew well in certain protected valleys in the little country. They were dingy from dust and weathered by the sun. They blended into the hot desert, making Loridian settlements hard to see from the air.

The Loridians had brought the weaving of hemp to a high art and shunned more permanent styled buildings. Although their settlements were more or less permanent, their national character remained stuck in the nomadic hunter/herdsman class while the world moved on. Rathmanizzar deliberately isolated his people, believing that Lorida had a higher purpose than to move with the rest of the world.

The insides of Loridian tents were hung with gay colors, reds, yellows, even reflective black, as if to make up for the sameness these semi-nomadic people had to live with in fending off the harsh exterior world.

Within the biggest tent a dark skinned, leathery looking, dour old man sat cross-legged on a red, cloth-covered mat. A worn turban rested upon his head. He looked tired. In front of him a man groveled on his knees.

"Speak, Ahmed."

"Word of the Holy Book, I have arrived only these moments ago with this news. Ben-Shirpa, a trusted comrade and family member in Gaza carried it to me. His contact from the United States of America has informed him that the killing of the woman Amber Pierce, who thwarted your plan to get the enriched uranium from America, has failed. She has disappeared."

"That is most unfortunate, Ahmed. The woman will be doubly hard to find now. Call a general meeting of the Kaneseth leadership for the setting of the sun. We will discuss the implications of this and what we must do."

"Yes, my master." Ahmed bowed and left.

Rathmanizzar crossed his arms and assumed an attitude of meditation. Never far from it, he closed his eyes and brought his world plan to conscious level. For this plan he risked all, his comrades, his country, his way of life. For this plan he fought the infidels. He needed uranium for this. He had the bomb plans and much of the special equipment he needed hidden away in a secret mountain retreat in the desert not far from Tubela-Ha. But for the uranium, although available from more than one source, none was as highly refined as the material he had tried to get from U.S. Atomics.

Quite to himself Rathmanizzar thought, so the American, Nick Trafalgar has failed. I must find out the circumstances of the failure. I need a strong contact in the United States of America, one who can be persuaded to assist the cause, but one I can throw away when the time comes to divest the cloak of secrecy from the holy plan. Is he not the one?

The woman, Amber Pierce, by her own hand has set back my time schedule by months. A strong and dangerous one! In the background of my dream I saw a woman's hand and a man's hand, white hands, hands not of the desert or of my people. Strangely, they were not bright like the vision of the jihad that will spring from the desert sands to work the will of Allah on the infidel. Could they have been those of Amber Pierce? And whose were the others?

It did not seem important when I gazed upon the shining purpose that will smash the unbelievers. Yet I must think deeply of this. All aspects of a vision must be seen clearly to understand. It is bothersome. Until I feel I have correctly interpreted its meaning, I must not tell my brethren.

Surrounded by the thousands of people in his desert community, Rathmanizzar could still feel comfort in the solitude of his moment.

8

"Quite a guy," Audrey said to her new partner.

"You don't know the half of it."

"Well, what now?"

"Get acquainted?"

"Umm..."

"Umm?"

"No repartee?" Audrey said playfully.

"I'm kind of old fashioned. Mama said go slow with girls."

"Your mama is a wise woman."

"Well, we could start there."

"Okay."

Richard decided to be a little impish. "Okay, but I'm not easy."

"Seems to me I said that to someone else in a past life recently."

"Audrey, allow me to tell you that you are one sweet looking chick."

"Glad we got that out of the way early. Of course, you haven't seen me in curlers yet. Talk about sweet..."

They both laughed.

"Hope we don't wake up Ted."

"We won't. Everything is insulated and reinforced. Did Ted tell you anything about the construction of this place?"

"Briefly."

"It's a fortress. Maybe overkill, but we need to be safe and undetected. Actually, this may be the safest place on earth. Completely unknown, except for a dozen people we don't have to worry about."

"You had them killed and thrown in with the treasure?" Audrey asked, wide-eyed.

Richard tried not to laugh again. He failed.

"Not necessary, but I can't tell you why."

"Why?"

"Some silly regulation...you know. Ted will tell you, I'm sure, at some point."

It was Audrey's turn to laugh. "We need this, you know."

Richard got serious. "Yes, we most assuredly do."

"Tell me what you can about yourself."

"Mid-western suburb, high school, good college, studied Western Civ, Biology, Physics, Electronics, world social patterns of the twentieth century, a little theater. Graduate studies focused on Molecular Biology. Joined a large pharmaceutical firm—you'd recognize it if you heard the name. Stayed, year and a half. I keep my eyes open. Saw some things going on the public would be interested to discover. I knew something needed to be done, but I didn't have a clue where to start. I only knew I hadn't told anybody and I wouldn't be smart to start. Stoic evidently has operatives in a wide network. Seems someone was watching me watching them, a young woman working as an admin assistant. She invited me out for drinks and felt me out. A week later she came to me with an offer and here I am."

Richard looked at Audrey and nodded. "Your turn."

"Born east, moved at seven to the West Coast. Schools pretty straightforward, college in L.A. Finished high in class. No graduate studies. Spent summers working with a circus, high wire, etc. Loved it! I ran three to seven miles a day. Got me interested in stunt work with both parents gone. Dad was killed while working in Saudi Arabia. He was a government contractor, something to do with the vast oil fields there. Dad wasn't home much and Mom said he had a sensitive job he couldn't talk about. I was seven then. After the government notified Mom we moved east to west. Mom was all I had after that. Had to grow up quicker."

Richard nodded sympathetically. "Sounds like I was dealt better cards."

Audrey smiled. "Thanks for the best wishes, but it wasn't all that bad. I really got to do a lot of things I would never have done if life had taken another direction. A drunk driver killed Mom two days before I turned twenty-one. It hurt a lot then, but I'm over it. I still graduated, but I cried a lot, especially during commencement. She never got to see me and Dad missed it all.

"After graduation I went up to Hollywood and looked around for stunt schools. Just before I enrolled in one, I met this guy who told me I looked like someone who enjoyed living on the edge. I guess I do. It didn't take much to convince me."

"Thought you'd never stop talking," Richard said, but his eyes were kind, and he correctly interpreted Audrey's need to leave the past where it was.

"Okay, smart ass. Now we know each other. Why don't you show me the digs?"

Richard laughed. "No time like now to get things done."

Audrey looked at him curiously. "Funny, that's one thing I remember Dad used to say."

He smiled at her and his eyes sparkled.

"Audrey, wife of mine. This is an assignment. But being as any day following this one we could, and likely will, be dead, I say live, live, live...while you can."

"Bravo! Show me the digs."

"This way." Richard stood and bowed with a flourish.

They left the War ready room, proceeding the short way through a long room that seemed to be a storage facility inside the building. At the end she noted an impressive array of storage batteries hooked into a lot of wiring that went every which way.

"What's all that, Richard?"

"It's the battery power setup. We can't use any other kind of power here. A gas engine would asphyxiate us, and the rumble of the engine would carry through the rock and give us away. Did you know that sound travels up to four times as fast in rock as through the air?"

"Duh."

"Oh, you did. Well, fewer of us do than don't. So there!" He made a silly hand gesture that made her laugh. The new relationship was starting out well. Richard didn't seem to be trying. She liked that.

"I didn't tell you, but I studied Physics and Geology. Good at it. Like to hunt down rocks when I can get off by myself, sometimes."

Richard said, "I like rock hunting and I like climbing, too. Maybe when Ted is through with us we could get off into the mountains and do some prospecting."

"Sounds good!"

They *really* liked each other.

"Now for the grand tour." Richard walked into the furnished area.

He gestured at pieces of furniture. "This is the Living Room. It is built for comfort. It is built for siege. Try moving any of the pieces."

Audrey grabbed at a love seat. It didn't move.

Richard went on. "The backboard of each has a steel plate in it. Makes an excellent place for defense, if it ever came to that. By that time we would have destroyed all the records kept here. There are some pretty important ones relating to the organization.

"There are usually two on duty here at all times, but because of your special rescue, non-essential personnel were removed night before last. They will come back three days from now when we are gone. They are good men and women, actually, one each on this shift. They don't need to know what's going on with us, and I can handle the duty assignment alone."

"Looks like a regular house. Even pictures of windows. Realistic outdoor scenes. A psychologist must have visited this place before the company moved in."

"True."

Audrey went over and sat down on the sofa. "Umm, nothing but the best."

"The organization spent some serious cash here."

Richard went over to the sofa and stood in front of Audrey. He held out his hands and pulled her up. "Time to continue the tour."

Audrey said playfully, "Maybe I'm tired. Had a busy night."

"Uh-uh," Richard came back, "the old man is tired. You're not allowed."

"Oh, really!"

"Way it is."

Audrey whined, "So I have to follow you around while you try to sell me furniture I wouldn't buy at a fire sale? Sorry. It's the furnished apartment for me!"

Richard's voice smoothed out. "Well, lady, this is your lucky day. The furnishings in this showroom are yours for the next two days, free of charge, and all we ask is that you leave a testimonial at the desk when you leave. Can you get more lucky?"

"Why no, sir. I can try out all this luscious stuff and not even pay for it? Oh my!" Audrey batted her eyes at Richard, which caused them both to roar.

Ted came out of the smaller bedroom pretending to rub his eyes. "Can't an old guy get any sleep around here? Do I have to find a motel?

Audrey became instantly contrite. "Sorry, Ted. Just getting acquainted."

"Rather well, from the sound of it." Ted smiled and Audrey knew he had feigned, too.

"I was about to tell Richard that somebody must owe you big-time at the Waldorf-Astoria. This is good furniture."

"It was in the budget, so we bought it. Isn't that the way it's done?"

"I guess."

"You young people go on about your business. I'm really going to turn in."

At that moment a chime rang softly but insistently throughout the building. Levity ceased. Richard ran toward the communications room, followed on his heels by Ted. Audrey ran a couple of paces behind.

"What is it?" she called with alarm.

"We'll know in a moment," Ted called back.

When Audrey came into the smallish com section of the...what... Situation Room, Richard's hands were moving expertly over the equipment, intent on discovering the problem earliest and oblivious to anyone around him. Ted pulled Audrey off to the side and spoke to her in lowered tones.

"Richard is one of our better electronic equipment people. The duty stations know their stuff, but Richard has a peculiar knack for it. He can run anything, which is one of the reasons Stoic wants your team-up. The set-up he's accessing gives an electronic view of the cliffs outside. Fine-shielded wire has been hidden and strung all over the face of the cliffs. It attaches to sensors and several miniature cameras that give us an outside overview, seaward, top, and sides. It's highest state of the art. It would take the greatest catastrophe, such as blasting the cliffs down, to render the system inoperable."

Audrey nodded.

"The stakes are that high."

"I'm convinced. Is there anything I can do?

"Not yet."

Richard worked at the equipment for about thirty seconds. Then he turned them. "Seeing outward from the cliffs is great, but it's impossible to see what's happening on the face of them. From what I can tell, a loose rock probably dislodged midway up, and took out a part of the screen. It's bad news because one of the cameras isn't functioning, probably went with it, and our seaward visual has been reduced by twelve percent."

Ted interrupted. "Probabilities?"

"The crisscross scanner across the bay that monitors movement near the precipice is functioning, and I ran the record back to yesterday. No evidence of movement outside of the inevitable seagulls."

"Good!" breathed Ted. "What do you suggest?"

A particularly telling talent for leadership showed in Ted. He could easily make command decisions, but would rather leave them with his operative. It built confidence and character, an essential element in operative training.

Richard responded, "I'll need to get out on the cliff face and effect repairs."

"Why not get the crew in here for that?" Ted asked.

"Because no one is supposed to know what's going on in here for the next two days. If we are to go in to the top looking for a double, we don't want *anyone* to know we are here. Therefore, I go out and do the repair."

"Excellent thinking, but you're going to stay here and monitor the equipment while Audrey, your fair wife does the job."

"Me?" Audrey looked astonished. "Why me?"

"You are an acrobat. You can replace the unit and repair the net easily enough. I'll give you a short course on what's necessary. Richard must be here to protect you and to keep a keen eye on the equipment, something he can do, and at the moment, you can't. He will check for ships or aircraft. Richard, did you check the Lodge?"

"Yes, it's clear."

Audrey looked Ted over and said, "One more surprise. Actually, it doesn't surprise me now. Very little surprises me any more."

"There are some surprises yet, Audrey. I want you to follow me to the top."

"The top?"

"We have land access."

"I gathered."

"You need to know the ins and outs of the facility and the protections we have on them."

"Okay, Ted."

"We'll wait until first light. This needs to be done as soon as possible, but we can't work with lights in the dark. We have special gear for cliff work. We'll get you a short-range radio. It's barely adequate for what we need to do, but we don't dare put more power to them."

"I understand."

"Okay. Better get some sleep. I'll do a wakeup for 0400. That will give us time we need. Richard, set the chime alarms again, and everyone hit the sack."

"Right."

They left, Ted to one bedroom, the "newlyweds" to the other. Audrey thought it might be awhile before she'd come down from the excitement of the previous evening, especially with a hunk like Richard lying next to her. Surprise! Richard planted a kiss on her womanly lips, and said, "Goodnight, Audrey," and rolled over.

"My God," she breathed, "a man of honor?"

She gave him a little push with her backside.

"Catch you later, husband."

There was an, "Umph!" from the other lump under the covers. She lay there for a couple of minutes listening to Richard's breathing become regular and deep. She found his breathing relaxing. The next thing she knew, the bed alarm went off.

Audrey lay for a few seconds soaking up the amazing past. She turned over, and sure enough, Richard lay there, looking at her. She gazed back.

"Morning, wife. Tell me, do you use litanies to keep you straight?"

Shock! "Yes!"

"Here's mine for today. 'This is only an assignment. This is only an assignment.'"

Audrey's gaze remained soft. "I know. I barely know you, Richard, but I couldn't hate you, I know that. I think it would be better if I didn't like you so much."

Richard looked at her with true affection. "Your thoughts are my thoughts, but we have to be true to our training. The company is number one. Training will keep us alive. I ask you to take that small part of you I have seen and put it into some small, protected place. I will do the same. When this assignment is done and we can manage some time off..."

Audrey nodded.

A knock came at the door. Richard threw off his covers and went to the door clad in his shorts. He opened the door.

"Room service? I thought I asked for the continental breakfast. Where's your cart tray?"

Ted smiled and said, "Come on, troops, time to get moving."

He turned on his heel and left the door ajar. The aromatic smell of hickory-flavored coffee wafted into their bedroom.

Richard turned back toward the bed and caught Audrey heading for the bathroom in her bra and panties. She looked over and stared at him. He stared back.

"Have you no shame?"

He looked behind him.

"No, I don't think so. Misplaced it, I think."

That struck her funny. Her lilting laugh pealed. She resumed her course into the bathroom and shut the door. Richard set out his clothes. His lot was easiest. He didn't have to rappel down the cliff and fix the net. He'd better tell Audrey to watch for sudden gusts. From its history he knew strong winds had blown more than one worker from his perch during the construction of the electronic web.

Audrey came out from the shower naked, a towel around her head. Richard took his turn.

On his way past he said, "I'm so glad you covered up that sexy hair."

She unwound the towel quickly and flicked his butt.

"Ow!"

"Get thee hence, varlet," she said.

He giggled. "You wait..."

"Hey, Ted! Richard giggles," she called through the open door. Ted started singing loudly. Audrey dressed quickly, went into the kitchen and sat at the table with Ted. He rose and poured coffee for her.

"Eggs, toast? Bacon on the side?" he said.

"Sounds good."

Ted got a plate and expertly served her two fried eggs from the skillet, grabbed a couple pieces of toast and bacon and waved at the marmalade and butter.

"I'm doing this to ingratiate myself to you so you'll do the cooking from now on." He smiled his lopsided smile at her.

"Oh, I'm sorry sir. I don't cook."

"A woman who doesn't cook...fie!" he said.

"Well, to show my appreciation for putting me in harms way today, I suppose I could make lunch. How do you take your arsenic?"

Ted got serious. "Speaking of harm's way, as soon as we've eaten, we need to get started. The equipment is ready. We've spares of nearly everything in the facility. It'll take twenty minutes, minimum, to get topside and past the protections. Another fifteen to set up on the precipice. Be light enough to work then. Repair should take about an hour, but..."

Why must there always be a qualifying "but," in their business? Ted pulled a small onionskin map from his shirt pocket. He pushed food dishes and kitchen things to the side and spread it out on the table upside down. Audrey looked it over. "This is the web. I marked the break. You'll rappel from here." He pointed.

Ted didn't bother to ask if she thought she could do it or even if she wanted to or if she had concerns.

Richard joined them dressed in khakis, looking rugged and virile. He went to the stove and scraped the remaining eggs onto a plate, grabbed toast, and sat down.

"How we making out?"

"Good. We're about ready to start. I'm going to educate Audrey now. I left a short-range radio by your equipment. Check in when you get set up."

"Uh-huh." Richard went to work on his breakfast.

The other two retired to the stock room and climbed into camouflage garb. Audrey's outfit was of cliff-side color, black and gray streaked. Ted donned a multi-green one-piece fatigue reminiscent of those used by jungle fighters in Costa Rica. They were heavily pocketed and zippered at the top.

Next Ted grabbed a body harness for Audrey, and enough rope to make the descent, the same color as the suit she wore. He passed her the items she needed. She hefted and held and looked them over critically. He told her what pockets to put various items in.

Ted went over what she needed to do and in what order. Finally satisfied that she had it, he motioned for her to follow him and they left the building.

At the door he gave her today's combination and told her that anything could happen.

9

About three a.m. Bernie tossed, overtired but unable to get any real sleep. Something invaded his consciousness! He sat up and pushed the cobwebs away. The cruiser! It had floated free. He made his way over to the sleeping Malfo and shook him. Nick's lieutenant came awake instantly. Bernie moved back quickly to avoid being cut by the fish knife Malfo kept in his left sleeve.

"What, fucknuts!" Alonzo Malfo came to in a flash.

"Chill, Alonzo! Tides in. We're free."

Malfo sat there for a minute comprehending the new information, and then, without a word, got up and tried the engine. It fired after three tries. He carefully swung the big boat around and headed for shore, clearing the bilge along the way. Nick loved his boat and only people he believed would take extraordinary care of it were put in position to use it.

Alonzo Malfo wasn't the real seaman his boss was, but he got Nick's nod, and in this organization, that kind of acceptance was power. Nobody better cross either of them. He put the dock to starboard and eased in. Bernie cast the lines and made fast.

Malfo disembarked first, followed by Homenio. They walked the dock and trudged the seventy stairs to the lower portico of Nick Trafalgar's palatial mansion. They moved through stillness. Neither man said a word. Mist had begun to rise on the water.

They climbed, only their own labored breathing giving life to this place, that only hours before had been the scene of the hedonistic excesses of the privileged and connected. They moved across the top of the huge, flat, open area. Greek statues on stone pedestals stood or sat mutely, punctuating the vastness with their bulk. Otherwise imposing, the two men hardly glanced at them.

Those thoughtful caricatures, muscular, in pain, carved in a plethora of fixations from a world that had died thousands of years ago, yet forced to exist here to continue to live in stone and marble meant little to the men. The stories they told were lost on men who lived in the now, and only by their wits. After the emotion eternalized on their stone faces, the many plant-filled urns seemed only to occupy space.

For one moment, Bernie reflected that one of those guys who studied people and history would go wild in a place like this. Closer to the surface, he thought with disdain that Alonzo Malfo wouldn't be Nick's right hand man if he had any imagination. Nick knew how to pick 'em. They'd do for him, because the boss was too smart to put in people who would question his authority or his direction. His top people knew what they needed to and were smart enough, but never smarter than the leader and they knew it. A perfect scenario for Nick, so Bernie needed to cool his heels and give lip service to secondary leadership.

At the juncture of the main house with the guest quarters, Alonzo pointed, and Bernie moved off to the left. Not invited, well, fuck him! In a moment it came to him that Malfo would hit the sack instead of going up to see the boss. He cooled off a little. He would bide his time, and when time favored *him,* he would make his move.

Maybe he should get some real rest. He moved into the soldiers' area, entered his room and looked it over carefully. Untouched. Bernie locked his door and crashed.

10

Behind the company building Ted and Audrey approached a granite wall. A four-foot, almost square opening that looked like natural rock greeted them. Blackness loomed beyond. Without a word Ted ducked under and disappeared. Audrey couldn't see a thing but followed silently.

In a few moments her eyes acclimated to deeper darkness. She made out a green glow at floor level, then three more ahead of her, further ones occasionally blotted out momentarily by Ted as he stepped along. Above her, at odd distances and heights she noted green rectangular glows. As they got to the last one they could see, more green glows appeared to her right on both floor and ceiling.

It happened again and again as the tunnel curved. Audrey guessed quickly that the ceiling varied in height and the upper green glows marked low points. Clearly they were meant to prevent brain damage. She glanced back. Yes, marked for the return trip, too. She reached out tentatively with her right hand and felt for the wall. She got her answer when her hand brushed against an outcropping.

Pretty obvious from changes in ceiling height, she knew. She could have asked Ted anytime, but she wouldn't do that. Figuring things out made her more confident. When questions needed to be asked, she would ask them.

The twists and turns were part of an old river course. As they moved forward she began to hear a sound, like swiftly running water somewhere near. Under, over, she couldn't be sure. Soon the tunnel began to vibrate noticeably. It made her uneasy.

When the sound became quite loud, Ted stopped. His shadowy hand reached up and pushed at something in the ceiling.

"Quick! Run!" He motioned for her to hurry.

She raced ahead. Once past, Ted stopped and speaking loud enough for her to hear, told her about the trap they had just crossed.

"A section of the floor is made to look and feel like the tunnel. If the person approaching doesn't neutralize the trap door, fifteen feet of floor hinged on the upside will drop them into the ice-cold river below. An unhappy death awaits. Even with the neutralizing switch we must get off it within four seconds. It's a defensive weapon. If we were being pursued, it could save our lives. The trap resets itself two seconds after it feels the last weight, giving a fleeing party an added measure of space in which to run or protect. Needless to say, anyone who comes here must be thoroughly familiar with our measures and countermeasures."

Audrey had seen death before, but an involuntary shudder gripped her as she pictured this particularly nasty one.

"Let's go. Watch your footing. It gets tougher, and slippery," Ted urged. They made an abrupt turn left and continued. Nice, Audrey thought, someone's shooting at you, make the turn, hit the switch and the pursuer gets dumped. Meantime the cave wall takes the shots. If she were designing a trap like that, it's just what she would do.

They had been gradually climbing, but now it became abrupt and more rugged. The green squares didn't illuminate much. Audrey figured they had walked nearly a quarter of a mile. She placed her feet carefully on the uneven floor and felt her way. Almost like walking a tightrope, she thought. Even so, they made good time. She gauged they must be about two hundred vertical feet above the sanctuary by the lake.

Audrey did a little mental calculation. The cliffs, according to her topography map were four hundred feet off the ocean. They were about halfway there!

Ted stopped. They'd entered a high, arching room. Audrey couldn't see its top. A metal ladder stood against one wall and rose out of sight. Ted did something in a small alcove. This time, without speaking, he pointed to what looked like a spring-loaded bus bar switch in the down position. He pointed to some camouflaged heavy gauge copper wires attached to the bottom of the ladder, one black, one red, one green. Ted started up and motioned her to follow.

"Slippery," he said.

The first of four ladders, this one ended fifty feet above them. After that Ted moved to another attached to an outcropping. To continue upward they had to move off the second metal ladder and cross empty space to grasp the third. Now they climbed the wooden variety, each perhaps twenty-five feet long. These ladders were in new condition, despite evidently having been in place for a long time. They leaned against a straight rock wall and stood on natural outcroppings. It must have been a hundred and fifty vertical feet in all. Audrey calculated that they were not far from the surface now. They had climbed for two solid minutes, eighteen minutes total by her luminous dial.

Ted spoke now. "I could have told you about each and every hazard, but the best way to learn is to be on the edge. How do you feel?"

"Fine. Got it. Much further?"

"You see the corridor?" He pointed.

"Yes."

"That's it." Ted went to the far end, uncovered a fish-eye peephole and gazed through. No one in sight. He turned to his right and did something to the wall, showing her what he did. Another panel opened and in red LED she saw a thumb print verifier. Ted placed his right thumb over the sensor. After a moment, with an almost inaudible click, a door on the opposite side of the panel opened inward.

They entered a very small room, large enough to hold maybe five people in a pinch. Ted touched a button on one wall and a monitor sprang to life, showing a sweep of the interior beyond them. It appeared to be a hunting lodge, a not unlikely style for this far out on Long Island. A hidden camera automatically and silently swung, giving panoramic views of the exterior. They saw no sign of movement.

"Looks okay," Ted said.

He pressed a button and a section of wall slid away. They entered the lodge.

"Owned by a consortium of contributors to the cause of world peace, we'll say. They don't come here. It's a perfect front."

Audrey looked around, but Ted was in a hurry.

"Let's get the job done. When we get back, we'll get you acquainted with the place." He began a running monologue, things to look for, innocence that was far from it, trappings of a hidden and deadly dangerous covert world. They made their way to the cliff edge where Ted found a well-rooted and sturdy tree. He carefully wrapped material around it to eliminate telltale signs of their passing. Enemies might find signs and deduce other things. Losing this place would be a serious blow to the organization.

"Optimize your chances. From the Manual. Now, get into your harness, and we'll get this done."

Audrey went to work.

11

At five a.m., Nick came awake in the darkness and went looking for answers. He called the night man and found that the Nicosia had docked around three-thirty. He searched out Alonzo and shook him awake. The knife went away as soon as Nick's lieutenant recognized his boss.

"Sorry."

"Don't be. Stay alive. Now, report." Nick pushed into Malfo's consciousness.

"Never had her. Her draft musta been at least three feet less than the cruiser. We reefed on the sandbar. Almost lost Homenio. Impossible to see anything in the dark when them big clouds go over the moon. Boat's okay, two of us okay. We start fresh. What else?"

"Lost a big chance to lay out a probable enemy." And, he thought, Rathmanizzar won't be happy. "You know what this means?"

"Sure. More care, back up, figure other avenues. Nothing new."

"Alonzo," Nick said carefully, "I have proof that the *lady* will become a serious thorn in the side of a business associate who is *very* important to me."

The stressed "very" caught Alonzo's attention.

"I don't know who she is, but something's going on out there I need to know about before I take the next step in my plan."

"She's just a bitch, Nick. We can fight it."

Nick blazed at him. "It's obvious, Malfo, that you don't know what the fucks going down!"

Whoa! What the hell?

"Nick, let me in if you want. You don't have to do it alone. I'm there with you."

The boss calmed down. "You get what you need to know. You know more than any of the soldiers in the organization, but not this. A few details, then I can let you in. Be there for me."

"Sure, boss, always. You know."

"Okay. I got a job for you. Come up to my office around ten."

"Sure, Nick."

"We're brothers, Alonzo, you're important to me. Soon, Alonzo, soon."

"Okay, Nick."

The boss left Malfo's bedroom as quickly as he arrived, an idea taking shape in his mind.

Now where *did* the woman go? It disturbed him. Sailboat disappeared into the ocean. Rocco. He'd get Rocco up with his twin-engine spotter this morning to run the coast and check out to forty miles. She couldn't have gotten farther out than that. Besides, it would be stupid. A storm's coming up from the south and she'd run right into it. If I know about it, she does too. He wouldn't put his cruiser out in that, and it was more seaworthy than a thirty-foot sailboat.

What if she wasn't alone? He didn't think of that before. Somebody else on her boat? Couldn't be! I had Bernie check out the boat before the party got underway. Nobody there, he said, and decked out all female, neat and tidy.

Did she know the coast? A secret harbor? Nah, couldn't be. I had the whole coast surveyed before I built this place. A lot of it's dangerous and much more is inaccessible. Rocks, quick mud, miles of salt marsh, even that fucking sandbar I keep clearing and it keeps coming back. That's why I planted here. No company unless *I* want company. And I got friends in the little towns for thirty miles along the coast who make a little scratch passing stuff on anytime they see something strange. So where the hell did she *go*?

At his study he immediately went to his phone.

"Rocco, I got a chore for you."

"That you, Nick?"

"Yeah."

"What you need?"

"Can you take your bird up this morning—like right away, like now—and cruise out to forty miles and along the coast toward Great South Bay? Looking for a sailboat. One of the women from the party last night got miffed and took off alone. She's a good sailor, but a storm's coming up and I don't want she should get hurt, you know."

"Right. Nick, the bird is down, maintenance, but I can get it closed up for take-off in fifteen, twenty minutes. That okay? Be about six-ish or so. Okay?"

"Sure, Rocco, I appreciate. If you spot her, dark blue hull, white sail, "Lucky Lady" on the side in white, fancy writing, call me by radiophone, just give position numbers, say 'em two numbers lower, no call signs, nothing else. That'll fake out the Coast Guard, if they're listening. We'll get her. When you get back drive up and we'll have a drink together. You got time?"

"I'll make time, Nick, for you. I'll be on 880.25 when I get up."

"Good."

"Roger, Nick, okay I bring my boy to work the glasses?"

"Little Rocco, you mean? Sure. And bring him up to see Uncle Nicky."

"Thanks. If the boat's out there, we'll find it."

"Good." Nick hung up.

He picked up immediately and dialed his dispatcher. "Ray, Rocco's going out to look. Stay on the receiver, 880.25. I'll be in my study."

"Okay, boss."

Nick hung up and sat back in his comfortable leather desk chair. He steepled his big hands and looked at them. Rathmanizzar, one dangerous son-of-a-bitch. Thinks I'm playing his game. I'm okay until he finds out I'm not, then all fucking hell's going to break loose. Why did he want the girl rubbed? He knows something I need to find out. He sat, trying to decide his next moves. It's like a chess game, he thought. He didn't even like chess, but it was just like it.

12

Ted tossed a safety rope over the side. It disappeared down the cliff, the camouflaged rope melding with the rocky granite. Audrey moved to the edge and looked out to sea. Nothing! She went over. Even with special boots, the cliff face was slippery in the early morning dew. She rappelled in short hops. Ted fed her line. When she got to the approximate site of the problem, she unhooked her short-range radio and called up to Ted.

"I'm about there. Don't see it yet. Richard, are you hearing us."

"Roger. Keep voice com to a minimum."

"Right." She looked over the rock area. "Going east."

She worked in silence for a minute or so, hopping to her right. Occasionally she saw thin wiring installed around crevasses of rock, very well hidden. Kudos to the construction team. Excellent work. In fifteen feet of sideways hopping Audrey found it. A piece of the cliff a couple of feet wide and four feet long had come away. Stainless steel pins were embedded in the rock. Evidently the crew who'd worked this part of the cliff had noted it but hadn't considered it dangerous enough to disconnect.

"I'm there."

No answer from either listener. Ted, topside, checked his watch. Richard kept a wary eye on his electronics. They watched the day brighten quickly.

Audrey removed pitons from her left pocket, drove them into two useful cracks in the rock and cradled herself. She went to work. She got out hangers, attached them to the newly exposed section, and carefully removed the replacement visual sensor. She affixed it, but left it loose enough to be repositioned later.

She donned gloves, located the torn leads, stripped and clipped them and covered them with special waterproof goop. The goop had a nerve reactant in it that absorbed through the skin. She eyeballed the coming day. She'd do it in two stages.

Amber searched for and located leads to the right and left of her. The three above her she handled with dispatch. Working quickly, Audrey made all attachments, extended wires where needed and hooked them into the sensor's connection board. She gave no thought to the two hundred-foot drop to the ocean. So far, so good!

"Ted, I need six feet down."

Ted paid out the line carefully.

"Two more." Her tinny voice came through to her man above.

"Stop."

She had located three leads at an intersecting point where they attached to the rock. Everything above had gone into the sea with the rock fall. She pried the wires out of their mooring, stripped and clipped them, and then reattached the junction. Audrey gauged the lengths she needed by eye, cut and stripped them and made them permanent. Then she brought out the special gloves and waterproofed everything. Satisfied, she pulled off the saturated gloves and stuffed them into a convenient crevasse.

"Up eight," she called softly.

The little pulley at her waist creaked slightly as Ted put tension on it. She rose toward the sensor. So far so good.

"Stop!" Richards' voice held urgency.

"Aircraft approaching from the north, flying low. Hug the cliff, Audrey!"

Both workers heard the drone of a small plane. It grew louder. Audrey put up the camouflaged hood of her jumper and made herself part of the mountain. Up on top, Ted pulled a camo-net over him and disappeared from view. Audrey turned her head slightly in time to see an old Rockwell Commander; its two engines thrumming in the peculiar way that such engines spoke to the air, clear the top of Spicer's Rocks by only a hundred feet and proceed out to sea. The plane continued south without a pause.

After an interminable time, Richard said, "Clear."

"Audrey, here we go." Ted started pulling again.

A moment later, "Okay, we're here."

Audrey quickly connected the three leads, pulled another pair of gloves on and waterproofed the rest of her work. She then pushed her feet out from the rock to inspect her handiwork.

"Done. Looks good." She moved to the side. "Your move, Richard."

"Good job, Audrey. Move the sensor a little to your left and up slightly..."

"How's that?"

"Pretty good. A tad more to the left...there! Whoa. Fits the parameters. Button it down. You've earned lunch."

"A 'tad', you say? My, how archaic."

"You better be nice, or I won't show you what I was going to show you tonight."

"Did I happen to see it this morning?"

"Oh, God, I'm so embarrassed."

"You were this morning...bare-assed, I mean."

"Okay, you kids, knock it off. Daddy is listening. Audrey, I'm going to haul you up."

"Ted, give me a sec to zip up."

Richard came out with his latest. "Oh my, sex on the rocks. How kinky."

"Knock it off, children!" But Ted didn't sound mad.

After a minute, Audrey called up to Ted, "Okay, haul away."

She started to rise rapidly. Once again Ted impressed her with his strength. Audrey bounced away from the rock face as she rose, rappelling upward. In three minutes she grasped Ted's hand and alighted on a horizontal rock surface. He pulled her quickly into the underbrush and then Ted spent a couple of minutes with the binoculars, checking behind the screen.

He said, "Quiet success is the best success."

They broke down quickly and made their way back to the lodge.

13

Ted showed Audrey around the place. The initial peephole turned out to be a view through the eyes of a big unlucky buck. "The two fish eyes have cleverly matched optics inside so that virtually every spot in the lodge can be viewed before an operative will leave the underground entrance."

The furniture was hunting lodge quality. Everything fit as to purpose and use. Ted pointed to the windows surrounding the lodge.

"They aren't quite one way glass, but they have a non-reflective tint to them, so that they don't flash notice to low flying planes or ships which could catch morning or evening sunlight just right. We don't want to draw attention to ourselves in any way."

The lodge had a working bar stocked with liquor. The refrigerator had its complement of Beck's, Heineken, and Bass beers or ales. Audrey looked around, noting everything, just as Ted had. She told Ted she had the picture. He nodded.

"Let's head back."

Ted took a last look around. Nothing out of place.

"You say no one comes here at all?" Audrey asked.

"Not from the consortium. This land entrance is only for duty staff. Literally no one else is allowed access or knowledge of it. The protected road that comes from the nearest highway is over a mile away. It empties out onto Route 27. The entire area is a private rich mans' compound and meant to seem that way. That means old looking fences and modern snoop defenses. People we know whom we have enlisted in the overt side of the company legitimately own estates on all sides of this place. They are compensated through stock options and similar means and have a vested interest in requests from the president of the company. All agreed to keep the cliffs and environs stranger free."

"Hmmm."

"Paranoia isn't appropriate anywhere, but we get as close to it as reasonability dictates."

"So I gather."

"Once back in the tunnel entrance, I'll show you our perimeter defense." Audrey followed Ted back to the seemingly innocent wall. An attractive bar filled the right side. Ted leaned casually over and moved the ashtray a quarter inch. The wall slid away as it had before. Then he moved it back. The wall closed as silently and smoothly as before.

"Now watch carefully what I do." He moved the ashtray more than a quarter of an inch.

Audrey heard no sound, but suddenly Richard's voice came out of the air above them. "I assume that was necessary."

Ted smiled quickly and spoke out into the room, "Sorry, Richard, I should have mentioned I would test out the passive alert system to Audrey while we were up here."

"My ears are still ringing." Richard sounded hurt.

Ted looked at Audrey and said simply, "The place is wired with more than listening equipment. In the unlikely event that an this lodge was "made" by an enemy, the operative below would look at the intruder, and if he or she didn't recognize the trespasser, the doors and windows would lock. The operative would release a sleeping gas and said unfortunate would soon be in bigger trouble than they had ever stepped into before."

Audrey said, "I've been running parallel to you. I can't think of anything you haven't thought of."

"Yes, it's well planned." He moved the ashtray once more the requisite distance. The wall slid open again and he moved toward it.

"That's casual defense," Ted said. They crowded into the tiny room behind the wall. Ted showed her the stud to press, and she did. The wall closed. They were in the dark again, obviously deigned to recover an operative's night vision before descending.

Ted went to the monitor. He turned the knob, and perimeter scenes jumped in. He showed Audrey the entire perimeter and then shut it down.

He took out his short range radio and said, "Testing, testing."

Richard's voice came back. "Go."

"Audrey, put your hand over the thumb sensor."

She did. She heard nothing, but Richard said "intruder" softly into the phone.

"Reset."

"Done."

"If it had been a real intruder, this small room would lock and refuse exit from either side. The intruder would be gassed, removed to our depot, shaved of all the information he had, and eliminated. It's war."

Ted put his hand over the sensor. The heavy steel door to the cavern opened silently and they entered. On the way down, Ted had Audrey neutralize each death dealing devise under his guidance. The trap door into the river bothered Audrey, but Ted assured her that nothing would happen to them if she followed his direction to the letter.

She had a thought. "What if one of our own was turned?"

"Excellent question. Each of the operatives is required to report every half hour using a computer key code only they know. If they fail to report, a contact at InFab is alerted and all remote codes are automatically changed until the situation is abated. Anyone stuck either in the lodge or the depot is trapped until released. All equipment, therefore, is also rendered useless for the duration. Backup personnel are never more than a half hour from the depot."

"Nice."

A half-hour later they were once again in the innocuous looking fortress at sea level.

Richard greeted her with a kiss that he planted solidly on Audrey's mouth.

"A privilege of the married," he said

He snickered when Audrey tried to belt him. "I learned how fast you were this morning with the towel."

"All right, you guys, you can get reacquainted later. Audrey, I need you with me for a few more minutes. Bring your gear."

Ted took his equipment and insisted that Audrey watch him put it away.

"Take an hour and familiarize yourself with everything."

"Sure."

"We are so close to Trafalgar that this depot is ideal for surveillance of his operation, a fortuitous plus for us. It also represents a danger."

"Yes. Should he ever find out about us, he wouldn't make many waves conducting a destruct mission."

"Exactly, although it would be much tougher than it might seem." Ted glanced at his watch. "It's only ten o'clock. Look around. Never know when we'll feel this safe again."

"Right."

Ted left her and went back to the com station. Richard told him everything was quiet. He set it on automatic and they retired to the living room. In an hour, Audrey made her way back. She plopped down with Richard in the love seat. Ted sat facing them in a leather recliner.

"Audrey, have you caught up to the enormity of what we've done here?" Ted asked.

"Yes, I'm with the program, and I have an idea what you want of me. I am thoroughly impressed with the facility and environs. How many people exactly have been involved in the building and outfitting of the East Coast depot?"

"An even dozen. More than Stoic wanted, but he sees realities and had to agree with the number. All of the "volunteers" were men and they were required to undergo hypnotic suggestion. Should our enemies locate any of them, the suggestion will cause amnesia and render them useless. We hated to do that, but protecting the depot is paramount."

"I understand. But only a dozen people, that amazes me. This must have been underway for a long time."

"Three years."

"Impressive. No leaks?"

"Hard not to, but we used a watch-on-watch suggestion as a part of the hypnosis, very subtle. We discovered one worker who had been tampered with, probably by the traitor we are trying to identify and neutralize. We deactivated and replaced him. It went smoothly after that."

"I'm not going to ask what you mean by neutralize, but I need to know how many in the top echelon know of this place?"

"Stoic and us three, plus the duty people, who actually know very little beyond their surveillance job. It isn't necessary for you to know how many are involved. Less known, less said."

"Whew!"

"The other four control depots are in other parts of the world. Only Stoic has those details. There is a tremendous amount of trust involved in the running of an organization of this type, although it would be foolish of any of us to ever assume that Stoic isn't aware of most everything that's going on. Still, he can't know all, and that is the Sword of Damocles that hangs over his head."

"That means four possibles. I'll need to know something on each of the four. Can do?" Audrey was deep in thought.

"That's the rub. Can't do. It has to do with the unique setup of the cells that makes the organization so dangerous to people like Rathmanizzar. Stoic, literally, is the only one with the information."

"I suppose we'll eventually meet him, won't we?"

"That's up to him. Do you know what he looks like?"

"No."

"I do." Richard, who had been sitting quietly listening to the exchange, now spoke up. "I met him once on an assignment."

Ted shifted his gaze. "Okay. What does he look like?"

Richard described the picture of the man at length.

When he was finished, Ted said. "You are correct. But you will never see him look like that again. Stoic is a master of disguise. I know you've heard that. Well, anyone in his organization below the top echelon who meets him he ensures will never recognize him again. I believe it's entirely possible that he uses a singular disguise for the top echelon, too, but maybe that sounds paranoid. Still, he is a very private man. You might just as well forget your description, Richard. If he decided to meet with you, he might use the same disguise for you and Audrey. He'd remember it. He has total recall."

"Sounds like an interesting man," Audrey said.

"Very."

Richard sat in his seat, looking a little uncomfortable. Ted got up and went into the kitchen. He called from there, asking if anyone wanted anything.

"Not me," said Audrey.

"Me, neither," said Richard.

Ted returned with a steaming cup of coffee. He set it on the end table next to his seat, and sat down again. "We need to get started. You both are going to need some changes, too. Richard, there is some special electronic equipment I brought in with me you haven't seen yet. I'll need about two hours or less to familiarize you with it. Audrey, you will need to get in on this also, as it's going to hook you two together like you wouldn't believe."

"What is it?" Asked Audrey

"Patience." Ted took his coffee and sipped it. "This is a rare thing for me, and I'm going to enjoy it."

"C'mon, Ted, you get us all interested and then you sit and sip coffee?"

"Patience."

Richard turned to Audrey and said mischievously, "Hey, why don't you and I adjourn to the bedroom while our master is sipping coffee. I want to show you something."

Audrey said in mock anger, "It isn't the thing you wanted to show me when I was hanging from the side of the cliff, is it?"

"Perish the thought. Ooh, perish isn't a nice word, okay, give the thought leave to go. Is that better?"

Audrey laughed and Ted smiled. More levity, more saving grace. It was redeeming.

Richard said, "I got really excited when you were hanging way up there above the sea. So seldom can we men get a woman into such a compromised position."

Audrey gave him a hard elbow in the ribs. "That's for thinking such thoughts."

"Oof!"

"Watch it! I'm not on the cliff now."

With reverence, Richard said, "Oh, how I love to watch it."

She jabbed him again. "Do men never learn?

"I hope not!" Richard moved across the seat quickly to avoid another jab.

The repartee went on for several minutes. Ted sat, taking an occasional drink from his cup and smiling now and then. Finally he uncrossed his legs.

"I wish this could go on forever, but we have work to do and we don't know how much time we have."

They turned off and followed Ted.

14

"Bernie, get Stretch. Time we had some fun."

"What's goin' down, boss?"

"Get Stretch!"

"Okay, boss!" Homenio turned quickly and left.

Nick entered his study on the mansion's first floor. His thoughts eased as he folded his big frame into the deep brown glove-leather chair behind his massive mahogany desk. Hundreds of literary works adorned the walls of the study. He hadn't read a single one of them and never would. Nick's idea of reading material involved spreadsheets and invoices, and especially bottom lines.

Dark mahogany wood, polished to a lustrous sheen glowed around him. A fit sitting room for a king, he thought. He enjoyed the heaviness, the substance; it was a thing he could touch and feel. It wasn't like dealing with people. With people you could never be sure.

He faced the massive inlaid black marble fireplace. White graining ran through the marble in interesting patterns. He studied it as he had many times before. Here was a place for deep thought, where big decisions that moved his life were made. He could feel a cusp coming, but he couldn't see it. Unknowns always bothered him.

Nick heard a soft knock at the study door. The boss got out of his chair and walked to it. He opened the door.

Bernie and Stretch stood there.

"You two come in here a minute." Nick stood back.

Bernie walked in first. He wore a blue polo shirt and had on khaki knee length shorts with a beige woven belt. His hairy legs were sun-bleached blond, although his lineage clearly came from darker Mediterranean genes. He got a lot of time in the sun, by the looks.

Stretch Monaghal was tall and thin, a couple of inches over six feet. His eyes darted this way and that in his thin face and they took in everything. On first impression he appeared gawkish, but he moved sinuously and he had a snap to his movements. A trained observer would instantly label him dangerous, a man to be handled very carefully. He had on black pants and a dark gray shirt. A silver necklace hung in the open neck. He had the look of a predator. He had another name amongst his fellows, Weasel!

"Bernie, you know where we put Tommie Boy last night." Bernie nodded.

"Stretch, we're gonna give a lesson this morning." Nick closed the outer door and locked it.

He went to his phone and picked up. "Ray, no calls. I'll let you know."

Satisfied with the response, he hung up. "Let's go."

The three passed through the study and went immediately to the right side book-wall. Nick pulled a copy of War and Peace out a couple of inches. A hidden door in the wall clicked open with a soft sound. The book-wall swung out, revealing a gray painted hallway. The three moved into a narrow corridor. The spring-loaded door closed silently behind them.

They turned to meet a set of stairs going down. There were a lot of stairs. They moved soundlessly on the carpeted part. At a landing halfway down the carpeting ended. The walls became irregular and cement stairs completed the journey. They were well under the house now and their steps rang hollowly. The walls were vaguely moist. At the bottom a soundproof door waited at the end of a short cement apron. Of heavy steel construction, it stared at them, silent and ominous.

At the side of the big door was a metal cabinet. Nick opened it and gestured. "Put those on."

Shiny yellow plastic, one-piece "duck" suits hung inside. Stretch and Bernie looked at one another, reached in and grabbed the one size fits all outfits and climbed into them silently. They zipped up the front and gathered at the wrists and the ankles.

In two minutes they turned to Nick, who grabbed a key from a metal peg left of the big door and unlocked it. He flipped the light switch nearby.

"Good morning, Tommie Boy. Did you sleep well?" Nick grated.

Tom Geacali lay on a mattress on the floor. He sat up when he heard the sound of the key in the door. A fearful look haunted his eyes. He climbed to his feet. His eyes got even wider when he saw the two guys behind him. He stepped onto the mattress and backed into a corner.

"Nick. What's this all about? What's goin' on, boss?"

"Well, Tommie Boy," Geacali didn't like the boss's tone of voice. "It seems you disobeyed my orders last night, and the little bird you were told to wine and dine has flown."

"Nick, I did what you said...what I do?"

The boss motioned the two men and they circled around and grabbed Geacali's arms. They were both smiling.

Nick balled up a ham hand and gave Geacali a vicious cut to the middle of his face. The hit man's nose started to gush. His legs gave out and he sank to his knees. Monaghal and Homenio struggled to bring him upright.

"God! Nick! No! What I do?"

"So you were spending your time trying to get a little ass, Tommie boy? That what I told you?"

Tommie took another hit. The force of the blow bruised Nick's massive hand, but he continued to smile. Blood covered Geacali's face. He pleaded now.

"Nick. Boss," he whined, "all I did was to grab her ass. How'd I know she's a fuckin' karate expert?"

"You weren't supposed to know, you flaming asshole!" Nick shot back.

Blood ran freely down Geacali's mouth and chin. The hit man's arms hung slack, his energy drained by fear.

"You were supposed to treat her nice until Bernie could *do* her." Nick kicked Geacali's outer thigh, just aside the knee joint. Bernie and the tall, wiry Stretch both grinned at Geacali's howl.

"You didn't tell me nothin," the hit man complained, "I didn't know."

"What I told you, fuckstick, was to bring her here and show her a good time. Where did I say grab? You fucked me up, Tommie boy, and guess who's going to pay for it?"

Tom's eyes went wide. He began to sob wildly. He frantically tried to pull away form the two men holding him. Nick motioned to the Weasel, who moved behind Geacali, grabbed a hank of the bloody man's nearly black hair and yanked it maliciously. Geacali screamed.

"Take all the time you want, Tommie Boy. You recognize a one-way road, don't you, Tommie Boy?"

Mortal fear sharpened the hit man's glazed eyes. He'd heard his death sentence. He tried to rise, to get free. Bernie kicked him in the stomach. Geacali doubled over. Stretch held onto the man's hair, and now, in the Weasel's hand appeared a straight razor. The hand and razor moved expertly along the side of Geacali's neck, front to back. Soundlessly, blood began to flow. As the razor crossed the jugular, blood suddenly spurted in all directions. Geacali's screams turned hollow and came and went. His right side turned red as the blood in his throat choked him. Nick jumped back with a malignant laugh.

"Bye-bye, Tommie Boy. Give the fucking Devil my regards!"

Stretch, watching Geacali's blood in squint-eyed, tight-lipped wonder, held the man's head and watched the life go out of him. Bernie grabbed the man's belt and held on until he felt the man's body relax and slump. Geacali's eyes glazed over and bad stench filtered up from between his legs.

"Tommie Boy shit his pants. Oh my!" Trafalgar uttered in mock sympathy. "Okay, you guys. You know what to do."

Nick reached into his pocket and tossed the only key to this room to Bernie, looked at both men hard, and then turned on his heel and went back the way he came.

The lesson wasn't for Geacali.

Nick thought silently as he climbed the stairs that a little reinforcement never hurt a thing. Had a couple of good soldiers here. Bernie redeemed himself today. Geacali didn't learn quick enough.

He thought for a minute—Mikey Dorneti—young, smart enough, maybe Mikey. Good kid, lot of potential.

Out with the old, in with the new. Not a revolving door, but if you wanted to stay in his organization, you better show you've got stuff. Yeah, Mikey, he'll do. Get 'em young; train 'em right.

Once back in his office, he visited his private bathroom, looked himself over and decided he'd missed the bloodbath completely. He sat back in his oversized leather chair and rang up the dispatcher.

"Ray."

"Yeah, Nick."

"Locate Mikey Dorneti and send him up to my office."

"Sure, Nick, right away."

Inside of ten minutes, there came a knock at the door.

"Come in, Mikey."

The door opened and a young, good-looking man of twenty-five came in. "You sent for me, Mr. Trafalgar?"

"Yes, Mikey. I've got a new job for you. Interested?"

"Well, sure, Mr. Trafalgar. What's the job?"

"Tommie Geacali had an accident, and I had to retire him. I want you to take his place. Want it?"

"Tommie? Too bad! Sure, what you want me to do?"

The boss smiled on his new soldier. "First thing you can do is start calling me Nick. Bernie Homenio will be your teacher. He's finishing up some work for me right now. When he gets back I'll have him look you up."

"Thanks, Mr...ah...Nick, I won't let you down." Mikey looked proud. When the boss said anyone could call him by his first name, it was an honor and a privilege. It meant he'd made it into the upper echelon of the business. It meant he had the bosses *trust*.

Nick looked hard at his young addition. "Yeah, Mikey, don't let me down."

"I won't, Nick, I promise."

"That's all for now, Mikey. You're going to make me proud, like a son, aren't you?"

"Yeah, Nick, like a son."

15

"Richard, check everything. Join Audrey and me in fifteen minutes."

"Okay."

Ted led Audrey into the depot's War Room. He manipulated the remote and she found herself looking at a representation of Stoic's organization. It looked similar in many respects to the spider leg arrangement of Nick's organization, except that most of the blocks were empty. In this diagram she saw a center circle representing the Head, Stoic. In a ring around the center were five circles. In them were written, "Man", "Woman", "Man", "Man", "Woman".

Audrey viewed it with interest. *Females, two, although why I should care is beyond me. The best people should get the best jobs.* It was good to see. *Must be a hang-up she didn't think she had from early life.*

Ted started talking, "Of course, the names and locations of the top group can't be known by the others, as I have said. I am in the favored position of knowing them all specifically because of this assignment."

"Why?" Audrey asked.

"I have to. Assume our enemies learned that the structure of the company included women. Stoic would not have put anyone in a position of extreme sensitivity without every one being as hard to crack as you would find me to be."

"Of course."

"It doubles the number of people our enemies have to look for, and, if they aren't that smart—something we can ill afford to believe—then they probably wouldn't be looking for women at all, right? If that sounds Chauvinistic, keep in mind that many countries of this world are fiercely paternalistic, particularly in Lobala."

It made sense.

She went back to reading the diagram. She noted that the organizational chart diverged from Nick's construction where a third level block blossomed with many lines leading to many smaller blocks.

"Those," Ted went on, as if he could see into her brain, "are the genius of Stoic. What he has done is to form secondary centers that only answer to the top five. I am fully in charge of my leg of this, yet by no means do I ever feel that Stoic is unaware of what's going on. For the most part the third level doesn't require super-secret treatment. Your previous contact was third level. The operatives know very little and happily go about their business, unaware of who they really work for. It's a big protection for them.

"They are, in fact, all employees of various businesses overtly run by Manson Rettick, titular head of International Fabrications, Inc. InFab is the holding company for sixty companies making up the bulk of Stoic's operation."

"Whew! I had no idea it was so big."

"Only the top five do, and now you and Richard. I briefed him on this before I "rescued" you. I haven't drawn it in, but there should be a small line jutting from my block to you and Richard that is connected to Stoic and me. Nobody else, get it?"

"Covert within covert, right?"

"Exactly."

"Um-hum. So, why you?"

"Could have been any of the five, but Stoic picked me."

The answer didn't satisfy her curiosity, but it would have to do. Ted went on.

"The pure fact is; you and Richard are the most important people in the organization at this moment. The entire operation is in jeopardy while the traitor remains in place. Whoever it is must be found and neutralized. When you two identify our common problem, it's Stoic's plan to take out a lot of somebody else's organization, hopefully more than one, before we actually remove our own cancer. Timing will be critical."

Just then Richard walked into the ready room. "Cribbage, anyone?"

"Draw up a chair." Ted replied.

Richard sat left of Ted, who resumed his monologue.

"Richard is up to date on everything so far, and now it's time we put the plan together. As you know, I've paired you two. Stoic thinks a husband and wife team will be most effective and I agree. He and I made up the profile I gave you. How are you coming with it?"

"Fine," said Audrey, "you have me acting quite naturally. But dark auburn hair, everywhere?"

Ted smiled at that. "A disguise has to be complete. Auburn takes into account your skin tone, ability to tan, etc. It doesn't require extensive skin treatments; in other words, it doesn't require you to try to be a redhead, freckles and all. Also, your profile moves smoothly into the physical part. Less likely to be caught acting out of character."

"You've thought it out, and you want me to be an auburn redhead?"

"Yes!"

"Well, 'ere oy go!" Audrey did a bad imitation of Mollie Malloy.

Ted looked at her and suppressed a smile that threatened to crack his serious face. "Precisely what I don't want to see."

"Kidding."

"I know, but in this we must be pure. From this point, you both must act the profile. Can you do that? It could save your life. Richard, how about you? Can you fall into the 'English' character I've outlined?"

"Yes, Ted," Richard replied.

"Okay. We have about thirty minutes before Audrey has graciously offered to do lunch."

Audrey gave him a dirty look. "You don't forget anything, do you?"

"Not much, Audrey," leavened with, "at least not when my stomach's involved."

"Yeah, right!" but she smiled.

"Anyway, let's role-play until we get hungry. I will join in and listen for cracks in the cover. I will also role-play the type of interview you likely will have with each of the four you will meet. Let's make it interesting."

They went at it for an hour, each getting into their part. Every so often Ted would stop the scenario and interject a correction. Less often, he would suggest a different approach. Near one o'clock Ted called it quits for lunch.

"Break time, children. Let's go eat. What do you think, Richard? Should we help her out, or should we make her suffer?"

"You guys go away!" Audrey said, "If you don't think I can whip up a mean tuna sandwich, you've got another think coming! Now stay out of my kitchen!"

The two men laughed and walked into the living room. She busied herself at the counter as they faded from sight. Dimly she heard Richard say, "Cribbage, Ted?"

16

The cement walled room measured twelve feet square, with deep gutters on its four sides and an uncapped four-inch drain that led into the sewage system of the big house above. The walls were fully waterproofed. Little could stick to them. The system ran underground down to the bay and emptied out into the ocean; the same type of system the big mansions on Bellevue Avenue in Newport used to use before they became illegal and were hooked into the city's sanitary sewer system. Nick Trafalgar wasn't interested in legalities, though, so his system functioned just fine. He'd had the pipes extended to a rocky outcropping under constantly pounding surf, which he found very useful at times. Whatever effluent gushed to the ocean through its twelve-inch pipe made it in microscopic pieces.

The shiny, gray walled room had little in it, just a mattress and a metal chair and cabinet, bolted floor and ceiling. Weasel pulled a heavy plastic body bag out of the cabinet. The heavy stainless steel cabinet closed with a resounding clang.

Bernie and Stretch removed all of Geacali's clothing, threw the body bag over his lifeless remains and zipped him in. They muscled the former hit man's body from the floor where he lay in his rapidly congealing blood. Stretch stood the body up. Bernie handed him the key, got his shoulder under the dead man's middle and hoisted him up.

Now Stretch unlocked and opened the other watertight door and they went through. He flipped the light switch and closed the big door. In the stone corridor Weasel pulled a large toggle switch that started to flush the killing room. He knew that pipes on the ceiling rotated rapidly, spraying water in every direction, cleansing, wiping out all traces of murder.

The corridor had a dank, watery smell to it. It had another smell, distinctly limey. The walls became rough. Soon they were in a natural cave well beyond the main house and deep inside the granite hills above. They made the lengthy trip watching their step on the slimy, wet floor.

The smell of lime grew the further they went. It pervaded everything as they turned into a side chamber and lay the dead man's body on the floor in front of a large depression almost full of water. The caustic smell wrinkled their noses. They didn't have much to say. Stretch unzipped the bag on the edge of the depression and rolled Geacali's body into the lime pit, taking care not to get splashed. The corpse sank to the bottom, stirring up sediment as it settled. Bernie and Stretch stood on the lip for a few moments, watching the lime begin to work. Abruptly they left.

Without a backward glance, the two soldiers grabbed the bag and took it another hundred feet down the descending corridor. The sound of running water got louder. They came out on a little ledge of natural granite. Beyond flowed swiftly running water only about a foot deep, but in a fairly wide channel of perhaps twenty feet.

The ceiling in the chamber vaulted to nearly six feet where they stood, but lowered to only inches above the water on either side where it entered and left the chamber. Stalactites hung from the ceiling. Stretch shined his light into the darkness. The shaft of light extended quite a way back, but the cave seemed to end at the far reach of the beam.

"Goddamn water's cold," Stretch complained as they dropped the bag and started washing it, inside and out.

"Cold as a witches tit. You heard that, didn't you?"

"Yeah. Fuck, it's cold."

"Let's get it done."

They washed the body bag carefully. With fairly good light from the waterproof overhead electric fixtures, they saw the blood leach out into a thin, dark stream that swiftly disappeared under the low ceiling downstream.

"Now, Stretch, splash water on me and I'll do you the same. They rubbed the telltale blood off their outfits, and checked each other over.

Satisfied, they returned to the killing room. Bernie shut off the flushing switch, and they reentered the now clean room, all traces of the mayhem of minutes before gone.

Bernie put the bag back into the steel locker, closed and locked the door. The two looked everything over carefully. They knew the mattress, similar to an outdoor chaise lounge, would drain and dry. They nodded in satisfaction and left by the door they'd entered. Stretch locked it, tested it, replaced the key. They removed their protective clothing, replaced it and started back up the long stairway.

"Glad that's done. Don't like it down here," Bernie said.

Stretch asked Bernie if he had any idea where all that water went.

"Don't know, don't care. Suggest you do the same."

Weasel shrugged. "Sometimes I think of cav'in. They call it spelunkin'. Did some as a boy. Would want a wet suit fer this one."

Bernie looked at Stretch sharply. "Stretch, don't! I don't want to hear no more. In this line I don't want to get to know nobody real well. Take a hint."

"Yeah. Yer right," he said.

They finished the climb in silence.

At the door to the book-wall, Stretch checked the peeper and saw the boss alone in his study. He didn't have company and he wasn't on the phone, so they entered the same way they'd come. They knew the rules. As the door clicked open, Bernie turned to the boss, who watched them enter.

"Done," Bernie said.

Nick looked them over. "Good. Okay, you guys beat it. I want a meeting with Malfo and you soldiers later on today. Don't stray too far. We got a problem I'm wrestling. When I got a handle on it, I'll get to you through Ray. He's on com. Got it?"

"We'll be around," Bernie said.

The two men left. They felt, knew, that Nick was pleased with them. Looked to Bernie like he'd overcome Nick's earlier displeasure. Of course, what just happened might be what the boss wanted him to be thinking about. He thought about it, all right.

"How 'bout some five card stud, Bern?" Stretch asked.

"Not now, you gamblin' fuck," Homenio replied. "I think I'm goin' for a swim."

"Where?"

"Up near the point-o-land. Water's clean. I heard storm's comin'. I'll get a couple hours anyway. Comin'?"

"Nah. Not my thing. I'm goin' up to the card room. Maybe Jocko's there. I can tap him for fifty, I bet."

"Later."

Bernie went to his room. He put on shorts and moccasins and grabbed his snorkel gear. He didn't bother with a bathing suit. He didn't feel like scuba diving. He didn't feel all that much like company, but it would've been okay if Stretch took him up on it. Before he left his room he called Ray and told him where he'd be.

"Grab a cell and I'll call you if necessary, Bern."

"What if I'm under for awhile?"

"I'll let it ring until you pick up. You worry too much."

Bernie liked Ray, as much as he allowed himself to like anybody. Ray would get him if the boss suddenly wanted him.

"Okay, Ray. Catch yuh later." He hung up.

Bernie walked through the wide, elegant portico. He squinted at the ocean. Looked okay to him. He was a strong swimmer. He made his way down to the dock and took the narrow footpath out to the point.

The path ran near the low cliff for a time, maybe twenty feet to the rocks and surf. A nasty fall, probably fatal, if you were stupid or careless. Then it diverged away from the sea and into the woods. The trees were not tall, mostly scrub, the kind that hang on in thin, rocky soil. Still, with moderate height cliffs out to the point and the extra height of the trees, the harbor got much less violence from storms. As the woods closed in, Bernie lost the house to view. The trees might have been eight to ten feet high, plenty. He felt relieved to be away even for a short time.

His thoughts rambled; how to stay on the good side of the boss, how close he had come because of that dumb bitch fiasco, how to displace that asshole Malfo, how to act stupid enough to stay in the position but smart enough to be there. But especially—he smiled at the thought—how to get rid of that vicious idiot Malfo.

After a little more than a quarter mile, Bernie came out onto the small beach he knew well. No footprints. He didn't expect any. He let his thoughts go, dropped his stuff, set the cell phone up in the sand at maximum volume, shed his clothes and took a running dive into the ocean in the one place he'd found the water deep enough. Nature at its best, he thought, that's for Bernie Homenio. Never get tired of being a nature boy.

He swam around in the cool water, then went back to the beach and got his snorkel and mask. He headed for the old wreck. There'd be plenty of interesting fish out there, too. A soldier he might be, but here he was in his element, not a goddamn cave dweller like Weasel. He never got claustrophobia under the water, but a dark cave—he shuddered.

He figured he'd be okay for a half-hour anyway. He didn't think Nick would need him for most of the day, but in a sense, he was on duty, and he didn't want Nick getting pissed with him again any time real soon. Like never! The boss had a very good memory.

The wreck was only a few hundred feet out, right on the edge of a drop-off. He had been here many times before, and being alone with his thoughts was his idea of fun. Nobody else seemed interested in swimming with him, even though he would have been happy enough to show them the wreck and all.

Maybe the kid Mikey, he thought, maybe he swims. He's a smart kid. I think Nick is interested in bringing him up. Who knows? Tommie went away, like forever. This could be his big break. Someday I'll ask him. Bernie didn't like being alone *all* the time.

After twenty-five minutes Bernie swam back to the shore. All quiet. He took off again, his pro-grade flippers giving a great surge to Bernie's speed as his powerful legs pushed him through the water. He surveyed the coast close in to shore, making sure his underwater watch kept him on time with his need to check the beach.

When he returned a second time, he found the phone still silent, but he noted rising swells coming in from the south. The ocean storm he heard about had started to affect the upper waters. Pretty soon, with new currents being pushed up from the south, snorkeling would get tough. And rip currents, he'd been caught in one once. They were a bitch! Yeah, time to quit.

Hey, I got some uninterrupted time off, he thought. Good! He sat around on the sand until he dried. Then he brushed off, dressed, and started back. On the way he looked at the summer berries on low bushes along his route and wondered if they were edible. With what I do, he thought, I should know about that stuff. How do I grab a book and look somethin' up like that? Everybody knows I don't read much, books anyway. I'll have to be careful, grab somethin' when I'm in town next time.

His phone rang. He pulled it out of his pocket and pushed "talk" in one smooth motion, "Yeah?"

"Ray, Nick's looking for you."

"Is he, like okay?"

"Yeah. Meeting. Nick wants the top to meet him in the big meeting room, including soldiers."

"Gotcha! I'm on my way back anyway. Be there ten minutes."

"Meeting's for eleven-thirty."

"Right!" Bernie answered, looking at his watch, "I got time."

Bernie heard the click as Ray disconnected.

The hit man pocketed the phone and went back to thinking about Malfo.

17

The meeting with The Word of the Book began at sundown. Rathmanizzar sat cross-legged on his blanket, arms crossed, a stern yet rapt expression on his face, as if something wonderful had occurred. The others, fifteen in all, crouched, sat or lounged on blankets and mats strewn around the central tent area, attention focused on the leader, flint-eyed men whose worn, dirty clothing spoke volumes on how they lived.

Rathmanizzar began without preamble. "Gathering of the leaders of my flock, I have had a dream in which the forces of good have overcome the forces of evil. A message has come to me from the spirit Mohammed. You have heard this before. You must hear it again."

A rumbling sound of approval came from the devout.

"The spirit has told me that Islam will triumph over the infidels of the world, and that the day is nigh. The spirit has given me the day, and has told me to reveal it to no one. It has said that the sons of Islam must redouble their efforts in a manner I will reveal to you this night. The judgment of Allah will crash as the waves of the sea upon the infidel. The infidel will be overcome as with the desert sandstorm. He will be brought before the spirit and judged harshly, and the teachings of Mohammed will spread to every reach of the world, and the peace of Allah will come to the believer."

A great outcry came from the assembled. The fanatic glint from thirty mesmerized eyes the leader noted with surety. They would lay their lives down for Allah and for Allah's messenger, for victory came nearer to them by the hour.

"The spirit has said that we must soon launch our jihad. The time is near! Listen, my brethren, to the plan thus revealed."

A greater outcry still! Men rose to their feet and moved and swayed to some internal rhythm. The leader waited patiently until his soldiers regained their stability and returned to their seats.

"To begin the jihad will require a different direction to our preparation. All that you have done to this time, all of it necessary and blessed by the great one has put in place elements of the fire that will devour the world. At the rising of tomorrow's sun, I, Rathmanizzar, will set in motion that new direction, and, before the next full moon smiles upon us our deed will be accomplished."

Another outcry! The leader sat silently until it subsided.

"You are the chosen. You will lead our brothers and those who attend them, making their positions as solid as Mohammed's mountain, so they cannot be dislodged. You, the leaders of the flocks will be the generals of the army of God."

More tumult! This time Rathmanizzar held up a hand for silence. The clamor subsided instantly.

"In the thirty days of Ramadan past, we have acquired the final instrument of the infidels destruction. In our hands will be the ultimate weapon. Soon I will reveal the date that will begin our holy war. We shall all strive together and we *shall* triumph against the forces of evil. Then you, my brothers, will take on the greatest responsibility, that of administering the former nations of the world.

"And now, I will tell you all, finally, of the manner in which the world will come to its knees and beg the faithful of Islam to release the infidels of their chains and become one with Allah."

The roomy tent filled as with one voice the prayers of the faithful. The silent majority sat in the next crucial hours and gathered to themselves Rathmanizzar's plan for world disruption.

When all had left, very late, the muted light of his eyes flashed and Rathmanizzar smiled in his darkened tent.

18

Audrey came out of the kitchen carrying three steaming platters. Ted and Richard looked up from an intense conversation. Audrey half-humorously expected them to be battling over cribbage, but when she saw their faces she could only ask if the war had started without her. She put the plates down in front of the two men quietly.

Mid-table sat some micro-electronic equipment and surgical instruments. Evidently Ted had just finished describing the use of them to Richard. He motioned Audrey.

"What have I missed?"

Ted said, "Not much. I'd described the equipment and just begun review of the surgical procedure for implanting these inside your skulls, so that you and Richard will be able to communicate while you are on your mission. Richard had a valid concern on whether the units could be jammed, and under what circumstances."

Audrey looked the micro stuff over with great interest. "Inside our skulls? Another little thing you haven't mentioned before...or did you and I just forgot? I haven't seen this advertised in a Sears catalog, have I?"

"No," said Ted, "even our Government would deny that such things exist. And they would be honest, because they don't have a clue about this lovely stuff."

He looked at them, first Audrey and then Richard. Their lunches sat idly by, forgotten. And Audrey wondered again at how little she knew and how she seemed carried along.

"This is the latest in micro-chip technology. Stoic acquired them through a contact in GEF's government controlled special products lab, the one it maintains at the space station. There would be hell to pay if they were discovered missing. There are only two sets of these in the entire world and 'these are them,' as they say. It's as super secret as anything gets. Us three, Stoic, his operative in the lab who, by the way invented it, and a couple of his superiors are the only people who know about it. Those superiors think the units are under maximum protection on the space station, inaccessible even to them.

That means," he said with unnecessary emphasis, "that no other part of Stoic's organization knows, either. It has to stay that way."

"Okay, I'm with it." Audrey gulped. "What now?"

Richard nodded.

"The micro-processor will be inserted up through your nose and will be lodged behind your left maxillary sinus. It will irritate for a day or so, but I am told that your bodies will get used to them because of the exterior shape of the device, i.e., your innards will heal around them. Because of human facial bone structure, the unit will be impossible to detect except by x-ray taken in precisely the right spot, which is highly unlikely unless someone gets wind of what we've done.

"The left sinus is very close to the Eustachian tube that allows you to clear pressure from your left ear. That viaduct, so to speak, will allow the unit to contact your inner ear. You will hear quite clearly, just as if the messages were coming into your brain."

Ted hesitated and then gave them the worst of it. "I'm sorry, but this is so secret that each unit has been programmed to self-destruct if anyone attempts to remove it, ever. That would cause internal damage to your faces, but probably wouldn't kill you. The units will be with you for life. If all goes well, you both will become a sort of counter-intelligence duo of the future. As you can see, Stoic and I have invested a great deal in you two."

Richard said nothing, but Audrey spoke up, "There is no other way?"

"Yes, there are other ways, but this is the best bet for our side, by far. You can refuse, but I hope you won't."

Richard looked at Audrey and said, "Well, wife of mine, looks like we're going to be joined in more than simple matrimony. I hope this marriage works out."

Audrey looked worried. "Yeah, I guess we'll really have to work at it, won't we?"

Richard looked at Ted. "For world peace, whatever that is."

"Ditto," said Audrey. "Let's get it over with."

Ted nodded. "My belief in you is justified. I am a hard-nosed guy where it comes to enemies, but never in my life have I put a friend or associate in harms way without them understanding all the implications of risk. Okay, *I'm* going to do the operation. I've read enough on facial surgery and have practiced on a few dummies. This will be the real thing. Come with me."

He got up and left the room, turned right and opened a large closet with a key from a small ring he took from his pocket.

Richard had wondered what was in there.

Ted spoke again. "You see before you a chair with straps for hands and legs and a brace for the head. You will each enter the chair and allow yourself to be strapped in tight. I will give you a shot, which will put you out for about ten minutes. It takes a bit over a minute to maneuver the micro-transmitter/receiver into place. Given no problems, when you wake up you will only have wicked sinus pain, for which you will take this." He opened his palm and the two operatives saw two small, white pills.

They said nothing.

"I will administer one of the pain pills to you and one to Audrey. Until yours takes effect, I'm not letting you loose from the chair. Understood?"

"Doesn't sound pleasant," said Richard.

Audrey stayed silent, but paled slightly.

"It's not, but I promise you, I will be as gentle as I can."

Richard turned to look at Audrey and said, "I'll go first, if that's okay with Audrey."

"Oh, be my guest. Gentlemen first, I always say, when pain's involved."

The two men smiled.

"Okay, Richard, step up here."

"I was only kidding!" he said, but climbed into the seat without hesitation.

Ted strapped Richard in and gave him the shot, then told him to count back from one hundred. He went out quickly. His eyes were closed, but the restraint held him face forward. With the chair on a raised platform, Ted could get under Richard's nose from the correct angle. He laid a bath towel on Richard's lap and up the front of his shirt, telling Audrey that there would be some blood, although not much, if he did it right.

She noticed no hesitation in Ted now. With the practiced movements of a brain surgeon, Ted deftly inserted the micro-processor/com device into a strange looking jointed instrument in his hand, and then gauging the exact distance, pushed it and the instrument up Richard's left nostril. At what he felt to be the right point, Ted twisted the base of the instrument and moved it sideways.

Blood immediately began running over Richard's mouth and chin. Ted paid no attention. He worked carefully but urgently, twisting and turning, moving and adjusting the instrument minutely, positioning it. When it felt correctly inserted, he carefully withdrew the long instrument, looked at it satisfactorily, and turned to Audrey.

"That does it. Think I should have been a surgeon?"

"Not bad," Audrey said, "but don't give up on your day job."

Ted smiled. Audrey had responded as perfectly as he could have wanted, because she now knew what was coming.

Ted took cotton and pushed it up Richard's nose to control bleeding. He kept a small opening for drainage and Richard's nose continued to leak.

"By the time he wakes up, the bleeding should have mostly stopped. I can't give the pill until he's awake. He'll be a hurtin' unit then, but it won't last long."

"Cribbage, Ted?"

"No, thanks, but I could use another cup of coffee."

"I'll get it."

"Thanks."

Audrey went into the kitchen, wondering if she should have gone through the procedure first. Blood didn't bother her normally, but she was beginning to get attached to the big lug in the chair and it seemed to make a difference.

"His refrain...'it's only an assignment' , it'll have to do for now." She grabbed a hot cup for Ted and made her way back to the closet.

"Thanks, Audrey," Ted said gratefully. "Another five, and I think your other half will be coming to. Then we can do you."

"Goody!"

Ted looked at her sharply, but saw that Audrey was just coping. He allowed himself a smile at her unusual aplomb.

Soon Richard began to stir. His muscles involuntarily bunched as the pain began to seep into his clearing head. He let out a groan. Audrey shuddered and empathized.

Richard's eyes began to clear. Ted waved a hand in front of his face and his eyes responded.

"Okay, Richard, I want you to take this pill and swallow it with some water. It is very strong, and it will help you. Blink if you can swallow."

A few moments passed. They watched his throat work. Finally Richard blinked twice, and Ted offered the pill, putting it on Richard's tongue and following it with a small amount of water. Richard managed to swallow.

"I know this is hard on you, but I can't release you until the pill begins to take effect. I can release the forehead strap a notch, though." This he did.

Richard blinked twice again, but didn't try to say anything. Slight tremors moved across his face. Audrey watched his conscious attempts to put down agony. She carefully kept her expression neutral. Ted and Audrey waited another ten minutes.

Finally Richard smiled ruefully and said, "Whoa! That's heavy stuff. I don't know if I should even say anything now, since Audrey hasn't gone through this yet."

"It's okay, Richard," said Ted, "she's seen the whole process, and it wouldn't be right to withhold at this time. She's going to kind of back into it, knowing what's coming. It'll be just as well if she knows the whole experience beforehand. I'm taking mental notes, too, so that in the highly unlikely event I ever have to do this or anything similar again, I'll have thorough knowledge of what's involved."

Richard began to sound better. "Ah, to be a Guinea Pig, a lifelong ambition!"

"Gone sour!" Audrey finished for him.

"The beauty of it, my dear…dear Audrey, is that I will never have to go through this again!" Richard fervently commented.

"You're going to feel silly communicating with yourself, hotshot," she retorted, "so you better hope I decide to go through with it!"

Richard looked at Ted pleadingly.

He spoke thickly. "She can't opt out now, can she, Ted? I mean, all that lovely pain. Look, Audrey, you and I are husband and wife. Woman, I command you to get up here and take the chair…after I've vacated it, of course."

Audrey gave him the finger.

"Children, children!" But the responses were right, in his mind.

Ted looked at his watch and started to unbind Richard's wrists and legs. "Safe enough now, I think."

As he finished loosening the last strap, Richard lunged out at Ted, grabbed him by the shoulders and smiled a bloody smile in his face.

"Your turn, matey!" he said, and then burst into an uproarious laugh, which he wished he hadn't done a moment later.

It startled Ted and he automatically started to defend. He realized in time and Richard did not end up across the room. Ted grinned sheepishly.

"Okay, Richard, you get one. You deserve it. You're the first of a kind."

Richard moved toward Audrey, who had been watching him closely. Instead of recoiling as he expected, she met him face to face and planted a kiss on his bloody lips. His eyes went wide, and then they became troubled.

"Audrey, don't fall for me," he said. "We can't afford it."

"Yes, we can," she stared into his eyes, "and I'm going to make sure you get through this, and you're going to make sure I do! That's the way it's going to be."

Richard became as sober as she had ever seen him. "God, what a woman you are! Rules change! I will do it, not because you say so, but because you are a wonder of my life, and I can feel it. Audrey, I love you!"

"I love you, too," Audrey said simply, not surprised that she meant it.

At the side, Ted filled with conflicting emotions.

19

Bernie Homenio arrived five minutes early. Several soldiers were there ahead of him. Nick's controllers were just beginning to filter in. Malfo the chosen—maybe the eventual pigeon, he hoped—strolled in and took a seat to the right of Nick's chair. Bernie noticed a new face, Mikey Dorneti. How about that, just what he was thinking. Mikey sat, eagerly attentive, and Bernie saw something close to love on his face.

The kid is going to be dangerous if he doesn't calm down, he thought. Maybe we all start out that way—maybe we all do. But the memory had been violated so many times by ugly business... ah...shit!

He entered the large meeting room, nodded to the few he knew as well as he knew anyone, and took a seat. This room was situated in the lower level of the house, off limits to Nick's wife, a woman seldom seen except in the upper reaches of the mansion. Hermona, same first letter, same number of letters as his last name, he thought, a real beauty in a washed out sort of way.

He knew Nick had explained to her that it was like he had an office downtown or in another city, and that she'd have to get past his security personnel to let her through. She never even tried. Maybe she didn't want to know where Nick's money came from, satisfied to live "upstairs" and not know...just not know.

Bernie had met her a couple of times. He'd been very respectful, but distant—treating her like a kept woman, maybe. He didn't understand it, but then, he wasn't Nick. He didn't have Nick's drives, or Nick's money, or anything else Nick had. He was a grunt, a soldier, and he better never forget it. Nick didn't!

The rest of the gang members had assembled and the low rumble of conversation continued at ebb, kind of like low tide, Bernie thought. What fearful camaraderie! They seemed to take their time getting there, but no way would they be late. Nick didn't like it and Nick was boss. They looked around and occasionally said hello to someone in the crowd.

Suddenly the room hushed and all eyes went to the front. Nick entered from a small door just behind the podium. He had a cup of coffee in his hand. He went to the podium and stood there until absolute silence reigned. It didn't take long.

"Welcome, my friends and associates. I have called this meeting of the company, because I have some very good news and I have some very bad news. I'll get the bad news out of the way immediately, because I don't like bad news with my coffee."

There was a wave of laughter in the room.

"The bad news is that an enemy of the company has gotten a temporary reprieve, and remains at large." He looked directly at Bernie.

There were a few muffled comments. Nick resumed his presentation.

"A couple of our locations have sustained damage from "vandals", which I interpret to be CIA or FBI. We have responded appropriately. They got nothin', and they won't, so long as you make sure *I* know about it. Don't forget that!'"

Trafalgar described the results of little initiatives and broad planning. After a half-hour of bringing his troops up to date, Nick started staring out into the crowd. They began to get uneasy, and they knew the time had come for the meat of the meeting.

"Okay! The company has a problem. It's a big one and it can mean success…that means we all get out of this alive…or failure…which means some of your sorry asses are goin' to be lookin' up at dirt," he said.

"I'm goin' to outline it for you once. That's all you get. Listen!"

Nick began by telling his men that the girl who'd left the party was too dangerous to live and that a business partner of his wanted her killed. He glossed over the details of the escape, and didn't point a finger a Bernie. He didn't have to. The soldiers knew. Rumors couldn't be quashed in an organization like Nick Trafalgar's.

Nick privately didn't care who caused the problem. Most important in a case like this was that a screw-up occurred at all. That needed to be pointed out. Kept them looking around and kept them sharper. He wanted all of his people on edge and fear accomplished it best. He didn't want them to trust each other.

He told them she had disappeared completely—in his view pretty near impossible—given the maximum speed of the ladies sailboat and the reconnaissance flight he'd commissioned early the next morning. He figured the boat must have made landfall somewhere along the coast, either camouflaged or deliberately sunk beyond the harbor. That would imply an accomplice, and that disturbed him a lot.

"Maybe the Fed...they're always crawling around trying to get something," he told the group, "but I don't think so. There's an unknown out there, somebody we don't suspect. You guys got any suggestions?"

After a little mumbling, finally Bernie raised his hand.

"Yeah, Bernie." Nick looked at him normally now.

"Boss, we could take a couple of the small speed boats out and head up and down the coast. We might catch somethin' from the water your plane couldn't see. We could do a two man, one lookin' with glass, one drivin'. I come in from the point like less than an hour ago, and the seas are comin' up, but they ain't bad yet."

"It's a suggestion, Bernie, but as far down the coast as you'd have to go checkin' things out, no way you'd get back before you'd have to hole up somewhere and ride out the storm. I caught weather before I came in. It's going to be a big blow. I don't want to lose any boats. Anybody else?"

More mumbling, but no one had any ideas. Nick continued on to his next subject with only a final comment on how they would eventually catch up with the bitch and then he dropped it. He wondered silently what Rathmanizzar would do about it subsequent to sending his coded communiqué.

"Okay, you guys. Next! Somethin' big—huge—is comin' down in the next maybe two, three months, best I can figure. Could be days. My ears are out there. We'll get the drift soon. Anyway, this organization is on the ground floor. Even the New York Families don't know, I'm pretty sure, and any word I get that one of them hears about it after today is going to produce a dead man, understand?" Nick looked them over, searching out their eyes, boring into them.

"You soldiers are going to start earning your pay this month. You controllers are going to get a first dose of real swinging business, and you're going to have to be up for it. You'll hear more later, after I'm finished with the soldiers."

Nick outlined the general direction things would take and then excused all but the controllers.

As they filed out, Bernie thought about what he'd heard, and wondered what opportunity might be in it for Bernie Homenio. Mikey Dorneti came out behind Bernie and tapped him on the shoulder. Bernie turned, and a big smile greeted him.

"I got the nod today, Bernie."

"Yeah, I know, kid."

"I can do this job. Nick's gonna be proud of me. He told me you was goin' to teach me the ropes."

It was the first he'd heard about it, but he didn't let on. "Sure, kid. Walk with me a bit."

Bernie kind of side-longed Mikey, gave him the glance, looked him over from the new perspective. Good-looking kid, pretty sharp dresser, nice Italian features, five foot eight, that darker Mediterranean color, like him. Maybe his parents came over from southern Italy or even Sicily, although he doubted *that*. He liked what he saw. An idea formed in his mind. He'd been out with many women, but he didn't have much use for them outside of using them.

He really preferred hanging with one or two guys he knew, or being alone. Bernie wondered what it would be like...

The other guys went on about their business. Mikey branched off with the older man and they strolled out to the lower portico.

"You swim, Mikey?"

"Yeah, like a fish, Bernie."

110

"We got a storm comin' up, but I got a special place to go when I want to think, or just swim. Let's go out there. Grab a bathing suit and maybe we'll swim, too." Bernie wasn't tired from his previous exertion, and he thought if he had to be a teacher, he might as well start in a place where he liked to be.

"Great! Be right back." Mikey took off like a rocket toward the room he had below the mansion.

The young man would soon get new digs, Bernie thought, up with the soldiers. He didn't think that was any great shakes, but Mikey would, for a while, at least. Might as well get the kid in his corner.

Bernie stopped in his room and grabbed his snorkel and fins and a suit, just in case Mikey was, like shy about naked swimming. He chuckled. Hey, he dressed up before. Snorkel and fins, that's dressed, ain't it? He went back outside and stood looking out to sea again, like he often did during the three years he'd been one of Nick's soldiers. It still didn't look rough to him. Not from here.

Funny, he thought, how many men of Italian descent ended up in a family or in an organization like Nick Trafalgar's, at least in America. Different in Russia, he'd heard. He wondered why. Italians did real well in middle management and doing hard work. We're sort of cut out for hard work, he thought. Very few except the Don's became the heads of big companies. They were much more likely to go into politics. He chuckled. Italians did well in politics. Usually got dirty, too. He knew they were easy mixers, but he also knew they never stayed satisfied. We're not brilliant, but we're smart. Lots of street smarts. Are we a type? He pondered that.

Mikey came back on a run. "Okay, Bernie, let's go. I haven't been out to the point before. It's nice? Do you swim often? I haven't got much chance at it since I came to the big house to, you know, help out."

"Yeah, kid. You'll like it. Yeah, I swim often." Regular chatterbox.

"Where's your flippers and snorkel?"

"I don't got any."

"I'll fix you up, kid. Got an extra set in my room. You know how to use 'em?"

"Oh, yeah, Bernie. I know. Left the stuff home when I told the old man to fuck off."

Bernie laughed, a short bark.

"I'll get 'em. When we get time, we'll go into town and I'll help you pick some good ones." Mikey stood there while Bernie fetched the stuff.

They retraced Bernie's earlier trip to the point. They both wore soft, comfortable moccasins.

"Lot of sharp rock out that way. Keep a watch for snakes. There's a few."

"Okay. Snakes don't bother me."

They walked the quarter mile to the beach. Nick hadn't been kidding. Nick kid? He laughed. Not likely. The surf was already noticeably higher now. Well, he'd been near the sea for three plus years and a city boy before that, neighborhood pools and stuff, Coney Island. It didn't surprise him. Storm surge. Storm comin' up from south, what he expect?

Mikey looked over the little beach. "Nice!"

"Yeah, Mikey. I'm about the only one comes out here. The guys know about it, but they'd rather play cards or hang around or use the exercise equipment in Nick's gym. Can't figure it. This is nature. This is the best." He swept his hand around, taking in the sea, the hazy horizon, and whitecaps that were now prominently part of the picture.

Dorneti looked Bernie over like Bernie had looked Mikey over earlier. Bernie could feel it. Hard muscled and tanned and looking good, he'd only just turned forty. Bernie wondered what Mikey had on his mind. Was he wondering what Bernie was all about, or did he have something else in mind? Bernie thought he'd test it.

"Mikey, I brought a suit, but I usually go skinny. You have any objection?"

"Don't matter to me, Bernie. I just always wore a suit. That's why I brought it. Figured that's how it came down. You wanna go skinny, no prob."

"Okay. Let's shed." Bernie dropped his bathing suit on the sand and peeled his shorts off. Then he picked up his fins and snorkel and headed for the water. Mikey stayed back, a little slower, like getting used to the idea. Then he shrugged, dropped his pants and peeled off his tee shirt and followed Bernie's example.

They waded into the water to wet their gear, popped their masks over the top and slid the flippers on. Neither of them paid attention to the other. Bernie didn't want to stare, because slow worked best, and Mikey probably remembered shower etiquette from back in high school. Don't look around unless you're interested. Eventually they'd both get around to checking out the other's equipment package; pretty natural.

They plunged in. The water shocked the system as always, but the Atlantic had warmed quite a bit since April. They soon found flippers essential because the oncoming storm produced significant undertow at the point, and because they had to blow out their snorkels often with the caps curling over the top as they swam face down.

After a few minutes, Bernie waved at Mikey, and motioned him to follow. He headed straight out to sea several hundred yards, and then pointed down, showing Mikey his wreck of an old steel hulled ship.

The kid looked at it and they both came to the surface. Mikey took off his mask.

"Getting too rough. Could we come back another time, after the storm blows out?"

"Sure, kid. No prob. We can see better when it's calm, and it's clouding up now anyway. Let's get back."

"Yeah."

They swam back. In less than the hour they were out on the ocean, it clouded over and the air had cooled considerably. A light breeze stirred—a portent of things to come. They shivered, but still stood and let the breeze air dry them. Then they climbed into their clothes and headed back.

When they got there, Ray, the com guy saw them and ran over to advise that the storm had been upgraded to a hurricane, and if they were through playing, could they help to batten things down, specifically the boats.

"By the way, Bernie, Nick told me to tell you Mikey's comin' under your wing, but I guess you heard it already."

"Yeah," Bernie said, "I heard it. We'll drop our stuff."

"Okay, hurry." The man went off to complete his errand.

"Stick with me, Mikey. This job comes with *this* territory."

"Right, Bernie," the kid said respectfully.
They headed for the dock.

20

"You're okay with this, Audrey?" Ted waited.

She smiled a little. "I'm not looking forward to excruciating, exquisite, horribly unendurable pain, but outside of that, I'm fine."

Ted thought she could handle as much pain as any man. Part of it had to do with her level of commitment to the job and the rightness of it. She believed! He briefly thought about whether he should have sequestered her somewhere when he started this, but inwardly shook his head. Audrey's presence, he felt, was critical to Richard coming through as well as he had. He had no qualms about Richard handling it, but he believed it helped to have Audrey nearby.

Ted said, "No time like now to get things done."

There's that phrase again. Couldn't be coincidence, could it?

"One each Audrey Penwarton, presenting for sacrifice, boss!" She gave a smart salute, and allowed Ted to escort her to the chair.

Richard sat in another chair outside of the enclosure in full view. He had carefully mopped up the blood on his face at the kitchen sink and returned to serve as Audrey's support group, with his head tilted back into the pillow from their bed. His eyes weren't quite glazed. He had no pain now. A prominent, not quite fiery dark red skin tone on his cheek seemed to be spreading up and around his left eye.

Ted strapped her down as he had Richard. He curled his hands around the back of her head and straightened out her hair before immobilizing her. He carefully kept his expression unreadable, but his hands were exceedingly gentle. He stepped back to look at his work.

From the tray at the side of the cupboard he got the Pentothal shot ready. Ted injected her quickly. Audrey felt the sting of the needle, but made no sound or movement.

"Count back from one hundred." The chief operative studied her face intently.

"One Hundred...ninety-nine...ninety-eight..." When Audrey got to ninety-two she faded.

Ted wasted no time. Having practiced on Richard most recently, he was quick and deft. He retrieved the special instrument from a tray of boiling water, cooled it and followed his previous procedure. Audrey had a smaller face and Ted's measurement accounted for it. He remained expressionless in total concentration. Audrey bled freely for a short time. The bath towel covering bib and lap caught it.

The operation took two minutes. Ted stepped back after inserting cotton to slow the bleeding, and he looked satisfied. Richard sat silently throughout, but now had to say something, although the powerful pain pill still had an effect on his speech.

"Nice, work, Ted. I think I would have been happy enough to go second, knowing what I know now."

"It probably wouldn't have made any difference from the standpoint of how it went. I felt confident enough. I practiced on cadavers and on a couple of live ones the organization planned to dispose of, using a dummy micro-com device. I didn't enjoy it, here or there, a job that had to be done; I treated it clinically."

"I understand. We've all had to do things we didn't want to, but it *do* pay to prepare."

"Yes, it does."

Ted pulled up another chair and sat with Richard. They waited fifteen minutes. Ted talked intermittently to Richard about how he felt throughout the process before Audrey began to show signs of consciousness. Then Ted got up and removed the cotton from Audrey's left nostril. Blood slowly seeped from it. Ted felt okay with the leakage. He kept the catchall on the front of the woman, and only loosened the headband after Audrey could blink as Richard had done earlier.

Her face screwed up with pain, but she didn't try to talk. She looked washed out and not pretty.

"Okay, Audrey, take the pill and you'll be pain free soon." Ted fed her the pill, which she washed down with water.

"Now that you have both completed the first step in your unique total communication project, I have a few things to share with you that will be important to healing and will avoid hemorrhaging when you least expect it, a condition which could be fatal.

"First, don't sneeze! The pill I gave you both has a strong suppressant, so you won't have to be concerned for five or six hours. After that it is imperative you keep uppermost in your minds that you do not sneeze. You can take a cough suppressant, but it has limited use.

"You will feel it necessary to sneeze, without doubt. I must point out that the two live subjects were treated same as you through the operation and given the pain medication afterwards, but were not told not to sneeze. As control subjects they did fine, but they both hemorrhaged and died because of uncontrolled sneezing following the operation. Point made?"

"Point made," they said simultaneously.

"Second, you will be at greatest risk in the first twenty-four hours. It'll bother you for about a week, but we should be able to move, barring any unforeseen problem, in forty-eight hours before the routine duty people are due back.

"Third, once you can lie flat without blood running down the back of your throats, you should get some sleep. That will help most. Once the pain pill wears off, even though you can take the extra strength stuff in the bathroom cabinet as often as needed, you're *going* to lose some sleep.

"Finally, the com units can only be turned on by a special computer program. That will wait until you are both comfortably unaware of their presence. The shot I gave you had a special clotting factor. It should be working on Richard now and you will join him shortly."

Richard mentioned that his bleeding had stopped entirely, and he had wondered at it, because although he knew his blood clotted well, it surprised him. Now that he understood, he relaxed.

"I feel strange," Audrey offered, "but it must be the pain pill. Like you said, Richard, it's heavy stuff. I think you were referring to the operation, but I mean the pill."

"Yes, it was heavy, too," Richard said.

Ted brought things back. "You had best lie down right away, Richard. We have a busy schedule ahead."

"Right, Ted." Richard obediently headed for the bedroom.

Once out of earshot, Ted said, "Audrey, you got through it fine. You had much less trouble than Richard did. Possibly I had a bit more finesse, but I felt you were the easier subject to work on. Anyway, I can see that the blood has almost stopped. You're getting some color back. How do you feel now?"

"Overall, not too bad. The pain is pretty much gone. I think you can release me, now."

"Fine." Ted disconnected her from the chair.

He held out a hand and Audrey grasped it. She rose and with Ted's help, descended the two stairs. Ted folded the stair inside and closed up the chair closet.

"Before we leave the facility, I will need you two to help me dismantle this and get it aboard your sailboat. When we leave, we go out the way we came in, just before the duty crew comes down. No need to leave anything for other operatives to wonder about."

"Okay."

"Looks to me you could take some sack time, about now."

"Good idea."

Audrey still looked washed out, but normal color had returned to the part of her face not covered in blood. Ted sympathized. He had done his best, but he knew more about the aftermath than he'd told them. His two throwaways had shown him that. Even though they were worthless scum, he had stayed true to his need to be clinically correct with them both as to the operation and follow-up. Then they died.

Ted didn't like this. In his credo, the imperative of the job was to find the source of the human cancer in Stoic's operation and excise it. Playing with or experimenting on people he didn't go for at all. But, he told himself; it is for the greater good. And, he supposed, the greater good has been served. Hope those kids'll be all right.

He watched Audrey's back as she walked out of the room and headed for the same bed, he assumed, that Richard now occupied. Pretty thing. He smiled at how human they all were, despite the job, despite the assignment. Well, as soon as Audrey had settled down and fallen asleep he would go in and monitor them. He didn't want them to know he planned to sit up with them like an old grandmother.

RICHARD O. BENTON

21

I've got to get another message to Rathmanizzar, Nick thought. What does he know that he didn't tell me about that woman?

His mind went back to their discussion at the Black Sea resort. They'd met there for the first time. Nick had made arrangements to visit a "business" site in Bulgaria, and ostensibly took dinner at the Budkovka, an exclusive Black Sea resort.

A dark haired waiter in formal attire led him to a table. The man did not speak a word, but was properly subservient and gracious as befitted the plush richness of the dining area. Seated at the table, he focused on a man of medium stature wearing the robes of a desert chieftain, clearly from one of the Muslim countries. Middle East? Africa? He couldn't tell.

The man nodded to him and then to the waiter, who offered menus and retired immediately. The man at the table spoke impeccable English. "You are Nicholas Trafalgar. Your features are known to me, as is your reputation. Sit, please."

The desert chief sipped water from a tall, rounded tumbler. Nick sat. He looked at his menu, but understood nothing of it. Rathmanizzar assisted him by describing the options, then he held up a hand and the waiter came over instantly. The American ordered his meal. After that the desert man got to the point.

"I have watched you from afar for many months. I have a proposition for you that will make you perhaps the wealthiest man in America. Does this interest you?"

Nick had done his homework. "I was already aware that we could accomplish much. I am interested in the details."

"Before I reveal my plan to you, I wish you to know that I have considered others as allies, but I have decided to offer you my enticement, instead."

"Rathmanizzar, you must tell me how I will help you. You have painted a pretty picture of the destruction of the East Coast families, and you have offered me other great incentives, but you have not told me what I must do to earn this 'glorious reward' you describe. I did not become a very rich man by accepting the rambling stories of any man, but by seeing him back up his words."

He remembered the light in the old man's eyes, and a hint of madness, perhaps, but Rathmanizzar spoke slowly and convincingly to his guest.

"You will help me by producing certain materiel and by opening certain doors in your country to me. Here is a list of the items I will need in order to produce the bomb. The uranium I will obtain through other sources."

Nick thought with special relish about the target of the bomb, a confidence revealed to him.

"You hate the Chinese, Nick Trafalgar, do you not? Will this not be a great satisfaction to you, to see the Chinese Empire destroyed?"

He handed Nick the list.

It had been like turning a switch. Trafalgar's mind traveled back to a time of youth when he had met a beautiful Chinese girl on leave from the Communist Chinese Peoples Republic. She had come to America to learn about rocket design, a thing that the gullible American political "powers that be" were willing to teach her in order to gain good will with the Chinese during the time of President Nixon. He was still a teen, and had been captivated by the sensitivity of the oriental beauty who projected a selflessness he had never seen before.

He wondered then, if life had dealt him different cards, where he would be in this instant, instead of meeting covertly with a known terrorist in an out of the way place on the Black Sea very far from home. Before he brought himself back to the present, he mentally shrugged. The gentle lady would have passed into the background of his desire, he was sure. But the Chinese should not have done to her what they did.

People thought some of the things he did were vicious! I have nothing on the Chinese, he thought. To have her raped and killed in the middle of a major street in New York's Chinatown and her lifeless body hung on a street post, arms outstretched, presenting a Judeo-Christian image to onlookers just because they suspected she might defect! Because they had discovered she had fallen for Nick, and he for her! A tinge of real remorse passed through him. Beautiful little thing...cruel country!

But, back to business. The past had already taken care of itself, and Nick looked to the future, his future, his glorious future, where he could call all the shots and run all the games.

"Yes. That would be satisfying. You have good intelligence on my early history, it would seem. No matter! That, at least, was no secret when it happened."

Rathmanizzar smiled slightly as Nick looked down at the list he had been handed. There was much more behind the smile than Nick would have fathomed in the meeting, had he seen it. But they were both very bright, if greatly twisted individuals. The leader of the Lobala Liberation Front could not know what thoughts were running through Nick's mind, either.

That night, as they sat at table, a large glass window overlooking the blackness of a Black Sea only occasionally punctuated by the glow of slow freighters on their way to some unknown destination, two men plotted different scenarios for their world. The low lights in the dining room of the rich man's resort accentuated the glow from the seaport town below. Except for a low rumble of conversation several tables away and two of the wait staff in the hall, they were alone.

The desert leader spoke only English to his guest, so the two men ignored the innocuous presence of a dark-skinned, dark-haired waiter cleaning tables nearby. Rathmanizzar, at least, was certain no one in the restaurant spoke English. Low-level conversation would do the rest.

"You are to commit the list to memory, and return it to me before we leave this table. Can you do that?"

"Of course." Nick handed the list back, watching the older man's eyes arch slightly. "In my business, a head for numbers is important. I have a very good memory, Rathmanizzar."

"That is good. You can produce the items on the list within, let us say, six months, delivered to the Lobala desert city of Tubela-ha?"

"It won't be a problem." Nick's mind was in high gear, figuring the logistics of the move.

The old man favored Nick with a rare smile. He lifted his glass of water.

"Let us drink to a mutually agreeable outcome to our plans for changing the power balance—in our favor."

Nick responded, "Yes, to a victory we both can see."

Rathmanizzar had looked at him searchingly. Nick could see that the man believed he was no fool. He was secretly pleased, because the desert man would be careful with him. Nick felt he had become more dangerous to him, but being the person Rathmanizzar was, he would see it as an advantage. The militant mind categorized people. The Lobala leader would respect him more and within limits, offer him more trust him. Birds of a feather...

Then the man put his hand on Nick's left wrist, firmly, the first time the other man had touched him. Even when the man had introduced himself, he had remained distant and aloof. Now...

"Nick Trafalgar, there is another thing I wish you to do. There is a woman who must be killed." Rathmanizzar looked more intent, and his eyes blazed. "Will you do this for me?"

"Tell me what you have to tell me. I will decide."

"Very well! Her name is Amber Pierce. She has been followed by one of my people and her whereabouts are known. She was responsible for disrupting some business I was conducting and it has cost me much time and work. I believe she is an operative for one of the American intelligence groups. I will give you information on her location. You may conduct this favor, as you would call it, as you will. Will you do this for me?"

Nick thought for a time, and then answered. "I do not like to mess with the Fed in any capacity, Rathmanizzar. However, I will do this for you. I will take your information and arrange what I can."

Nick came back to himself. He smiled. Everything went well at the resort. The materiel he had been asked to produce was grouped and sent surreptitiously to Lobala in the following months. The terrorist had moved it from there. Nick suspected that it was already in China or very near, although he wondered about the method of transport.

Then a frown appeared. Nick knew he was still under the gun with Rathmanizzar because he'd had to report failure in his mission to kill the girl. Damn Geacali and damn Homenio...but I'm boss; it falls to me. Tommie paid his price, and he'd make Homenio pay in other ways for a long time for this.

I'll ride that little bastard, he thought. It's not over yet. Shit happens, and I'm the shit that's going to happen to Homenio. Hmm...wonder what'll happen if I give him to Alonzo for a couple of "simple" jobs? Alonzo doesn't like the little bastard, grates on him. He laughed, and a black and white mean streak surfaced through his cultivated demeanor.

RICHARD O. BENTON

22

In the desert city of Tubela-ha the leader was alone again with his thoughts. He wondered why Nick Trafalgar had failed to eliminate one small female. Ineptness of his associate? A failure in his organization? Another agency he didn't suspect? A traitor? No! He was certain of his contacts in all his far-flung organization, that they believed in the cause as fully as he did.

Anything was possible, of course, and the American was of a different type, one who would not be swayed by the words of The Book. But he had not cultivated the leadership of his organization and spent much time on his foreign contacts assuring himself that they would all move in his directions with an expectation that he would miss something important. His mind moved back to the meeting at the Budkovka in Varna.

Rathmanizzar had seen a picture of Nick Trafalgar. He'd read the limited dossier on him. Trafalgar impressed him in the degree he had covered his tracks once he entered the night world of illicit business." The dossier was sufficiently impressive to know that the man bore watching. In his low-key discussion at table he'd found the man to be bright and quick. He had only shown a small part of himself in the revelation he had offered to the LLF leader.

There was little reason to believe that the man would reveal himself in any way unless he wanted to, which implied cunning. Nick Trafalgar had wanted to impress the leader with knowledge that he wouldn't be trifled with. He believed that Trafalgar would search out what he could of Rathmanizzar.

The leader smiled a grim smile. He would not find much, not Nick Trafalgar, not anyone. He had built his reputation carefully, a presence mysterious, like an elusive bit of smoke or sand. Except for his most trusted, no man saw Rathmanizzar unless he wanted him to.

The desert man reviewed the essence of that meeting. Yes, he made the contact he needed, and yes, he was most pleased to have an intelligent if dangerous man in his camp as an associate. He did not want stupidity. The two men were worlds apart in their thinking, but most importantly, he believed he understood Nick Trafalgar.

He must be sure his "associate" did not become aware of the projections he had for the governments of the world following the detonation of the bomb and China's declaration of war on everyone outside of China. Yes, that land was full of insecurities, and he, Rathmanizzar, was going to see that the world paid heavily for not taking China more seriously.

The Lobala leader was politically savvy. The top leadership of China would not be in Peking when the bomb went off. He wanted an angry response to the tragedy to be immediate, to not wait for an interim government to form. Given that, Rathmanizzar was certain that present Chinese leadership would respond in the way he projected.

He expected rapid destabilization of the major world governments, but it would be the reverse of his desire to see China dissolve in chaos.

His thoughts shifted to the man that had been brought to him after the meeting, after Nick Trafalgar the American had departed the resort following their dinner. He was one of the wait staff. The man was dark-haired, of less than average height, but very broad in the chest, like many of the Bulgarians who lived in the seaport town of Varna. His agent thought the man had acted a little out of character; that he had stayed near the table Nick and the leader were using too long. He'd trailed him after the man left the resort at the end of his work detail.

The agent, Talmud Ben-Sichah, had summoned another and the two had accosted the man as he scurried away over a bridge into the poorer side of town. When they hailed the man, he had turned and tossed something small over the stone side of the bridge and had started running. They caught him and detained and tried to question the man, but he pointed at his tongue and would say nothing.

He carried no identification, very suspicious in that part of the world. They were unable to get him to talk and decided to bring him before the leader. Whatever he threw over the side of the bridge into the water they were unable to find in the dark.

Curious about the man because Rathmanizzar believed no one knew of his whereabouts at the time, he agreed to see him. He questioned the man, who looked scared, and kept pointing to his tongue and making throat sounds. The leader decided he must be mute, but that too much rode on his secret visit to Varna. He told his man to kill the uncommunicative waiter and dispose of him quietly. Ben-Sichah cut the man's throat immediately and the two men removed the body under cover of darkness.

Rathmanizzar did not know he had murdered Stoic's man Balkan. He instructed his men to look again in the morning light for whatever the man had thrown over the bridge. They did not recover the item.

The leader did not know that Balkan's assistant watched him being picked up but could not intervene. He recovered the spy camera and the miniature recorder wrapped in plastic and sent it to Stoic with a report of the events of the night. Stoic finally got a good picture of the mysterious and elusive Rathmanizzar while cursing the loss of a good agent. Part of the tape was damaged and unreadable, but Stoic learned enough to become aware of the plot to construct a bomb and to detonate it in a highly sensitive city—somewhere.

Emotionless, Stoic mentally hung out another reason for ridding the world of this and all terrorists. Balkan's body was never recovered.

RICHARD O. BENTON

23

Ted sat with his charges through the night. He watched for signs of a coming sneeze. Audrey and Richard were probably at this moment more important than he, and he wasn't going to let anything happen to them. They were young and strong. They'd be okay.

Audrey seemed to be doing better than Richard. It didn't surprise him. Richard's implant had been tough. He felt sympathy for them, especially Richard, whom he knew was going through much more than he'd let on in front of Audrey. Brave kid, he thought, but caught the fatherly thought and put it down.

The pain these operatives had gone through to prepare them to ferret out a traitor in the organization was enough and Ted knew it was the very beginning. They would be utilized to team other situations later. He couldn't mention his desire to create a super team. He couldn't let on what their full capability would be; he didn't know himself. The implants were experimental!

By three a.m. his charges were breathing normally, and Ted was certain the blood leaks from the damage he had done had begun to heal. Richard tossed about. The pain medication had worn off, and even in sleep his body felt the discomfort. Ted woke Richard carefully so as not to disturb Audrey, who still apparently felt the effects of the pill. He fed Richard a lesser pain medication and in a few minutes Richard drifted off again.

The narcotic pills had both been of the same dose, but Audrey's body weighed considerably less than Richard's, and she had taken the procedure better, so Audrey got the benefit. Ted gauged the time and decided they were right on schedule.

He got up, stretched and went into the kitchen to make coffee. He peeked in on them and then went to the communications room to check the net. All quiet, nominal. The dead of night gave him time to think about his best approach and pick the right time to lay the whole thing on them.

Time for the next chore. With a last glance at the sleepers, he headed through the tunnel to the underground lake.

Two hours later he returned. When he'd sent them to bed, he had gone into the Com room and put it on silent signal. Around five-fifteen the blink alarm went off and with only a glance at the sleeping two, he dashed back to communications and ran a quick check of the equipment.

A sweep of the area showed him a wild sea kicked up by the storm from the south. Nothing could be out in that so close to the shore, so he turned off the blink system, cancelled the alarm and logged the incident. He then checked on the sleepers.

Ted decided not to wake them until they both came to naturally. His stomach growled several times. Rather than take a chance on disturbing them, he cut his appetite with crackers and cheese.

Two more hours passed before first Richard and then Audrey began to stir. The smell of food would help, so Ted got up and made noise in the kitchen.

Soon an anguished cry came out of the bedroom from one Mr. Richard Penwarton.

"Hey! What is this, a train station? Can't a guy get a little sleep around here?"

Making jokes already. Maybe he had underestimated Richard's recovery time frame. He remained in the kitchen making noise and sang a little off key.

"Get out'n that kitchen and rattle those pots and pans...oh, get out'n that kitchen and rattle those pots and pans..." Ted glanced at the door to the kitchen, waiting for an entrance.

Renewed grumbling came in Richard's baritone register and then silence. Ted left the stove and walked to the entrance of the bedroom. Audrey's lips had very effectively shut him up. Ted grunted and returned to the kitchen.

He gave them a few minutes to pull themselves together and then called out, "Breakfast in ten minutes."

No answer. Ted made a big pile of flapjacks out of the box recipe and covered them. The cooking smell moved out of the kitchen and pervaded the compound.

A few seconds shy of ten minutes, they both appeared in the doorway in light colored "his" and "her" robes. Richard had his arms around Audrey's waist under her perfect breasts, and they walked slowly in sync. Audrey looked pale. It was clear she wasn't feeling good, but she didn't say anything. Ted took his cue on how to deal with them from Audrey.

Richard didn't look good either. The left side of his face was now brutally purple. It would be a couple of weeks before that would fade. Ted thought privately that Richard's looks alone could put the operation back a few days. It was *that* important. He'd have to wear make-up.

Amber said, "Ted, I've decided not to go through with it after all. Sorry. Will you have me killed now so you can operate on some other unsuspecting female?"

He looked at her sadly.

Audrey burst out laughing, but stopped immediately. "Ouch! That hurt. I'd better play it straight for awhile."

"Sorry, Audrey. I need to go over some additional do's and don'ts, but your levity was an invitation I couldn't refuse. You'll need to tone it down for a couple of days while general healing takes place. We have to be out of here tomorrow. We're going to another place closer to headquarters, a few hundred miles from here. You two must not be seen or the plan may fold. I figure it could be two weeks before you can start looking for our traitor. For now, you need to rest and learn."

Richard spoke up. "I've been thinking. Your plan was to take the Lucky Lady out through the sea entrance. I wonder if that's wise."

Ted said casually, "You haven't taken a look at the 'Maiden Voyage I' lately, have you?"

Richard caught the inference. "Ah...you've been hard at work while we've been sleeping our lives away, have you, Ted?"

"I took a few minutes to make a few changes."

Richard and Audrey made for the door, but Ted stopped them. "Uh-uh! Eat first! Sit!"

The two came back and sat. During breakfast the three tried to keep it light-hearted, studiously avoiding comment that would cause them to laugh.

Finally the meal was history. They got up and pitched in with the cleanup. Ted protested that he could do it, but Audrey said that moving around aided healing and they knew she was right.

Immediately after, they left the building and headed along the serpentine route back to the big cave. They went slowly and it wasn't fast enough for Audrey. She wanted to know what Ted had done to her boat.

Soon the narrow way opened up into the giant cave, and there in front of them, with Ted shining the light of a five-cell flashlight over the hull and then up to the top of the mainmast they beheld a sailing vessel they had never seen before. It had a maroon hull and the white sail had a distinctly cream color to it with striping. A big maroon "R" painted on it matched the hull color.

"I don't believe it!" Audrey cried, "How did you do this so quickly? This is amazing."

Ted answered, "I prepared to make changes from the moment you left the boat and entered the compound. The first night I pushed the sailboat out about twenty feet and anchored it with ropes. Then I took the dinghy we keep here and loaded the paint sprayer onto it. As a pre-pressurized unit I've had experience with, it took little effort to let the gentle current here at the slip carry me slowly fore to aft and do one side, and then the other. It's a fast drying nautical paint that will pass normal inspection and should be good at any reasonable distance.

"Painting the sail was the tougher job, but I used a long extension and basically painted by the numbers. You have noticed that the sail is cream colored now, as well. That goes well with maroon, and *viola*, a completely hidden ship."

Richard appeared awestruck. "Is there nothing you can't do?"

"The new name was simplest. It's a contact paper decal, nothing more. As I said, I started the night we arrived, after you two went to bed. The sail was toughest, but with the right equipment..." Ted said. "I finished that part last night when I was sure you were going to be okay."

"I'm amazed," Richard said. "Do you sleep?"

"I get by without much. I've been around boats all my life and I got plenty of practice scraping and painting hulls as a teenager before I got the call."

Audrey said. "What about the water line?"

"After I hefted out a few hundred pounds of movable equipment, including the anchor, your lucky gal was riding as high as it needs to in the cave. There is no swell in here, so I could paint right to the waterline and the bottom is black. There is no worry about paint residue floating out the exit because of the surf at the base of the cliffs. When we leave we need to take the special equipment I brought. That has to find its way back to Central or be scuttled if we're threatened. When I returned everything to the boat after the paint dried, it settled a few inches. The box and our weight will help, too. No one will notice."

"You thought of everything."

"Hope so."

"Thought of everything."

"Think so."

Richard said, "You're taking good care of us, Ted. Maybe we'd better get back in and start boning up on profiles, and such all."

"Good. We can talk and study in the living room where it's comfortable and we don't have to move around much."

"Okay," came from both.

They made their way back to the depot. Ted excused himself to get the profiles from the War Room. He returned with them and a black metal box twelve inches on a side. He carried it by a metal handle on its top, and Ted seemed to find it quite heavy. He sat in the brown leather easy chair and set the metal box carefully on the end table next to the chair. He handed the profiles to Richard and Audrey, who sat on the large lounger. Then he turned his attention to the box, which he began to manipulate. He offered no explanation.

Ignored, the two began to study stage II of their new identity. Pretty soon they heard a click and the front of the box opened. Ted said nothing, but he did sit back and relax, hands behind his head, eyes to the ceiling.

"I'm going to take a power-nap. Wake me in an hour. Don't peek and don't touch this unit."

Okay, Ted."

After fifty-five minutes Ted woke up on his own and looked at his watch. He bent forward and began work on a section of the open box that Richard and Audrey couldn't see.

A couple of minutes later, Richard, referring to the profiles, looked over at Audrey and said, "Done! You have these firmly in your mind?"

"Uh-huh."

"What now?"

"That's up to Ted, but he seems engrossed with his toy, and I for one, don't want to disturb him." Audrey couldn't believe how the British English accent he had cultivated seemed to straighten him up. She went looking for the stiff upper lip.

Ted looked up. The faces of the box they could see were all dull, flat black.

"No problem. A minute or two more..." He reached over to his side and grabbed two files and handed them out. "While I'm finishing this, study these."

"These..." turned out to be more profiles, this time of the four top echelon people they were going to have to investigate. There were no names attached to the information given. Audrey looked at Ted expectantly.

"You will recognize each individual if it comes to your having to meet all four. If you don't have to meet them there is no reason why you should know them, *ever*. Get it?"

"Right." They returned to reading. Another minute and Ted sat back with a satisfied grunt.

"When we leave, this box becomes the single most important thing in our lives, at least for the next week, or until we can use it to activate your advanced internal communication systems. You will each need to know how to open it—it's booby-trapped—and how to access the sequences that will activate the implants. I am familiar with it, and you will need to be intimately familiar with it, too."

"The weight of this small unit is, in part, due to the C-4 high explosive that is wired into it. There is enough explosive to blow the three of us and anything in a fifty-foot radius to little pieces, about as microscopic as the top-secret apparatus within. That's by design. Now, you about finished with your sketches?"

"I am," said Richard.

"Me, too," Audrey followed.

"Let's move to the table," he gestured, "and I will introduce you to the other half of the greatest advance in communications technology ever invented."

They looked at him.

"Yes. This little baby and the units healing inside your heads right now I told you were developed on the International Space Station that's floating above us now. Actually, only the electronics were fashioned there. Stoic arranged for the box to be built in one of his machine shops. Stoic pieced it together himself. As you can imagine, if he couldn't get access to what he wanted, no one could. Wanna see?"

"Uh-huh."

The three stood and walked over to a steel card table. They sat in cushioned metal chairs, the box now closed again, ready for demonstration.

Ted began his narrative. "The apparatus was built strong enough to withstand considerable force. There is only one box, and this is it. As you know, you can slam C-4 around all day and it won't detonate, so this unit can take quite a beating."

He focused on the part he'd opened before. There was a key lock at the top.

"The key lock is a ruse. Anyone trying to pick the lock or use any kind of a key in it will automatically set it off. Anyone trying to bore into the box from any part of it will set it off. There is no way to get into it without doing exactly what I will show you now."

Ted's hands moved to the sides of the box. The folded metal edging had a waviness to it that extended from top to bottom, but only on the side with the door.

Ted slowly and precisely pressed on the left side using his index finger only, two inches from its top, and then on the right side the same way, two inches from the bottom. Then his hands moved to opposing positions and he repeated his procedure. Keeping his hands in contact with the metal of the door, he moved both index fingers diagonally until they met at the center. He held them there. In about three seconds there was an audible click, and the door released.

Ted breathed a sigh. "Beneath the metal of the door is a pure lead sheath, part of the reason for the weight of this baby. Attached to that sheath are heat and pressure sensitive micro-switches. The unit can't be x-rayed either. The sequence I showed you is the only way to open the unit without causing it to explode. Once you begin the opening process, you must not remove your fingers from the door, or it will explode. Once the heat sensitive switch in the center senses your final command, the door will unlock and the fail-safe will reset and you can work the apparatus, sending the final command to the micro-processors in your heads and you will then be fully operational."

"Fully operational implies that these 'things' we have implanted in our heads are more than just communication devices, am I right?" Audrey queried.

"Yes it does," said Ted. "From what the inventor told Stoic, the full capability of the units will amaze you. As I said, Stoic and I are the only people on earth, until you two, that have any knowledge of this equipment. It will not injure you, but in addition to being a communicator, it will add immensely to your discernment abilities. I may go over that with you earlier than I had planned, but won't discuss it until all chance of a physical hemorrhage is gone and healing has progressed sufficiently. Another day, I think. In the meantime, how are you both feeling right now?"

"Brutalized," said Richard.

"A little weak, but okay," Audrey said. "Breakfast helped a lot."

Ted said a little sympathetically to Richard, "The procedure was tougher on you than on Audrey. You'll get through it okay. Could take longer."

"Yeah, I figured."

"Best to keep your minds active and not thinking about your implants. Now, since you are able to focus on the profiles, you aren't going to have trouble becoming experts in opening this box. Who wants to practice first?"

"Ladies first," Richard said with a little bow.

"You are so gallant, monsieur." Audrey curtsied, and then said to Ted, "Ted, got anything I can take for my raging headache?"

Richard jumped in on that, "Me, too!"

"Sure." Ted produced a small bottle with some pills in it from a shirt pocket and gave them each one. "These are strong, not like the knock-down pills I gave you initially, but I don't want to use any more than I have to."

They nodded. Richard went into the kitchen for water, and brought the glass back to share with Audrey.

"Here, wife, you first."

"Thanks." Audrey downed the pill with a sip of water and handed the glass back to Richard, who did the same.

Ted could see they both pretended feeling better than they did. He said nothing.

Richard began the next scenario. "Audrey and I have gone along with everything you have put in front of us, Ted. You are intimately aware that we are not followers. Audrey hasn't said anything to me, but I sense she is in my camp on this."

"You don't have to sense it, I'm there," Audrey said.

Richard continued, "We need you to talk straight to us. We don't believe you have held back anything without your reasons, but I want to cut to the chase. Lay it out for us, all of it."

Audrey said, "It does go for me, too. I have never met a neater, more interesting person in my life than you, Ted. Well, maybe Richard, but the jury's still out on that," she smirked at Richard, "whom I sensed I could follow with impunity. But it's not enough. I want answers, too."

"Okay, I give up. But I do want you to wait until nearer the end of the day before we sit down and I spill my guts. Right now I think you both should be moving slowly and getting as much rest as you can. I wouldn't hurt me to get some rest. I was up all night mothering you two."

Audrey looked at him sympathetically. He did look tired.

"Late in the day," Ted went on, "we will get the stuff out of here that the duty operatives shouldn't see. We'll put it in the sailboat's lower hold. We'll be ready to sail just as the staff descends the ladders from the Lodge. They are coming in at midnight."

Richard spoke up, "You know there's a hurricane raging outside?"

Ted said, "Yes, I know. I checked the weather projections earlier and it's slated to blow itself out in the next ten hours. It came up the coast fast. Right about now it should be over us. That's good because it'll keep people at home.

"The weather should be just right when we leave. We won't have to worry about storm surge, being on the backside of it, so we'll be well hidden as we leave. It won't be an easy passage, but we'll make it. I figure we'll be well out to sea and past Nick Trafalgar's lookouts by first light. Then we'll come in closer to shore and pretend we're checking out damage as we head for the New Jersey coast."

"Sounds like he thought of everything," Richard said to Audrey.

"Yep," Audrey responded, "I have a feeling, Richard, that you will be more than a partner to me, and I like the idea, but do you know how I think of Ted, ever since we first met?"

"No, how?"

"I met this mystery man in the moonlight, only two days ago, and he has become a lot to both of us, but he's still my Moonlight Man.

Ted smiled. "Moonlight Man, now there's a misnomer for you."

But he seemed pleased.

24

Senator Hartfield left with his wife Sally along toward noon of the day before the hurricane hit. Nick had time to meet with the Senator for an hour before they departed. He left Sally in their palatial third floor suite to finish their packing. She seemed unable to go to a party or on a vacation, no matter how mini, without bringing half her trousseau. The Senator ignored her foibles, because he loved her dearly.

Nick knocked on their door around ten-thirty, following his staff meeting. Sally answered the door. She looked good, although a bit pallid and Nick thought the lady had probably taken a few Excedrin to care for the morning after.

"Good morning, Sally. Sleep well?"

She grimaced, but then smiled at their host. "Hi, Nick. I hope I didn't make a fool of myself last night. I sure did have fun, so they tell me."

Nick laughed. "You had a good time, Sally, period. You may grace my castle by the sea anytime."

Sally was delighted. "Why, thank you, sir. But I'll bet you're here to see that stuffy old husband of mine, aren't you?"

Nick smiled. "I wouldn't call him stuffy, but I would like to borrow him for a few minutes. I believe I mentioned to him last night that I had a rare gun collection, and he said he'd like to see it. With your permission..."

"Of course, Nick." She called back to her husband, "Robert, Nick is here. Are you decent?"

"That's what the "D" in my middle name stands for." The Senator appeared around the corner of the door.

"Your middle initial is 'A,'" Sally corrected, "The 'D' is for dolt."

Hartfield swung around and gave his wife a smack on the butt. "That'll teach you, woman, to trifle with me."

Sally Hartfield let out a little screech, and disappeared into the interior of the suite. In the back of his mind, Nick saw how their closeness would help him get what he wanted from the Senator.

"Good morning, Senator." Nick shook his hand. "Did you sleep well?"

"Yes, Nick, very well indeed. And don't let that wife of mine fool you. She can put it down like a soldier. Still, she was a bit pale around the gills this morning, I noticed." He laughed.

"You're a lucky man, Senator."

"Yes, I am. So, what's your pleasure, Nick?"

Nick winked at the Senator. "I thought I'd show you that gun collection of mine before you go. Do you have time?"

"Certainly." He turned into the room. "Sally, I'm going with Nick for awhile. You be okay?"

Nick heard Hartfield's wife, her voice muffled by the distance to their bedroom say, "You go ahead. I'll finish the packing and maybe read. Take your time."

"Okay, my dear," to her, and to Nick, "Let's go, Nick."

The Senator pulled the door shut and the two men walked down the long, wide, hallway to the sweeping circular marble stairway and descended. A few steps shy of the first landing they met Maurice, one of the household staff. Nick told him to arrange to get their guests baggage down to the front as soon as Mrs. Hartfield was finished packing.

"Yes, sir," the man said, and went on his way.

On the second floor they entered a large room, long but narrow, with columns, similar in many respects to the layout of the entire mansion. In this room the tones were muted and ran from scarlet reds down through maroons and finally to one draped wall covered entirely with a scene from a Roman battle. It was multi-colored within, but its predominant color was black. Below the frieze were several glass display cases.

"You really do have a collection of pieces, don't you Nick?"

"Would I lie?"

The Senator looked at him sharply. "Not about this, evidently. But, you are a big business man and you have obviously done well in life. I bet you didn't get where you are today without turning a phrase or two in a direction that helped you along, did you?"

Nick laughed loudly and slapped the Senator on the back. "Who hasn't?"

Now the Senator laughed. As they stood over the glass cases, Nick gave Senator Hartfield a verbal tour of the gun collection. Hartfield was suitably impressed. As Nick finished, he stepped back and described the wall hanging as a priceless antique from Rome.

"I paid a lot for that. Very fitting place for it."

"Yes, it is."

"Now Senator, there are a couple of chairs at the other end of this room that face toward the ocean. They are outside on the balcony behind the scarlet drapes. It's a favorite place of mine when I need to sit and think, and rarely, when I want to discuss something with someone important to me. It's private."

Hartfield looked at him but said nothing. Nick walked with him to the drapes, held them for his guest, and they stepped out into the summer air. There was no breeze at the moment and the air had that hushed, drawn breath feel that gives the sense of an impending event.

"Storm coming. Might be quite a blow. The latest I heard was that it was on the edge of becoming a hurricane."

"That so? That would be one of *nature's* big things. What's on *your* mind, Nick?"

Nick moved his plush chair so that he could keep an eye on the Senator and read him non-verbally. Nick was exceedingly good at reading people.

"Senator, we were discussing the upcoming Appropriations Bill last night. My reading of it is that were it to pass, several of my businesses, notably those in scrap and concrete would accede to a more favorable environment for sales, and that would be a big help. What is more important to me, however, is that there is a clause in it that would limit my growth in the heavy metals industry and certain radioactives. It's an area I got involved in about a year ago, and it looks like it could be very lucrative. Clause 4-c would have a deleterious effect on my move and I could lose a couple of million I have invested in it."

"What would you have me do, Nick? I rather favor that clause."

The Senator's body language was innocuous until Nick got to the clause in the Bill relating to the heavy metals and radioactives. Hartfield tensed, just slightly. It told Nick that Hartfield had guessed the reason Nick had invited this particular Senator to his party. The Senator may have just realized the rest of it was fluff, that he was the *real* reason for the party. Nick hit him hard now.

"You, in fact, were the author of that clause. I want the Bill to pass, because if it doesn't I stand to lose in other ways it isn't necessary to discuss. But I want your clause dropped or changed to read as follows." He pulled a typewritten piece of paper out of his pocket and handed it to Senator Hartfield.

The man took the sheet out of Nick's hands and read it briefly. He looked at Nick incredulously.

"I can't do this. How do you come off trying to tell me how to run my office? I'd rather let the bill fail. I won't withdraw it, and I've a good mind to report you to the police."

Nick answered reasonably, "That is an option, of course, but then I might feel it necessary to send a few photos I have to a national scandal sheet I know. Here's one I have with me. You may recognize it, although the angle is different from the angle you were working from at the time."

He pulled a photo from the same pocket and handed it to Hartfield.

"Politics, eh, Senator? Sometimes it gets in the way of a good man."

Senator Hartfield's face got white. "You wouldn't…"

"Then there's that lovely wife of yours. A thing like this…well, it could put a crimp in a marriage. Of course, you've probably regretted it already and told your good wife, but then…there's that lovely wife of yours…"

"No! No! It would ruin me. She'd divorce me…my career, oh my God, what have I done?" He stared at Nick Trafalgar, and now fear was mixed with hatred. "What did you mean, 'then there's that lovely wife of yours'?"

"Forget it. I'm sure any momentary problems in our budding relationship will be smoothed over and you and your wife will feel very safe in the future. Your children, too, of course." Nick hesitated, and in the right next moment said, "Won't they...?"

Hartfield looked as if he was going to cry. Nick kept looking at him with a fatherly expression, although he knew the man was five years older than Nick. He kept reading signs from the man, satisfied that he'd just put a United States Senator in his pocket.

"I've never been compromised. I did it to myself." The Senator wasn't looking at Nick any longer, but through watery eyes at the ocean beyond. "What do you want me to do?"

"Remove clause 4-c from the Appropriations bill and work your butt off to get the Bill passed. Tell them a lot more is riding on passing the Bill than that clause and you will gain the votes you need for passage by taking it out. The hang-up is not in the House; it's in the Senate.

"You are a well-respected Senator. You have charisma. You can do it. I will have little contact with you after today, but my eyes are everywhere. Don't think about it. Live a normal life. Your secret is safe with me but don't cross me. Maybe you can help me again in the future but I have no intention of becoming a thorn in your side. I mean it. I highly value your independent mind. Be independent and go on with your life."

Hartfield looked at Nick again, a beaten man. Still, Nick saw a glimmer of hope in his eyes. Nick thought his final words helped to ease the pain and maybe gave the Senator back a bit of his self-esteem.

"Look out onto this beautiful world we live in, Senator. There is much to live for."

Hartfield got out of his chair and went to the low marble balustrade. He looked out over an ocean a hundred and eighty feet below him. He finally spoke in a subdued voice, filled with regret.

"Being in politics is a worthwhile endeavor, if you can keep yourself clean. But it's so easy to slip...so, so easy. I've been around a long time, Nick. I never slipped before. It was a year, a lousy year ago, and it's going to follow me for the rest of my days. One thing!"

Nick said in a gentle voice behind him, "It's just business, Senator, just business."

Hartfield turned pathetically and looked Nick over. "Yeah, Nick… just business."

Senator Hartfield turned and walked through the scarlet drapes and back to his room. Nick sat still for another ten minutes, and then got up and walked to the first floor, across the central atrium with its two story white marble colonnades, and a slight smile played across his lips. He timed it correctly. He arrived outside at the curb of his circular driveway in time to say goodbye to the Senator and his wife as they prepared to leave.

Sally Hartfield bubbled. She said to Nick, "Don't forget us when you have another party like this one, Nick. You'd ask us back, wouldn't you?"

"Of course, Sally. Your husband and I had a few minutes to discuss our mutual philosophies and it turns out they are remarkably similar. I'm certain my secretary will have your names on the top of my list."

"Oh, good!" Sally cried.

Nick held his hand out to Senator Hartfield, and after only a moment's hesitation, Hartfield took it.

"It is amazing, isn't it," he said, managing to keep the bitterness out of his voice, "how quickly the fortunes of luck and life can turn in directions one least expects."

He turned to his wife. "We will definitely be seeing each other in the future, Sally."

Hartfield grasped his wife's arm and guided her into the waiting limousine. He got in and signaled the driver to move away. Nick waited motionless while the vehicle quickly became a small aspect in the acres of green lawn on the treed estate. He noted how the driver slowed and braked before driving through the open iron gate past the guardhouse, and then disappeared onto the roadway.

"Yes, Senator, but you still don't know the half of it." Nick turned on his heel and headed for his office, his mind already on other things.

25

The two students studied their character alterations seriously. They practiced, criticized, role-played, and in a very limited time frame, tried to fit themselves into new roles without slipping.

Richard was exceedingly bright and had already picked up on the part, becoming so well versed it seemed he'd become another person. The Rolph of the past, with a last name Audrey never even got to hear slipped away, and Richard became the only person Audrey ever knew. It became difficult to remember the nuances of the person he had been. Richard became, eminently, Richard Penwarton, right down to the shaded English accent.

Audrey wondered more than once if Rolph/Richard had done this kind of presto-chango before. It amused her to wonder if the Rolph she had met wasn't some other kind of construct, but she decided nothing would be served by inquiring. She knew her performances weren't as good as Richard's. She'd always known there might come a day when she would need another identity, but it didn't come easy.

She grabbed her stubborn streak and willed herself to prevail. She role-played her new self until it came out her ears. She improved with time, got the semblance of an accent down to where Richard started to believe her and Ted stopped good-naturedly shaking his head.

The long sessions got longer and the time shorter.

Finally Ted interrupted them. "You are just about there. I don't need to tell you that you need to *be* the part. And I don't have to remind you of the stakes."

Audrey shoved Amber Pierce far back in her mind and became Audrey Penwarton. Amber didn't like it particularly, which is why she gave Audrey such a difficult time, and Audrey had to essentially convince her original self that it was okay, that some day she could resurface when things got better. Finally Amber allowed herself to be subverted.

Audrey knew that in Psychology there were many case studies; people whose personalities had been shattered by horrific trauma. The mind split them into two or more quite different people, each acting as *self* during periods of control. She knew there were those who could switch abruptly, depending on the stimuli, from one personality to another and back just by the suggestion of a gifted hypnotist.

Ted put it to them this way. "The mind," he said, "is without doubt the most complex thing in nature. It is probed, abused, stressed and strained by everyone. It has been studied by scientists of one ilk or another for thousands of years, but not so thoroughly as it has in the last hundred years. It still eludes the understanding of Man.

"Nature has imbued in the mind a primal need to its own preservation. Although voluntary command of the consciousness can override prime directive, as it were, it is a most difficult thing to accomplish. You speak of changing your mind, but it is an altering of opinion based on the strength of outside stimuli that causes the need to alter a course. That kind of change is superficial and the prime directive—to preserve the essence of the mind—is not touched."

"So how do we overcome our original personalities, such that they never surface during an operation such as this?" Audrey had to ask.

"There are two aspects to it. The first is repetition. Repetition deepens new neuronal paths in the brain, and helps to create habits. The second is the conscious mind's command to itself to find a new way, where failure in the old way is assured. This can be done through the profiling of a personality, which is what you have been doing."

"I understand."

Richard broke in, "I studied a good lot of that in my Psych courses, but it wasn't my meat. I was much happier taking things apart and then trying to put them back together again. Then, of course, there were the women."

"Richard!"

"Sorry, love. Like Ted says, every time I failed, I had to search for a new pathway." He smirked at Audrey.

She smacked him on the arm with her open palm. It hurt her more than it hurt him. Ted looked at his watch and noted that it was past time to eat. Like a well-oiled machine, the three moved into the kitchen, prepared a hearty steak supper and sat down to eat.

"After dinner let's take a little time off to just vegetate. I get the feeling this might be our last supper together," Audrey said.

Ted looked at her, "What makes you say that?"

"Well, I sense it's just gone too smoothly. You know what I mean?"

"Yes, I do," Ted said, "but we are in as safe a place as we could be, barring being found out by any of several hundred good and bad organizations throughout the world."

Richard had to get in his two cents. "That all?"

"You don't think the Fed wouldn't give a lot to have a place like this, or for that matter, even know about it?"

"Don't they?" Richard spoke up to a nagging feeling.

"Richard, to the best of my knowledge, and of Stoic's, no. No one knows. And none of the other four top people know of it, either. But keep in mind that all secrets are transitory. The more people involved, no matter what their level, the greater chance of a leak. Stoic wants this to remain one of our super-secret bases, because it has great utility, but you can bet he has a plan for the day when we are discovered."

"I'll bet."

"And the Families on the mainland, what about them? How about our friend Nick Trafalgar? Imagine how happy he would be to find our depot, and how ecstatic he would be to find our little Audrey, barely five miles from his big house. Our best bet is to stay unknown, that is our cloak, but you are both familiar with cause and effect. Someday we'll be found out. Then it's up to Stoic. Comprendé, Senor y Senorita?"

"Si," Richard said.

Audrey said nothing.

"Now," Ted said, "Let's go through it one more time, and then we'll quit and pack Audrey's sailboat. After this, that will probably seem like fun."

"I'll vote for that," Audrey said.

They got up and moved around for a couple of minutes. Richard kept a running dialogue accented by his new British inflection, and the other two had to keep from laughing.

Finally, Richard sat down and said, "Okay. I'm ready."

"Good, you're very convincing," came from Ted.

They went through it all again. Audrey was passable, but she didn't have the flair for it that Richard had. Still, at the end, Ted nodded agreeably, and pronounced them both ready to begin.

"Countdown in effect, as of now."

"Right."

"Let's go and start putting things away on your sailboat, Audrey."

Ted led the way into the War Room. They collected anything that wasn't part of standard depot materiel and moved it close to the exterior door. Then they went into the secondary room where the chair closet was bolted to the floor and took the better part of an hour dismantling it.

"It was built strong," Ted said unnecessarily.

"Noticed," said Richard.

Audrey proved to be lithe and strong, even under the weather as were both she and Richard. She assisted where she could, sometimes taking more than the men thought she should, but they said nothing.

They packaged and boxed, toted and carried under Ted's direction. After three hours they'd finished the task and were ready to sit down for the night.

"Good going, gang," Ted said wearily.

"Thanks," from Audrey, "Can I die now?"

Ted said, "Uh-uh. Whose going to pilot the sailboat?"

"I don't know. Let me look around—nope—nobody! Guess we'll have to stay."

"No can do. We have to move on."

"I know, Ted, I know. But the body says stay and I'd like to listen to it for awhile."

"We'll break for two hours and sit around. Then we've got to go. Our relief is two hours away."

"We understand," said Richard, and he put his arms gently around his new wife and gave her a squeeze.

Audrey looked up from her helpless position at Richard and said, "Let's lie down in the bedroom together."

She looked at Ted. He nodded, and they left him standing. When they were gone, Ted sat on the comfortable lounge sofa, and set his watch for eleven forty-five. Then he too lay down and did his best to relax. Soon he was sleeping softly and soundly.

At eleven forty-five Ted's watch started thrumming his wrist and the man came instantly awake. Oriented, he got up and called to the still sleeping couple. He silently berated himself for putting these two in the position they were, but what choice did he have?

"Sixteen bells!"

They stirred and dragged themselves out of bed. No one felt like speaking. They stripped and remade the bed together, throwing the soiled linen into the laundry hamper. Ted had made sure anything with their blood on it went with them. They dressed for the voyage and took time on the head. As usual, Ted had anticipated that earlier. At five minutes to twelve they said a silent goodbye to their safe haven and marched out of the depot building.

Richard felt constrained to say, "Ted, you logged everything?"

"Yes. Not to worry! I know you feel responsible. Those following will be happy enough."

"Thanks. I do feel that way."

"One of the reasons I picked you," Ted said.

"One more thing," Audrey said.

They turned to her.

"The duty staff will see us leave in the Maiden Voyage. What about that?"

"First, Audrey, a good question. The duty staff is trustworthy and they will follow directions. I left a note in the communications room for them to leave the visual monitors off for a half hour, enough time for us to clear the point. Once around we'll hug the coast for another half hour. No one will see this sailboat exiting the cave.

151

"Curiosity won't get the better of them?"

"No."

"Okay, then."

They wound the gray, serpentine route back to the ship.

"All shipshape and ready to go. Captain," he looked at Audrey, "shall we pipe aboard?"

She smiled at him and said, "It's your call, Admiral, but don't you think a pipe would be a bit shrill in this cave?"

"Point taken, Captain. Let's aboard then." They walked up the plank, pulled it onboard, and battened down whatever needed it.

Would you like to take it out, Admiral?" Audrey asked.

"A pleasure! Start your engines." Of course there was only one, but theatrics seemed right.

"Cast off the lines, mate."

Richard looked at Ted. "I assume you mean me, Admiral. Why don't you say "grunt" and do away with that high-falutin' stuff?"

"Okay, grunt, ship the lines and we'll be off."

Richard cast off the lines. Ted applied power to the little engine and made a wide turn in the underground lake. They headed for the one and only exit. As the opening became discernable in the remarkably low light they were showing, the speed of the vessel also picked up. Ted cut back on the power as soon as he was in the middle of the channel, and let the subterranean river propel them into the ocean. They exited alarmingly fast.

The pulsing roar of breakers on the ocean side replaced the noise of the stream. It became too difficult to hear. They slid through the natural opening to white fury melding with white noise. The moon shone bright through puffs of fleeting scud from the blown-out hurricane. Ted found the swell heavy but manageable. He went back to full throttle and gave it his total concentration. He kept the rudder straight for a count of fifteen, and then turned the wheel hard a-starboard for a count of five, then straightened the ship out again.

For the next fifteen minutes he weaved one way and then another. Evidently flying blind, he took them out according to a pre-conceived, pre-memorized path. The sky didn't cooperate. Enveloping darkness and racing clouds turned the moonlight on and off with regularity.

152

To Ted's credit, they hit nothing. As they picked up the buoys, he relaxed and held on until they slid far enough around the point.

"The seas are still rough, but calming. Want to take over, Audrey?"

"Sure." She took the wheel and headed them straight out into the Atlantic, away from the receding storm. "How far out should we go?"

"You can gauge it. We don't want it to look at first light like we had tried to cross the ocean in this, but we want to get out far enough so that it's easy to swing back and cruise the coast. We could put out the front jib to pick up some forward motion, what do you think?"

"That would work for now, but I don't want any more sail until we get less bluster."

"I agree."

"Look, Ted, I think I'm good for a couple of hours at the helm. It'll keep my mind off some...discomfort."

"Go for it. Do you want another pain pill?"

"No, I'll be fine."

"All right, then, I'll go below. Richard, why don't you hit the sack?"

"I want a few minutes with my wife first."

Ted nodded and went below.

"Audrey," Richard said after Ted was below, "I am beat. You can't be any better off than me. Will you be all right?"

"Yes, Richard. I'm back with my baby, and everything's fine. I'll lock the wheel down and come get you in two hours. You know these rigs, don't you? I'm surprised I never thought to ask before."

Richard went cornpone. "Yew askin' a old farm boy from the mid-west where the corn grows like a ocean if'n he kin steer a boat with nothin' around but water? Is thet whut yew askin?"

Audrey laughed out loud. "My God, Richard, where do you get those voices?"

Richard laughed, too. "I mentioned I did some theater during college to pass the time—you know."

"How you are!" She exclaimed. "You make me feel almost inadequate."

Richard looked at her as seriously as he could muster. "Audrey, there is nothing about you that is inadequate. If we get through this, I want to see if I can handle a life with you. I mean it."

"We'll get through it. If there's a God in heaven, we'll get through this. Even if there isn't! Now you turn around and march. Get some sleep. You're going to need it. Ted needs sleep as much as we do, so I want to give him a break. Go!"

Richard reached out and held her smaller face in his hands and kissed her gently.

"That's what I think of being told what to do by my woman... anytime!"

Audrey returned the kiss and then pushed on his chest until they separated. With a smile but no further words, Richard went below. The Maiden Voyage I glided over diminishing seas, a lighter, occasionally moonlit darkness against the blackness of the night. Audrey rode the sea alone, queen of her realm, a contented smile on her lips.

She couldn't put down her smile. Neither could she put down the yearnings of love that bubbled up inside her. She looked at her waterproof Indiglo watch. Twelve-thirty! So much had just gone down, but now it had a dreamlike quality. Time to wind down. She gave herself back to gentle thoughts.

26

She turned the nautical receiver on low, just enough to hear over the sound of the plowing bow. Not much to do but steer. She tried to catch something on the past hurricane, news of damage, tidal flooding, and distress calls. Too early.

Her mind drifted into her new persona. Her hands automatically felt the needs of the boat as the swells normalized. She looked at her watch again with momentary shock, nearly two-thirty a.m. Audrey realized she'd totally disconnected. She willed herself out of her dreamlike state, turned the sailboat east and locked the wheel, heading toward Spain for a couple of hours. Audrey went down to wake Richard.

She could see he slept soundly. She liked looking at him in repose. "Richard."

He came awake instantly and grabbed Audrey, pulling her down onto the bed with him.

"Hi."

"Hi, yourself. Behave!"

"All shipshape?"

"Yup. You okay?"

"Sure. I'll take something for this headache, but I'm really not feeling bad now. What's our heading?"

"Due east."

"Okay."

"Want me to maintain that?"

"At three-thirty come around one eighty and head back towards this start point. We'll retrace our path to show up near the mansion around six-thirty. Ted wants one more early morning look in the light at Nick's place."

"Isn't that dangerous?"

"A little, but Ted says he wants to cruise past about a half mile out of the bay and see what he can see. Okay?"

"Okay." Richard got up and Audrey stayed down.

"Later."

Richard walked up the steps from the cabin and unlocked the wheel. He sat in the Captains chair, checked the compass and then looked around him. The moon had set and the sea turned dark, matching the cloudless sky he had come up to, except that with the storm now past, a crystal sky teemed with stars. A warm breeze blew gently across his naked upper body and combed through the curly mat of chest hair. It felt good.

He held the wheel lightly, feeling the sea on the rudder and watching the compass. Richard allowed himself to relax as Audrey had done earlier. His face still hurt and the swelling hadn't gone down much. The bathroom light had shown serious bruising, but no more errant blood; he felt a bit better than he had. His thoughts turned to Audrey and he smiled. She may look fragile, he thought, but...

At three-thirty he turned the craft and headed back toward a point in the ocean opposite Spicer's Rocks. He relished feeling alone, surrounded by water, having nothing to do but feed on his thoughts. The left side of his face was a gnawing, ever-present ache. It helped a lot to keep Audrey on his mind for the majority of his helmsman's duty. Remarkable girl, he thought, never a one like her before. She definitely has something. I'm glad we're a pair, no matter what happens.

Richard wondered what it would be like being hooked up to Audrey's communication system. Ted had implied there was more to it than he had let on. Wonder what that is? What did he mean by "discernment abilities?" Why did they have to wait a full week? Was it really for healing, or did Ted hold back on something he needs to find out for himself at the moment of truth? How powerful were these units? Placement evidently was critically important. Could it be what Ted had said? Plausible, but it didn't wash.

There were many questions, and Richard knew he would only get answers when Ted decided to offer them. He shrugged mentally. Faced with no other options, he'd wait. Mulling these things over made work for Richard and passed the time. Before long his watch said five-thirty; time to wake Ted and for him to get back to bed.

He locked the wheel as Audrey had done earlier and went below. Ted slept lightly and came awake as Richard had. They conversed in soft tones for a minute or so and then Richard returned to the wheelhouse and went back to watching the dark seas and the glorious night sky.

Ten minutes later, a much older, well tanned and weather beaten man, perhaps in his late sixties or early seventies came up from below. He ascended the stairs and smiled at Richard.

"Well, sonny, here you see a seafarin' man. Got my sea legs fifty years ago. I'll take over the helm, youngster." The man said, a slight quiver in his voice.

Richard laughed out loud. "Perfect!"

Ted smiled and said, "I wanted to get another look at Nick's place before we leave the area. No point in inviting disaster, in case they have boats out which I doubt, but it pays to prepare."

"Good idea!"

"We need to arrive at the secondary depot in Maryland near Washington, in four days time. Stoic has informed me that one of the other four chiefs is using the facility, so arriving too early would not be in our best interest. Taking an eastern route, doubling back and cruising the coast will time it right. Also, if you can handle it, I've altered my thinking and may decide to activate your units on the boat. We'll see when we get closer."

"Oh."

"I can take the wheel. If anything happens, I'll start singing, "Blow the Man Down" as gustily as a seventy-year-old might to alert you. Make the bed and hide in the bilge, just in case we're boarded. Make it look like there is only one person aboard. I doubt it'll come to that, but, let's just say I was a good Boy Scout."

"Bet you were, Ted."

"Nice following breeze right now. I think we can get out the mainsail and trim the jib. Want to help me with that?"

"Sure."

The two men got to work and finished in minutes. Ted suggested Richard go back to sleep for as long as he could. The work of setting sail had brought back the old headache and he felt excessively tired. Below, he checked through the cabin and made sure a stark minimum of things would need doing to camouflage them, just in case. Then he carefully crawled into the bed with Audrey so as not to wake her.

That didn't happen. She came full awake and wrapped herself around him.

She looked him in the eye and said, "Where you been, husband?"

"Topside counting stars."

"And how many did you count?"

"I lost count." He made a move to get out of bed. "I better get back up there and count 'em again."

"No, you don't! You're stayin' right here, pardner!" She gripped him in her arms and held him tight.

"Oh, you're so masterful!" he cried.

Ted called down from topside, "Hey, you guys, we're only ten miles off the coast. You trying to call attention to us?"

"Oh, that's father. We better be good!" said Richard.

"Knock it off!"

"Yes, father." They called up, but they did subside, relaxing together until Richard could come down from his previous exertion, and then they drifted back to sleep.

About nine-thirty they woke to Ted's quavering voice singing of "Blow the Man Down." Richard came alive instantly and informed the rudely awakened Audrey about Ted's signal. They quickly made the bed and hid themselves in the lowest section of the boat. Richard grabbed a gun from his pack and as an afterthought affixed a silencer to the weapon. Then they played hidden mouse and listened.

After a few minutes, they heard Ted's muffled voice calling out to someone who had arrived in a powerboat. Richard thought it had the sweet, throaty sound of a Donzi.

Neither could make out what was said, but after a few minutes, the speedboat roared to life again and cut away from the sailing vessel. The sound faded rapidly. After five minutes, while Ted put distance between them and the center of Nick Trafalgar's empire, they became aware of a tap-tapping sound. Audrey recognized it as International Morse Code. It said, "Clear...clear...clear." Ted kept his position at the wheel in case someone might still be watching him in binoculars. Very careful man!

They removed themselves from the bilge area, Audrey with a cramp. She sat back on their bed and rubbed her left leg until it faded.

Richard went to the cabin stair and called softly above, "What we got, Ted?"

Looking straight ahead, Ted noted conversationally that they had had a visit from two of Nick Trafalgar's bad boys, Alonzo Malfo and Bernie Homenio. He told them what transpired and suggested that if they were all slept out they might join him, but that he thought it wise to not show up on deck for another half hour.

"Bet you could handle a hearty breakfast."

"Yes, that sounds good. You and Audrey want to rustle up some grub?"

"We have to pass a the half-hour doing *something*, don't we?"

Ted laughed and in his quivery voice said, "Sounds good to me, sonny. You call me when you're ready."

"No kidding, Pops!"

The heart of danger loomed closer. Ultimate seriousness would be required. None of them felt impropriety in continuous banter and Ted encouraged it. It allowed him to continuously take the emotional temperature of the two.

The clatter of pots and pans in the galley was lost in the big ocean, soaked up by sheer distance. After ten minutes, Ted smelled the familiar odor of bacon and eggs. It reminded him he hadn't eaten for many hours. He gave it another ten and then called to the two below.

"We're out of range, now and nothing is flying low overhead. The coastline is largely uninhabited here. Why don't you join me? It's a lovely day. By the way, bring food."

He heard a loud chuckle from below, and then Richard's voice. "We've got him where we want him now, Audrey. You have that list of demands?"

"In my shirt pocket. I can take it out of my pocket by myself, thank you."

"Just trying to be helpful," Richard grumbled.

"Just trying to help yourself."

More grumbling.

"Richard, there is a hungry man up there. Don't you have any manners?" She'd not forgotten to practice her new accent. Richard nodded approval.

"Okay, okay! You sound much more real, by the way."

"So I wasn't real before?"

"I'll never learn!"

Audrey gave him one of those pretty, "No, you won't!" smiles.

Ted heard foot falls on the teak stairs and Audrey appeared, moving smoothly onto the deck. Her willowy shape made Ted look a moment longer than he might. She carried a specially made tray with places for four glasses or cups, and a center section shaped like a platter piled high with scrambled eggs, properly garnished with parsley. On the sides of the tray were depressions filled with perfectly browned link sausages.

"I am truly impressed," Ted said, sniffing deeply.

Richard appeared behind Audrey with a carrier, silverware, napkins and three plates, also of sturdy Melmac.

"I came up last because of the view," Richard smirked.

"Do you want to wear this breakfast, Richard?"

"No, mi'love, do you want me to be good?"

Audrey thought about this for a moment and then said, "No, I guess not. I'd better keep your lascivious character out in the open where I can see it!"

"Lascivious! I'm shocked and dismayed."

"I'll bet!"

Ted watched and listened silently. The two young operatives set up the table behind the wheelhouse and efficiently spread out the breakfast feast. The sailboat paralleled the starboard shore about half a mile away. The swells from the storm were nearly gone, but breakfast remained a challenge.

Three voracious appetites consumed everything. Ted opined he could have eaten even more and that Richard and Audrey had outdone themselves. "Maybe," he mused out loud, "*that* was why I chose you."

It pleased Audrey, and she said so.

Richard nodded to Ted and said, "In the Roman tradition, we are treating every meal as if it were to be the last. We ought to eat really well for awhile."

The thought was sobering, but Ted continued to smile.

They finished around eleven-fifteen. Now eighty-five degrees with the last of the storm clouds already well to the north, it left the sky cloudless, brilliant blue and clean. Only near the horizon did they see a faint trace of haze that would build through the hot day. They moved with the coastline, keeping a half-mile from shore. They searched the shore with binoculars by turns.

They altered course now and then to get a closer look at an odd feature or damage caused by the departed hurricane. They listened to the radio and picked up information on conditions from Long Island's local stations with an occasional ocean weather forecast thrown in.

At one point they heard a distress call from a foundered sailboat. They discussed going to the rescue, and would have announced their presence and E.T.A. but they caught a reply from a Coast Guard ship so they continued, relieved to remain inconspicuous.

They took revolving shifts at the wheel. The ocean had calmed and the Maiden Voyage I pushed along at eight knots with the sprightly breeze. The fresh wind pushed occasional tops off the swells, giving an artists view of little whitecaps in all directions. Ted figured they'd be in the Babylon area by eight p.m. and put up for the night in the water outside of Robert Moses State Park. He knew it to be a regular parking place for sailboats. They'd fit right in and make their run across congested New York Harbor in the morning.

"We're making good time. It won't hurt to hang back," Ted said.

Ted finished a six-hour stint at the wheel, enjoying himself thoroughly, but let Audrey take over to preserve the schedule. He and Richard got together for some cribbage. Tiring of the game after an hour, Richard asked Ted if he thought it might be okay to work out some, or was it too early in the healing process. Ted nixed the idea, although he said he felt Richard was coming along well enough. He suggested that if Richard felt he could handle a moderately vigorous exercise program, to start on it tomorrow.

"Matter of fact, Richard, I'll join you."

"Good. I'm going to grab some sun," Richard replied.

Ted looked at the cribbage board and shrugged. "Suits me."

Richard's still swollen face made him look uncomfortable.

"You can handle a couple of these," Ted said, getting out the plastic pill bottle. "Be a hero later."

"Thanks." He tossed them down and went topside. He gave a lopsided smile to Audrey and a "Howdy!" and went aft.

"Want me to flip you over when you're done on one side?" she called.

"No thanks, but if you're into a little roll on the deck after your watch, wake me up."

"Enjoy your sleep,"

"Old married couple—no fun anymore..." Richard groused.

"You're so deprived," she shot back.

"Now you sound like my mother."

"Oh great—this conversation is really heading down!"

"I like my mother."

"That's not what I mean."

"I know what you mean. I'm just trying to get in the last word."

"Unlikely."

"One of these days."

"Keep dreamin."

Richard grumbled and subsided. He reached into a compartment under an aft deck seat, carrying it to Audrey at the wheel.

"Smear some grease on my back, won't you, love?"

"That I'll do. Love that big brown body. Never liked burnt toast." She applied a generous amount of sunscreen to Richard's back and legs and rubbed it in.

When she stopped rubbing, Richard took the tube.

"Thanks."

"Think nothin' of it, ducks."

He glanced at her but didn't bite. He yanked a blanket out of the aft chest and spread it out, rolled up his shorts and lay down. The sun rode high in the mid-afternoon summer sky and the heat blazed.

The only clouds now interrupting the clean blue were far south. Heat lightened the blue sky and haze covered the horizon.

Audrey went back to her gentle thoughts. She wanted nothing more than to capture the serenity of the ocean. She had no illusions about the ordeal to come and she knew the others felt as she did. She continued south of the coastline, practicing her new accent in low tones.

The flat face of the ship's clock brought her out of her reverie when the boat rolled slightly and flashed a sudden glint into her eyes. She peered past the reflection and noted that she'd been steering her lovely, altered sailboat for five hours. She looked aft at Richard. He'd fallen asleep.

Her watch said four-ten. Better get him up. This close to shore she couldn't lock down the wheel and let the ship run free. Richard could bring them along to Robert Moses State Park. Couple of sails in the distance; nothing up close. No powerboats she could see. She noted a large rusted tanker spewing smoke, a glaring ugly spot on the quiet ocean's beauty. It plied near the far horizon where sea and air melded from one blue through the gray haze and back to dark, ocean blue.

She glanced at her map, found a landmark, plotted their position and marked it with her erasable highlighter. Right where Ted wanted us to be.

Audrey went over and shook Richard awake. His back showed only a slight redness from the heat. Nonetheless, after all that time under direct sun, she told him to lie still and went to the first aid cupboard, got out sunburn lotion, which she applied judiciously to his back and legs.

"Glad you greased up earlier, Richard." she said.

"Still tired, thought I might fall asleep."

"You're fine." She slapped him on the shoulder.

"Ow! It's genetic. I tan quick. That hurt, you brute."

"You deserve it."

"Why?"

"'Cause you're you, buddy-boy!"

"I heal fast, in any event. Miraculous healing happens here, Audrey, my dear."

"Right! Can you hear the skeptic?"

"I thought I detected just a wee bit. Well, it's off to work I go, to quote a famous dwarf."

Richard got up and made his way to the wheelhouse, sat in the captain's chair, unlocked the wheel. Remembering the words by Robeert Louis Stevenson of an old Sea Chantey he sang in college, he began to belt it out. The words rolled across his eyes.

Sing me a song of a lad that is gone,
Say, could that lad be I?
Merry of soul he sailed on a day
Over the sea to Skye
Mull was astern
Rum on the port
Eigg on the starboard bow
Glory of youth glowed in his soul
Where is that glory now?

Sing me a song of a lad that is gone
Say, could that lad be I?
Merry of soul he sailed on a day
Over the sea to Skye
Give me again
All that was there
Give me the sun that shone
Give me the eyes
Give me the soul
Give me the lad that's gone

Richard's rich baritone wafted across the sailboat and down to where Ted had been napping and woke him.

Audrey, who had made her way down to the second step of the cabin stairway stopped and turned. She looked at him with love. What a guy, she thought, and then she silently repeated their litany; *it's only an assignment...* And she thought how much more difficult it would be if at some point they both allowed, even for the briefest moment, their emotions to override their intellect and training at some critical time.

Down in the cabin she met Ted on his way up.

He looked at her and said; "I see conflict in your face, Audrey. Don't be too concerned about having strong feelings for Richard. You two are more of a set now than any two operatives of any organization in the world. I assure you of that. When you both discover your full potential, there will be only one way for the two of you for the rest of your lives."

Audrey tried to speak, but Ted held up his hand and continued. "When I pulled your files and decided you were a match, I agonized over how to approach it. Finally I decided that the benefits so completely outweighed the downsides that I would just bull it through. I thought of you as two individuals, and then I thought about the safety of the world and the contribution you could make. I never wanted to play God. I hope you will never hate me for the decisions I've made."

"I couldn't hate you, not now."

Ted looked away from her. "I want to destroy the evil in the world, just like Stoic does, yet I know it will never happen, because evil is a part of the human condition. Second best is to be an effective fighter against it. That I try to be! There are people I can affect, turning them into weapons against that evil, example, you and Richard. I live with the knowledge that the fine people I have turned into weapons may be taken out by others with weapons of their own."

He turned back to Audrey. "I truly wish there were some other way."

"Well, Ted, if there is, nobody I know knows it. Now, may I go to the bathroom?"

Ted burst out laughing.

"I can't even sermonize timely," he said ruefully, turned and walked away, shaking his head.

27

The hurricane caused no appreciable damage to the dock, mansion or boats. Nick's private army could be utilized in any manner for extra chores. In the wake of the storm, the ocean became calmer. Bernie thought about the swim he'd had with Mikey and his new feelings. He idly watched clean scud arch across the sky as it followed the storm. The deep, brilliant blue the storm left in its wake, made him feel especially good. His watch said seven a.m. Bernie decided to look Mikey up.

He found him in the Card Room, one of the more popular places in the mansion. Several of the guys were playing five-card stud, and a couple of hard faced guys in the corner were slapping down blackjack cards. Mikey stood outside the larger group, watching. He looked around when the door closed.

"Hey, Bernie, what's goin' down?"

"Got a job for you, Mikey."

The other men looked up briefly and went back to their hands. That made Bernie happy, because he didn't want to draw attention.

"Yeah? What is it?" Mikey asked.

Bernie didn't answer, except to say, "C'mon."

When they got outside of the card room and Bernie glanced around the empty hallway, he said, "That shit is boring. I wondered if you were up to a swim again. I'm interested in seeing if the hurricane caused any shifting of the wreck out beyond the point. Wanna come?"

"That the job, Bernie?"

"I don't want the other guys knowin' what I'm up to. Fuck 'em! Don't throw too much of yourself at those bad boys. Good policy! You know?"

"Guess you're right. It's a new ballgame, you know, more serious stuff."

"Yeah, kid."

"I'd rather swim than play cards any day. You wanna go now?"

"Why not?"

Mikey went up to Bernie's room with him while Bernie picked up his gear. He casually looked around to see if the way was clear. He didn't want to be stopped now. That feeling of excitement he had when they'd been out last came back strong. Strange, but good.

"Let's go, kid," he said.

They left by the center patio, walked seventy stairs down to the dock, turned left and hiked to the secluded beach. The sea looked quite calm and Bernie thought he remembered the tide would be going out. He'd forgotten to check the schedule before they left, but what did it matter?

He saw beach erosion, not bad, though. Could have been a lot worse.

He called to Mikey, "Last one in...!"

They dumped their equipment on the sand, stripped quickly and with a yell, Bernie ran into the ocean. A few feet out he dove cleanly and disappeared beneath the waves. Mikey dove in right behind Bernie, grabbed his leg and pulled. Bernie came around and scuffled with him. After fifteen seconds or so underwater they both sputtered to the surface.

"Fun, man!" Mikey said.

Bernie stood in the chest high water and put his arm around Mikey's shoulder. "Yeah, man, it sure is."

The younger man twisted out from under. "Let's go see the wreck, Bernie."

He waded out of the water and grabbed their gear, tossing Bernie's to him.

"Sure, kid, let's go."

Slow and easy, he told himself. He didn't want to frighten the kid, and even though he felt strongly about Mikey, he didn't feel reciprocation. He could wait. He began to devise a plan. Time off, why not? He'd been steady. Nick wouldn't say no to a couple days off.

Donning their gear, they swam out to the wreck. They dived in various places and finally headed for shore near nine o'clock. Pretty clearly Mikey had become more comfortable about being skinny with Bernie, but he wasn't like, jumping into Bernie's arms. Bernie, for his part, treated Mikey like any of the others.

They were lolling on the sand catching some rays when Bernie told Mikey it was time to head back in case they were wanted. Bernie stood up and looked seaward. He spotted the top of a sail off in the distance coming from the east. It gave him an eerie feeling.

"Mikey, quick, get dressed. We gotta go back now."

"What's the trouble?"

"You remember that bitch that was all the flap three days ago?"

"I heard something. What about it?"

"I think I may have spotted her sailboat just now. If we hurry, we can get back to the mansion and I can tell Nick. We ought to check it out. Never hurts to show the boss you're bein' observant! Wouldn't he be happy if I came up with her?"

"I guess." Mikey pulled his clothes and clogs on quickly.

Bernie had a feeling! "Let's go!"

They grabbed their stuff and ran the quarter mile back to the mansion. The sailboat passed the little harbor about a half-mile out. He picked up a pair of binocs and tried to see more, but the sailboat was too far away to be sure. Still the feeling persisted. He got Ray on the phone exchange and asked for Nick.

"Here you go, Bernie," and he connected Bernie to the boss in his study.

"Yeah?"

"Bernie here, boss."

"What?"

"Boat coming from the direction I think the bitch maybe went. Saw it out on the point, ran back. Seems kinda familiar, but it's far out. You want I go out there and check it out?"

There was a long pause, and Bernie began to sweat.

Finally, Nick said, "Get Malfo. Tell him I said check it out. Take the Donzi. Malfo drives."

Bernie breathed a silent sigh. "Sure, boss."

Click.

He went to find Alonzo Malfo and caught him in the Card Room playing seven-card draw. Bernie quickly told him the boss's pleasure. Malfo gave Homenio his "You're nothing but a turd" look, but Bernie shrugged it off. Malfo got the prize for being a mean bastard. Bernie believed Malfo wasn't too smart, not as smart as Bernie Homenio thought *he* was anyway, and someday Bernie'd make him eat some of *his* shit. He smiled.

Malfo got up without a word or a backward glance, threw his cards on the table and left the room.

One of the guys at the table said, "Alonz...you done?"

Disgusted, Malfo threw his hands up and didn't look back.

The player said, "Guess so," and went back to his game.

The other two at the table said nothing.

Bernie followed Malfo out. He could keep up the appearance until the right time. They walked across the big patio and down to the dock. A short, stocky man in his mid-forties, Alonzo Malfo looked fit enough at a glance, but a lazy streak developed after his promotion and now he had a protruding belly and fleshy arms and legs. More and more he waddled.

Bernie, behind him all the way, kept thinking, Nick will see it soon. The little bastard has lost his edge. Brother be fucked! Nick will start wondering soon, and then—it's only a matter of time.

A little smile played across Bernie's face. He had an agenda. He'd freeze out the little turd and dispose of him with his own fish knife.

"C'mon Homenio, let's get this over with." Malfo didn't look back.

They got into the Donzi and Alonzo started it with more success than he had with the big cruiser a couple of days before. The boat glistened, bright red, a sleek racing boat, sweet as money could buy. Dirty money still looked green. The women who frequented Nick's place, doing their thing to promote the party atmosphere Nick wanted were quick to jump in and hair flying, grab a little piece of this action when they could get it.

This time Malfo waited for the highly tuned engine to warm. After three or four minutes he told Bernie to cast off. He carefully put it in reverse and backed out. Carefully engaging forward, he eased in the throttle, powered the craft away from the dock and straight out into the bay. Nick's lieutenant took what scraps he could get from his boss, and this ride, this awesome ride was one of them. This baby would do eighty miles an hour on a glassy sea.

The waves were not glassy by a stretch, but Malfo knew the boat could handle it. He pushed the throttle to half and the Donzi almost jumped out of the water. Bernie had the left seat, and casually held the port rail. The power nearly threw him over the seat. He yelled and grabbed wildly for the front seat lip. Malfo laughed his ugly laugh. Nick had told him to push Homenio whenever he could.

"Pretty fucking funny, Alonzo." He shouted over the deafening roar of the big twin engines.

Malfo laughed harder. He leaned over the wheel and chuckled and chuckled. The boat sped on. Waves slapped hard under the hull and Malfo had to keep a tight rein on the wheel. The sea threatened to pull it away from him at this speed. He rode as high as he could handle, barely safe, barely in control, a real rush.

Bernie didn't enjoy it. Malfo pissed him off. He knew Malfo would as soon chuck him over the bow and run him over with the props as look at him. He also knew that whatever happened out on this sea, Nick would side with his lieutenant. He swallowed his anger and deepened his resolve to kill the little bastard as soon as he could do it and help himself in the organization at the same time.

Bernie fanaticized about what he planned for Malfo as they moved swiftly toward the sail now a mile away from them and closing fast. As they neared the sailboat, Bernie noticed that the color of the sail was cream and the "R" stood out prominently. He began to have doubts. But the boat was of the same type as the bitches' boat, he was sure. He thought, camouflage? But he said nothing.

Malfo started to look disgusted. "Hey, Homenio, that look like the ladies boat?"

"Same type, long jib, cant-angle mainmast. Colors are wrong. Couldn't see that well from the mansion, Alonzo. Thought it worth a try."

"You thought, Homenio—you thought?"

"Well, Nick thought it was worth a try, too." Bernie put a little whine in his voice.

"Yeah, well, you got me out of a good game, and there better be somethin' to this, Homenio!"

"C'mon Alonzo, Nick wanted the bitch bad, you know that. If Nick thought it was worth it, don't go puttin' it all on me, okay?"

Malfo glared at him. "If it ain't nothin', Bernie boy, I'm going to ride your ass from now into next week. There ain't many who don't know Nick's not happy with you. Keep it in mind."

"Okay, Alonzo, okay. I'm out o' line, I guess. I'm just tryin' to redeem myself, that's all. Give me a break. Okay?"

Malfo laughed, "Sure, Bernie, you redeem yourself, yeah, you redeem yourself. You do that!"

Malfo turned momentarily away from his steering. As he looked back he saw a large swell dead ahead, the cap blowing off in his direction. He had to cut power or be launched into the air and maybe over-rev the twin props. Nick wouldn't like that. If he dumped it, he'd be up shits creek.

"Shit! Leave me the fuck alone, Homenio! Gotta do this right." He slowed their headlong pace and renewed his concentration in front. Bernie held his breath to keep from laughing. He could barely keep his face straight. He had to look away.

They closed the distance to the sailboat rapidly and soon moved starboard of the bigger boat. Bernie wasn't feeling too good now. The hull of this boat was clearly maroon and the sail clearly complemented the rest of it. An old guy at the wheel looked down at them.

Malfo hailed the sailboat. "Captain, mind if I ask where you came from?"

In a quavering tenor voice, the captain said, "Normally I do mind, sonny. You have a reason for asking? You're *not* the Coast Guard."

"Ah, no sir, we're not." Malfo thought fast. "My employer asked me to come on out and ask you because we tried to raise you on the ships radio on standard frequencies, but got no reply. One of his workboats got caught in the gale and you came from the direction where we think they were. He thought you might have seen something, some debris, maybe."

"Radio's on the blink, sonny. Blasted thing interrupts my thinking anyway. Glad I can't hear it. Can't say I saw anything in the water this morning."

"Oh, I see, sir. Well, if you'd like we could come aboard and see if there was anything we could do to help."

"You're welcome aboard sonny, but you needn't bother unless you're carrying a full repair kit in that little boat. On my way to pick up the wife and daughter in New York Harbor. Doing what they do best. Off on a spending spree! Good for them! Gives me time to myself. Know what I mean?"

Alonzo Malfo laughed. "Yes, I do. Well, we won't trouble you further. Happy sailing."

"You too, sonny."

Malfo swung the Donzi carefully away from the bigger craft and as they distanced themselves from the Maiden Voyage I, Bernie turned to Malfo.

"Didn't you want to just board her and look around, Alonzo?"

"No, fuckstick! I'm not going to get in and push around on somebody's boat lookin' for nothin' we'll ever find and have the guy file a complaint with the Maritime Authority. You already got Nick on *your* ass. I'm not lookin' for the same!"

"But what if they was in disguise and the bitch is in the cabin?" Bernie tried not to sound exasperated, but in fact, he wanted on that boat. It didn't look like the bitches boat, but he had this nagging feeling. Even up close, well, he'd looked the sailboat over when it came in, after Tommie had escorted her up the long stairs. It seemed *so* familiar. "What would the harm be in takin' up the old farts invitation?"

"Look, Homenio, there's nothin' there. Leave it the fuck alone."

Bernie turned away so Malfo couldn't see the hate in his eyes. After they cleared the sailboat and had put considerable distance between them, the little lieutenant opened the Donzi up viciously and only slowed down again as they entered the sheltered harbor. They docked. Malfo got out without a backward look and headed up the stairs.

Bernie hung back, almost vibrating. "Little rat bastard pissant little fink."

He couldn't think of enough bad names to call Malfo. He took out the little pig-sticker he carried and as Malfo disappeared onto the patio Bernie drove it deep into a wooden piling again and again, imagining it was Malfo's chest.

After a couple of minutes, he went out and sat at the end of the pier looking out across the bay into the limitless ocean. Fifteen minutes later he'd calmed down enough to go back to the mansion. On his way up the stairs, he vowed to kill Alonzo Malfo slowly and painfully while looking into his eyes. Bernie *so* wanted to see his terror, to realize of the moment of his death.

28

"Word of the Sacred Book, we have received another message from the American, Nick Trafalgar. He has asked for additional information about the American woman. He says he is certain he will be able to find her and wishes background information."

Rathmanizzar sat in contemplation. After a minute, he raised his head and looked at his chief disciple. Ahmed bent forward, forehead touching the mat on which the leader sat, his dusky white desert cloak spread out behind and to the sides. He spoke with a reverence accorded only the most holy.

The leader spoke. "Inform Nick Trafalgar that he is released from his sworn obligation to me concerning the death of the woman. Present matters make the woman unimportant to the plan. Perhaps his talents will work more effectively at another juncture. Send that message this day, Ahmed."

"Yes, my leader, my Word." He rose, bowed low and left.

Rathmanizzar bent and picked up his much-used copy of the Koran and turned to a certain, often opened page. He removed a piece of parchment and became absorbed in it. The normal sounds of Tubela-ha faded before his recurrent revelation. From his own writings he read, "and the infidel shall bow to the power of the Word, and the Word shall become as thunder, and the sound of the thunder shall wipe away the transgressions of the faithful upon the earth, and the light of Mohammed shall shine forth upon his people. The believer in the Holy Book shall be the instrument of Mohammed. It shall be he that brings forth the thunder, and in the light that prevails thereafter, he shall become leader of all men, and bring them forth into the salvation of the light. And he who believes shall lead the final jihad and become its standard bearer."

Rathmanizzar closed his eyes. Once again he saw the dream. Once again he reveled in the glory that he saw. Once more he saw the white hands in the background. But after contemplation, still he could not ferret out the message.

"Mohammed, the greatest prophet, your vision is mine. You have chosen me to lead your Jihad and I shall lead. Your dream is my dream. Allah's will be done." He spoke in measured tones and bowed low, as if to an unseen presence, as had his disciple, before him.

He returned to his lounging area and sat silently for several minutes, musing. Then Rathmanizzar, Word of the Book, went to his sophisticated electronics equipment in a nearby tent, composed and encrypted the following message to his China contact. "Materiel has arrived at capitol city. Release the flotilla."

The leader stood, drew a desert cloak about him, went forth from his tent and moved about his people. Having received the adulation of his followers for years, his responses were automatic, but, because he believed he would become the savior of all of mankind, they were genuine.

Rathmanizzar left Tubela-ha by its front fortification. The man raised his arms and the guards rapidly opened the doors for him. As he passed through he told the guards that he went to communicate with God and that he wished no interruption before he returned.

The guards bowed low and the leader passed through. As the desert was a dangerous place, they would watch over him on his solitary sojourn. Never would the leader catch a glimpse of the watchers, yet his protection would be total.

The peace and serenity that comes from belief in a mission of goodness brightened his face. Onlookers at the gate watched silently as their leader disappeared into the desert.

Rathmanizzar was gone six days. During that time he never gave voice or thought to his own safety. Allah would provide. During that time he saw no one. He knew the desert and the desert treated him well. He thought of his communion as a pilgrimage and a testing.

While in the heat of the day and the chill of the night, he lost eight pounds. His robes kept him from becoming dangerously depleted. Nonetheless, when he returned, the tent city of Tubela-ha rang with the news of his coming.

The leader had a message from Allah for his disciples.

Ahmed Al-Salud joined his leader at the opening of his tent. The other disciples pressed close. Rathmanizzar kept his head high and those near him saw rapture in his face. His eyes were exceedingly bright and the mania that had beset him through deprivation his followers interpreted as a signal of divine contact. Their hopes rose as they prepared to hear the revelation of The Word of the Book.

The leader went to his pillows and sat. His disciples sank to their knees and deep-bowed their fealty. He raised his arms and began an intonation to invoke the spirit of the occasion. This went on for several minutes. Rathmanizzar lowered his arms at last and the men sat back expectantly. The leader looked searchingly at them.

"The time to move is now. The spirit of God has visited me. God has told me that he is ashamed of the evil that exists in this world he has created. He has told me that it is a time for cleansing, and he has appointed your leader to begin the cleansing. He has given to me to offer my disciples the holy mission of that cleansing. He has shown me what we must do. Go out among our brethren and call an assembly of all in our city. I will speak to the people of Tubela-ha of the sacrifice we will shortly make, and of the glory that will come of it. All glory to Allah. Allah, akbar. Allah is the only God, and God is good."

The men entered rapture. As one, they rose to their feet and the multi-voiced sound of a ravenous beast propelled through the tent walls, spreading rapidly outward into the desert city. The men outside heard the cry and carried it along until it reached the desert itself, where the sound disappeared in its vastness.

Quickly things began to move. Ahmed informed the leader of a message just received, that all was in place in the city of the catalyst. The disciples of The Word of the Book began spearheading the movement with Rathmanizzar at its blood-chilling point. Coded messages went out from state of the art equipment well hidden from the prying eyes of dozens of roaming civilian and military satellites. Each man in each cell in each country smiled as the long awaited message came to them; a smile that came as close to ecstasy as any desert man could feel. Each man told his cell the good news and word spread with the power of a desert sandstorm.

North to Europe, west to the Americas, east and south the message rang through complex electronics, and there came a breathless pause, and a culmination. "To the soldiers of Tubela-ha throughout the world, rejoice, the jihad begins. Gather your people, ready your weapons and your hope for the glorious final days of the infidel. Be ready for a cataclysm that will spark the new order. Thus has spoken 'The Word of the Book.'"

And to Ahmed Al Salud, Rathmanizzar spoke. "It is here, my friend, my confidant. As our people move to channel the power of the movement into directions of our choice, terror will come to the world, and in that terror, we will succeed." His eyes glowed.

"Yes, my master," Ahmed said in a low and reverent tone.

"See to the beginning. Our statement will be made at the time the sun is highest in the China sky." Ahmed al Salud bowed deeply and left.

Rathmanizzar sat in his now empty tent, the words of his belief carried by his chiefs and echoing in his mind. An inner peace took hold of him, yet there nagged at the edges of his mind that one image of the white hands on the mosaic of his dream.

"It has meaning," he mused, "but what meaning has it?"

The leader had sent out his forces in a firm belief that the time was now, and that they would prevail. Why, then, did this bother him so?

Rathmanizzar sat still as a rock. His dream moved in front of his eyes like a huge cape, a living thing, dark but for its highlights. The brightness showed armies of believers moving toward a center point, toward one shining eye. This he believed to be the eye of Allah, the all seeing, all knowing. Rathmanizzar saw himself below the eye, in white flowing desert robes, arms outstretched, standing on a glowing missile from which emanated a soft and deadly light, dripping blood, as his image called on the faithful to join him in the final jihad. In the mosaic he saw other motion, too, alive, undulating, like a writhing mass of snakes, never still. And at the edges of the dream fabric were those hands, and now they seemed brighter than when he reviewed his dream last. And they had begun to curl!

It gave him a start. He felt glad his disciples had left. It could not be that they should see their leader seeming perplexed. No! But the nagging feeling he'd had before became stronger. The dream was changing, and that meant something had happened. He wondered if the hands could be of the American woman, Amber Pierce. By the Curse, why couldn't Nick Trafalgar have eliminated her! And whose were the other set of white hands?

It's begun, he thought, I do not wish to stop it now. It's moving and has taken on life of its own.

Yet he worried.

All of the tendrils of his far-flung organization would soon be exposed. They had the power of faith now. They *must* possess the power of arms when the world became aware!

Rathmanizzar thought of the years he had spent developing his sensitive contacts, the recruiting, constantly addressing his dream, the chances he had taken for the love of Allah. Groups of five men fed each cell, one key man, always a member of his city of Tubela-ha with contact to other cells nearby. The others, soldiers only, living in apartments in all important cities of the world, blending with the population, hiding in unlikely places, beneath molestation or notice, law abiding in any country where they resided. On that the leader insisted.

And the bomb! Such care, how slowly he had moved to obtain the necessary material so as not to call attention to the government security forces of the major powers. He had succeeded so well! Not twenty-four hours from this time the world would be at war, each state fighting the other states and no one would guess until it was too late where the power lay.

The Word of the Book smiled again. He could think of nothing he hadn't addressed.

But again he felt the chill. The hands, the hands...

29

Robert Moses State Park stood off the bow. The sun had dipped below the horizon but the refractive lensing of the Earth's air envelope pushed red and orange above it; colors that undulated and changed slowly. A thin cloud moved into the sun and split the image in two equal parts. Other brilliantly outlined clouds near the horizon painted the dying day pink. The high scud above glowed and faded to gray as light diminished with distance.

The three voyagers watched, and Richard said solemnly, "'Red sun in the morning, sailor take warning. Red sun at night, sailor's delight.' I have wondered in the past where that old saying came from. Now, with weather radio and the sophisticated equipment we carry onboard, we can know what's coming long before it arrives. It's so easy. Isn't it too bad we can't guess on the outcome of our coming trial?"

Audrey took him up. "Richard, we'll do our best to get through this. For myself, I wouldn't want to know the outcome of anything before it happens. I leave that to God or the Future, or to the great "Whatever" to know. How dull this world would be if we knew before we lived it. Not for me."

Ted said, "We are heading into extreme danger, but you wouldn't want to know if you or Richard, or I for that matter, will come out of this?"

"No, Ted, I wouldn't. Somewhere I read that the very act of testing something alters any natural result that would otherwise obtain. Maybe there is only one reality, and maybe there are an infinite number of them. I don't care. I'll use my skills, take my chances, and whatever will be, will be."

Ted smiled at her. Just how he thought.

Richard considered that. "Yeah, I have to agree. Life wouldn't be very interesting if you knew what was coming."

The three stood and watched until only faint pink remained and Venus blazed down at Earth as it set, with Jupiter still high in the southern sky. Soon the stars took sway. The moon hung at last quarter, its bright half showing high near Jupiter. Each quietly appreciated the night.

When they talked it came hushed, not for fear of being heard, but because the quiet sea had set the mood.

They finally decided to retire. Audrey would take first night watch. They weren't out of the woods yet. Ted told them he would stay up awhile and he'd call Audrey.

Richard took Audrey's hand, but she had caught something in the way Ted had said that.

She said, "In a few minutes, Richard."

"Okay." He continued on.

Audrey turned to Ted and said, "It's hard for you, isn't it? There's nobody but the organization, is there? I used to feel that way, until you drew straws and Richard and I came up. Now I realize there is much more to life than only duty."

Ted stared at her.

"Ted, you can't lose more than your personal self when there is no one else who cares. I don't mean Stoic and I don't mean the organization with however many there are in it. That kind of caring is for a cause, for rightness, for freedom, to help beat back the wave. I'm talking about another human being who cares about you so much you can feel it in every waking moment, someone you care for so much that you carry the hurt of it in your chest always, someone you would willingly but not carelessly lay down your life for. Someone who adds that little bit of heart to everything you do, so that when the almost inevitable happens, it's all right, and you can let go. You know you had done your best, that you were appreciated in the deepest sense."

She finished speaking and realized that all the words had come out in a rush. Ted continued to stare for a long moment. Then he turned and went to the rail and gazed out at the dark ocean, unseeing. She followed hesitantly. After awhile he spoke.

"There was someone a long, long time ago, Audrey. Such feelings can be good, but they carry the sharpness and dangers of a double-edged sword. She was a woman so much like you that it's painful to talk about her. I loved her so much that if Stoic hadn't saved me at the last, crucial moment I would be dead now.

"For that I grieve every moment of every day in a special place inside. I have been hurting even more ever since I decided you were the one who had to go into this assignment. It didn't stop me. I could make no other decision. Stoic assigned the responsibility of finding the traitor to me. I am honored by his trust and I won't let him down. You and Richard are our best hope. I am convinced of it. Of all the people in my part of the organization, you two were, could be, the only choices. But it doesn't stop the thoughts I have or the memory I wear." He touched his head.

"I'm so sorry, Ted. I didn't know."

"You couldn't, Audrey. It's okay."

They stood at the rail for another ten minutes. Audrey stayed, feeling that her presence helped Ted somehow. Finally she told him she needed to get below to get some rest. Tomorrow would come altogether too soon.

Ted nodded and said, "Goodnight, Audrey. Go to Richard. He needs you, too."

In that moment Audrey knew that she'd done it right. She leaned over and kissed Ted on the cheek. Then she moved silently away and disappeared into the cabin. Ted stayed at the rail. Two small tears welled up and he blinked them away without moving. He stayed there for a long time. His cheeks glistened until the gentle night breeze dried them. No one saw his iron control crack. That couldn't happen.

At ten o'clock the statue became a man. Ted descended the stairs and stripped to boxers. He went into the couple's bedroom and shook Audrey awake. She got up instantly, stretched and stood, and told Ted she was awake and to, "Get some rest."

Audrey dressed quickly, shorts and halter-top and left the cabin. The night wasn't black. About half of the waning moon showed low in the southwest, a dim bulb shining dimmer as it set. It gave off less light now than it had three days before when this strange, nightmarish dream had begun. As the moon lost ground, the stars gained. Brilliant stars now shone above and reflected like a million Christmas bulbs on the ocean. When the Moon finally set the night sky would return to thrill her as it had thrilled people for eons.

When it disappeared, she checked her watch. Eleven o'clock. She turned with her back against the port rail and gazed into the heavens. It can't be all bad, she thought. All that beauty must have meaning. All those points of light, each one a sun more or less like our own, some bigger, some smaller, some red, yellow, orange, some blue and some white. So much variety!

She turned portside, leaned on the rail and stared at the horizon. Stars above, total blackness below. Suddenly she heard a faint creak behind her. The men were sleeping below and the sound hadn't come from anywhere near the cabin. She tensed and extended her senses. She felt a presence and heard breathing and her senses cried, "Danger!" Without thought, she turned cat-like and jabbed with her fore and middle fingers, going for the star shine glint. There was a scream!

30

Alonzo Malfo reported to Nick. "It was nothin', Nick, not even close. Old guy on his way to pick up his wife and daughter on a shopping spree in the City. When we got close the boat was the wrong color and even the sail wasn't white, more a cream color with a big "R" on it. I told Homenio to tend to his knittin' and don't go off half cocked again."

"Okay, Alonzo, it's a slow day. Why don't you go back and play some more cards?"

"Yeah, Nick, think I will." He left.

A half-hour later Nick got another call from Bernie. He was still chaffed over the way Malfo treated him and still not convinced about the sailboat they'd approached. He had an idea and he could follow up on it himself. If he scored, he'd come up with the bitch and Nick would be real happy with him. No more "Bernie Boy" then.

"Sorry, boss, I thought it was a good shot."

"Bernie, I'm not as pissed as before. At least you tried. The rest of these fucks just sit on their asses playing cards. Forget it."

"Thanks, Nick. Look, I got no jobs right now, and if you don't need me for somethin' I'd like to take a couple of days off. That okay, boss?"

"Yeah, I can spare you. Where you going?"

"I want to take a car into the City and visit a couple of good places I know," he lied.

"Go ahead. Get outta my hair for a couple. Do you good."

"Thanks, Nick. Appreciate."

After he hung up with the boss, he looked up Mikey again. He took him aside and asked if he would like to take part in an adventure where they could both score big time. Told him he'd got an idea that the sailboat Malfo let go without boarding maybe had a couple of others on it who didn't want to be seen.

"Even if it ain't so, I got a couple ideas that might pan out when I get to the City. Couple guys I know from one of the old families in New York, we're still in touch, now and then. Nothin' else, we got a couple days off, you'n me. Waddya say?"

"Sure, Bernie, but what about Nick? I should ask him?"

"You're too low on the totem pole for anybody to miss you yet, but we'll tell my friend Ray, just in case."

They looked up Ray and Bernie outlined the plan. Ray laughed at them, but said he wouldn't tell anybody.

"You're on a fools errand, Bernie." He watched the two unlikely sleuths as they left the room.

Bernie and Mikey signed out a car at the front gate and left immediately. Bernie drove and Mikey surfed the radio channels for heavy rock stations. They picked up Rt. 27 and headed toward New York City. After a half-hour Bernie poked Mikey in the passengers seat excitedly.

"There it is!"

Mikey looked and sure enough, the sailboat that had passed the mansion could be seen far out in the Atlantic beyond the sea break. Bernie stopped and got out with the glass to look it over.

"Definitely the same one. We'll follow it. I doubt they'll get as far as New York Harbor. Too congested. My guess is the old guy will stop long before that, maybe around Ocean Beach or by the State Park and make the run into the City in the morning, if that's where he's really goin'."

"Whatever." Mikey wasn't into this Sherlock Holmes thing like Bernie and the good rock station he had on powered over Bernie's words so he really didn't hear him, anyway.

"Hey, Mikey!" Bernie ejaculated.

"Hey what, Bernie?"

"Goin' to the City...goin' to the City...goin' to the City!" He spoke to the rhythm of the rock song currently blasting on the radio.

"Yeah, man...goin' to the City."

"Gonna have fun...gonna have fun...gonna have fun!"

"Yeah, yeah!"

"Gonna catch some mother fuckers...yea, yea, yea!"

"Yeah, yeah, yeah!" Mikey felt the pulse.

Their excitement level went up. Bernie played to Mikey's instincts. The young guy would never have been allowed in if Nick didn't have a hold on him...something in the past. It occurred to Bernie to try to find out what Nick had on Mikey. So he played it up, movin' and groovin' to the music, and with every sidelong glance noting that Mikey seemed more excited. After awhile he changed the message with his own.

"We're bad-ass mother fuckers, yea, yea, yea!"

"We're bad-ass mother fuckers, yeah, yeah, yeah!"

"We're gonna do that white bitch...yea, yea, yea!"

"Yeah, yeah, yeah!"

"We gonna bring back gold to the big boss, yea, yea, yea!" He reverted further into Rap.

"Yeah...yeah!"

The song ended, but the rock station, typically afraid of losing its audience, laid the next selection right over the ending and the raucous rhythms continued. Bernie thought about this practice at some level, all the while moving and grooving to the music. Funny, he didn't even like that shit, but when he saw Mikey groovin' to it, it was where he'd be comin' from, right now.

"Hey, Mikey!"

"Hey, Bernie!"

Using the same rhythm he said, "How you come to be with the Big Nick? Yea, yea!"

"Got in a bit o' trouble in the Big City three years ago, my man. Goin' behind, up the river, friend, not a good place for a youth like me—lawyer knows Nick called him—told him he had somebody would be good for his organization. Nick was lookin' to bring somebody in—an' that somebody was me. He pulled a little here and there, and lookee' here I am!"

"Cool, man," Bernie said. "What you do...can you tell?"

"Nick says to me, 'Don't tell nobody.' But you're my friend, Bernie, I can tell you."

"Yea?"

"Killed a kid, young teen. Sorta gang war thing. Stuck a bowie knife in him and ripped him up as far as I could. Asswipe never cut me; Mikey's too quick. But they got my ass and were puttin' me away when Nick sprung me. I owe him, big time."

"Yea, I hear you, kid."

"Why you in, Bernie? You take out a family member or somethin'?"

Bernie wasn't ready for this. He hesitated. Oh, what the fuck, why not? Maybe get closer, this way.

"Dropped a match into a barrel of gasoline. Lottsa years ago, now. Just a fun thing, me and some friends, but it caught on a warehouse and the whole fuckin' thing went up. Belonged to Nick. I help him now, and he lets me live. He's good shit, Mikey. Gotta work for him. And I want more, too. And I'll get it, because Bernie's a smart guy. Don't underestimate Bernie Homenio, Mikey!"

"Yeah, Bernie!" Mikey shouted above the high volume din of the radio.

Bernie brought his free hand around and they clasped hands and shook above their heads. A good moment!

"We're gonna do well, Mikey, you and me." Bernie returned his attention to the road.

"Yeah, Bernie. Real glad you were assigned to help me into this new job."

Bernie looked at him. I could just kiss you, he thought. I feel so funny, Mikey, bet you don't even know.

"Hey Mikey. Let's stop awhile. We're getting' ahead of the sailboat and there's a point up there with a restaurant," he pointed, "where we can stop for a sandwich and keep an eye on its course. I figure I got an idea where it's going. No fuckin' way it's going into New York Harbor tonight, unless I miss my guess. That's daytime stuff."

"Where you figure he'll stop for the night, Bernie?" He really didn't hear Bernie when he talked about it before.

Bernie didn't hold it against him. "Somewhere along the sea break outside of Great South Bay. Depends on how quick the captain wants to get there. If he's real, and he's picking up his wife and daughter, I'm figuring he'll lay over somewhere along Robert Moses State Park and make a run into New York Harbor early in the morning. Time-wise, that's about right. Now Mikey, if he's not real, I don't see much else happenin' anyway, because a man's got to be a fool to cross the channel at night. Dig?"

"I dig, man. You got it figured, Bernie."

"Yea, kid."

They continued on, bopping and swaying to the music. At the cutoff for the restaurant, Bernie pulled off and parked. He chose a window with an ocean view and with luck, got the perfect table. They sat and ordered something light with a couple of beers. Bernie brought his map with him.

They were on 27A now, trying to stay as close to the shore as possible. It took longer to traverse the roads they were on, but necessary to catch sight of the sailboat every now and then. If the old guy told the truth, they'd catch sight of his sail every fifteen to thirty minutes along this road. So far that's what happened and Bernie felt good.

They ate, finished their beers and left. The map told Bernie's it was going to get harder to stay with them, but he still bet the boat would stop at the state park overnight. The sailboat didn't seem to be deviating and it gave Bernie confidence. Finally he elected to try to get ahead of the boat. The map told him that Robert Moses State Park access road provided the only entrance to Fire Island National Seashore.

Mikey and Bernie drove out Rt. 27A until they could pick up the Sunrise Highway, and made tracks for the State Park. They arrived two hours later and found themselves with nothing to do, the sailboat far behind them.

"Wanna swim?" Bernie said to Mikey. "What the hell?"

"I got no suit." Mikey said.

"Neither do I."

"So what...like there are people around?"

"So let's go spend some money and get some new ones."

"Right."

They drove north and found a small store that specialized in aquatic equipment.

Around six p.m., tired of swimming and hungry, Mikey suggested they dress and find a place.

"Yea, let's do that."

They checked out the park, found out when it closed and scoped out the beach security force New York money had decided was adequate for the area. Then they left to find a nice restaurant where they could get a good meal and a few pops. They found The Purple Onion not far away and spent a good hour chowing down.

31

Bernie told Mikey he was sure, based on wind and tides, that the sailboat couldn't possibly pass that point before eight o'clock, the state park's closing time. All they had to do was to get back into the park before they closed the gates.

"I'm bettin' the old guy will park right out in front of the place."

"Why, Bernie?" Mikey asked.

"I think he'd want to park where he could see shore lights."

"Oh."

After dinner and a few beers they returned. Bernie parked outside of the state park's chain link fence. They walked in and told the attendant that they had lost something in the sand when they were there earlier and would it be okay to go and try to find it. They wouldn't be long.

It was already past eight and the attendant wanted to leave. She said, "Just go ahead. I'll leave the gate open a crack. The night guard will shut it later."

"Hey, thanks," Bernie said. "We'll just be a few minutes."

"No problem." She got into a rusty Olds 88 with a bad muffler and drove away.

"That's a break," Bernie told Mikey.

The two men quickly located the guard shack and saw the security guy sitting in it with the TV blaring. Evidently there wasn't much to do this far out from the City. They hiked it to the water and squinted searchingly out to sea, but saw no sign of their prey. They checked out the rowboats tied together with a chain and decided it wouldn't take much to get one free, in the event they had a chance to try and board the sailboat.

"Go back to the gate and close and lock it, Mikey. The guard will think the attendant checked and decided no one's in the park and he'll be less likely to check things out."

Bernie frowned. Something else...what? Yeah!

"Mikey, get the jack handle from the trunk before you come back."

"Why?"

"Might need it."

"Okay, Bernie." He left the grassy hummock and crept up on the gate, keeping an eye out for the guard.

In five minutes he slipped back noiselessly. "All okay." He handed Bernie the jack handle.

"Good man! Now we wait."

About quarter past eight, as the sun hung above the horizon they spied a sail. Bernie looked it over with the glasses and pronounced it their pigeon. They hid in the grass and watched it slow.

"The fucker is stopping. Good news, baby!" Bernie said excitedly.

They watched silently until the boat came dead in the water, and someone tossed the anchor over.

"Mikey," Bernie said, "there's more than one person on that boat. I knew it! You know what that means?"

"What?" Mikey returned in a whisper.

"The old fart said he was alone, cruisin' the coast to pick up his wife and daughter, remember? The old bastard lied. We just struck gold!"

They could see the black outline of two slim figures on deck against a dimming blue sky. In the glasses Bernie was certain he could see two and thought there might be a third, but he couldn't be sure.

At eight-thirty the guard came out and made cursory rounds at the beach, checked the boats and the picnic area. He evidently decided it would be another boring night and retired to the comfort of his TV, leaving the door to the security shack open. Light spilled out along with plenty of sound, but as Bernie and Mikey waited, they could hear no other sound along the beachfront.

They stayed hidden until the sun set completely. The stars had come out and the waning moon brightened. Now they moved out to the boat rack and took the chain off the end rowboat, easy as pie. The four screws holding the eye came off in a quick yank of the jack handle. It made little sound.

They talked in whispers. Slowly they dragged the rowboat near the water as far from the shack as they could and left it behind a grassy hummock. Mikey scuffed the drag marks out of the sand and they hid the boat chain. Bernie reasoned that it would be easy to see a missing rowboat during the day, but not at night. Oars were another problem. They were locked in the rental shack with other swim gear. They'd have to break the lock to get in.

"Mikey, take off your shirt."

"Huh?"

"To muffle the sound. C'mon, take it off."

The guard shack was some distance away and they succeeded in prying their way in without being heard. Bernie picked out the oars while Mikey stood outside and watched for signs of movement. Satisfied they'd not been heard, Bernie tossed the jack handle into a tuft of tall saw grass. If it made a sound, it wasn't louder than the onshore breeze.

They carried the oars to the boat and installed them into the oarlocks. Now to wait. With the binoculars, Bernie checked from time to time on the guard shack and again on the boat. The old guy seemed to want to stay up all night, but around eleven o'clock he went below. The moon set, too.

Bernie took that to be the man's bedtime. They checked out the guard shack a last time and pushed off into slightly choppy seas. Mikey rowed quietly. The oars made a small sound as they dipped the water, but Bernie didn't think it would carry far. The mild breeze turned over a few waves here and there and masked their approach. When they were almost there, Bernie shushed Mikey silently and he took the oars out of the water.

Another figure stood on the far side of the deck, gazing out over the ocean and staring at the stars. Bernie bet a "C" note it was the slim figure of a woman. He pointed and Mikey noticed, too. Bernie had his gun in his right hand pocket, ready to go. He motioned Mikey close and whispered into his ear.

"I'm going to board near the bow. My weight won't cause much movement there. I can move along the port side low and whoever's there—I think it's a woman—won't see me. I can take her before she turns. Be ready to jump aboard. Then we'll see what we've got."

"Okay, Bernie, you're the boss."

Mikey rowed another two minutes when Bernie said quickly, "Stop!"

The oarsman stopped, oars in mid swing. He looked a little frightened.

"Put the oars in the water and duck!"

Mikey couldn't see what Bernie saw, but he did it.

Bernie sweated it for a couple of minutes. The girl had turned and if she searched the water near the sailboat, he thought she could see them. They held their breath and made themselves small. After awhile, the girl turned back to the port rail and in a few moments, Bernie gave the signal to move ahead slowly.

Mikey pulled the oars as silently as he knew how. They gained on the bow of the sailboat under the port lip. Bernie reached out a hand and held them away from the boat. Mikey carefully shipped his oars. Then Bernie eased the rowboat around so he could stand in the center and slowly pull himself aboard.

Bernie felt sure that the little breaking whitecaps would mask their noise. The sailboat made little noises, too, the kind that comforted seafaring folk. The woman remained leaning on the port rail, evidently lost in her own thoughts. To Bernie, she seemed at peace with the world.

He gave Mikey a thumbs up and rose carefully until he stood upright. He grasped the railing and gently applied his weight to it. In one slow, smooth motion he put a leg over the rail and muscled his body up and over, carefully feeling for dry deck with his sneaked foot. Soundlessly he brought himself to the polished deck down in front of the rigging and sail house.

He held his breath and watched both accesses to see if he had been heard, but the woman apparently hadn't. Good! Now to creep up and grab her around the face and mouth and yank to throw her off balance! What could be simpler?

Bernie worked his way port to the cabin well. A small step down put him eight feet from her. He could be seen anytime if she turned. He took a step, then another. If his luck held, he'd have her and she wouldn't be able to scream and alert anyone else on board. He patted his pocket and felt the bulge.

Mikey got into position to jump aboard as soon as Bernie said, "Psst!"

He sat in the boat in almost breathless wonder. His friend Bernie would pull this off. He could feel it. What a guy! What a good friend! What balls he had!

Bernie moved behind the woman and stood to make his move. One more step and…a loud creak where he put his foot. No more time! He lunged! In that final second he felt triumph. Then…

The woman turned like a cat. Two fingers on her right hand held rigid searched and found his eyes and pushed. White pain screamed in his brain! His arms went to his face but never got there. She brought her left hand around and, with the heel of her hand she slammed up under his nose. A practiced uppercut; a killing maneuver! Bernie's nose buckled under the force and shards of bone were blasted into his brain. He screamed!

Mikey sat in the rowboat. His brain froze. He couldn't fathom the sound, the scream. It seemed to come from a long way off and skim across the water. Bernie, what went wrong? Oh-mi-god, what do I do now?

Run, run! He had to get out of here. He grasped the oars and started to dip them into the light chop.

Too late! Looking down at him he saw a man in maybe his late forties in skivvy shorts. The man looked grim and he looked deadly. And if he didn't look deadly enough the forty-four magnum in his hand with the long silencer made up Mikey's mind for him. Without a word, the man gestured. Mikey shipped his oars, not caring about noise now. He raised his hands and as the man stepped back, he climbed aboard. Still without sound, the man gestured toward the cabin, and Mikey crossed the deck, hands over his head. He went down the stairs and into the cabin. Another man, younger, but very muscular and looking extremely capable waved him in.

Not a word had been said in the last—eternity—he thought. I'm a dead man; he suddenly knew it, like it came to him from some unplumbed depth of the universe. What could have gone so wrong? Bernie? Where are you? I want to see Bernie! His mind called to some part of him still numb from shock.

"Hey," he said haltingly, "like, what's happening here? C'mon man, I didn't do nothin'. Lemme go. Hey! You listenin'...?"

The silence unnerved him after the awful scream. Mikey knew it was Bernie's voice, and since that moment, there had been no further sound from him. Was he bound and gagged? Was he dead? Where was he? Why wouldn't they say anything?

The big, younger guy had duct tape in his hands. He motioned silently and Mikey put his hands behind him. Should he yell? Who would hear? The young man made the decision for him by putting a four-inch strip of the same tape across Mikey's mouth. Then the man pushed him down on the bed nearby. Mikey sat, trembling. Not good, not good at all.

The older guy grabbed binoculars, went topside and looked searchingly toward shore. They were quite far out, and the thin, reedy sounds of the TV, diminished by distance, but still loud enough to hear even in the cabin, told Mikey the guard didn't pick up the scream. They'd set the rowboat adrift. It would be pulled down the coast with the tide.

Mikey heard no other sounds from above for a minute. Then he heard the sailboat weigh anchor. The steerage motor started and he felt motion. They were getting under way. In the middle of the night? Nick's new man was terrified. I'm done, he thought. But why did they tie me up? Information, that's what they want. But I don't know nothin'. But they don't know that. Mikey grasped the thin edge of hysteria. Where's Bernie? I want Bernie. He started to sob. It wasn't supposed to end like this. He cried freely, sobs racking his body. Just like that, Mikey Dorneti, beaten.

The older man came back down followed by a woman. Through his watering eyes he thought, God, what a beauty! But what cold eyes! The big guy went up and evidently took the wheel. Mikey could feel the motion of the sailboat, but he couldn't tell direction.

The woman came over and ripped the tape from his mouth. She wasn't gentle.

Then she spoke. "You're buddy was Bernie Homenio. Who are you?"

How did she know? Of course, Bernie had been right all along, this had to be the woman Nick wanted offed! She said "was." So Bernie was dead. So was he, then.

"Mikey Dorneti."

"Well, Mr. Dorneti, tell all, *now*, please." The older man wasn't the old guy Bernie told him about. Could there be four, he wondered? Might it have been a disguise? He wondered if he would ever find out.

Mikey spilled his guts. He told them about Nick, about Bernie, about his recent promotion and how Bernie was assigned to train him into the position as a part of Nick Trafalgar's hit squad. He gave his best guesses as to how many men and women were stationed at Nick's place, how many vehicles and how many rooms? Secret rooms? He didn't know. It all came out.

The older guy said, "Just about the figures we had. There's more to the mansion than he knows about. I doubt he knows much more."

The woman, whom he now associated with the name Amber Pierce, what Bernie had told him, said, "He's seen us, Ted."

"Yes," Ted replied. "What would you do?"

He wouldn't make the decision. It was Audreys. Ted's interest lay in how an operative would approach the cusp of a problem and how quickly they would respond.

Audrey said, "Are we through here?"

"Yes."

"Okay." She went to the medicine chest and came back with a syringe. She handled it professionally, letting a little out of the end.

To Mikey she said, not unkindly, "You'll feel a little prick, and then you'll go to sleep. This is not a poison."

"Why are you doing this?" Fear filled Mikey's eyes.

"You know why."

Without another word she injected him and stood back. In less than a minute or so Mikey's eyelids got heavy and he nodded off.

Audrey looked at Ted. "He's ready."

He nodded and went over to free the man's hands. "We'll be out in shark waters in another twenty minutes. Then we can dump them both. Nature will do the rest."

"I didn't lie to him." Audrey seemed to feel better about that. She absently massaged the heel of her left hand.

Ted groped for proper words.

"Audrey," he said, "I would expect you to lie to save your life. That's on the same order as, 'He who fights and runs away...' That you find it difficult to lie when a lie isn't called for, I consider a huge plus in your character, a defining characteristic. Those who would bring us down and those we would overcome don't have that.

"We are forced to commit murder from time to time in order to prevent much greater damage to our world and the people in it. We should always agonize when we have time to reflect."

Ted put his arm around Audrey's shoulder. "I couldn't be more proud of you, my girl, if I was your father."

Audrey thought, well, that answers one nagging question.

Sudden action and now the waiting! Would she ever get used to it? Twenty minutes crawled by.

Richard called down. "I think we're far enough out. No shipping anywhere to the horizon. You ready down there?"

"Yes, Richard. Toss Bernie overboard and then come on down and we'll get rid of this one. Audrey, you want to take the wheel? After we dispose of our cargo, we'd better get back to our berth outside of Robert Moses Beach."

"Okay, boss." Richard locked the wheel and went aft.

"You think that's wise?" Audrey said to Ted.

"Yes, the guard on the beach certainly saw us stop and drop anchor before we lost our daylight, and I feel confident he didn't hear Bernie scream, so we want to give the same scene to the only possible witness before we weigh anchor and move on. No ripples!"

"Right." Audrey headed for the stairs and disappeared onto the deck.

Presently they heard a heavy splash. In a few moments Richard passed Audrey and went down into the cabin. Richard and Ted manhandled the limp figure of Mikey Dorneti up onto the deck a couple of minutes later and dumped him over the side.

Audrey said to Ted, "He won't come to before he drowns, will he?"

"No, you gave him Pentathol. That dose will keep him under until the ocean does its work."

"Good. Never liked this."

"None of us do. Try not to connect emotionally."

"Yeah!" She whipped the wheel hard over and came about.

32

The sun rose in the east, a beautiful, clear orb, too bright to look at after a couple of seconds. It climbed rapidly above the horizon as it had for billions of years. All three were up to watch the sunrise, but in no hurry to leave the area. Radiational cooling had brought a chill to the air and the sea was calm. They drew in big, deep breaths of morning air and it felt good.

After awhile Audrey went down to the galley and started to make kitchen noises. Richard told Ted to take it easy; he and Audrey would prepare breakfast.

Ted studied the shoreline through the binoculars. The rowboat had drifted away and he couldn't locate it. He wanted to stay until the night guard's relief came. If the missing rowboat wasn't discovered early, they would be a totally innocuous presence on the water, innocence personified, just because they tarried. If someone came out and questioned them about it, they knew nothing, and "we hope you find it."

Ted suspected from the clatter below-deck that they were doing it deliberately to put a guilt trip on him. On some level he loved the little things they did, the human, funny things. He remained introspective and let it go.

Finally, Audrey called up to him. "Want to eat on deck, or down here?"

"Up here is good," he replied.

In a couple of minutes the smells from below got much stronger, and the two appeared with food trays.

"Smells delicious."

"Don't think you're getting off easy. You're doing the dishes!" Audrey said with a smile.

"No problem, kids, Daddy can do."

They laughed while they set out places on deck. By the time they finished, the sun rode high in the east and had turned a brilliant yellow.

Ted saw the night guard's relief come in. He watched him take inventory and discover the missing rowboat and the broken lock on the equipment shack. Now the two were running about. One of them had a cell phone and appeared to be talking to someone with animation. The other one had a pair of binoculars, looking at Ted watching him. Then he searched from horizon to horizon.

Soon a motorboat left the little dock from the beach maintenance area and headed their way. It arrived as Audrey and Richard removed the breakfast dishes. A thirty-something young man in a bathing suit with a blond beard hailed them.

"Ho, Maiden Voyage I."

"Hello. Nice day, can we help you?" Ted offered.

"We're missing a rowboat and somebody broke into the equipment shack last night. Just wondered if you had seen or heard anything."

"No, not a thing. That happen often down this way?"

"No, not often at all. Well, thought I'd ask. Have a nice day"

"You, too. Hope you find whoever did it."

"Oh, we will, probably just a high school kids prank. I'm sure we take it more seriously than the kids do. Well, off I go." He turned the powerboat around expertly and departed. Soon he arrived back at his dock, a small moving dot.

"Well, there you go, guys. All set. Now we can leave leisurely and get on the next leg. By the way, you two need to practice some more. Couple of times I noticed you lost your English accent."

"Good idea. Old personalities die hard." Audrey said.

"Blimey!" Richard declared.

"Don't overdo it," said Ted, "You two come over here in the sun. I want to take a critical look at your healing."

The two came over and shoved their faces at him. Ted looked at them closely. Audrey looked good, almost no exterior residual from the operation. Richard showed some darkness on the left side of his face, bruising that Ted thought would disappear adequately in his time frame. Another two days and he thought he'd be able to activate the communication devices without causing problems. He'd let on that there was more then just communication involved and he wanted to find out what their total capability would be as much as Richard and Audrey. If he could integrate them while still sea, he had a strong feeling if would be wise to have them at full potential.

"Audrey, you're looking good."

"Why thank you, sir. Thought you didn't care."

He ignored her. "Richard, you have a bit to go. How does it feel internally?"

"I can handle it. Much better than yesterday."

"Good. Okay, why don't you two do a little role-playing after we weigh anchor? I'll take the wheel."

"Sure." They went off.

He watched as Richard weighed anchor, stowed it in the forward hatch and spread sail. A light breeze filled the sail enough to send them on their way. Ted glanced at the map and took his heading. They'd have to be watchful once they started to cross New York Harbor. Huge ships moved in and out all day and all night. Out as far as they would be sailing he figured only the big ones could be a problem.

The young operatives retired below and left Ted alone on the bridge. He reviewed the past four days. He and Richard had arrived by car, towing a small open boat with a large covered parcel tied into it. They came through the Lodge after the duty people had left. He smiled. Richard's was Rolph, then, but he certainly hasn't been Rolph since. Ted was aware of Richard's abilities, but he stood amazed at Richard's omnipresence all the same.

Richard had immediately taken over the equipment, while Ted studied his maritime map of the bay's underwater rock structure, getting it firmly in mind. That night he took the car and boat and drove to a secluded site about where the cliffs began to rise impressively out of the sea a mile from the lodge. He hid the boat and went back to the cave through the Lodge. When Richard gave the all clear he took the powerboat from its dock in the cave and ran the dangerous approach twice for practice. He had no real problem but got close enough to several hull-ripping hazards to believe in the importance of running them carefully.

Once finished, the two went back through the Lodge and drove to the boat. He took great care with the covered parcel that enclosed the special chair. Ted couldn't take a chance of losing the only copy. They made their way down the mostly overgrown dirt road to the boat and Ted took to sea, first dragging the carrier off a ledge and into forty feet of water, then running the gauntlet of the rocks for the last time that night.

Only one incident in connection with their third running marred a perfect score, when the towed boat scraped a rock and got momentarily hung up. Ted cut the powerboat hard a-port and managed to pull it off. The boat wallowed for a few seconds, but finally came around and with a sigh he repeated in his reminiscence, Ted completed the trip. Richard drove the car back to the Lodge, parked, and returned to the depot.

Once Ted made it inside the cave, they'd dragged the special chair into the depot building and set it up. By that time his watch said seven a.m. and time to hit the sack.

That evening, Ted dressed up, disguised himself and showed up at Nick's big party. While there, he mixed and kept a low profile. He was a businessman from Atlanta—he knew Nick had a business there— and by flitting around and staying away from the house staff, no one got wind of his uninvited guest status. He learned a few things about the place and kept his eye on certain guests.

While moving around he noted with interest the presence of a man he thought he should recognize, but he couldn't get close enough to listen in. He made a mental note to check the man out if he had time. His primary function, to prevent Amber/Audrey's murder, took precedence.

Ted knew where Amber was and from a distance Ted had seen the curtains part and saw Amber's momentarily disgusted face. She covered her expression quickly and then slipped slowly and watchfully into the crowd, heading for the patio. She, too, stayed away from staff. He correctly surmised the "date" had gotten hung up somehow and, being in a better position to leave unnoticed, made his way to her sailboat. He'd gotten there twenty minutes before she arrived and tried her tightrope act.

He willed himself back to the present. It was shaping up to be another beautiful day. Maybe he should get some real sun later on deck. Although he worked out a lot, clandestine work normally didn't get him outside to the degree he wanted.

He decided they'd put up for the night along the southern New Jersey shore. He looked at the map and triangulated their heading and speed.

"Right there."

His finger pointed at Ship Bottom. Perfect! Two days to the safe house. Barring problems, he'd be able to personally activate the microchip devises about mid-afternoon of the second day.

He'd say nothing. Ted's kill team would have time to learn their full potential at sea. Better yet, they would have more than the originally allotted time to integrate themselves as a unit. That was something he had mentioned offhand earlier so they would be aware, but if the inventor was correct, their implants would be far better, well, at least far more intrusive than they had any idea. He hoped they could handle it.

He said it to himself as often as he said it to others. To visualize the whole of something free from confusion was to best understand it. This "thing" could literally change the world. Would it change his charges? Would the change be good? Would they be controllable? So many questions, so few answers.

One step at a time. He sheltered his thinking along a more innocuous plane. Ted deliberately attempted to meld with the visual scene. He couldn't think about Stoic or the organization for a while. They were on radio silence. Only Ted and his two students must know where they were.

Ted kept the wheel for five hours and as the day approached two hours past noon, he called down below.

"You two must be just perfect by now. C'mon up."

Audrey poked her head up through the stair opening. "You rang?"

"We still have a way to go, but we're creeping up on it. I can almost see the Jersey shore in the glasses."

"You have a destination?"

"Ship Bottom, about twenty-two miles above Atlantic City."

Richard appeared beside Audrey. "Audrey promised a night on the town at Atlantic City. You mean, we can't go?"

"I did not!" Audrey said indignantly.

"Well, I thought you did. Maybe it was the lumpy bed...ouch!"

"More where that came from, matey!"

"Okay, okay! I give up."

"C'mon up, you two. Somebody needs to spell me."

"Me...M...E...me." Richard smirked.

"Richard!" Audrey tried not to sound like it tickled her, but it did.

Richard took the wheel. Ted went to the stern and laid a blanket from a sea chest down and stretched out on it.

"That looks good, Ted. Enough room for me?"

"Sure." He moved over a couple of feet.

Audrey went to put on her bathing suit, throwing an aside over to Richard. "Don't be jealous, big boy. It's just Daddy."

"No problem, Audrey, my dear. I have some Playgirl magazines here. I'll be involved for some time. Knock before you come in."

"Oh, you horrid man! All you ever think of..."

"Huh? Me? Such injustice..."

"Right!" Audrey continued downstairs and disappeared for five minutes.

When she returned, Richard's eyes bugged out. "My God, and I thought you looked good naked! Ted, take a gander at this."

He whistled. Ted's head came up and he looked smilingly at Audrey. "Nice outfit. Guess that's from a cupboard I missed when I came aboard."

"I doubt it, but thank you, gentlemen. Always does a girl good to get a few whistles. Means we're keeping the pounds where they belong."

The two men laughed. Audrey went to join Ted and lay down beside him. Richard checked the course and called back to Ted.

"ETA?"

"Not to worry, another five, six hours, depends on wind. Forecast predicts light breeze, although it'll change direction toward sunset. Audrey can take it from there, say around five-thirty?"

"After all, it is my boat!" Audrey chimed in from the stern.

206

"Yeah, yeah!"

The two in the back spent a short time applying sun lotion to each other's backs and then lay face down and went to sleep. Richard checked out the radio channels on low to not disturb. He found nothing worth listening to. None of them expected to hear anything about the two thugs who'd met their untimely fate, and based on what Mikey had blurted out that it would be at least another day, probably two, before Nick would become interested in the whereabouts of Bernie.

Then he would discover that Mikey had gone with Bernie on his sojourn to the City, and being perceptive, Nick would smell something rotten. Nick would put out the word and Ray would tell him of Bernie's plans. While idly thinking about it, Richard visualized Nick going ballistic on Ray, then going to his study and making a few calls to contacts he had in the City.

"Yeah," Richard murmured, "that's about the way it would come down." He smiled.

The coastline had disappeared hours before, as Ted turned southwest to cross New York Channel. Richard kept an eye on the compass and kept the heading, occasionally watching for shipping. On the map he figured they were about even with Asbury Park. He would alter course and head due south when the Jersey coastline came into close view. Meantime, they sailed like they were on a lark, without a care in the world.

The afternoon passed blithely by. Around four o'clock they were still four miles out from the New Jersey coast, now visible as a dark line of muted, hazy grays. No sounds came from the stern, and Richard glanced back from time to time. Still sleeping. He checked them over and decided they were handling the sun well enough. He unlocked the wheel and took over again.

He'd turned the radio off two hours before as a distraction. He wanted to hear the sea and enjoy its muted sounds. With half-lidded eyes, Richard appreciated the unique singularity of life and the moment. He looked out to sea to gauge the height of the sun and compare it to his watch when he noted a thin, dark line along the horizon. It didn't look quite right. Something about it seemed too stark. The earlier marine weather forecast didn't call for bad weather, and there weren't many clouds about. Richard wondered.

He turned the radio on again and suddenly the airwaves were filled with sound.

33

"Warning, warning, tidal wave...tsunami, tidal wave...tsunami! Warning, warning...all shipping alert! New Jersey coast in great danger between Point Pleasant and Atlantic City. One-foot pressure wave traveling two hundred miles an hour. Coastal impact twenty minutes..." Richard stopped listening and yelled to the others.

"Everybody up, pronto. Tsunami! Hurry!"

Ted and Audrey were up and running before he finished his short but urgent message. They closed in on the wheelhouse as Richard turned the volume high enough so all could hear. Audrey spoke first.

"Give me the wheel, Richard, we've got to get away from shore. The thing'll kill us if we don't. How much time do we have?"

"Radio said twenty minutes from the coast. But they said it was only one foot. Is it a problem?" he said as he got out of her way.

Audrey spun the wheel hard and the Maiden Voyage I turned west-southwest. She headed directly for the oncoming wave.

"Got to get as far from the coast as possible. Ted, check the map. What's our depth? She turned to Richard. "One foot in the deep ocean will pile up a lot of water as the sea shelf narrows, Richard. Five miles out it could be ten to twelve feet, and grow enormously larger by the time it hits shore."

"Yeah, think I read that somewhere. Sorry, I forgot. Can we make it out to five miles?"

Audrey looked worried. "I don't know."

She consulted the map and checked their position. "We're right on the edge of the worst of it."

Ted said, after consulting the Loran, "There's less than two hundred feet of water under us."

"Potentially we could get hit with a ten-foot wave. I don't know if we can surmount a wave that size. Ted, what do you think?" Audrey said.

"I think I'm going to take a big chance and activate your internal units right now!" Ted headed for the cabin fast.

Richard and Audrey looked after him quizzically. They were both thinking the same thing. Audrey managed as tight a turn as she had ever done, and more quickly. She started the steerage motor at the same time.

"Richard, see if you can release the front jib. There's enough wind for it to help. I'm going to try to get eight knots, maybe nine with the engine pushing. I'll try to angle away from the wave a little and then face it when it's on us. Maybe we can catch an extra two minutes. It's our only chance!"

Richard ran forward and started fumbling with the relatively unfamiliar fastenings. Just then Ted came up the stairs carrying the black box. He saw what Richard was doing, set the box on a side seat and went to help Richard with the jib. The two working together, it only took a minute. He went immediately back to the box and began to key in the combination.

The ocean was relatively smooth. The long swells were only five to six feet, but this far out and now plowing the ocean to get as far out as possible, they started to slap waves. Ted focused his full attention on the unit. It only took one mistake.

The front came down.

"Audrey, if you are set for five, lock the wheel and let's get this done. Richard, if you can sit over to my right, you can install the contacts above and below the maxillary sinus on your left side. Audrey, as soon as you get here, grab the other set of contacts and do likewise. It's going to be tender." Ted carefully removed the wires.

Richard took his, quickly removed the sticky tape covering from the end of each contact and attached them. At that moment, the Maiden Voyage I plowed into a large swell, head on. The sailboat shuddered, slowed, picked up momentum again. It angled over seventeen degrees and slid down the other side. Ted had to grab the open box and hold it firmly to prevent it falling to the deck. Richard grabbed for it, too, but the boat righted.

Audrey came over and sat. Holding the unit with one hand, Ted handed the other set of wires to her. She followed Richard's example and told Ted to go ahead.

Ted said, "One minute. More info. When I press the activation button, you will feel a tingling on the left side of your faces for about twenty seconds. Then you may feel, I was told, some heat in the area of your faces where the implants are and a crawling, needle-like sensation. Don't put your hands to your faces or crinkle your noses, or anything else. Just bear it. Sit on your hands if that helps. That will be your internal units powering up. The sensation should pass in about two minutes, and you are activated. Try to keep your minds blank—thoughtless, if you will—during that period. I was cautioned about that, but don't know the reason for it. Just have to trust the inventor on that one. Ready?"

He covered, with considerable personal pain, the knowledge that he had lied to them this once. The scientist-inventor had told him of the hair-fine, self-seeking filaments that on activation would feed out of the top of the units and seek certain nerve bundles in the cortex of their brains. Further questioning had yielded no satisfactory answers as to what would happen. The scientist shrugged and told Ted that he didn't know what would happen, not really, but he suggested that the subjects not be told of that feature. Ted understood. He thought he had covered it well enough.

He snapped out of his reverie.

Ted got a synchronous yes. He looked at them, and pressed the button. Nothing seemed to happen for a moment. Then, without a word, the two operatives eyes got big. They sat stock still, totally motionless, while the sailboat pushed outward, leaderless.

Richard's left eye began to tear. His hand automatically started for his face. By force of will he brought it back to his lap. Tears fell down his cheek, but he didn't move again. Ted glanced at Audrey. She seemed all right, although she was undergoing trauma, too.

A little over two minutes passed.

Suddenly, Richard said, "My God, Audrey, was that you?"

211

No word came from Audrey, but Richard turned and looked at her, and then at Ted. Audrey was a picture of concentration.

"Good God Gertie!" he exclaimed. "I'm hearing her thoughts. Lord above, Ted, you didn't mean this, when you said "increased discernment capabilities, did you?"

"I wasn't sure, Richard. The inventor intimated that such a thing was possible with the right match, but I don't think he knew, either."

Nonetheless, Ted was awestruck. Richard turned to Audrey. He didn't say anything out loud but seemed to be concentrating. After a minute, Richard looked disappointed. "You didn't get that, Audrey?"

"No."

Then she concentrated again and Richard said, "She just said don't try so hard."

"Yes," she confirmed.

Ted listened to the exchange between his two new super communicators. A thought occurred to him. "Look, Richard, your healing hasn't gone as far as Audrey's. It's possible that she can project to you and you can't respond, but it is likely that with more healing, you'll be able to project, too."

Ted looked worriedly out to sea, and brought up the other important thing. "I got you both up and running because we're about to be hit with a tidal wave. I really suggest that now you've been activated, you put it aside for now, and let's see if we can survive the wave."

Richard and Audrey looked southeast. The line that got Richard's attention wasn't much bigger, but that meant nothing. Nothing could stop it! Audrey went back and unlocked the wheel.

"Hope New Jersey authorities got everybody back far enough. Wonder how much time they had?" Richard said.

"At the moment, we are closer in harm's way, Richard, but we at least might be able to overcome the wave. The shoreline will be devastated, especially the area including Ship Bottom. They are right on the sea break. We might as well review the contingency plan." Audrey said sadly.

Ted said, "I agree, Audrey."

"As a precaution, we'd better get out the life boats, too. What do you plan for the activation mechanism, Ted?"

"Been thinking we need to get rid of it and to render it harmless. I wouldn't want to chance someone finding the box and having it explode in their hands. There is a timer I can set for five minutes." He reached into the still open box and made the adjustments.

Ted then closed the front and hefted the heavy box over the side. "We're somewhere between one-eighty and one eighty-five feet, according to the depth finder, about thirty fathoms. In five minutes the wave will be right on top of us and at the same time the box will explode. That ought to cover the explosion. We'll continue on course for four minutes and then turn to face the wave. It'll be tight, but I think we'll be okay."

Four minutes later, the tidal wave wasn't a line anymore. Audrey gasped! It raced at them with incredible speed! She turned quickly toward it! With only seconds to go and nearly square with the wave, the little thirty-foot sailboat rose suddenly, higher and higher toward its crest. The top broke as it passed under them. The boat gave a lunge and a shudder and spun quickly sideways down the sluice on the other side.

Immediately, the secondary wave hit the boat! It tilted, further and further. Audrey let out a scream!

Ted yelled, "Grab anything!"

The former Lucky Lady went over on its side, out of luck. With a resounding smack the sails hit the water. All three were propelled into the cold ocean, just as the black box sitting in nearly two hundred feet of water exploded.

The explosion sent out its own pressure wave. All fish in the vicinity were killed outright and began their long float to the surface. A tiger shark that had stopped to nose the box was blasted into pieces the size of the destroyed microcircuits. When the pressure wave caught them, luck only kept them from being killed. The distance Audrey had managed to get away from the detonation site diluted the wave enough, but left the three momentarily disoriented.

Through this haze, from well behind them came a shuddering vibration and a plume of white water erupted high into the sky. The tidal wave passed unconcernedly by.

As the sailboat capsized, it threw Richard into the cabin bulkhead. His head hit hard. Ted, better prepared with a tighter grip, held on and grabbed at Richard with his legs as the young operative washed by. Missed! He watched Richard carry over the side and disappear into the watery greenness.

"No!" he shouted.

Audrey still had hold of the wheel and had had enough previous experience in rough weather to strap in. She heard Ted and forcibly pushed the haze out of her head. She saw Ted let go of his hold and vault over the side after Richard. She oriented herself and looked around for a life preserver. The closest one flapped on its hanger above her head. She unstrapped and grabbed it down.

Her fingers slipped. She seized it again. Got it! She tossed it in the direction of the two men, went after the other one to port, found it under water and retrieved it expertly, attaching a half-inch line to it. Holding the ring under one arm, she jumped into the water after her men. Bright sunlight of mid-afternoon gave her some depth of seeing in the water. She held onto her lifeline, continuously dunking, trying to locate them.

For a couple of minutes she saw nothing but blue-green ocean water. She started to get more scared. This couldn't be happening!

"Ted, where are you? Richard, this isn't funny? I know you like to kid, but this isn't the time for it!"

Then she screamed. "Richard! Ted! Please, not now."

Her boat; now Richard and Ted! Frantically she decided to cast off and start diving when she felt a tug on the line behind her. She turned, tears ready to come. She saw Ted holding Richard's head above the water. Richard sputtered and groped around haphazardly.

Ted called above the noise of the sea. "Audrey, it's okay. I've got him. Give me a hand and we'll get the big lug up onto something solid."

"Oh, God, I was beside myself. Hang on."

Audrey swam over. Between the three, with Richard being able to assist a little, they pulled themselves up the side of the capsized boat and lay there breathing heavily for several minutes. Richard heaved seawater. Finally the spasms abated and Richard just lay like a dead fish.

Then, suddenly to her mind, Audrey heard Richard. *Audrey, I love you. I thought I was all done just then. Thank Ted for me. The strength of that man, you don't know.*

Audrey laughed a little, first in relief and then harder at the convoluted way Richard chose to tell her it had all come to him and he could do it, too. She gulped.

"Ted, Richard says thanks."

Silence, then, "Richard, you can do it! That's great!"

Ted ascended to heaven again. If nothing else in the world happened to do one better than this, ever, he'd remember this moment.

"God, the beginnings of the world's first super team!"

"Yup," Richard said out loud. "It's actually pretty neat. I can project what I want Audrey to hear, but my thoughts are still my own. Lucky thing, too. Wouldn't want Audrey to find out about Trixie."

Audrey jumped in, "And who's Trixie?"

"Oops, she heard me! Now I'm in trouble." Richard's slanted sense of humor returned with a vengeance.

Ted interjected, "I hate to break it to you, but we are on a sinking ship and it might be a good idea to inflate the life raft and get out of here."

"Yeah," Richard said, and then coughed hard for a minute more. That got rid of the last of it. He lay still, catching his wind.

When he recovered, he said with a smirk, "Good idea. My clothes are all wet, too."

"Cute!"

Ted spoke to Audrey. "You have an exact fix on our position, Audrey?"

"Yes, I took the coordinates as we turned into the wave."

"Good. There are things aboard I don't want anyone not connected with the organization to find. When we get ashore, we'll need to arrange for one of my group to locate and raise your boat on an ASAP basis. I don't think we have much to worry about. I'm certain the tsunami has caused much damage to the New Jersey coast. Rescue and recovery efforts will focus there. Let's get started."

"Right."

The sailboat gradually but noticeably sank lower in the water. They unlashed the rubber life raft and Audrey pulled the pin. The raft could handle five people. Oars were Velcroed to the inside floor. They climbed aboard. Richard, now sufficiently recovered, grabbed the oars and threaded them through the rubber eyes. He waited for the order to row.

They were less than five miles out but they were low in the water and could no longer see the coast. They'd have to gauge the sun.

"Wait, I want the sextant." Ted told them he'd get it.

The others nixed the suggestion, but Ted remained firm. He told them that the sailboat might sink while they talked about it.

"It's important to me."

Audrey conferred with Richard and they both threw up their hands at the same time. Ted laughed and jumped over the side of the raft. After two and a half minutes the two started to get worried. Suddenly, Ted broke the water and held it up.

"It wasn't where I put it." He handed it to Audrey and pulled himself aboard. "Okay, Richard, pull hearty, mate!"

Audrey said, "Ted, you've got some mighty powerful lungs."

"High school swim team. Stayed under a minute longer than anyone. Instructor came down to pull me out. Waved him off."

Richard began to pull away from the stricken vessel. Just as he did, a large burp came from the cabin and the Maiden Voyage I settled further in the water and began to slip.

Audrey began to cry. "I'm sorry, guess I'm not as tough as I told everybody."

"No need," said Richard, "I feel like it myself. She's a great boat."

"We'll get her back, Audrey," said Ted, "Right now we have to focus on saving ourselves and getting to our destination. We're going to have to do it overland, so the rules have changed, but we'll get there. Then it's back to business."

"Oh, that," Richard offered.

He pulled hard on the oars, sending them up one wave and down the next. Ted gauged the sun and suggested Richard move two points to starboard. He complied. Richard got into a routine with the oars, and even after two hours, when Ted suggested he felt good and he could row for a while, Richard said no, that he felt fine, "Enjoying myself."

Audrey thought they had moved to within a mile of the shore by then. She thought she saw columns of haze in the direction of travel and mentioned it could be fires on the mainland. The others agreed.

She had had a lot of time to think about where they were, where they were going, what awaited them, the dangers, the whole magilla. Every now and then she projected a thought Richard's way and he responded without breaking his rowers cadence. She loved the new abilities, but decided after awhile that it wasn't nice to keep Ted out of the loop, and suggested this to Richard.

So, out of the blue, when nobody had said a word out loud for thirty minutes, Richard, in his inimitable style, blurted out, "Of course not!"

Ted looked up from his reverie and smiled. "Practicing?"

"Yup," they both said, and the three laughed at how one ludicrous comment had tied them all together again.

Ten minutes later they could see the coast at the top of each swell. After thirty minutes they pulled up on a beach and saw utter desolation.

"God! Wiped clean!" Audrey commented.

All the beach homes along the coastline were gone. They could see debris piled helter-skelter in the distance, perhaps half a mile inland. Broken white hulls of several boats were piled amongst the debris. The land sloped upward from the beach here, so the wave had dissipated quickly. They could hear sirens in the distance and recognized the smoke they'd seen out at sea rising in several places. It seemed a good bit further west. They saw no sign of life nearby.

Richard pulled the raft up onto the beach and Ted removed his sextant. They started inland, silent now, looking around. After awhile, Ted said he thought they were near Monmouth Beach or Oceanport. That would put them in range of Long Branch and close to the Trenton connector.

"If I'm right..." he finished.

Their footprints led into raised areas where only two or three hours before had grown tall, wiry saw grass, the stuff that will cut you if you're not careful. They need not worry now. Saw grass and brambles along the northeast shores of New Jersey were all part of the debris from wrecked boats and homes they saw in the distance.

They plodded on.

34

The south side of Long Island in Nick's harbor felt little of the tsunami. The major wave impacted New Jersey and little else. The weather and oceanographic people opined that part of the deep-sea shelf had suddenly collapsed, causing a seaquake and releasing the wave. Ray first heard about it while monitoring ship to shore radio, and called Nick. Nick told him to alert the complex and get some guys down to the harbor and batten down, just in case.

"Right away, Nick," he said.

The boss went to his wall safe and pulled out his organization chart. He studied it for a moment. As he remembered, there were two locations he had interests in that might potentially be affected. He gave Bernie brief thought and decided that the little idiot would have to fend for himself. He told Nick he was going to the City. He doubted New York would be seriously affected, based on what Ray had said, but he decided to turn on the small TV he kept in his office.

Rarely did Nick use his TV. He turned to Channel 4 for the local news. The tsunami blocked out all other news. A local meteorologist showed a satellite image of the coast of New Jersey that covered part of Long Island all the way down to the Delaware water gap. He started with a dot showing the seismic origin of the wave and then drew a computer line across the ocean in front of it toward the U.S.

coast, quickly showing where the pressure wave would travel and where it would hit with devastating effect.

Nick sat at his desk, picked up the phone and Ray answered. "Ray, get Bruno Aiello on the line for me."

"I'll call you right back, Nick." Nick hung up.

Three minutes later, the phone rang and Nick picked it up. "Bruno, Nick here."

"Nick, how you doin'? I know what yer callin' about. We're okay here. I got the guys out tyin' shit down, but Jaime, you know Jaime, he says the wave won't get three miles inland, not where we are. I think we're okay."

"Good to hear, Bruno. Maybe your products are going to be in great demand down your way. That makes me happy. You know I like to be happy."

"Yeah, Nick, happy. Don' you worry. On my life, we okay here."

"Okay, Bruno. Talk later." He hung up.

Nick decided not to call the other New Jersey business he had his fingers in. From the sound, it wouldn't be bad inland.

He picked up the phone. "Get me Stone. I'll hold."

A moment later Nick's accountant was on the phone. "Yeah, Nick?"

"Called Bruno. Been meaning to look over his numbers. Bring them up, will you?"

"Sure, Nick, on my way."

The boss sat back and watched more TV. Soon he heard a quick knock, and the door opened. Stone came in.

"You heard about the tidal wave about to hit the Jersey coast?"

"Yeah."

"Let's you and me discuss ways to make lots of money out of this."

"Sure, Nick. Brain trust, huh?"

"Yeah, Stone, brain trust!" He laughed.

They talked and Nick questioned some numbers here and there for a while. Nick left the TV on in the background. When they were told the wave had hit the coast, they stopped and the two men watched television for twenty minutes.

"A fuckin' wave thirty feet high!" Stone whistled.

"Yeah. Pushed those cottages, some of them pretty big suckers in half-mile, some places. I can smell a lot of money coming out of this, Stone." Nick's face took on a mixture of pleasure and greed.

Nick finally tired of the TV and turned it off. Stone and the boss talked and jotted figures for another hour. After that he told Stone to get back to what he was doing and went back to thinking about how much he was going to profit from the disaster in New Jersey. He shoved the Rathmanizzar problem out of his mind.

As he sat, he decided he had a little chore for the kid he'd just promoted. Dorneti might be able to prove himself to his boss and justify Nick's faith in him. Of course, Nick would kill him as look at him, but if he turned out good, why not? Be a good test. That's how a man got value in the organization.

He picked up the phone again. "Ray, send Mikey Dorneti up. I wanna talk to him."

There was a hesitation. "Nick, Bernie didn't tell you he was taking Mikey with him?"

"No, what do you know, Ray?"

"Shoot, Nick, Bernie says to me, like, 'Hey I'm taken' a few days off. I'm taking along Mikey to show him some spots I know.' I says, 'Sure, Bernie,' but I'm thinkin', Bernie boy, bet yer sweet on that young buck, an' I laughs to myself. They leave and I don't think no more about it after that."

Nick exploded. "Thibbert, what the fuck! You know my rule! Everything gets to me. Everything! Homenio is sweet on a kid? He's going fucking queer? What the hell's going on here? Sounds like we're going to have another meeting on the rules according to Nick Trafalgar! What else you know?"

Ray thought, holy shit, Bernie never told the boss! He held the phone twelve inches from his face and winced and waited to see Nick crawl through the phone.

When he stopped, Ray said, "Nick, I didn't think nothing was wrong. Bernie told me he got time off and they were going into the City to have some fun. Then he tells me he's pumped up about finding that bitch you wanted, an he thinks he can find her along the way. He says he'll make a big hit with you when he grabs her and brings her back. I laugh under my breath; it's so far out. I figure he's tryin' to make some time with his new friend and I put it out of my mind after they leave."

Ray sweated through a long silence. Then Nick said, his voice again under control, "Ray, I gotta think about this. I'll call you back. I'm not pissed at you. I'm pissed at myself for not seeing what's going on around here."

He hung up.

Where did Homenio say he'd stay in the City? Did he say? Nick knew when Bernie and some of the other boys got a little time off they went down to little Italy and screwed around. A lot of the guys were Italian, some were "Gricks" and some were Miks. Matter of fact, Stretch was a Polack. Did he care?

"Yeah! Concha Doro, that's that place." He got on the horn to Ray. "Ray, call the Concha Doro Hotel down in Little Italy. I think that's where Bernie was going. You think so?"

"Yeah, maybe. He didn't tell me where, but he's been there before. I can check and see if he made a reservation."

"Let me know."

"Sure, boss."

Nick set the phone down and spoke to his bookcase. "I'm going to frost his ass. I didn't say he could take anybody with him."

In a few minutes, Ray called him back. "Nick, Bernie registered there, but he didn't show up yet."

"He should have been there yesterday. Ray, do me a favor. Check with some of the guys and see if there are any whorehouses he frequents. Maybe he stopped over. You think of anything else, make some calls. It doesn't make sense though, if he's got Dorneti on his mind. Anyway, check it and get back to me."

"Okay, boss."

He hung up. Nick bent to the numbers he'd asked Stone to bring him. Not bad! Let's see what kind of hay Bruno would make in the month succeeding the disaster. Building materials would be in high demand. Maybe a few things'll happen at the lumber mart over in Hammonton. I could arrange it. Bruno wants to expand over in that direction.

An hour later Ray called Nick again. "No dice, boss. Bernie and Mikey never got to the City, all I could find out."

"Maybe he had an accident, or something. He took a pool car, didn't he?"

"Yeah. I checked with the gate. He took a maroon Ford Taurus. I got the plate number. You wanna send one of the boys out to find out where it got to."

"First check with the Staties. See if they got a line on it, or the two guys. Suddenly I don't like this. Was Bernie packing?"

"Don't know, Nick. He likes that little piece of his. Could be he took it, but I don't know, like I said."

"Yeah, well, keep your ears open, and find out what you can."

"Right, boss." Ray got busy again. First he checked with the State Police barracks in Levittown.

"I'm calling from Trafalgar Imports. One of our cars has been out too long and I wondered if you might have a report on it?" Ray gave the dispatcher the plate number.

"Hang on, sir." Ray could hear rapid typing on a keyboard.

"Yes, sir, we have a report. Hang on."

Ray waited. A new voice came on. "This is Sergeant Smith. I have the report."

The Sergeant said, "It's yours all right. Owner listed as Trafalgar Imports. Who was driving?"

Bingo! Hit on the first try. The plate number had been reported on an apparently abandoned maroon Ford Taurus outside of Robert Moses State Park.

"One of our representatives, I believe," Ray said.

Ray asked if it had damage or any other remarkable thing about it. The police said no; they'd found it locked and undamaged, so far as the local police report showed.

The Sergeant asked Ray what he could tell them about the driver and any passengers. Ray deferred, saying he had to check with the pool to find out who had taken the vehicle.

The Sergeant said, "You knew the car was missing and don't know who took it?"

"I'm just the messenger, Sarge," Ray said smoothly, "My employer got a call from the front gate with the stats on the daily use of vehicles, like he always does. He calls me and says one of the cars is real late. Track it down for me. He doesn't give me any more info. I say okay, and I give you a call."

"Let me talk to your employer."

"He's in a meeting at the moment. I can't get to him, but I'll have him call you, or I'll get back to you. That be okay?"

Just then Ray heard the dispatcher nearby say something to his superior about an accident. The Sergeant told Ray he had to go and just to get back to him.

Ray told him he would.

He dialed Nick. "Boss, the Staties have a record. The car was found on the road outside of Robert Moses State Park. Whadda you wanna do?"

"Let me think." Nick reviewed what he knew and made a few guesses. "Where's the car now?"

"At the impound lot in Wantagh."

"Tell the cops we'll send a couple of guys down to claim the vehicle. Call the gate. They'll have the necessary papers. Tell the Weasel he's got a job to do. Tell him to pick up the car and nose around the beach area and see what he can find out. Tell him to take one of them poker-playing assholes along as a driver. Maybe Homenio did stop there with Dorneti. Maybe somebody saw them. Get what you can."

"Right, boss." Ray hung up and went to work.

35

Ted, Audrey and Richard reached the beach road. Two feet of sand lay on the paved road now, except in the places where the wave had swirled or gone around a low impediment or the road was gouged with little sections of blacktop showing at the sides. The process sand and gravel under-fill of the street showed darker, markedly different from the light beige New Jersey coastal sand. It made an odd contrast.

"A lot of work here," Richard said.

"Yes. Hope there wasn't much loss of life." As he said it, Ted tripped on something barely sticking out of the sand on the far side of the road.

He stopped and started digging with his toe. Then he bent to it, using both hands. He uncovered the thing, a beach shoe with a foot in it. Richard and Audrey looked on in silence. Richard bent down and started to pull sand away with Ted. They rapidly uncovered a woman in a beach robe with nothing on under it. They were able to extricate her by pulling simultaneously on an arm and leg and rolling her over on her back. She was in her twenties, blond, but with a dark, nearly black pubic muff that suggested a top-end dye job.

Richard said, "She was *pretty*. A real shame. Looks like she tried to run too late."

"Yes. Was! Reminds me, when we clear here we'd better cook up a plausible story on how we happened walk out of the devastated area intact."

Richard countered with, "Might as well just tell the truth. We survived the wave but lost our boat. Our beached lifeboat should be proof enough. I suppose we could say it was a powerboat, and we don't have to give the exact location of the wreck. That should keep things safe for our guys salvage operation. No need to mention the explosion, unless some news helicopter or commercial jet happened to see the plume from it. Doubt it, but worst case; if we were ever connected, we could say we had a fire on board, breakfast grill that got out of hand. We got off in time, but the boat exploded."

"Nice try, Richard. Some of that might work, but an inquiry would want to know why our fire extinguishers weren't working, and so on. I'd prefer to not be seen at all. There is bound to be a lot of confusion. Anybody who sees us coming out of the devastated area will bring us notoriety. Hopefully, we can get past curious eyes without drawing attention to ourselves.

"I think when we near the connector, we should pretend we're helping save belongings out of the wreckage of some home on the periphery of the devastated area, and then cop a ride to Trenton or somewhere we can get a rental car. We'll say we have relatives there we can stay with. We need to remove ourselves from the area as soon as possible."

"Okay, you da boss." Richard shrugged.

"Let's roll."

As they went on, Audrey noted a large strip of marshy land on their left, flattened and swirled and gouged in great, haphazard wounds. She thought it could provide cover. A tangle of trees in the distance looked uninhabited, even before the tidal wave came through.

"Ted?"

He had been making his way toward the remains of a group of buildings. He turned.

"Yes, Audrey?"

She nodded to her left and raised an eyebrow. Ted stopped and thought.

"Good. Anywhere in this direction we're bound to find a shore road. That will shield us longer. Unlikely any people there at the moment, but the curious will be getting past the authorities pretty soon. Let's go."

They angled away from their route. It had been impossible to walk without leaving footprints, but now grass and rock poked up here and there. Ted told them to start covering their tracks as much as possible. They nodded and went on. The going got tougher, but they bulled their way through, around and over upturned trees and slowly made their way across them. Finally, before them they saw a large open space and then a road.

Typical of access roads to nearly every beach on the East Coast the road followed the curves of the land. They were nearly a quarter mile inland now, and still hadn't seen a soul. It couldn't last. The wave had pretty much spent itself in this area. Inland to the west what they could see looked better and better. The low shrubbery was intact and the trees stood where they belonged. Small, single family homes stood vacant, doors ajar, as if a whole population had panicked and run.

They moved carefully around a low hill and curve. Suddenly, in front of them they saw a police car and old blue Chevy. Audrey stopped instantly and motioned the others back. They ducked into the shade of a straggling forsythia bush. The police car slanted sideways on the access road, deliberately blocking it. The officer lounged on the cruiser's trunk, talking to a couple of locals. He wore the requisite, typical shades; a short sleeved khaki summer uniform shirt, and long, light green trousers. That made him a local constable. The cop didn't see them, and the other two had their backs to them.

"We don't want to get shot as looters, guys," Audrey said. "The area is fairly desolate. Let's work our way around this curve and approach them from the other side."

They pulled back silently and went around, working southwest. They had enough cover so they only had to stoop low in a couple of places. Clearly the constable had been assigned to keep people out of the area, and didn't expect anyone to come out of it. Two hundred yards south, they came to the road again. No one in sight this time.

"So far, so good," breathed Ted, "Now, we double back and approach him from the west."

Audrey and Richard were conversing at their higher level.

Richard spoke. "Ted, why don't I amble back there with Audrey. As a couple, we will attract the least attention, and be least suspicious. We might convince the locals to take us at least part of the way to Trenton, or at least someplace where we could find a working phone to call for transportation. You wouldn't have to explain the sextant. What do you think?"

"Not a bad plan," Ted looked at the sextant in his hand and thought rapidly, "Now I wish I'd left it on the boat. It did help us to shore, though. I'll make my way up the road a mile or so and then turn and double back, make it appear I'm heading for shore. Fifteen minutes, max. You get those people to bring you up this way and recognize me as an uncle, trying to find you two. They'll take me along, too. You tell them you're trying to find your cousins, who have a place down here, but your car broke down and you walked several miles and finally found somebody, and you're not even sure where you are now. Ask the constable to take you to your car. He'll refuse, can't leave his post, but will probably help convince the two that are talking to him to take you some ways. Might work."

"We can do it."

"Remember, it doesn't matter where they take us initially, so long as it's away from shore."

"Right."

"Okay." Ted strode off at a fast walk, keeping an eye out for signs of life.

Audrey and Richard waited until Ted was out of sight, then they walked north on the parallel road back to where it joined the beach road. The old Chevy still sat there. Evidently its owner didn't have much else to do, and the two guys were keeping the cop company.

About a hundred feet away, Audrey called out, "Hey, officer."

The constable turned and looked at her. He spent some time looking at her, matter of fact. The other two were a bit older. They looked at her appraisingly, too. They noted Richard in passing, but they were acting and thinking like men, Audrey thought to Richard.

Why do men have to think like men, Richard

He tossed back, *My guess is that they* are *men, Audrey. Just a guess, though. Why do women try to look attractive?*

She turned and smiled at him, noting that the others had noted it, too. Something else she'd begun to notice too, in the past few minutes. Beyond the mind link, another awareness had begun to manifest itself. Audrey began to see outward, to be aware of surroundings even behind her. She examined it and told Richard.

She projected. *Something new developing.*

Concern? he linked.

She outlined it for him and then projected, *No, not as yet. Let you know. It feels awesome, like a bubble surrounds me, projecting outward. Everything it touches comes back to me in it's own spatial position. I discern movement, too. Much better than eyesight!*

Sounds good. Okay, we're here.

The officer spoke first. "You strangers around here. Can't get any farther toward shore. This is it."

Audrey said, "Officer, our car broke down up the road. We were coming to pay a surprise visit to my cousins, the Thatcher's, but the radio said a tidal wave, the one with the Japanese sounding word hit and we were worried about them. Nobody around and we figured we could walk it from where we were but I'm not even sure we're in the right place now. Do you know them?"

No, Ma'am, I don't. Charlie, Jake, you know them?"

They shook their heads. "Sorry."

"I wanted them to meet my new husband. God, what are we going to do now?"

The constable looked sympathetic, while attempting to look through her clothing. He glanced at Richard, who slouched a bit to look less virile.

"Where them cousins of yours live, lady?" Charlie asked.

"Sandy Lane, in Spring Lake."

"Yer north o' there. This's Belmar. But I heard it's wiped out total, lady."

"Oh dear, Richard, I told you we shouldn't take the cutoff where we did. Oh, what a mess! Oh, I hope Sandy and Lori are okay."

To Richard she projected that they were nearly ten miles south of where Ted had thought. She also thought a caution. She wasn't convinced about this constable, and the other two seemed seedy. C'mon, I thought we were civilized up here in New Jersey. Strong vibes came from all three now, and she didn't like them.

Richard, she thought, *Look a little sappier. I think these Jersey good old boys are thinking naughty thoughts.*

Richard slouched more and put a small silly grin on his face.

Audrey linked, *If we can't get transportation one way, we'll get it another.*

I hears yuh, honey. You pick the time, I'll pick the place.

She spoke to the officer again. "Well, could you at least give us a ride to a gas station with a phone so we could get a tow. Could you do that, officer?"

"What's your rush, sweetie?" Now he called her 'sweetie'.

He stood up straight, a man well over six feet tall and he looked fit. He started to smile. Audrey put down a laugh at the picture poster he effected.

"Charlie, Jake, what do you think of this pretty little gal here?"

"Mighty nice," said Jake.

"Think you could convince the husband to move along, or you think he might like to watch?" Charlie offered.

The constable smiled bigger. "I think that could be arranged."

Audrey went on full alert. Her impressions now came from the group as a whole. They took on a curious coloration to Audrey's eyes, a hue of red, like a danger signal, faint, but definite. She glanced at Richard. No color change there! How odd!

She projected, *I think he's going to go for his gun, Richard!*

She anticipated the man before he had clearly formed his thought, yet she wasn't reading his mind. It felt more like foreseeing intent, yet clearly not foreseeing the event. Another feature of the implant? How lovely!

Suddenly Richard stooped low and lunged at the constable. He grabbed the man's gun hand as it jerked the weapon from its holster. He caught the constable off guard. Richard's rush carried him behind the man, and as he moved, he brought the constables' arm up behind him. Richard twisted, putting his full weight and momentum into it and he heard a satisfying crack and pop as the constables' shoulder dislocated and the humerus snapped.

The man uttered a sharp cry. The two other men, Charlie and Jake had already moved in to help the officer. Audrey leapt and spun on her left heel, catching Charlie, closest of the two in the neck with her right foot. He went down like a rock, windpipe collapsed, Adams apple crushed. His hands went to his throat, but only whimpering sounds came out. His eyes bugged out and he strained to get breath he would never get again.

Richard had turned the constable around, as the officer dropped the weapon from his useless arm. His cry ended as Richard got his neck in a vice grip. The man jerked one way and another, but nothing he could do made Richard give up his bulldog grip. The constable got redder and redder as he strained against the strength of his assailant. Finally he slumped with an audible sigh. Richard held him for a few seconds, then twisted his neck, hard, heard a crack and let him to the ground.

Jake, who had charged forward thinking to grab Richard from behind, went sprawling as Audrey's kick sent Charlie's body into him. He got to his feet, and in his hand flashed his fish knife. Short Jake, a man likely in his early fifties, and wiry, evidently knew the ways of short knife fighting. Audrey knew how deadly sharp fishermen kept their knives. He spun around and reached for Audrey with a big curve of his arm at elbow level. Audrey leapt and folded in half as the knife went past her, cutting the front of her shirt. Close, very close! As she straightened, her left hand came around, extended, and went for the nerve at Jake's neck. She closed with his body, grabbed the spot and with her other hand seized his left shoulder.

Audrey squeezed. Jake became limp and fell to the ground, momentarily paralyzed. Audrey found a large rock nearby and finished the job. Richard looked at her in something resembling awe.

He said into her mind, *Don't ever get mad at me, love. I couldn't handle it.*

She replied in kind, *Not you, teammate. You I love. Them I didn't.*

He spoke into the air, making his voice gruff, "And you better keep it that way, sister."

"Levity later. We better get rid of the evidence, Richard, don't you think?"

"Yeah, good idea. You have lots of good ideas."

Well, here's another one, once again in mind link, *there is a swamp beyond the culvert over by those trees over there. We can dispose of all three there. We'll put the constable in the end of the*

culvert and get the other two further off into the swamp. We'll cover
the tracks to the yokels, but leave a faint trail local enforcement will
pick up on. I can handle Jake. He's small. You get the others. I'll check
to see if the keys are in the old car.

"Gotcha. You figure the sheriff may not look further than his
man."

"Right."

They went to work, and in five minutes, they'd removed the
human presence. Audrey got sand, covered the blood traces and
brushed the area with a nearby leafy, battered branch. They left the
cruiser alone and avoided touching it. The radio muttered off and
on as the dispatcher made calls to other cars in the fleet.

Audrey was about to head back to the Chevy when she heard,
"Carl, where you at? All okay?"

No answer. "Carl, pick up."

Louder, "Hey Carl, where you be?"

"Oh, damn, where that man?" She left the key open for a few
seconds.

In the background they heard a man's voice, "Probably took a
leak. Try him in five."

The radio went quiet. They got in the Chevy and left. As they
rounded the curve before the road straightened out, they saw Ted
jogging toward them. They stopped to let him in.

36

Ted looked at them both. "You had trouble."

It was a statement. Richard answered it.

"Yes. Seems New Jersey has its share of good old boys, too. Wanted to play with Audrey, and Audrey didn't want to play. We had to dispatch them. No choice. Just as we left, the constable got a call."

"That's too bad." Ted became silent for a few moments. "Let's get rid of this car at first opportunity. We need something clean. This got a radio?"

"Seems to be broken. I don't think the sheriff knew his constable was jawing with locals, though. Didn't sound like it."

"That's good. That probably gives us twenty minutes to half an hour, max. Keep the speed down. We don't need attention."

"Right."

They drove on in silence.

Here and there they noticed people. They weren't moving around much. Evidently they'd all heard on radio or TV they were to stay in their homes and leave the roadways open for emergency vehicles. The area held middle class single-family homes. The people in them listened to authority and largely obeyed it. They saw shock, too.

For a couple of miles they stayed on Monmouth county roads. This used up eight minutes of their assumed timeline. Finally they got on the Trenton connector. Richard checked the gas. They had a quarter tank, but he didn't want to stop anywhere nearby in case someone knew the car or its owner.

"I think we can make it to Trenton, or at least much of the way with this old boat. Runs well."

"No," said Ted. "Won't be long before someone discovers the problem we left back there. When the police dispatcher checks again, they'll send somebody to check on him. You didn't leave any prints."

Audrey looked at him, "Of course not."

"No, of course you didn't," Ted said.

They got onto the connector without trouble. They noted a state police car on the far exit ramp; the state police were checking on people trying to exit. There wasn't any traffic at the moment. The bored officer on the other side glanced at them and then turned away.

"Only locals," mused Richard.

Ted said, "Mmm."

On mind link, Richard said to Audrey, *Aren't you going to mention the foreseeing intent thing you have developed?*

Not right away, she sent back, *I want to see if it develops any more and just what it does, how it operates. Also, I want a bit more time to go by to see if this is unique with me, or if you will develop it, too.*

I understand. I trust Ted implicitly, Richard linked, *but he did say a couple of days ago that we must include everyone in our suspicions. Still, I would withhold from him only for the reason that he might be compromised somehow and give away something important about us that could be to our sole advantage. Sounds to me we'd better whip up an agenda of our own by link.*

Agree, Audrey said shortly.

There followed a rapid-fire discussion that they only suspended when Ted said, "You two are very quiet. Can I assume a lot is going on?"

"Yes, Ted. We are improving our linkage and running a few test programs of our own to see what we've got."

"Interesting. Can I get into this?"

Audrey answered, "Ted, we have complete trust in you, but we both feel that we were teamed up to spearhead an operation you started that has implicit dangers. We could be compromised in unknown ways. Will you trust us to tell you what is appropriate to the three of us only? We will tell you everything we've just discussed if you request, but only if you request."

Ted thought on that for a long while.

Finally he said, "You're right. I've put all of the eggs in your basket. I don't like not being in the know, but I understand you. I will agree. I know you have a mind link. So far as I know that is all. I will want a full accounting after this mission, however."

"That's all there is, unless something else rears its ugly head, Ted. Thanks." Audrey didn't feel good lying to Ted, but he would believe her, and worst case, he couldn't give up what he didn't know.

"Don't thank me, you two, if I saw any hole or other danger in what you're asking, I would override and insist."

After a short silence, Audrey said, "We understand."

They approached the exit for Neptune City and passed it. Ted calculated how long they might travel in this stolen vehicle based on his knowledge of local police procedures. He told the others he didn't think it would be long before the sheriff would send someone, and it was safe to think that a car was already on its way.

"I think we'd better get off at the Candlewood exit and ditch this car. We can check a phone book for rental companies. Hopefully there's one near there. Otherwise there may be a bus running that will break the possible chain to this car, anyway."

"It's five miles ahead, Ted," said Richard, noting the sign for Candlewood and Freewood Acres ahead. He glanced at the gas gauge and noticed it was approaching empty.

So far their luck had held, but they knew all hell would break loose once they found the local constable in the culvert. No chance he wouldn't be found. That would cause a media flurry, even without somebody to blame although they could count on its being toned down with disaster stories all around. On the outside, the sheriff wouldn't know of the two locals until their wives got tired of waiting for their men to drag in for the night. By that time the three operatives should have disappeared completely, leaving a mystery for the sheriff's department in Neptune. But, they couldn't count on it.

At Candlewood they found a small shopping mall and parked in amongst the shopper's vehicles. There were no rental agencies in town, but they found a Greyhound stop down near the end of Main Street. And with a bus heading for Camden due at seven o'clock, only an hour from then, it would be perfect and just the break they needed. Audrey suggested they get out of their beach clothes, shorts and open neck polo shirts, and the men readily agreed. They found a small clothing shop on Main Street.

"We'll shop here, take our packages out and change over at the Mickey D across the way." Ted nodded in the direction.

First Richard and Audrey went in. Ted followed in three minutes and pretended not to know them. There was only one clerk on duty, but she managed to split her time between the two. Ted bought a light colored pair of slacks and a striped long sleeved shirt. The clerk boxed them up for Ted, and he paid cash and departed.

Audrey ostensibly shopped for Richard, but while waiting for him to come out of the dressing room, "accidentally" found a nice dress she thought Richard would like, and taking the sales lady into her confidence, she had the woman put it away for her. The saleslady wanted to talk about the big news, the tidal wave, and she was ready, but these yokels didn't seem to know about it, so she discreetly paid attention to business.

"He'll just love it! I know." She said in a high, slightly shrill voice.

Richard came out of the dressing room wearing a pair of dark, casual trousers, double pleated in front. He posed for Audrey.

"Oh, Ralphie, they look so good on ya." Audrey said, barely able to keep from laughing. "I saw a sheute ov'a here maybe you'd like."

She led "Ralphie" over to a shirt rack. "I think it'll fit those big, massive shoulders of yours, don't ya think?"

Audrey looked adoringly at him.

"Yeah, doll, ya got good taste." Richard said in a deep baritone.

Otherwise he had little to say. They completed their shopping. Richard paid cash as Ted had earlier. Audrey had the clerk give her, her package. Richard raised his eyebrows.

Audrey just said, "Lattuh, Ralphie, lattuh."

She grabbed his arm and they walked out. They repressed a chuckle as they imagined what the clerk must have thought of them and pictured her shaking her head. "It takes all kinds…"

Once outside Richard checked his watch and they hurried to MacDonald's. They found Ted sitting in the back section with a cup of coffee and a spread of food and drinks. They passed Ted without looking and headed for the bathrooms, changed quickly, storing their beach clothes in the bags. They would be useful later.

They slid into the booth with Ted and munched out. All three were very hungry and the Mickey "D" fare slid down fine. In low voices they told Ted about how they had put on an act for the clerk, and Audrey chewed her French fries noisily.

Ted laughed, "That wasn't necessary!"

"No...fun!"

"Yeah."

They finished quickly and left by the side door. They were pretty sure they hadn't been noticed above the normal notice all customers got. They made their way across the parking lot, jumped the low barrier and went through the lot next to it. Then they crossed the street and made their way back to a late running pharmacy. The sign above the door said, Greyhound Stop. Purchase tickets inside.

They got tickets to Camden and sat around until the bus arrived fifteen minutes late, no doubt due to shoreline problems. They got on and shortly left. The bus made a stop in Lakewood, then later in Lakehurst, and sped on to Camden. Once off they walked out into the nighttime city and lost themselves. No one they had talked to or purchased tickets from would likely remember them. They found a three-star hotel and put up for the night. They used altered ID's, but the clerk didn't notice or care. They opted for separate rooms this time, Ted by himself, the newlyweds in another room. They'd rested on the bus, but all agreed a nice bed was what the doctor ordered. Still, they joined Ted in his room and watched the eleven o'clock news.

The tidal wave and aftermath were the big stories. Severe damage all along the coast. All the little towns along the breakwater devastated. Ship Bottom wiped out entirely. Atlantic City shore area had moderate damage, but the casinos for the most part, were in business. Further south the damage seemed minimal. The north central Jersey shore got it worst. Boats left in the water were hit very hard. Marinas were a jumble of high value matchsticks.

Toward the end of the broadcast, they heard a brief mention about three murders in the shore town of Belmar. The police were looking for leads.

"Wish that hadn't happened," Ted said again.

"Nobody felt good about it, Ted."

"I know, I know. We trained you to kill," He shrugged, "Okay, gang, let's go over tomorrow's plan."

They would go to Baltimore, again by Greyhound, and then rent a car for the remaining journey to Churchton, Maryland. They felt safe now and they thought no one could guess their route. They had been scheduled to arrive at Churchton's dock at six p.m. and make their way to the safe house on foot. They would make it handily by land.

The safe house would be outside the village proper on a low hill in the town's most exclusive area. It was known to all in the area as the Captain Church house, the village named after this pre-revolutionary war man.

"I have a password that will allow you access to the house and grounds. I will have to disappear and report to Stoic. I will return within a day. If I do not, something bad has happened in the organization. You will proceed directly to International Fabrications head office and ask to speak to Manson Rettick. His personal secretary is Laura Baumert.

"She is a member of my organization. Manson Rettick is *not*! That's important. Once again, only Stoic knows this. She knows you're coming, but not when, and she won't have a clue about what you look like.

"When you see her, wink, and say, "Manson wishes to see us."

"She will recognize that as an oddity, because no one calls him Manson. She will then respond with a wink and you will know she understands you two are the special operatives she's been alerted to. If she does not wink, there's trouble nearby, and you should excuse yourselves and leave on some pretext. I don't care what you say, but get out of there.

"If all is well, Laura will see that you receive a proper introduction to Manson. She will arrange for you to be hired on as a husband/wife consulting team dealing with the advanced electronics used by the upper echelon. Stoic has set this up with Rettick. That's how you'll get almost instant access to the highest and most sensitive areas of InFab. Then you're on your own. Got it."

Audrey and Richard linked a message.

Audrey said to Ted, "We got it, but we have to say we're rather fond of you, so do come back."

"Just planning contingencies, guys. I've been out of contact with the organization for a week now. That's a long time."

"We get you," they said.

Ted looked sad and a bit worn, "Nearly time to move on."

"Well," Richard said as he stood, reached out and took Audrey's hands, pulling her from the comfortable chair, "Might as well live it up while we can. Audrey, your husband requests your presence in bed."

"I feel a massive headache coming on."

"I promise not to get near your head."

"Not even kissy, kissy? Maybe I'll take an aspirin to ward off the horrible thing."

"What horrible thing were you thinking of warding off?" he said innocently.

"Why, my headache, of course. What horrible thing were *you* thinking of?"

Ted spoke up, "Get out, you two. You're making an old guy jealous."

Audrey immediately looked contrite. She shot Richard a silent message.

He shot back his own. *Hey, girl, he married us.*

She countered. *Watch it, or I'll make it legal.*

Suits me fine, he said.

She smiled at him and then at Ted. Out loud she said, "Ted, we want to get married. I mean, really! Does that work for the plan?"

"Don't know why not. You are linked in a unique and special way. Is that what you want?"

"I don't know. Seems to me we are married in a truer sense of the word than any mortal marriage I can think of."

"True enough. Richard, what are your thoughts on the subject?"

"I don't think it would make a difference to me, but if Audrey thought it was the right thing, I wouldn't hesitate."

"Well, decide for yourselves. What is marriage anyway, if not a close union, a marriage of the minds? On that score, nobody anywhere has one up on you two."

Richard looked thoughtful, and then said to Audrey, "Ted is our witness. Audrey, will you marry me, to have and to hold, until death do us part?"

Audrey looked startled. It all came down to this, whether in a church, a grassy outdoor setting, by a lake, or in some ridiculously common place. Like jumping over your sword, any testimonial would do if the heart was in the right place.

"Wow! You get right to it, don't you Richard? Well, let me think for a second while I...that's a second. Okay! And I want to do this right, as you say. Richard, will you marry me likewise, to have and to hold, until death do us part?"

"I will," he said solemnly.

"Well, I will, too. Kiss me, honey." There followed a long silent interval of lip-lock while Ted looked on.

Finally, Ted stopped the ordeal with a wry smile and congratulations. "Duly noted by the official who thought this union a good one in the first place. Now, get out! *I* want some sleep tonight!

Richard and Audrey grinned at Ted and left for their room.

37

Stretch grabbed Johnny Quinn from the card room, took a pool car and headed out. They both wore dark casual slacks made of a slick, shiny material like gabardine. Quinn wore a red polo shirt with a wide white stripe front and back. He was a small man with kind of scrunched up features, all in the center of his face. His nose, his most prominent feature, showed heavy rosacea damage. T'was from the drink, he'd say. He had quick hands that seemed to be moving all the time. Johnny's sandy red hair and freckles gave him the classic Irish appearance and his bare arms were freckled and pink, the kind that only grudgingly tan.

The much taller Weasel wore a maroon polo shirt of solid blue. Deeply tanned, his hair slicked down and shiny, it made him look like a Vitalis ad. Odd, because Stretch, a good swimmer, only occasionally went swimming outside of his spelunking avocation, but he did get a lot of sun, nonetheless. The two had a Mutt and Jeff appearance together, but nobody better say anything when they were together. Quinn was obsessively sensitive to his height and had a mean temper to match his face.

At the gate, Mal gave them the extra set of keys for the Taurus and handed them an envelope.

"Registration and proof of ownership," he said.

Ray had suggested they take a mobile phone with them. They grabbed one and headed out. The trip at highway speed took just under an hour and a half. They had left at nine-thirty. Traffic wasn't heavy on the limited access highway and they made good time. The New Jersey coast might have been a mess, but Long Island had no problems.

Stretch wasn't much on talk. Quinn tried. For the most part he got grunts from his passenger. Finally he gave up and just paid attention to driving. They got to Babylon about eleven and stopped at a little diner to take a leak and grab some coffee. Then they headed to the Police Station.

The Desk Sergeant turned out to be the same one Ray had spoken to earlier. They cleared the release of the car with as little conversation as they could manage and got directions to the impound lot.

"Your employer is Nick Trafalgar," the Sergeant said.

"Yeah," said Stretch.

"Heard of him." The Sergeant gave the two a long look.

"Yeah?"

He looked like he was going to say something else, then decided against it. He busied himself with papers for a moment, then called to one of the men in the office, "Jake, take these two 'gentlemen' to impound and get them their car."

"Okay, Sarge." The officer grabbed a key off a rack and motioned for the two men to follow. Looking back, he said, "You got keys for it, don't you?"

"Not to worry," said Stretch.

He led them out to the lot in front and got into a cruiser.

"Follow me."

The impound lot turned out to be three blocks away, near the east edge of town. The cop pulled up beside the gate, got out without so much as looking at the men and opened the gate. Johnny Quinn spotted the Taurus about the same time as Stretch. They moved toward it. The town cop stayed by the gate.

Unhurriedly, Stretch moved to the car and walked around it. No damage to the eye.

"See anything?" he said to Quinn.

"Nah. Looks okay."

Stretch looked at the officer who seemed uncomfortable, maybe a little irritated and definitely impatient, and said, "Looks okay."

"All right, you guys take the car and beat it."

"You gettin' off shift? You in a hurry?"

"I'm not interested in smart mouth from you clowns, just get the car and beat it."

Stretch stared hard at the young cop. His eyes said, "I'm going to remember you, asshole." Leisurely he unlocked the car and got in. He turned the key. Quarter tank of gas. The Ford started right away.

"Nuttin' wrong," he said to Johnny, "I can't figure."

"Yeah," said Quinn.

Stretch made a decision. "Johnny, you take the other car back. I'm goin' down to the Park and nose around."

"Want me come, too? Two heads, ya know."

"Nah. I don't see nothin' here, but I'm going to look around anyway. Tell Ray to let Nick know I'll be back before night."

"Okay, Stretch, way you want it."

"Yeah, Johnny, way I want it. Leave me the phone."

"Right." Quinn went outside the gate, grabbed the cell and handed it to Stretch, got in his car and left.

With another withering look at the cop standing at the gate, Stretch drove off, heading south. As he drove away he looked in his rear view mirror. The cop flipped him a bird and then closed the impound gate.

Stretch laughed. He made a mental note to give the guy some pain next time he came through.

His route took him to the wide access road to Robert Moses State Park. It didn't take long before he saw the shore and ticket house. The Atlantic Ocean spread out in front of him. He stopped and paid the small admission, drove to the parking area, and locked up. He noted where all the man-made structures were and identified them in his mind. Then he walked the beach and the dunes for a few minutes before he went over to the guard shack.

"Hey!" The young man gazing out over the blue ocean on a backless stool started and then looked over at Stretch.

"Yo, man, can I help?"

"Looks pretty good from the tidal wave here," he said conversationally.

"Yeah, no prob here, mister. Couple extra feet, all at once. That's why the sand is smooth over halfway up the dunes. Coulda been a lot worse. Heard Jersey shore got shit on."

"Yeah, heard that, too."

Stretch looked out at the water. "Seafloor up any?" he asked.

"Calmed down by now."

"So no damage, then?"

"None to speak of. Rowboat got taken last night. Probably kids prank."

Stretch thought how few years separated this kid from the ones he was obviously referring to. Had something to do with a job and responsibility, he thought. He smiled a little. He had a job, too, but this kid would run for the hills if he had any idea what Stretch did. That made him smile bigger.

He thought about the rowboat. Maybe a kids prank, maybe not. He felt, sensed, it coulda had something to do with Bernie and Mikey.

"Ha-ha! So when did that happen?"

"Who knows? Overnight guard found the broken chain at first light on his last round. About five-thirty, I figure. Then he discovered the break in the equipment shack and got on the horn. It's happened before. Boats back already. We always get 'em back."

"Yeah, kids," he nodded sympathetically. "So anybody out on the water last night?"

"Why you interested, mister?" The young guard looked at Stretch with more curiosity now.

"Oh, nothin'. I been here before," he lied, "seen sailboats out on the water. Just wondered. This is a good place."

"Yeah, not bad. Nobody said anything to me about boats out last night."

"Just wondered. So how long you on?" he smiled.

"Till three, then the Soop takes over until the night guy gets back at eight."

"Hey, good talkin'. I'm goin' down to the water. Can't stay long for now. Workin', you know. I'll probly come back after work for a swim. Kinda checkin' out damage from the wave for now. Maybe we'll catch up again."

"Sure, Mister. I'm Duke."

"Reggie. Good tuh meet yuh."

"Okay, Reggie, have a good one."

"You, too, man." Stretch went on, angling away from the rowboat area. He'd come back to that after he made it look good for the kid. He went down to the water. Still no sailboats in sight. Not usual, but considering what happened across the bay...eh?

He wandered for ten minutes, looking around. Just as he turned to leave, he caught a glint of dark metal in amongst the saw grass. He looked furtively around, but nobody was paying attention to him. He dug the metal out of the sand, scratching his hand on a local bramble.

"Shit!" A jack handle! No rust on it, either.

He ignored the blood starting to bead out of the scratch. I'll look funny carrying this off the beach, he thought. He grabbed a handful of sand and rubbed off any print he might have left on it, then tossed it back further in the weeds and grass. He headed back past the rowboat cache.

The first boat in line showed signs of the screws holding the attachment plate having been ripped out. Probably the one, he thought, and it looked like he'd just tossed away the instrument somebody used on it. He'd bet on it! He looked it over carefully, but saw nothing else odd about the rowboat. He bet the oars were back in the temporarily repaired equipment shack. He looked at it thoughtfully and made a decision.

Weasel left the park hurriedly, glancing at his watch just as he saw the kid look away from his gaze seaward, and wave at him. The kid would think he'd overstayed himself and had to get back to work. Good.

He went to his car and opened the trunk. No jack handle. Everything else there. Stretch got in and left the park. At the ticket gate, he stopped and told the vaguely pretty young woman in a sleeveless state park uniform that he'd just stopped to check out the park because of the tidal wave, but that he'd like to come back after work to swim. He wondered if he could get back in free later, since he had paid once today already.

"When do you get off work, sir?" she asked.

"Six," he said.

"I'm on until we close at eight," she told him, "I'll remember you. I'll let you in."

"Hey, that's great. Thanks." He gave her a big smile and drove on, making the turn onto the Ocean Parkway toward Jones beach, driving aimlessly. He pulled off in Oakbeach and found a seafood restaurant, "The Best Catch". His stomach started to growl. He'd eat there, but first…

He dialed the mansion. Tony was spelling Ray for his lunch hour. "Tony, Stretch. Let me talk to the boss."

"Hang on, Stretch." Long pause. Nick came on.

"What?"

"Boss, its Stretch. We got the car and I'm nosin' around down here at Moses State Park. I think I got somethin'. It's not much, but I want to stay until the supervisor comes on at five and ask him some questions."

"What have you got, Stretch?"

"Well, I talked with one of the park police for a few. I found out somebody took a rowboat last night. I'm sure it was Bernie and Mikey. Way I figured it; they wouldn't have stopped at the park unless Bernie had a hunch he was playin'. I know he was burnin' inside for losin' the bitch. They found our car right outside the gate. And guess what I found in the saw grass on the beach?"

"Don't make me guess, Stretch."

"Yeah. Well, it was a jack handle. I checked the trunk and the tire's in there. The jack handle's missing. Bernie and Mikey took the rowboat, and there's only one reason he would do that."

"Go on."

"There had to be a sailboat off the coast here last night; had to be! He musta thought it was the one."

"What do you propose?"

"The Super comes on at five. I figure he questioned the night man pretty good, and it would about clinch it if he remembers the night guy mentioning a sailboat off the coast, put up for the night, and Bernie leaves his car here."

"Where does that lead, Stretch?" the Weasel had Nicks interest now.

"If Bernie was right, the woman'd be makin' for the City or the Jersey shore. I don't think the City. She wouldn't know what we got around the docks, and I don't think she'd chance it. It's the Jersey shore, then. It would prove she's alive and runnin'. If I get real lucky, maybe I can get even more."

"What do you mean?"

"I don't know now, boss, but I got a feelin'. Okay, boss?"

After a short pause, Nick said, "Yeah. Go ahead. Dig what you can. Call me."

"Will do, boss," Stretch disconnected.

Nick sat in his study thinking. Stretch seems to be outdoing himself today, he thought. Up and comers are good. Maybe...

He tabled the thought, but it would come up again. Stretch might bear a little extra watching. Malfo had started to piss him off lately.

38

The Weasel went into the restaurant and spent an hour eating and mulling. He had deliberately parked on the other side of the lot as far from the restaurant as he could. The large, unpaved parking lot angled back some ways. He wasn't bothering anybody, and the pace of life in Oakbeach was slow, so he decided to nap until four p.m. He set his alarm watch, got in, cracked the windows four inches, put the drivers seat down as flat as it would go and soon drifted off.

At four his alarm woke him. He sat up, disoriented. When the fuzz cleared he opened the drivers door. The interior of the car had heated up despite the open windows in the still air and he was covered in sweat. He decided he'd better go shopping. The stores would still be open on the shoreline. Right now he looked out of place, not like someone who wanted a relaxing swim. He put his seat upright and fussed with his hair until it didn't look like he'd been sleeping on it.

He drove out the driveway and turned left toward the main part of Oakbeach. Stretch found a place on the street, parked and got out. He saw a small clothing store halfway down the strip. The area had that weather-beaten look of most shore towns. Most people called it nostalgic. He thought it could use a good paint job.

He walked down the lazy main street and went in. Racks of clothing greeted him, taking up the majority of space and making the aisles too narrow. He smiled at the owner's obvious intent in making his stock visible in too small a place. The sales clerk came over right away. Only the two of them were in the store. Before him he saw a pretty girl, mature, probably twenty-eight or twenty-nine, he guessed. She had a bright smile and lots of tan.

"Welcome to the Oakbeach Swimtank, sir. Can I help you?" She tried not to look bored, but Stretch was accustomed to looking people over and noted it as the first thing about her.

"Yeah. Sure. I want to buy a bathing suit." He looked around. There were some bright, loose-fitting beach shirts on a rack nearby.

"Tell you what. I want to look around. I'll give you a holler, okay?"

"Sure." The woman retired behind the counter.

Stretch took his time, picking colors and sizes. Then he went to the other side of the store and picked out a pair of beach loafers. Finally he called over to the girl.

"I'm about ready, miss."

She came right over. He'd picked out not-too-colorful, but still bright beach trunks and matching loose button up shirt in yellows and reds and told the girl he thought that would do, but could he try it all on?

"Of course, sir. The dressing room is over there." She pointed to a curtain.

"Thanks." The woman returned to the counter. He looked her over with more than a little interest, now. She was well rounded, a bit fuller than hit his taste, but shapely, with muscular, yet very feminine legs. She was wearing a yellow cotton dress cut above the knees. There was some kind of yellow flower in her hair. To his mind, she had other, even more appealing attributes. Why was it that at first impression he felt she wasn't very much aware of them? He liked that kind of innocence. It excited him.

He entered the dressing room and put on the new beach clothes. Good fit first time around. Well, he knew his sizes. He slicked his hair in the mirror. He looked himself over and decided that even with a thin face, he looked attractive.

I'm thirty-four, and he thought, why not?

When he left the fitting room, he carried his pants and shirt in his hand and went to the counter. The girl gave him a bright smile and he said. "I'll take all of this. Fits good! I'm going out to claim some beach time. I'd like to wear my purchases out of the store. Would you cut the tags off for me?

"How are you paying for the purchases, sir, cash or credit card?" Evidently she wasn't asked to cut peoples tags off while they wore the outfits very often.

Stretch caught the nuance. "Oh, is it not done, here? I'm not from here. I'm sorry. Let me go and change back."

The girl fed into his feigned distress. "Oh, no, sir. I'm sure it'll be all right. But I would like to complete the transaction before cutting tags."

"Oh. Silly of me." He took out a wad of twenties and let her "accidentally" see several hundreds mixed in. He set them all on the counter and pretended to look through the pockets for his license.

"That won't be necessary, sir."

"Call me Stretch. Everyone else does." He smiled a big smile and the girl colored slightly.

"I'm Barbara," she said.

"Well, Barbara, you're a very pretty girl." He said it casually, while counting out bills. No doubt this was by far the largest sale of the day, and he could almost see her calculating the commission.

"Well, thank you."

He said no more and pretended that he was only interested in the sale. She gave him his change and closed the register.

"May I give you a bag to carry your other clothes in?"

"That would be great."

Barbara reached under the counter and came up with a shiny plastic bag with shopping handles. "This is the largest size we have. It should do it."

"You bet."

She put the clothes in the bag, and then got a pair of scissors from under the counter. She came around and paid attention to cutting the tags carefully. When she got to his neck she asked him to lean over the counter, she couldn't reach high enough.

"Six-two, Barbara."

She laughed, "They grow 'em tall where you come from."

"Funny," he said, "that my four brothers and three sisters are all your height. Guess they needed me for a lamp post."

He laughed good-naturedly, and she laughed with him. "My goodness, eight in your family?"

"Yup!" he lied. "You're five-six, right?"

"Yes, I am."

"I'm pretty good guessing like that. Yup, they're all of them, to the last one, five-six. Always amazed me. Maybe they found me on their doorstep and didn't have the heart to tell me."

Barbara laughed again. "You have a nice sense of humor, Stretch."

Stretch decided that it was time to go. One more thing! He reached out and shook her hand. He didn't press hard, just firmly. "Nice to meet you. Really nice."

"Thank you. Nice to meet you, too."

It was pretty easy to see how much he'd flattered her. Now to leave, but with a twist. Stretch picked up the bag with his parcel of old clothes and went out the door. The heat hit him like a wall. He turned immediately as if he'd forgotten something, and came back through the door. Barbara still looked at him with a slight smile on her face.

"Barbara," he said, "I'm here in the area only for a couple of days, and I've got to get back to Greenwich where I live, but I'm all alone here."

He hesitated, as if he knew he'd overstepped his bounds and then blurted out, "I wonder if, well, if you're not doing anything tonight, would you let me take you to dinner? I don't want to eat alone. I do it too much of the time."

Barbara looked shocked, but he could see her trying to decide if she could chance going to dinner with a funny, total stranger. She had already noted that he had no gold band on his left ring finger, but that didn't mean much, these days.

"Oh dear, I don't normally go out. I don't know what to say." She looked at this thin faced man, kind of attractive in a plain sort of way, yet all the same, he seemed dynamic, an action kind of guy.

"It would mean a great deal to me. But if you say no, then I will understand. After all, you don't know me at all, and if I were you, I'd be careful, too."

That seemed to decide her. Tell them you want them, then tell 'em they'd better not. Gets them all the time. How to back into a trusting relationship through denial. He almost laughed while he watched the decision form, but he kept his face looking hopeful.

"Well, Stretch, if you don't keep me out too late, I'd like to go to dinner with you."

"That's great. No, I won't keep you out late. Let's pick a really nice place. I can afford it. Where would you like to go?"

"Well, how about The Conch Tree. It's kind of expensive, but I've always wanted to go there."

He smiled. "The Conch Tree, it is. Uh, where is it?"

"Over in Fair Harbor, on the shore road from Robert Moses State Park. Maybe twenty minutes from here."

"When do you get off work?"

"At five, but I'll have to go home and change. It's dressy."

"No problem. Would you like me to pick you up, or do you want to meet somewhere?"

She looked troubled, but then brightened. "I'll meet you at The Conch Tree at seven, all right? I'll draw you a map. Not very hard to get to from here. The restaurant is right on the beach. It's really beautiful and elegant there."

"Sounds terrific! Okay, then, I'm going to go down to the Moses swim area, kinda promised myself, but I'll be there, don't you worry."

"Oh, that's excellent. It's less than ten minutes from the Park."

Her face clouded. "I was thinking you'll need a dinner jacket. Do you have one?"

"No."

"The clothes you came in with, they're fine. The place is swank, but if you didn't bring one, I think they'll put you in one at the door, I'm sure I heard that."

"Okay."

Barbara looked so pleased, he thought. This was going to be a better than average night, he promised himself. Maybe he wouldn't do her at all. Maybe...

Stretch left a second time, turned and waved briefly, a brightly transformed man.

"Mr. Beachman," he thought giddily.

After leaving the shop, Stretch's thought processes returned to normal sleaze. Suddenly he remembered he'd told Tony to let Nick know he'd be back by evening, and it was pretty clear he wouldn't. What could he say to Nick? Nick was smart. He couldn't tell him he'd found some snatch for the night. As he got back into the car, he figured he'd look into the Moses Park Supervisor's recollections before he chose how to approach the issue.

Decided, he drove off.

39

In the morning around ten, Ted called the honeymooner's room. He had to wait longer than he'd thought.

When Audrey finally picked up, Ted said, "You two going to sleep all day?"

"No, Ted," she said, "I had enough trouble with the big lug and I didn't think to take the phone into the bed with us."

"Ha-ha. Audrey, you guys hungry? I think we can still get breakfast downstairs, if you want."

"Lemme see." Ted heard Audrey in the distance asking Richard if he felt like being a bear for food. He heard a faint roar. Audrey came back to the phone.

"He wants me back in bed. Says there's an experiment he wants to try. We'll meet you in the restaurant in twenty minutes, okay?"

In the distance, Ted heard, "No experiments. Get dressed. We're going to breakfast with Ted."

Faintly, Ted heard "Killjoy!" and laughed.

"Meet you there." He hung up.

True to her word, Audrey arrived looking bright and natural, followed by Richard, who looked a little disheveled, but rather happy.

Audrey moved to her chair and stood, waiting for Richard to seat her. Richard caught the nuance and couldn't help saying, "Oh no, it begins already!"

Audrey simpered. "Aren't I worth it?"

"Uh, well..."

"I don't recall hearing any doubt in your voice earlier."

"I get a strong feeling that it's not about winning. It's more about how bad you're losing."

"And don't you forget it."

"C'mon gang," Ted broke in, "Let's eat."

They sat. They spoke in quiet tones about what had come down. Nobody in the group felt there was the slightest chance Nick Trafalgar or any of his hired scum could get to them now, but they wouldn't leave it to chance.

At eleven, they checked out, disposing of clothing they wouldn't need. For the time being, they'd travel light.

The three looked for all the world like everyone else in New Jersey. They weren't actually due at the safe house until six p.m., so they would use the day to catch up on current events and waste some time. They bought a Wall Street Journal at a cigar store near the hotel entrance. At the Greyhound station they bought tickets on the one o'clock bus to Baltimore. Ted called ahead for a rental car.

They planned to arrive in Baltimore at four, pick up the rental and drive the hour and a half to Churchton. They would stop on the outskirts and check things out. Elements of Stoic's organization should not overlap one another. They would arrive at the appointed hour without a stir.

They spent their free hours in local stores looking at merchandise. They picked up a couple of things. When they arrived at the bus station and claimed their tickets, the TV above the ticket window said "on time." Another tribute to the healing power of a big country after a disaster.

They sat separately and arrived without incident. From Baltimore center the drive to Churchton took them through Annapolis. They picked up route 214 and later, route 468. They wended their way south along western Chesapeake Bay, a pleasant ride.

Audrey and Richard found Churchton a beautiful, picturesque small town with a long history. Visible evidence of change was everywhere. The pressure of living near Washington, and Baltimore to a lesser extent, saw Churchton building into the countryside from its ancient core with nice middle-class homes. Most were large, tasteful and well cared for. Churchton overlooked a Bay rife with shipping. A bedroom town for most purposes, many of Washington's elite lived there.

The most prominent home in all of Churchton belonged to a direct descendent of Delutius Church, a seafaring man who had settled on this spot two hundred and twenty years ago. He obtained a charter from the English king and positioned his estate to command a spectacular view of the bay. On the long, sloping hill that eventually disappeared into tidal foam where the bay met land, he had his slaves clear four hundred acres.

The sea accounted for the biggest part of the area's food supply in those days, and with general lawlessness and pirate trouble to his shipping, Church imported workers whom he allowed to live on land surrounding the spot where he built his mansion, so long as they would answer the call to fight when necessary. He employed them in his fishing fleets and to run his estate and his slaves; it made the perfect set up and he prospered. Later, when he freed some of his slaves, he gave them small parcels of lower surrounding land and offered them sharecrop work to stay.

Church was smart. He'd created a buffer between his estate and the sea from which almost any danger that could hurt him could be expected. Yet, as a solitary man, when he began to allow others to build below his estate, to preserve his almost fanatic need for privacy, he had two hundred of these acres walled in stone. Thus it stood today.

The house, also of the same stone, not quite a castle, but an unusual, one-of-a-kind edifice, stood unique on the hill. It combined the drafty coolness of European castles with the down home woodsy comfort of the frontier, which wasn't at all far away in those days. European and frontier influences were in stark contrast, yet somehow he managed to make them work together.

Originally the castle mansion comprised eight rooms. They were huge and ostentatious for the time. Later two ells were attached, adding twelve additional rooms. Now it was a unique, twenty-room mansion draped in mystery and folklore. Wendell Nutting, Delutius Church's direct ancestor currently owned the mansion. Interestingly, he was also a silent partner in International Fabrications, Inc. through a holding company.

Unbelievably safe from the physical standpoint, massive, eight-foot stonewalls surrounded the property. The solid stone mansion and its human security, augmented with absolutely state of the art electronics, made it complete. More a fortress than a simple dwelling, only a handful of people knew it. Finally, below the captivatingly interesting structure above ground, a labyrinth of tunnels led to unexpected, hidden places within the growing town below as it crept silently around the edges of the estate.

Audrey looked it over. The organization's got lots of money or lots of friends, probably both, she thought. She didn't see a single weed in the manicured lawn. She searched for one; she really tried. She stifled an urge to kick off her shoes and run in the grass like she did as a child, grasping and pulling tufts lightly with her experienced and agile toes. She threw Richard the image.

Richard glanced at her and smiled. *Might like to try that myself, later on*, he projected. The kid in him ran quite close to the surface at times.

At six on the dot, Ted rang the gate bell. An ethereal voice, tinny, without character, but probably male, said, "Yes? May I help you?"

"Yes. Thank you. I'm here to make a delivery from The House of Weeds."

There was a pause, and then, "Enter now!"

Ted pushed the metal gate strongly. It opened and they passed through. The gate closed quickly and locked with a loud click, like a bolt being shot home. Ted walked rapidly up the sidewalk adjacent to the cobblestone road toward the building in the distance. Audrey felt they were being watched. It came to her in an extrasensory way. No reason for it, but she knew. She said nothing and acted normally.

We're being watched by electronics. Richard said on the link. Audrey had not sent him any message.

A new ability, Richard?

Yeah. It's like fuzzy, not really a color, but it feels like green. You got anything like that?

I knew it, but I only felt it. You can see it?

Yes. It seems to be area specific; that is, I can kind of tell where the units are and how they are wired. The brightest point would be the unit, itself.

Great! Have you caught the, uh, intent thing I've got, yet?
No. Haven't seen that one.
I'm beginning to wonder if our physiology is dictating what is enhanced and what is not?
Could be, like, who knows?
Wonder what's next?
Stay tuned. Shame we can't tell Ted.
I know, but it's best for now.

Ted had reached the main door to the mansion with Richard and Audrey close on his heels. As he reached for the door, it opened. A massive black man stood there in dark, baggy pants tied with what looked like a sash chord. He had on a long sleeved white shirt with the sleeves rolled up, which showed massive muscles as far as his elbows. He had to be at least seven feet tall, and broke the scales over three hundred and fifty pounds. He looked extremely fit.

Richard looked up at him. "Always somebody, isn't there?"

The giant stood silent. Ted looked at him.

"Gorgonzola," he said.

"Welcome," the giant said, and grinned. "You guys just can't say it right, can you?"

Ted smiled, "I tried."

"It's Gorzongala." He laughed uproariously, and waived them in.

They entered a dark interior entranceway, a foyer of sorts, large, with high ceiling and oddments placed along the walls. An old-fashioned umbrella stand stood near the door. Next to that sat a huge blue Ming Vase on a short stand. Audrey wondered about its placement, but did not doubt its authenticity. The surrounding walls were massive, intricately carved, clearly crafted in a disappeared age. The foyer extended twenty feet inside the front door, and led two steps up to a carved glass doorway. Both doors were closed.

"I am Kunta Kintay." He laughed again, "No, I'm Clarence. Pay me no mind. You transients are the only fun I have around here."

All three laughed.

Richard said, "Want to trade places?"

"Nah, I'm just having fun. This is the best job I ever had. Mr. Nutting lets me get away with a lot, but I'd die for him, so I guess it evens out."

"Nice to meet you," Richard said, "Glad I don't have to fight you as entrance fee."

Clarence laughed again, a deep belly laugh, harmless and telling. "Come, meet the master of the house."

He led them into a huge living room filled with ancient horsehair furniture, predominately red, in what appeared to be new condition and tastefully arranged to take advantage of the room dimensions. Beyond it they went into a hallway that led to the north wing. The guests tried to note everything as they passed through. They would compare notes later.

40

It seemed like only a few minutes later that Stretch entered the Robert Moses State Park main gate again. He drove up to the ticket taker. The same girl was taking tickets in the booth.

"My, how you have changed." She said, all blue eyes and golden smile.

"I'm a chameleon," he said good-naturedly.

She laughed.

"Go ahead," she said. He drove through.

At the parking lot he found a spot in amongst the parked cars, got out and locked up, noting the position of his car in the lot. Stretch made his way to the beach. His waterproof spelunking watch said five thirty-five. Good timing. The supervisor would be settled in and accessible.

After passing through the sandy, well-trod narrow approach portal, the whole beach area widened out. Inevitable tufts of hardy saw grass struggled to grow on either side. He thought it was so "northeast seashore," such a common look. Beyond the seawall, the barbed grasses and pricking thistles with their pretty pink and purple flowers made the long stretch of dunes patently inhospitable.

Stretch moved to his right as the expanse of the Atlantic opened out, heading for the little guard shack. The door was open and he saw no one. As he arrived, a man about Stretch's own age, deeply tanned and rugged looking appeared from around the end of the shack.

The man looked at Stretch and said, "Hi. Need some help?"

"Uh, yeah," Stretch answered, "I'm trying to find out if my employer's sailboat might have been off the beach area yesterday. You the supervisor?"

"That's me."

"He hasn't called in, and he usually does once a day, every day, even on vacation. We were worried because of the tidal wave, and my supervisor asked me to scout the Fire Island preserve as far down as I could. We knew he was headed west off the coast. Tryin' to pick up his trail."

"How can I help?"

"Well, I stopped by earlier and the young fella on duty told me the guy on last night would probably remember anyone who parked out for the night. He also told me one of the rowboats had been taken. I figgered maybe you questioned him about it and maybe... Well, I'm just tryin' to be thorough."

"I see. Well, there was a boat off the park just beyond the breakers. Three people on board. I had to come in this morning awhile because of the rowboat and the break-in to the oar lockers. I went out in the powerboat to see if they had heard or seen anything last night. They hadn't."

Stretch's mind worked furiously. *Three people. I thought it was just the bitch. That's interesting.*

He smiled at the park supervisor. "You said three?"

"Yeah, three. Why?"

"My super told me the big boss was traveling light. I mean, by himself. What they look like? He might've picked up clients to wine and dine. He's done that before without telling us grunts."

"Guy in his late forties, I'd guess. Other two younger, maybe late twenties or around my age. I'm thirty-one. Very pretty redhead, more auburn, I'd say. Raised my temperature some, I'm here to tell. The guy was big, good-looking lout, wouldn't want to fuck with him, and I'm in pretty good shape. Didn't look mean, just capable. What kind of business you in, mister?"

Stretch had to think fast again. "It's a, uh, dating service. Compatibility Partners. Very fast growing. You heard of us?"

"No, not really, but I'm single. Maybe I'll look you up. Got a card?"

Oh, shit, Stretch thought, what now? Then he said, "Oh, yeah, not on me. Look, I'm goin' for a swim, now I'm here. How about I give the girl at the ticket booth my card for you when I leave. They're in the car."

"Yeah. Super! Thanks," he winked at Stretch and laughed, "You never know."

"Nope. You never know." Stretch said, "I'm goin' swimmin'. See yuh."

"Okay, man, take care."

Stretch left and moved down a largely empty beach and dropped his stuff on the sand. A lot to think about. So there were three of them. Who were the two guys? One forties, the other maybe thirty? He didn't dare ask too many questions back there.

I'll stop by after I think this out and get some more, he mused. He looked at his watch again. Five of six. He ran into the water, diving just before the shock of the chill water on his legs hit him. He numbed up quickly; best way, he thought. When he came up he stroked strongly out toward sea. Eastern Cuba was the next landmass south, a long, long way from here.

As he worked, his body compensated for the chill, and soon he felt good, comfortable. After two minutes of intense effort he stopped, and treading water, turned and looked around. He'd told Bernie he didn't cotton to the swim thing, and he didn't, really, but he enjoyed it today. He'd swum well beyond the buoys marking the edge of the controlled swimming area. He knew that was for kids, but there were few around at this time of day. Most of the beach mom's had packed up their kids and headed for home.

He didn't figure the lifeguard on duty would bother with him, and he was right. He let his thoughts come. Stretch had no description of the girl. Bernie had said she was striking, beautiful, a real hot number, and also a blonde. What else did he say? He told her she had blue eyes, a perfect face, classic beauty, very shapely. The park supervisor said much the same thing about this babe. But he said this woman's hair was auburn. Hey, they all color their hair. If she was the same one—Stretch thought it a bit of a long shot—except for what Bernie must have been thinking, because the stupid Wop never came back from who knows where and he'd left his company car intact, locked and unmolested just outside of Robert Moses State Park's beach entrance.

One thing Stretch knew for sure. Bernie feared Nick. He woulda called. Okay, now the others. A forties guy and a younger gorilla. Stretch flipped over in the gentle waves and started back using a lazy backstroke. It brought him slowly nearer shore. After the first few strokes his body went on automatic and his mind resumed his analysis.

The older guy...the older guy might be a boss. Maybe he could tell Nick a bunch of stuff. If I get anywhere with this, he thought, I wonder if maybe Malfo might have something to worry about. He laughed into the air, sobering immediately. I got to get a description of each person, much as the super on the beach can remember.

After a few minutes, Stretch felt a difference in the waves and knew he'd come near to shore again. He turned over, felt for the bottom and found himself in four feet of water. With the tide out and the sound of the muted breakers barely registering in his mind, he turned his back on the ocean and wandered in to shore. There he walked a bit to dry and then grabbed his stuff and headed for the guard shack again.

"Hey!"

"Hey."

"Hi. I was thinkin', we must have a file on the two the boss picked up. I should call Carl at the office and tell him Mr. Hinkley grabbed another couple. He'll be real pleased that we're on top of things when he's away. Could you describe them to me? I can pass it on." Stretch turned on his friendly charm.

"Well, best I can. I could describe the girl all day long. Sight of her made it tough to walk for a while when I got back on sand if you know what I mean?"

Stretch groaned inwardly, but laughed out loud. "Yeah, know what you mean. All them hormones, eh?"

"Yeah, hormones!"

Stretch never got the guy's name, so he simply said, "Okay, buddy, anyway, so go ahead."

"The girl was a real looker, like I said, red hair, blue eyes, probably five-six, five-seven. All female, but a lot under it, too. She didn't move around much, but she looked at me, and that lady's got a lot upstairs, I think. She wasn't a bimbo."

He stopped, apparently relishing the morning view in his mind.

"Yeah, yeah?" Stretch said. He was getting a little impatient. "The boss I know, but the other guy?"

Maybe he'd take a chance later getting more on the forties guy, but at least he could get some impression on the big guy. "How about the other guy?"

The super started to look embarrassed. "A big guy, that's all. Dark hair I remember, but you know, I'm not into guys and the girl pretty much had my full attention. The guy was big, looked powerful, and as I said, good looking, moderately tanned, I don't know, just a big guy."

"Okay, okay, what the boat look like?"

The park supervisor started to look suspicious. "You don't know the boat?"

"The boss is successful, he's got two. Carl didn't tell me which one."

"Oh, I see. I remember the name, Maiden Voyage I. The sail was a cream color with a big "R" painted on it, and the hull was maroon. Sweet looking boat."

"Okay, I know the one. Thirty-footer, right? Ten-foot beam. Polished mahogany deck." He took a chance.

"Yeah, that's right."

"Look, thanks. I appreciate. I'll call in on the car phone when I get changed." Stretch covered his confusion well. He was sure this boat was the Lucky Lady", even though it was dark blue with a white sail when he saw it in the harbor during the party. He decided not to ask any more questions about the forties guy. Least he was thinking on his feet.

"Sure."

"Well, just wanted to get wet. It was good. You got a nice beach here, buddy."

"Name's Luke. Have a good one."

"Yeah, you too, Luke."

Stretch turned on his heel and left. Once out of sight, he checked his watch. Now six-twenty. With The Conch Tree about ten minutes away, Stretch had just enough time to change and slick down for his date. And enough time to give Nick a call. Perfect!

He went back to the car and got out his earlier outfit. Nobody was about, so he changed beside the car. He combed out his stringy hair, checked himself over and picked up the phone.

41

Tony picked up the incoming call in two rings.

"Tony, Stretch. Boss available?"

"He's got Stone in with him right now. This important?"

"Ring him up and see if he wants to take a break for a minute. I'm on a trail."

"Okay, Stretch." He rang Nick. Still in his study about nine hours now, Tony figured. Something going on, he thought, but Nick talked to you when he wanted, and you talked to him when he wanted.

"Yeah, Tony," Nick came on.

"Stretch on the cell phone, Nick."

"Okay, I'll take it. Stone, a minute..."

"Sure, Nick." The Weasel could barely hear him in the background.

"Stretch, how you making out?"

"Pretty good. Got some info from the super, as I said. Guess what? There are three of them."

"Tell me."

"Forties guy, and two younger, the girl, and a big muscular gorilla. The girl matches the description of the bitch who was at your party all the way, but she's a redhead now."

"No shit?"

"No shit, Nick. Gotta be the same broad."

"Why?"

"Listen, Nick, I thought this out a lot before I called you. The timing is perfect for the boat to be at the State Park down here. It was the only one layin' out that night. The girl fits the description, except for the hair. That's easy to change. The sailboat is the same size, same hull design, same sail design, but it's maroon now and the sail's cream color, with a big "R" on it.

"Doesn't sound like the same boat to me, Stretch."

"I feel it, boss. You know I got some good hunches before. I got this one. I feel it! This is bigger than maybe you thought. These people went to a lot of pain not to be found. But I got this sixth sense about it. Bernie like vanished. Right here! Dorneti, too. Boss, I don't think they're hitchhikin' back. I think they're dead. I think Bernie and Mikey are dead. I think there's a lot more goin' down than maybe you thought."

Nick interrupted Stretch. "Lemme think a sec."

Stretch got quiet while the boss took some time. He held a couple of minutes. Finally Nick came back on.

"Stretch."

"Yeah, Nick."

"Keep nosing around. Come up with something. Sniff it out. You surprise me. This kind of surprise I like. Call me tomorrow. You want me to send you one of the boys?"

"No, Nick. I'm okay. If it gets hotter where I'm sittin', I'll let you know. Right now I'm okay."

"All right, Stretch. Good work. Tomorrow."

"Yeah." Click.

And yeah, he thought. I got me a night off with a nice healthy frail. He checked his watch. Time to drive over to The Conch Tree Restaurant. He felt good two ways. Got a date, that's rare, and the boss is noticin' him big time. And that never happened before!

Eight minutes later he drove into the restaurant parking lot followed by two other cars. He noticed a lot of big, expensive cars already in the lot. Stretch parked the Ford behind the restaurant in one of the few remaining spaces. Busy restaurant means good food, he thought. He looked around to see if he could find Barbara. Nowhere in sight. He got out, locked up and went to the awning that led to the front entrance.

She stood to the side of the front entrance. She looked terrific. Evidently she had some nice clothes, because she'd dressed to the nines. For him, he mused. It made him feel good, especially after his call to Nick. She wore a lacy white thing over a silky blue dress. Her arms were bare, but the dress itself accentuated the positive and he liked what he saw. Black web pumps and black patent leather high heels completed the outfit. Gave a nice appearance to those legs. It made Stretch feel a little plain, but he had no time to think about it. She gave him a brilliant smile.

"Wow!" he said. "You look really nice, Barbara."

"Thank you, sir," she replied. She gave him her arm and they marched through the high oak double doors.

The hostess stood behind a tall podium of sorts. She smiled when they stopped in front of her.

"Attire is formal, sir," she said, "What is your jacket size?"

"Forty-four long, ma'am."

The hostess motioned and a young man hastened over. "Please bring our guest a forty-four long, John."

The man looked at Stretch and said, "I'll be a moment, sir."

Nice manners, classy place, thought Stretch. Not in my league, but I can fake it.

The coatroom had a separate section in which they kept formal attire, many sizes for the few who came unprepared. They must do a bang-up business for them to keep all this stuff handy for guests. John came back quickly and helped Stretch into the dark gray striped jacket. Ha-ha—perfect fit! Stretch reflected that they'd have to be really prepared, to enforce a rule like that, and they were. Made him feel like a million bucks.

The hostess led the two to a table near a large window overlooking the ocean. Candelabra style lights adorned the ceiling, keeping the light low and intimate. The sun shone above the horizon through puffy, late day clouds, making them dark, without color. She placed two menus in front of Barbara and Stretch and murmured pleasantly that their waiter for this evening would be Harvey, who would be with them shortly. Then she retired to her podium.

Stretch looked his date over, smiled and then looked the restaurant over.

"Quite a place, Barbara."

"I know. I always wanted to come here. There are some very famous people who frequent this restaurant. I heard that the governor eats here when he's down this way from Albany, and famous musicians and actors come here all the time. Isn't that wonderful?"

Stretch tried to eyeball some of the nearby guests, but saw no one he recognized from the media or from any of the Broadway shows he had seen.

Barbara hesitated and then said, "Oh Stretch! I hope you don't think I'm taking advantage of you, going to a place like this."

"Not to worry. I can afford it and now that we're here, I'm glad you picked it. I feel like a million in this." Stretch brushed his knuckles several times across the lapel of his borrowed, high quality dinner jacket and Barbara laughed.

The waiter appeared, apologizing for the wait, although there had been none. He placed fine linen napkins on their laps, the lady first. Then he stood tall and asked if they would like a cocktail at this time.

Stretch looked at Barbara for her lead, and nodded. She said she'd like a glass of good white wine. Did they have Kendall-Jackson?

"No, Ma'am. But we specialize in good French wines. May I choose for you?"

"Okay."

"I suggest Auxey Duresses Les Clous Leroy 1999. It is our house wine, but it is a very nice vintage. It does not have the bouquet of the American wine, it is smoother. You will certainly like it. However, I must tell you, our wines are only available by the bottle."

Barbara looked at Stretch again. Big time, here! He didn't even dare ask the price. He nodded.

"That will be fine," Barbara said.

He turned to Stretch. Stretch had already decided he wasn't going to ask for a Bud, so he told the waiter that the lady's drink would suit him fine. Harvey left.

To make conversation, he said, "You like French wines?"

Barbara looked momentarily stricken. "Oh, Stretch, I've never had one before. I just wanted to. Is it all right?"

"Sure, anything you want," he said, "and don't hold back. I don't get out often. I'm enjoyin' this."

He favored her with a smile he genuinely felt. "Want to hear something?"

"Sure."

"I never had any either."

"Really?"

"No."

"Oh, this is such an adventure!"

Stretch let one hand rest casually on the table. Under it, with the other hand, he caressed the knife from the outside of his pocket. At the moment he didn't feel at all like he did earlier. He'd actually begun to like this bright and pretty lady. He decided to let the feeling carry him as far as it would. Maybe she'll save her life tonight. He smiled gently. Let's see if she can win a game she doesn't know she's playing.

"Yeah, it is."

They took time to look at the menu. The selections were in English, but the flavor of the restaurant was deep sea, and they noted a number of Cajun menu items, too. Blackened Sea Bass, how about that! Stretch's mouth began to water. Cajun! Oh, man, he thought, I been a time away from that kind of feed.

The waiter returned with the bottle and a short table topped with an ice bucket. He uncorked it at the table and poured a small amount into Stretch's glass. Somewhere he'd heard you pick the glass up and sniff it, like for bouquet or something, so he did. He smelled it and then tasted it. It was real nice. He nodded to the waiter, who proceeded to fill each glass to exactly one and one half inches below the rim. The golden liquid sparkled in the low lighting.

"What you think, Barbara?"

"Oh, gosh, I need more time. There is so much here."

"Take your time."

He nodded again at the waiter, who took his cue and left, after wrapping the bottle in the ice bucket with a linen table napkin, retiring to a place where he could watch his tables and keep track of his livelihood.

Stretch picked up his glass and held it forth. Barbara picked hers up and brought the two glasses together with a delicate "clink." They took a sip.

"Oh, this is a *good* wine, Stretch," she said, "a *very* good wine."

"Yeah. I like it, too."

Stretch let Barbara sit for a couple more minutes, and then said, "Ready?"

"I think so. I think I'll have the prime rib. But everything looks so good."

"Would you like to come here again some other time, Barbara? I mean; if we hit it off, well, you're very pretty, but you know, that's not everything. Well, you know, I have some business down this way. Not all the time, but some. I'd be coming back." Stretch thought he was doing a great job of appearing humble and awkward in front of this lady. He could see her eating it up. She must not get much around here.

"Oh, Stretch, could we? I mean...yes, if it works out." The last of what she said seemed an afterthought.

"Sure. I mean, well, let's just have a good time and see where it goes, okay?"

"Yes, let's."

"So, you're ready?"

"Sure."

He looked toward where he knew the waiter would be. He knew that if he looked in his direction in a place like this, the waiter would come over instantly. How different from the feedbags he frequented. He was used to almost making an ass of himself just to get a waitress attention. Class places. Good thing! Gotta do this more often.

The waiter saw him and fulfilled his prediction.

"Yes, sir." He kept an eye on both, but looked to the lady first.

Stretch said, "Go ahead."

"I'll have the prime rib, Harvey."

"A good choice, ma'am. And how would you like that cooked?"

"Medium rare, please."

"Very good. Salad or soup of the day?"

"Salad, please." The waiter ran off the selection of dressings, and Barbara picked Parmesan Peppercorn.

"Baked potato, our special home fries or Chef's slaw?"

"What's the Chef's slaw? Never heard of it."

"It's a special cabbage blend, red and white, with certain spices you would love but I cannot list for you, a secret of the kitchen."

"It sounds wonderful. We are here tonight for the first time. I would enjoy a taster, but I will have the baked potato, with butter and sour cream, is that okay?"

"Yes, thank you. Very good, ma'am."

He then turned to Stretch, who'd watched the process with concealed amusement. "And you, sir?"

"I have to have that Blackened Cajun Sea Bass. Made my mouth water just thinkin' about it." Stretch looked expectantly at Harvey.

"Excellent, sir. It's one of our specialties. And will you have soup or salad, sir?"

"I'll go with the salad, same as the lady's, that'd be fine. And I'll try those fries."

"Thank you. I'll put the order in and be back in a moment." Stretch nodded to him again.

Harvey left and they sat back to enjoy the wine.

"Stretch, I can't believe I'm here with you in this fantastic place. I don't even know you. I mean, you're nice, and good looking, but I don't know anything about you. Want to trade secrets?"

"Sure." Either way, Stretch thought, it wouldn't hurt a thing. "Ask away."

Barbara seemed a little embarrassed. "I don't mean to pry, but what do you do? You said you live in Greenwich. That's a pretty ritzy town."

"Yeah." He decided to give her the same line he gave the Park supervisor. "Well, I actually work for a guy who has a dating service."

She gave him a strange look.

"Oh," he smiled, "I'm off the clock now. Don't get worried. I'm not recruiting tonight. Matter of fact, that job is one of the reasons I don't get out much, although it pays really well."

He stopped to let that sink in. Barbara relaxed a little.

The waiter came over then and set a small, steaming, newly baked loaf of bread on the table on a cutting board. The knife and butter container were part of the ensemble. Barbara stopped talking while she watched the process. When Harvey left, she finished the thought.

"I guess I'm like everyone else. It's hard to really feel comfortable with someone if you don't know them," she said.

"Sure, I know. And how do you get to know them if you don't let yourself give it a chance, especially with someone you don't know. It's like 'damned if you do, damned if you don't,' right?"

"I guess so."

"I suppose you got to take a chance sometime, right?"

"It boils down to that."

"So let's have a great dinner and we'll go from there."

She smiled at him, "Seems we have no choice."

He paused and then said, "So let's hear about you."

"I work at Oakbeach Swimtank, as you know. I've been there pretty much since I graduated from Bablyon Regional High, uh, several years ago."

"I'm guessing that'd be about ten years, right?"

"Oh God, am I that transparent?" She thought for a moment, and said, "Ohmigosh, I'm sounding just like my mother. I don't want to do that. Sorry!"

"No problem."

"Anyway, I wanted to go to college, but the money was too tight, so I had to get a job. The owner is nice, and I just sort of stayed. Pretty dull, huh?"

"Nah, not really. Everybody's got to do somethin'."

The patter continued, each one thinking they were learning more about the other, and each feeling more comfortable because of it. As Barbara told the truth, Stretch fabricated right down the line.

Dinner arrived and it was wonderful, exquisite. Barbara's prime rib was perfect, and the Cajun dinner Stretch ordered was hot and seemed to melt in his mouth. Silence reigned for the first time since they'd sat down. The wine went down fine. Stretch ordered a second bottle against the protest of Barbara. He told her he could afford it and that this was a real and a rare treat for him, and not to worry.

"If I get giddy, it's your fault," she said, with a little laugh. Stretch figured a heady wine and a good time filled with excitement guaranteed giddiness.

Stretch generally threw down a few beers every day while waiting for assignment—Nick didn't seem to care, so long as they could perform when he wanted them too—and found this wine going to his head, too. He had to keep watch over his tongue.

Having eaten and drunk like a king and queen, they settled back in their chairs, and as they did, Harvey was right there to clear the table. The dishes disappeared quickly, without fuss, and Harvey returned with his practically invisible crumb scraper to deftly remove clear crumbs from the linen tablecloth. Harvey then handed them each a dessert menu.

"Ohmigod!" said Barbara, "Where is there room?"

The waiter smiled, "May I suggest something?"

"Sure," Stretch said, now feeling pretty expansive, "Lay it on us."

Harvey, thinking what a peasant this guy was—the girl was foxy, though—went expertly through the dessert menu. Then he mentioned the specialty of the house, something like Death by Chocolate, but with an ice cream core gently embedded with a shot of Liquor 54, looking like a glass chimney above the sinful dessert below.

They both decided on that. Harvey knew his clients well, it seemed.

Afterward, Stretch and Barbara sat silently looking at one another, too full to speak. The waiter left them alone for several minutes and finally approached them to ask if their meal had met with their satisfaction, and would there be anything else?

"No," said Stretch, looking first to Barbara to see if she'd agree, "You couldn't have done better, and everything was great!"

"Thank you. I'll bring the check in a moment."

"Yeah, that'll be good," Stretch said.

Harvey returned with the check, laid it gently on the table facing Stretch, and retired to his position. He seemed to be looking away, but they knew one eye followed their table always. What an excellent waiter.

Stretch looked at his watch, eight-fifteen. He glanced at the check and saw a big number. Well, what did he expect? He took a couple of hundreds and a fifty from his wallet and paid it, making sure Barbara noted the size of the tip he left. He returned his borrowed formal coat and escorted his date out to her car to the kind best wishes of the hostess, and a "Come back soon, folks."

"Thank you, we will."

They left, walking slowly out to the back parking lot. Stretch reached out and tentatively took Barbara's hand. She grasped his.

Stretch had planned to entice her onto the beach and then slit her throat down by the water. In another place, in another time, that would have been the perfect ending to a perfect evening for the Weasel.

The thought excited him earlier, but now he had strange, mixed up feelings about this nice lady. Shit, man, I can't do this. I'm fucked up, he thought.

Stretch thought about his job and how often he might be able to pull away to meet with Barbara. What would he tell Nick? He considered how much grass his ass would become if he screwed Nick over. You didn't *do* that!

They arrived at her car. She unlocked it and got in. He saw she owned an older Camaro, an '89, but free from dings and rust. It looked very good under the remaining light of the waning day.

His mind fought itself, but in the end, he simply said, "Listen, Barbara, I gotta go back to the job, but I had a really good time, and I think you're terrific. I'd like to see you again, if you would be willing."

Barbara looked up from the car seat and spoke through her open window. "Stretch, I'd like to go out with you again. You were a real gentleman and I had a wonderful time. Why don't you call me when you can? Come a little closer."

Stretch leaned down into the open window and Barbara raised her face and kissed him lightly on the mouth. Her breath carried the odor of after dinner mint. Stretch felt momentary surprise; he'd given it no thought. His mind had been in another place, and slight shock registered on his face. Barbara wrongly interpreted it as naiveté, not connecting the fact of his stated employment with his action. She liked what she saw and it made her feel dreamy.

"Yeah, I will call you again, soon as I can. Uh, you don't want to walk along the beach for awhile before you leave, do you?"

"Why, sure." She got out of her car, took his arm, and they set off.

A five-foot seawall separated the back patio of the restaurant from the sandy beach area, the restaurant itself some distance closer to the road out front. Couples could be seen sitting around small square tables sipping after dinner drinks and enjoying the breaking coolness of the evening.

A wide wooden stairway made its way down either side of the patio to the sand. Walks on the beach were encouraged as part of the Conch Tree's ambience. In the late afternoon light Stretch and Barbara could see others in their evening finery walking slowly, taking in the wonder and glory of the setting sun. A well thought out place for ladies to leave their high-heeled shoes at the base of the stairs—beach slippers provided—encouraged those who were willing, to retain the mood. They gladly shed their foot-ware for such a bonus and moved onto the sand to watch for the coming night. The gents could too, if they desired, but most kept their shoes on.

The private beach area was nicely combed and kept. Totally class, kept running through Stretch's mind. If he began to take time off on a regular basis and beat it back down here to spent time with this girl, he'd have to be very careful nobody got wind of it, or they'd hound him. Hell, Nick would probably put an end to it anyway, and he belonged to Nick, right? He filed it.

At eight twenty-five they had filed out of the restaurant and onto the beach. The sun lay dead across the horizon, a huge red orb, distorted by the atmosphere. A single, thin evening cloud cut the bright blaze in half. Stretch wondered about that. He'd seen knife clouds many times. They could look at the sun now for a short time without being bothered by the brightness. Barbara leaned into Stretch's right side naturally.

They stood near the water listening to the low, lapping waves and the occasional heavier muted roar of the ocean crashing over distant breakers. The setting sun cast its deepening red glow across the water. Stretch let his arm find its way around Barbara's waist and he held her to him. She didn't protest.

It was only minutes before the sun's last glint melted into the horizon but time seemed to slow perceptibly. With a start, Stretch realized he'd never in his life done this thing before. Oh, he'd had women, enough of them, but he could not remember having any feelings for a woman save lust. This was new and different. It troubled him, but he knew he liked it.

"Barbara," he looked into her blue eyes, "I gotta go. I don't want to. I never felt this way before. Lookit how old I am. I don't believe this. Look, I want to see you again. Okay?"

Her eyes glistened with the light of the floods that came on just after sunset. The Conch Tree now shifted gears to handle its late evening crowd. Oblivious to those around her, Barbara shifted around and put her arms on Stretch's sides and kissed him again. Stretch was more ready this time and let the kiss linger for a timeless moment.

When Barbara let go, she said, "Yes, Stretch, you can see me again. When?"

"Won't be for awhile. When I get back to the job it's going to be a lot of work for the next month. I can give you a call, if you'll give me your number."

"I have a pad in my car. I'll write it down for you."

"Good. We better go."

Barbara put her shoes on and they walked back to her car. She found part of a pad and a pen in the glove box, wrote the number and a best time to call. Before entering her car she turned and raised herself onto her toes and kissed him one last time, quickly. Her lips were moist and downy soft. Stretch felt a thrill course through him. A night for honest thrills, like, so different! He wasn't prepared. That made it best of all. He wanted more, but held back.

She got in and with a wave, drove off. Stretch stood for a long moment, considering how Barbara had won the game after all, a game she didn't even know she was playing. He smiled.

42

"Mr. Nutting, your guests have arrived." Clarence spoke into a ship's pipe leading to the upper level. Nautical paraphernalia abounded, although Audrey didn't take notice of that ancient form of voice communication until Clarence did that. She looked around again. Really great place, unique!

"Send them up by the north stairway, Clarence, and thank you," came a gentle voice that sounded one with the ancient equipment.

Richard thought, how odd. This place is a fortress in many ways, state of the art electronics outside, yet the accoutrements within are what I would expect in a seven-masted Spanish galleon or a British Man-O-War.

The big bodyguard turned back and grinned. "Such a nice man, Mr. Nutting. You heard him, up that set of stairs, folks."

He pointed and the three moved off. They passed a pair of deeply carved oaken doors, wide open now, but appearing strong enough to ward off small cannon fire. Immediately they were on a set of wide, shallow rise steps that wound upward and curved as they went. Shortly the gloom on the stairwell brightened and they entered a foyer lit by one window well above their heads. Here another set of massive oak doors greeted them. They were closed, but as they reached the foyer they heard a click, and the doors swung noiselessly open, presenting a long, dim hallway to view.

Ted walked quickly through and the others hurried after. The door closed silently behind them. Audrey heard a faint but audible click much like the first, and would have bet anything that there was no way out behind them. Ted confirmed it in a voice just above a whisper.

"Believe I told you this is a fortress of sorts. Keep your eyes open, and I think you'll be impressed."

"Kind of what I was thinking, Ted," she murmured in the same voice.

The gentle voice of Mr. Nutting came to them, "And we can hear *everything*."

Ted looked back at Audrey and smiled. Richard remained silent, but looked everywhere and missed nothing. Curiously, he hadn't noted anything close by with his new capability, but he shrugged it off. After all, he'd just begun to be aware.

He projected to Audrey that they might do well to keep their facial expressions neutral and give no hint of their conversations. He suspected that they were not only being listened to, but watched as well, watched very closely.

Audrey shot back agreement. She looked around, getting a flavor for the uniqueness of the place. Every five to seven feet on either side of the wide hallway stood a tall warrior holding a spear in its right hand. They were exquisitely carved in a highly polished dark wood and the features, though too pinched and small to be real, were decidedly lifelike. They stood seven feet tall, feet resting on a one-inch pedestal on the floor. The Indian warriors looked unconcernedly over their visitor's heads.

About midway down the long hall, a short, very fat man of oriental mien appeared from a doorway, gave a small bow, and silently motioned the three inside. They entered.

"Welcome to Churchton Manor, my friends." The man spoke to them from the center of a huge bed. Light covers were pulled up to his mid-chest, and his arms, thin and old, lay above the covers. He wore sunglasses. Audrey immediately projected to Richard that her aural sense told her the man was blind, that the glasses hid the fact that he had no eyes, just sockets. Richard projected back that he'd had to exercise great control not to respond physically to that comment.

We're going to have to practice in this mode or we'll give ourselves away, she replied mentally.

Agree, he shot back.

Mr. Nutting spoke again, "My man is a deaf mute, and totally trustworthy. Clarence downstairs would give his life for me. That goes for the others of household staff. There aren't many. It doesn't take many people to care for an old man. Now, so we can talk and give away no secrets, give me some names I can use to address you. We are friends here. You may call me Wendell."

Ted spoke up immediately. "I will be 'Chet', the woman will be 'Carol' and the man with me will be 'David'."

"Thank you, Chet. Tell me, how was your trip to Churchton?"

"Most interesting. Have you heard of the tsunami that hit the New Jersey coast yesterday?"

"Yes, I have means of keeping abreast of the news. I would be interested in your perspective on it, however. News reports tend toward the spectacular. It's like selling newspapers, like selling anything."

Ted smiled. "Well, we were boating and got caught in it."

Wendell lifted a thin hand off the covers, his five fingers reaching in the air. "Interesting, yes, very interesting. Tell me more."

"We were sailing west south west from a temporary assignment and had just finished crossing New York Bay when we got word on the marine radio that an undersea earthquake had caused a tsunami. Word had it; it was traveling at two hundred miles an hour and would overtake us in minutes. We were about four miles from the Jersey shore in a sailboat. We turned in the direction of the pressure wave, hoping to put deeper water between us and shore. The wave that hit us was a capper ten feet high and that capsized us. The boat sank. We eventually made our way to the shore in a rubber lifeboat, skirted people, found transportation, and made our way south to Churchton to keep our date."

"Excellent, Chet! I perceive there were more interesting aspects to your adventure, too. We need not discuss them." He smiled.

Ted laughed. "In this work there always are."

"Even in my latter day attempts to serve, yes indeed, there are," Wendell replied. "David, let me get a sense of you."

Richard spoke for the first time since they'd entered the building and had bantered with the giant. Taking his cue from Ted, he spoke in his previous voice, not the one he'd cultivated for his and Audrey's mission. The job was to entertain their host, as he saw it, while revealing nothing of them that could be culled by an enemy, even in this secure place.

"Nothing much to say. We've been together awhile, and expect to be for a while yet." He stopped.

"I detect that you would prefer to defer to Chet in most things. Would I be right?"

"We all think independently, but at present we listen to Chet, yes."

I'm stopping there, Audrey. I am detecting some kind of monitoring equipment that may be checking out our voice profiles.

Got you, hon.

"A good answer. Now, last but certainly not least, Carol. How are you handling what you are in the middle of, my dear?"

"Fine. It's nice to make your acquaintance, Wendell." Audrey stopped. She had also reverted back to her original persona. When the silence began to lengthen, Wendell Nutting moved back into it.

"You don't seem anxious to contribute, Carol." His stress on her assumed name rose slightly.

"I have little to say," she replied and while looking around, said, "lovely home."

"Yes, thank you. You are probably wondering why I am passing such inanities between us. I will explain in a moment." He reached for the phone next to his bed and as his hand touched it, it rang. He picked it up, listened for a moment and replaced the phone on its cradle.

"Your voice profiles are a match for our records. You are who you say you are. Knowledge of the password to gain entry to Churchton Manor can be found, bought, or tortured away. Voice profiles are hard to disguise and almost impossible to alter, no matter what you do on the surface to cause change. Welcome to my home, gentlemen and lady."

"Thank you," said Ted.

You see, it works, Richard passed over in his link with Audrey.

Yes, one more, maturing ability. When will it end? Audrey projected laughingly and lightly.

Anything more on your end? he thought back.

Maybe, just an odd feeling. I'm trying to get a handle on what's developing. Let you know as soon as I do.

Okay. Richard looked around haphazardly.

Wendell spoke from his bed, "We'll keep the names Chet came up with. I, of course, know your current names and that you are on your way to the 'Citadel', as I call it, ostensibly for conferences. Stoic asked me to see that Chet got a move on as soon as we were certain. No vacation for you, I'm afraid."

"Something's up?"

"You are to go with Clarence to the waterfront tunnel. He will transport you to Deale where I have a fast speedboat for you. Go to North Beach Marina. Stoic will meet you there. All hell's breaking loose!" Nutting stopped.

"Clarence," he called.

The giant appeared from behind a curtain at the far end of the room. In his hand was a 9mm Luger style pistol with silencer attached. It looked like a toy in his hand. He casually laid the weapon on a table next to him. "Yes, Mr. Nutting."

"Take Chet to Deale and wait for him."

Yes, sir. Let's go, Chet." Clarence walked to the door and disappeared out of it without looking back. Ted disappeared with him.

Now, Carol and David, let me see to your comfort."

The fat oriental reappeared behind them. Wendell said, "You must be hungry. My man will take you to our upstairs dining area. He reads lips. You may tell him what it is you would like to eat, and if it's in our pantry, he will provide it for you. His name is Chou-Ting. Please enjoy our hospitality. I am sorry I can't join you, but I'm stuck here."

"Thank you," they said.

Shortly they were led into a small dining room. About the size of a normal household living room, its ten-foot walls were paneled in what looked to Audrey to be Brazilian Rosewood. She loved that stuff, but knew it was exceedingly expensive. Serving paraphernalia nested in one corner of the room near an ancient dumbwaiter.

Sitting lightly on a nearly wall-to-wall Persian rug were four elegant oak tables. A setting for two, fine 1810 silver, linen napkins, beautiful gold rimmed plates and crystal glasses adorned the table closest to one of three large, low windows, and they noted that it commanded a view of the long slope to the property wall, and thence from there to the ocean. Richard also projected to Audrey that the window appeared to be of one-way glass.

Interesting.

Thought so, too. Wonder how much danger there is here, how many outside organizations have wind of this place? Not many, I'd wager.

We get paranoid when the other side makes us; that's sure enough. But face it; the best preparation makes for fewest casualties, she thought.

Yup.

Audrey stood expectantly at table. Richard seated her and then seated himself. They looked long at the ocean, both thinking that Richard had nearly drowned not more than twenty-four hours before. They turned, aware in their uncanny way that Nutting's man was waiting to take their order.

Richard said, "Fish, meat?"

Chou-Ting nodded.

How about a couple of rare steaks, Audrey linked.

"Filet Mignon? Rare? Baked potatoes, butter and sour cream, chives, garden salad?" The man nodded. Richard looked at Audrey and she nodded at the waiter.

The man left silently.

Richard took Audrey's small hand in his and they returned to gazing out the window at the scene below. They passed the time in mind meld, looking out the window.

You're definitely going to be easy to shop for, Richard.

Probably. Long as I'm covered...

Not bad uncovered.

Aw, shucks.

Don't feign embarrassment. You know you're good.

Nice day out there.

Humility doesn't become you.

Audrey projected a picture to Richard, one a tangle of arms and legs, heavy breathing and slick rhythmic motion. Richard reddened. Permeating her lust he caught an overlay of love, a wave of emotion that softened the picture and curled its edges. It faded into an old tintype, and washed away.

Wow! Like that for you?

Yes, send me a picture.

I'll try, but I don't think I can beat that one. Richard projected.

Wow right back!

Wonder of wonders, Audrey, I love you in a way that can't be matched by any of the disabled, lonely, unconnected people of this world. They can't know what we've got. Even Ted, we can't tell him.

No, you're right. We can't share this with anyone, not now, not yet. Maybe…not ever.

Their aura announced the return, still outside of the door, of Chou-Ting. Richard linked the thought that the ability seemed to be expanding.

Yes, it does, Amber thought back.

Chou-Ting went to the dumbwaiter and pushed a button. A faint hum told the two their dinner was on its way up from the kitchen. Efficiently, the little oriental served them, stood back waiting, and left at Richard's "Thank you, Chou-Ting. It looks excellent!"

Both sensed they had a free evening with nothing to fear in this place. They therefore enjoyed themselves, relished the meal and made light spoken conversation, knowing they were being eavesdropped. After twenty minutes, Chou-Ting came back, cleared their dishes into the dumbwaiter and sent it down. The manservant then motioned Richard and Audrey to follow him, and he brought them back to Nutting.

"Enjoy your meal?"

"One of the finest. Thank you."

"You are welcome. Come sit by me. Let us talk." The two operatives found chairs on the right side of his bed and sat.

"You are a couple of sensitivity, Wendell began, "I can't see you, and behind these dark glasses, I sense you are aware that I am blind, but more, that my eyes themselves have been removed. A rare type of cancer…"

Audrey ventured into the breech, "We didn't know, of course, yet you are right, we suspected. Richard and I are both sensitive individuals, one reason why we are together in this assignment, and the signs we noted on our first meeting caused us to feel that way."

"There are people throughout the world who have special power. My hearing is very acute, for instance."

"We know that the loss of one faculty may enhance another over time, or with training."

"Yes, that is true, Carol. Tell me, if you can, what you plan next?"

"We go to meet a highly placed official in our organization, I think."

"You don't know?"

Richard interjected, "It isn't something we need to know until time."

"Ah, David, so good of you to join," Nutting shifted his gaze to the big man, his sockets seeming to bore into him, "Tell me, are you aware of the assignment you are on?"

"Yes."

"And what is that?"

"I can't tell you."

"Why?"

"Because you don't have a need to know," Richard said simply.

"Quite right, David. What I know I don't share, you don't share what I have no business knowing, and this was a test, of course." Wendell Nutting smiled.

The two operatives conversed rapidly in mind-speak, but sat verbally silent, waiting for what would come next.

Nutting continued, "This is a way station, but it serves an important position in Stoic's operation. It is used for weeding."

"We see, " Audrey said. They'd suffered a moment of alarm at the direction this seemed to be taking, but now they relaxed a little.

"Well, you have much of the day to yourselves, I would think. May I suggest you take a walk in the gardens behind the mansion? They really are quite lovely. My man will take you to your rooms and see to your rest for the night. I would not expect Chet back much before early morning, if that." He pressed a contact on a small remote he kept near his right hand. In moments, Chou-Ting appeared, knocking once lightly on the doorframe. They couldn't figure how Nutting did that, some kind of electrical stimulus to a hand or some other part, perhaps.

Wendell didn't explain, but spoke directly to the oriental, "Chou-Ting, see to the comfort of our guests. You may show them around if they wish, or they may delve into the history of Churchton Manor in the Library or enjoy the grounds with impunity for their time here."

He turned to where Richard and Audrey sat. "Do you like dogs?"

"Yes, we do," said Audrey. "Why?"

"I've an old black Lab mix out back, best friend a man ever had."

"I'm sure we'd be happy to make his acquaintance."

"Her."

"Her."

"Wish I could come out there with you. Sometimes I have Chou-Ting bring her up here, but mostly I can't do that. It's her arthritis. Her name is Sassafras, like the old sassafras tea people used to serve. Call her Sassy Girl. Eighty pounds of love. She predates losing my eyes…great friend…" his words trailed off and the two young people could sense the pain and longing he felt for things changed and things past.

Like a shadow, it passed and he was himself again. "Well, you run along now. I don't imagine there are a lot of places you can let your hair down, but you can here, so feel free."

"Thanks." They left with Chou-Ting.

The man led them along the corridor and at the end he stopped and opened a door for Audrey. He pointed across the hallway at another similar door and nodded at Richard.

He quickly mind-linked Audrey, *Best be separate tonight, my love?*

Not on your life, buddy boy, she retorted, looked at Chou-Ting and said, "He's with me."

Audrey took Richard by the hand and led him into her room past the house servant. He raised his eyebrows slightly, then stepped back with a smile, reached in his pocket, produced a key for the room and retired noiselessly back down the corridor.

The room was large and ornate, old Federal style, the furniture mostly dark and rich looking. They noted a large dresser with an old-fashioned silvered mirror. It had plenty of drawer space. Two hassocks adorned the further reaches, and there were three chairs and a writing desk. The bed looked comfortable, but they made no move toward it. A bathroom with white, checkered tile and gold fixtures at the far end sported a high porcelain bear-claw tub with rubber stopper. It seemed as dated as the room, but everything shined with obvious care. A modern shower nestled in a corner at the far end of the room.

Tonight, thought Audrey. They left.

They spent a couple of hours in the Library. An old, leather-bound collection of Voltaire's works especially interested Richard. Audrey picked out a copy of Tom Sawyer and sat in a comfortable lounge chair to read. They carried on sporadic and innocuous verbal conversation to make it look good, but the bulk of their discussions were all in mind-speak and related to their upcoming assignment, what Wendell meant by "All hell's breaking loose," and wondering when Ted would make it back.

Later in the afternoon they went into gardens formed as a rather good maze. The back part of the estate was fenced off and one reason why trotted up to them, sniffed them a "you're okay" and then trotted alongside the two as they explored the maze.

"Hello Sassy Girl," Audrey said. "Treating you well, are they?"

Sassafras wagged her tail. "The best," she wagged, and regarded them with a bright, intelligent look. She seemed a bit stiff in the hips, but appeared nothing but friendly and moved along with them.

"Bet old Sassy Girl here doesn't get as much company as she used to," Richard offered. He bent down and scratched behind her ears, which she loved. The collar she wore had a lump in it and Richard examined it carefully while talking to the dog. When he finished, he linked Audrey.

Transmitter, very high tech, how interesting!

You get the feeling that everything in the place is wired for sound, don't you? Audrey replied.

And for video, I'd lay money on it.

Glad to be on this side of it.

Mmm.

Behind the maze, woods extended for a couple thousand feet. They walked as far back as they could. Sassy Girl soon tired of the walk and turned back, wagging them a friendly goodbye. They smiled after her. She ambled away toward the maze, her tail swishing lazily, her hips sashaying in time with it and soon she disappeared in the underbrush.

Just as well, Richard linked.

Nice old girl, she replied.

At last they found an open area extending as far as they could see in either direction, denuded for about fifty feet, and another tall stonewall like the one in front of the estate. Richard's new sense identified several trees in the area with tiny, well-hidden wide-angle audio/video cameras spaced to provide maximum coverage of the entire perimeter.

Very thoughtfully and carefully planned, he thought.

Yes, she replied, *note the thin pathway, nearly straight as an arrow for maybe a thousand feet, ending in what I think is a tall tree from here. Lot of brush around, but it's a straight shot from there. Casually, now, let's move to our right as if we're wondering how far the wall goes. When we get to the next arrowed straight path, I'll sense it and let you know.*

What do you have in mind?

My red sense has been heightened for the last couple of hours ever since we left the mansion. Every now and then I see a faint glow in amongst the trees, as if someone's stalking us. Another one by the tree at the end of the long path, she sent a picture, *I can see faintly. Something's going on. Don't start acting suspicious. Go with it.*

But I need to know what you are thinking.

I'm thinking that we may be in a trap.

Really! Where did that come from?

I'm convinced that Wendell is all right, and I'd bet on Clarence too, but I'm not convinced about Chou-Ting, although he didn't show on this damn radar before. Remember I said I felt the sense was like foreseeing intent? Maybe not quite that, but like it.

Yes.

We haven't seen any other house personnel. What if they have been compromised? Maybe by the woman or man we are supposed to neutralize. This facility is used by all factors of Stoics operation, right?

I guess.

Let's nose around and satisfy my curiosity. You have any weapons?

Just my brawn tonight. Sorry.

No problem. We can handle most things that might come up against us, long as they don't surprise us too badly.

I'm with yuh, honey!

43

During their walk, Audrey and Richard spoke briefly of the trees, what flowers they saw. They held hands. Their trained eyes and ears took in everything else. The sun dipped low in the west, and shadows overlaid the forest. In minutes the mansion's outline put them in full shadow. Audrey suggested they split up and try to flank the closest person, doing so where he or she couldn't be seen by the person at the tree.

That should be easy enough, Richard linked. They angled off; then Richard exclaimed that he had to sit awhile, stone in his shoe. Audrey opined in a low but carrying voice, that she'd seen an unusual flower "over there," and pointed, and left Richard to catch up after he got his shoe back on.

Her aural sense put the stranger thirty feet to her left. The image remained fuzzy, reminiscent of but not like an infrared image. As she bent over the flower, she ducked and disappeared to the follower's view. Doubled over, she made her way cautiously and silently, circling the image. Then she moved in and jumped. A quick karate chop to the neck, and the man went down without a whimper.

She flipped him over. A stranger, medium height, fair complexion, wearing dark jeans and a black tee shirt that said USDA Prime on the back in faded letters. He had a long steel-jacketed five-cell flashlight that vaulted out of his hand when he fell. Good weapon, Audrey thought.

She rifled his pockets and came up with a six-inch switchblade, some change, and a lottery stub. In his hip pocket he had a wallet with nothing in it. Apparently he'd removed all trace of his identity; no doubt leaving it somewhere it would be hard to find.

She noted he was young, probably about her age, give or take a year. Clean-shaven, not bad to look at, although some acne damage remained, probably from his teen years. He still breathed. She wanted him alive.

Richard, come over and look what we've got.

You okay?

Of course!

Be there in a minute. Have to look to any other watchers like I'm being nonchalant.

He arrived under the minute. She handed him the knife. He stared down at the man, then bent down and slapped him awake. As the man came to he flipped open the switchblade and lay it alongside the man's jugular with just enough pressure to make his point.

"Any sound out of you I didn't ask for will leave you bleeding to death. Understood?"

The man nodded.

"You speak English?

He nodded again.

"Make this easy on yourself. Tell me what you're doing here and why. Keep your voice down. Your first lie I will clearly see and you will be dead. Now, begin."

No cold-rolled steel here. The man started to shake. "The Chinaman, he told me to find you and track you. If I got a chance, I should kill you. There's big money in it. I owe, you know, like...I gamble. I thought this was a way out. I'm desperate, mister." His eyes got big. "You gonna kill me?

Richard ignored him and asked, "How many are out here in the woods?"

"Three, me and Chuck and Taliman by the tree yonder. We work in the kitchen and do care-taking."

"Your name?"

Buddy, used tuh be Budney...just Buddy. Glisome..."

"Well Buddy, used tuh be Budney, you got a new job. You're going to get the attention of Chuck, quietly, and have him join our little gathering. I'm an expert knife man, and your back will never be far from your knife. Understand me?"

"Uh, yeah, man. I don't want no trouble, mister."

"You got more trouble than you can imagine. Don't forget that— on your life!"

Buddy looked terrified. Audrey linked her opinion that he would do as ordered.

"Get your guy's attention. Just talk to him. Don't warn him. You're first, then him if you do."

"Sure, mister, I'll do it. Oh shit! Sorry, ma'am."

Audrey kept silent. Richard pointed and the man moved away. By quick-link they moved to each side, keeping their man in view and circling toward the near object in Audrey's mind-sight, which she continually projected to Richard.

Richard, on the other hand, found his mind vectoring the picture he received and triangulating to his exact position. Another ability, or an extension of the one he'd felt earlier? It came to him more easily, he found, when he didn't try to focus on it. Good!

"Hsst..."Buddy got his mate's attention.

"What you want, Buddy?" Richard and Audrey were opposite the two now, and closed like silent wind.

"Had to talk to yuh," Buddy said.

"Yer supposed tuh be watchin."

"Got a problem."

Richard and Audrey coordinated their move. Audrey suddenly rose into the other man's view from behind and to the side of Buddy, distracting him, just as Richard came from directly behind him. Richard's hand closed on Chuck's mouth, held him in a grip of steel, and whispered in his ear, "Not a sound. You're not dead and won't be if you make no sound when I release you. Nod your agreement."

Chuck couldn't believe how quickly this watching game had suddenly turned bad. He nodded. Richard released the pressure.

"Now, why?" Richard addressed them both. Chuck and Buddy were both dressed alike in non-reflective dark clothing. Right down to black sneakers, not cooks wear. They looked like they'd done this type of watching before. That didn't settle with the operatives' opinion that the two were flunkies of the lowest sort and seemed relatively naive.

More than meets the eye, Audrey linked.

Where's the third guy?

Still at the tree, no wait, he's moving toward us now. He's redder than these two. Bet he's watching the watchers. My aural sense tells me he's got a gun!

Okay, I'll watch these. Have fun. Audrey moved silently away.

To Buddy and Chuck he said in a low voice, "Sit tight. Make no sound. You can still die."

The prisoners sat on the ground and Richard hunched down, all but disappearing behind the tall greenery of a fern thicket. Audrey melted into the surrounding forest. She moved wide, catlike, circling the oncoming Taliman. She sensed his drawn gun. At a huge shagbark hickory near the path where she expected the man to pass she paused, noting that she could still sense him, even with the tree in between.

As the man approached, he slowed and trod quietly, his feet carefully picking their way. Audrey, doing the same, inspected the ground around the tree for dry twigs and stumbling hazards. Then she moved silently around behind him as Taliman went past, looking furtive, listening for any sound.

The man is more professional than the other two, she thought to Richard. No answer. He wasn't about to break her concentration.

Once in place, she leapt again, as she had done before with Buddy and caught the bigger man turning at the slight sound her move made. Her down-turned hand smashed his left neck. He reeled, but didn't go down. He twisted and brought the gun up. Only Audrey's inherent quickness saved her from a savage blow to the head. His .38 police special roared in her left ear. As the man came around, Audrey closed with her opponent. She caught a faint whiff of early morning cologne residue. She inserted her right leg between his two and grabbed his shirtfront. At close quarters she brought her knee up, hard!

With a yelp, the man folded and Audrey chopped him again. This time he stayed down. Richard arrived then, looking scared, but still professional.

"What happened?" he said.

Audrey shot him a quick mind link. *The others?*

When I heard the ruckus, I grabbed them both and knocked their heads together. They'll be out for quite awhile.

I'm okay! Let's see what we've got here. Audrey bent down and retrieved the gun.

Richard assessed the man on the ground. While he lay on his face, Richard grabbed his dark shirt and ripped it off him, tore it into strips and tied him up, hands and feet. Richard flipped him over. The remnant he stuffed into Taliman's mouth. Then he dragged the unconscious man to a couple of small, close growing trees and put his back up against them. He found a still-strong dead branch about five feet long and smooth nearby. He shoved it horizontally between the man's arms, making it impossible for him to move or get up. Then they waited. It wasn't long before their prisoner came to.

He wiggled and checked his bonds, decided he wasn't going anywhere right away, and subsided. He glared hatred at them but made no sound.

Audrey linked, *Foreigner! You'd better do this.*

Right, Richard shot back.

Richard positioned himself in front of the man, leaned forward, hands on knees and gave him a hard stare. He looked at the man for a minute or so, but said nothing. An obvious hard case, Richard felt a little psychological silence might help. Audrey stood to the side, looked on but remained out of the picture. Richard removed the gag.

"Your name?" The man said nothing.

He's going to be tough. Don't forget the shot. Could bring anybody. I don't sense anyone yet.

Go check on our other charges. I'll work on this one.

Okay. Audrey left and found the other two accomplices. They were still out. Taking her cue from Richard, she tied them together back to back with strips from their shirts and drove a small limb she found locally as deep into the soft ground as she could between them. That ought to keep them there until we get back, she thought.

She returned to Richard to find him applying pressure to the left hand of the prisoner, bending it slowly and painfully backwards. The gag was back in his mouth.

Hate to do this, but we have little time, and something big is going down. He'll understand how serious I am very soon.

295

Richard felt a projected wince from Audrey, but she linked, *Do what you need to. We didn't start this.*

The man's hand went further back. Still no sound, although Richard could read the pain in the man's eyes.

Very hard case!

Not much longer, Richard countered.

A loud crack sounded, and the man screamed into his gag. Richard calmly dropped the broken hand to another muffled scream, and grasped the ties holding the man's right hand behind him. He freed it and began the same process on the remaining hand. He heard a muffled sound and removed the gag.

"No, effendi, no more."

Effendi...Arab, Turk? Audrey linked.

Turk, probably.

"Your name?"

"Effendi, I cannot. I will die." Richard began to slowly apply more pressure to the right hand. The man whimpered.

"Who is your boss?"

Silence.

Back and back. Crack! Another scream.

"Who is your boss?"

"No...no...stop, please." He cried piteously.

"Who do you work for?" Richard reached for the man's leg.

"Chou-Ting...UH..." He jerked suddenly and slumped. Richard stood and looked at the man, then leaned over to feel his pulse.

Dead! Had to be post-hypnotic suggestion of a high order.

Suicide operative, only possibility. He had to believe it would or it wouldn't work. Who would do that in our organization?

I don't think Stoic would. It would be against his credo.

Then who?

I don't know. But we'd better find out. We can't trust anyone in the compound. Maybe Nutting; I can't believe he's mixed up in this, but nobody else. And we've got to get into our assignment. Looks like the mansion and at least some of its staff have been compromised. And, "All hell's breaking loose!" Remember?

Let's make our way back to the mansion through the maze. We have to find out who else is involved.

I'm against the idea, Audrey projected, *We need to get the hell out of here, and I think the back fence is the best bet. We'll travel overland and try to pick up Ted before he gets back.*

Not going to work. Something stinks in Denmark, and I mean to find out what's going on.

You're decided?

Only choice! To get back in here would be nigh impossible. Ted is likely okay. Not sure about Clarence, but that can come later. Nothing we can do there. At least we're inside and I'm afraid we may have some more dirty work to do.

Guess so.

Let's go. They made their way back to the two still unconscious prisoners. They didn't look like much.

I don't want to kill these two. I think they are too low on the totem pole, but we've got to do something with them, Richard linked.

They've seen us, Audrey shot back.

I'll have to do it.

They are enemy.

Check around to see if you can identify any audio or video units nearby.

Audrey quietly scoured the area, but couldn't find any in the gathering darkness, except near the trees, with the video units facing outward, toward the wall.

Nothing I can find. You're about a hundred feet in from the nearest A/V unit.

Okay. C'mon back.

When she returned the job was done. Richard didn't look happy. He had quietly wrung their necks. Audrey kissed him and sent him a love package with curled edges.

Thanks, honey. We'd better go.

Yeah.

They walked slowly back to the hedge maze and around the far side, staying fifty feet from each other but as closely linked as if they were one body. Audrey shot Richard vectors continually. She didn't seem to be trying; it felt natural. As they got close to the house Audrey let Richard know that she could discern people inside the house, but none outside.

Where are they?

I sense three. One is near the door we exited. He's got a gun in his hand. Two others are at a lower level. Wait...one is leaving, going upstairs fast. I can't see Wendell, but he might be in danger. Let's move.

Right!

They silently approached the mansion and headed for the door, ducking close beneath the windowsill. Once there, Audrey tested the door and found it unlocked. Richard positioned himself in the darkness beyond the door, off to one side, switchblade open and ready.

I'll have to be very accurate this time. When I say, yank the door open.

Ready.

Okay, now!

Audrey grabbed the door and flung it open. "Crack! Crack!"

Audrey saw a flash in the air and heard, "Oogh" as Richard's knife dead centered the man's throat. Richard dived into the low light of the interior and grappled for the firearm, which hit the floor about the same time. The man's hands immediately went to his throat, pain and amazement on his face. Blood trickled down his neck and shirtfront. Richard stood, gun in hand. He projected *"All okay,"* to Audrey, who joined him.

The injured man lost all fight, futilely clawed at his neck and tried to breathe as blood ran down his esophagus. Richard used the butt of the gun to his head, and the man stopped moving. The blood continued to flow, a slow and darkly spreading pool beneath him.

Next, Richard linked. He retrieved his knife, wiped the blade on his soiled trousers and folded it expertly. He dropped it in his right pocket.

Wendell! They ran to the west side stairway and took the stairs two at a time. Just before they cleared the landing, they heard a shot and something heavy hit the floor. They stopped. Richard carefully looked beyond the dark glassite door entrance to the hallway. One of the doors stood open, a wooden stopper holding it. Richard peered slowly around. The body of Chou-Ting writhed on the floor, blood beginning to flow freely through his thin black shirt, dark red suffusing the material.

Hang on, my dear, gotta see if anyone else comes out.

298

Waiting. I don't sense anyone else in there, but I get a fading impression of Wendell.

Okay, here I go.

Richard stood to full height and cautiously but quickly inched along the edge of the wall, using the thin Indian figures as cover. Finally he stood over the now quiet body of Chou-Ting. Richard glanced into the room and ran in suddenly.

Wendell Nutting had bled copiously into his sheets. The man wasn't moving. Ready for anything, Richard took in the room while making for the bed. Too late! Nutting, too.

He bled out, Audrey. Not pretty.

No, sad. How about the Chinaman?

Dead. Damn! Big problem, honey! Anybody left alive in this place?

Someone in the lower level is all I can sense.

Okay, let's go.

Richard took the lead and Audrey followed as they ran back to the stairwell and down, making as little noise as possible.

Where?

That door, she pointed. Made of deep tint walnut, it seemed to be a natural part of the building, but Audrey sensed that it was newer, a recent addition. They opened it slowly. No sound. Richard clicked on the light switch. Two naked overhead bulbs lit the way. At the base of the stairs stood a massive door, somewhat like the vault door in a bank. Before they could figure out what to do, the door began to open. A slim man came out, saw them and dived back in, trying to close the door behind him.

Richard grabbed the door and wrenched it back. It took all his strength to halt and reverse its momentum. Without thought, he launched himself into the room in time to see the man pick up a heavy weight of some sort and smash it down on the console in front of him. Richard seized the man by the hair and ripped him backwards, away from the equipment. The man spun around with a yell, the heavy weight still in his hand. Richard hit him full in the face. The weight spun out of the man's hand. He fell like a rock and lay on the floor, stunned.

Pretty impressive, Richard! A regular one-man army!

Richard stood, letting his pulse get back to normal.

Thanks. All in a day's work, I always say, pip, pip! Think Brit. Oh, Richard!

Let's see what we have here. Evidently it's the central electronic surveillance equipment station. Wonder how much damage he did?

Richard began to look the equipment over as Audrey bent over the unconscious man. He lay face down and seemed out cold. A thin trickle of blood oozed out under him from his broken nose. She turned to see if she could help, and just then, with a lunge, the equipment operator rose on his knees and made a dash for the door.

Richard reached in his pocket and in one smooth motion, pulled out the switchblade, pressed the stud and flung it point first at the retreating back. The knife made one quick turn in the air and drove deep into the man's left upper back. He cried out and fell. Audrey got through the door before Richard and pounced on the man. He'd made the turn to the steps but got no further. With a ragged breath, he lay still.

Good shooting, Richard. You sure you need me in this assignment?

More than ever, my love. Got a strong feeling a lot more's coming down before it goes back up.

I expect so.

Before retreating into the Communications vault Richard made a quick trip upstairs and removed the two bulbs in the overhead lights.

What's that about?

Might slow somebody down a little.

Oh. They went back, closed and locked the door.

"Now, Audrey, let me take a look at this stuff. Occurs to me he went for something sensitive. I'd bet it was a link to his or Chou-Ting's boss. Hope he didn't destroy it." He bent over the equipment again.

Audrey left him alone in his thoughts and looked around at the equipment and the room. No places to hide, shelves for equipment, books, manuals. It wasn't a large room, but it appeared inviolate. She would have bet money the exterior walls were just as impregnable as that door, too.

Richard spoke, "As I thought, my girl, it was a link and it's been destroyed. I hope that didn't alert our quarry on the other side."

"Wouldn't be good," Audrey replied. "What now?"

"We're safe as we can be for the moment." Richard flicked a few switches and images came up on seven, ten-inch monitors ahead of the operator's position.

"Okay, we've got perimeter views." Audrey looked at them with him.

Seems quiet. By the way, why did you switch to speech? Audrey linked.

Not a good idea to rely too heavily on the mind link and forget to talk normally some of the time.

Balance in all things, right old bean?

Yup.

Got you. Doubt we could be heard here, but if we discuss things not relating to the link, we'll not chance blowing our secret.

Richard nodded. He tried other buttons and switches. "No internal house views and no sound, from what I can get of this equipment. I'll try some more stuff."

Ted should be back with Clarence very soon, I think. Clarence could be dangerous, although he didn't glow, you said, Richard continued.

No, but this thing seems to work for intent, and if he had no malicious intent, I'm not certain he would show something. Look at what happened with the guy outside. I saw nothing coming there.

That's true and a little disturbing.

I'm pretty convinced there must be some kind of aura around everybody—something most people can't see—like an ethereal extension of themselves. My sense seems to pick up on certain vibes. This transmitter/receiver in my head appears to catch them. Darker vibes seem easier to get, so to speak, so I pick up on them more easily. It's really odd, but it greatly augments my natural abilities.

I can agree. Okay, let me see what I can do here. He turned back to the equipment.

44

Ted reappeared at one a.m. through the tunnel from the waterfront with the giant Clarence at his side and both in a great hurry. The entrance from tunnel to house was hidden in the mansion's ancient basement behind what appeared to be a large pile of miscellaneous debris, but it all moved quietly on a rotating platform, closing again as they walked through and shutting out the dankness of the tunnel. They walked to the first level and found the mansion in shambles, a dead man only feet from them. He appeared to have been stabbed in the neck. Ted looked furtively at Clarence. Horrified, Clarence had already started to bound up the stairs when Ted urgently called him back.

"Clarence, quietly, slowly."

Clarence stopped and the mad glint in his eye disappeared. They made their careful way to the living room, where Clarence went to a hidden cupboard and removed two Lugers, handing one to Ted butt first.

"They're loaded, safety on," he whispered.

Ted relaxed a bit. Clarence seemed to be on his side in this. Ted had studied the man for quite awhile while they were together. He knew that Clarence was fanatically loyal to his boss. He put the thoughts down but kept an eye on the big man. They moved as quietly upstairs as they could. The place seemed lifeless. At the top they came on the second body, another man Ted hadn't seen before. He had a bullet in his chest.

Down the hallway, partly inside the master's suite they saw a short, fat man. He lay face down and there was a bloody hole in his back. A sharp kitchen knife lay nearby, blood on the blade. He looked like he'd tried to leave the room hurriedly when the shot got him.

"Chou-Ting!" Clarence whispered.

"Clarence, one by one," Ted said, indicating the doorways along the long hall. No one in any of the rooms.

"Now Mr. Nutting's room. I'm smaller. Cover me."

"Okay, Chet." Clarence looked around for any movement, and then focused on Ted as he went through the door. Ted looked in quickly and then motioned for Clarence to follow.

Ted's worry in not being able to contact Wendell Nutting from Deale an hour before was well founded. Nutting lay in his bed, his throat cut, coagulated blood soaked into the covers. He touched the body. Rigor Mortis had set in. Not over four hours dead is my guess, he thought. Audrey and Richard were nowhere to be found. A 9mm Luger lay on the floor beside the bed.

"Looks like Chou-Ting cut Mr. Nutting's throat and left him to die," Ted said, "Wendell must have had a pistol under the covers and with what strength he had left, shot Chou-Ting in the back as he left the room. His aim was as good as his hearing."

"Looks like I'm out of a job. I loved that old man," Clarence said, his voice cloudy.

"You're still part of the organization, Clarence. Let's see if we can find my partners. Hope they're all right." Ted didn't reveal to Clarence the terror he felt.

"Yeah, Chet. Nothing we can do here."

"Call me Ted. You'll work for me, now."

"Yeah, Ted, whatever," was the dispirited reply. Ted glanced at him and said nothing. The man was grieving. Ted had to keep both man and situation under control and under wraps.

"Go to the front windows and check out the area. I'll check the back."

"Right." Clarence left.

He came back in a minute. "All quiet."

"Okay, where is the electronic surveillance equipment kept?"

"Basement level, special room, metal door, not easy to get into."

"We'll go there next. Do you have access?"

"No, Chou-Ting headed security. It takes a security card. Wait..." Clarence rifled through Chou-Ting's pockets, then patted his body all over. "No card. Have to wing it."

"Let's go, then." Treading lightly and carefully, the two men made their way downstairs. The opposite stairway had two bodies on it. Clarence checked them. Nothing helpful.

"This way." Clarence peeked around a doorframe, gun drawn, then moved to a dark walnut door, opened it carefully and looked into total blackness. The smell of death hung in the air, sickly sweet. He flipped the switch and pulled back instantly. Nothing! No light. Clarence looked back at Ted, who gave him a nod. He grabbed a small blue vase from a nearby table and tossed it into the opening. The vase shattered but no other sound came from the stairwell.

Ted whispered, "From the look of the place, I think we should try it."

"Okay, boss." Clarence jumped quickly, but quietly into the stairwell for so massive a man, followed by Ted. Ted shut the door behind him to eliminate being silhouetted.

They hugged the outer stair wall, sliding along, backs to the iron pipe railing. Clarence led four steps ahead. Near the bottom, the giant black man hit something with a foot. He bent carefully and found another dead man lying partly on the stairs. He ducked low and made his way carefully around the body to reach bottom. He felt for the massive door he knew was there and ran his hand around the doorframe, catching the lever. He turned it carefully. It stopped immediately. Locked! It needed a key-card.

Someone was still in there. Ted caught up with Clarence. In a whisper Clarence told Ted what he'd found.

"No other way out?" Ted whispered back.

"No, the Com room is relatively recent. It's built like a vault. It would take dynamite, a lot of it, to get in."

"Okay, let's knock anyway."

"You sure?"

"Yes."

Clarence knocked. A brief silence, then, "What do you want?" came from the speaker over the door.

Richard's voice! Ted smiled. "Richard, it's Ted. What's your status?"

"Ted! Hey Audrey, look who's outside our door!"

"What are you waiting for, Christmas? Open it," Audrey's voice came sweetly.

A sound like the clank of pistons, and the door slowly opened. As dark inside as out, Richard called to Ted. "C'mon in. You alone?"

"Clarence, too. He's working for me now. No others." The light over the door flickered red and outlined Ted and Clarence. They entered the Com Room.

"Close the door, Ted," Audrey said. She sat spread-legged on a metal chair, leaning on the back of it. She held a wicked looking gun on them, silencer attached. Ted did as he was bid.

"Lock it."

He did. "What's this?"

"Called taking care. We're sure of you, but not Clarence. Clarence, sit in that chair over there," she indicated with a wave of the muzzle. The big man sat. Richard dialed up the interior lighting.

"Now we're all cozy. You want to sit, Ted?"

"I'll stand. Let's hear it."

"Okay." Audrey quickly recounted their adventure of the day before. When she finished, Ted looked over at Clarence. "For the price of your life, give it all."

"Boss, I don't know any of this. Mr. Nutting hired me, was good to me, I loved him. This other crew that was here were vouched for, Mr. Nutting said. Most been here six months or so. We always have change in personnel, time to time. I been here longest, four years. Chou-Ting for two. All quiet, working the way it's supposed to. Don't understand it. They're all dead?"

Ted ignored him. "Continue."

"No more. I protected Mr. Nutting..." he paused for a second as the picture of the dead man came to him again, "and acted as a household servant. Got along well enough with the others..."

"How many," Richard interrupted.

"Seven. Seven is all the big boss said the mansion needed. Cook, communications man, caretakers, and Chou-Ting to run things and watch security."

"But he was a deaf-mute."

"The man saw everything. His problem wasn't a disability. Knew where everything was, could read lips from a long way off. Spent a lot of time in the surveillance room. Everything was wired for video and audio. He had a man down here nearly all the time, Taliman the Arab. Oh, and Trevor, he was thick with Chou-Ting, too. That's him outside the door. Those three were smarter than the grunts, but nothing to suspect them for. Treated me okay, and Mr. Nutting never said a word to me about being worried."

"Given a choice," Ted said to Clarence, "What would you want to do, now all this has happened?"

Clarence visibly got red. "I want to find who was behind this, the bastard who caused all this. I want to kill him!"

"You don't think Chou-Ting was the top man?"

"No. It's a feeling, that's all. I got nothing to base it on."

Richard and Audrey had been in rapid conversation in mind-link. She detected no red or pink aura around Clarence and passed that on to Richard.

If you think he's okay, tell Ted, but not about your ability.

Of course not, Richard. Here. She handed Richard the gun and motioned for Ted to come to a corner where they couldn't be heard.

"Ted, I think he's telling the truth. I asked Richard about it and he thinks so, too. We're up against something bad in the organization, but we think we should trust him."

"A new ability, Audrey?"

"No," she lied, "just our training."

Ted looked at her for a moment, but decided not to pursue his nagging feeling. "I think so, too Audrey. I'm not often wrong about body language, and Clarence really cared about the old man. He was very hurt by what happened. I think when he said he didn't understand what happened here, he was also being truthful. We could use him. Let me finish this up."

"Right."

"Oh, incidentally, why did you wait until we got to the door to let us in?"

"The house circuits are out...damaged. The guy you found outside the door inadvertently let us in. When he saw us he dived back in. Richard grabbed the door before he could close it. He did something to the equipment with a heavy paperweight. Nearly succeeded in bringing the whole Com system down. We pulled him off the stuff and knocked him down...out...I thought, but he came to and bolted for the door. Richard tossed a knife into his back. We still have periphery views but no sound. Richard was working on it when you appeared outside the door. Evidently a separate circuit for the door."

"Ah. And why'd you end up here?"

"Most logical place. We managed to neutralize the household and searched as far as we dared, found nobody. Decided we'd get the best views from communications. Obviously, that was before the damage. Then we figured you'd eventually get here and search this place out when you saw what had gone on upstairs. We were pretty sure we'd neutralized the whole crew."

"Right you are," he said.

They went back to the larger section. Ted acted as if the conversation hadn't occurred.

"Clarence, if I help you find the person who did this, I want you to go along with any order I give. You may not understand it, but it'll be necessary. Agree?"

"You bet, boss, anything you say."

"Richard, you can put the gun away."

Richard handed it back to Audrey who took off the silencer and returned the weapon to a storage closet.

Clarence finally smiled slightly, "Well, let's get going then."

"First, we're going to get this Com equipment going again. How about you and Audrey rustling up some grub? Been a long day, and it'll get longer. Damage control first, we'll give it half an hour. Then we've got to get serious. And fast!" A new note of urgency sounded in Ted's voice.

Audrey and Clarence left. Ted locked the vault type door behind them.

"Richard, can you fix it?"

"I think I can jury-rig something. That's what I was working on when you arrived. I found a cabinet with some spare parts. The guy killed what I think was the private link and ruined a modulator for the house system. It's a little different from the outside system, but I have one I'm trying to modify. Couple hours, I think."

"Keep working at it, but I'm not sure we have that much time."

"Want to fill me in some?"

Ted thought about it, and said, "Yes, you can tell Audrey."

Richard linked her immediately.

Listen. I'll feed this as it comes.

Okay.

Ted resumed, "I'm going to leave Clarence here to keep up the front for awhile. We need to get into the parent company as soon as possible and ferret out the traitor. We've got to prevent further damage and get information we need. Stoic got wind of Rathmanizzar's move to begin his Jihad. That implies Rath has his bomb and it's probably at or nearing its destination as we speak."

Audrey to Richard, *Where?*

"Where?" Richard asked.

"Stoic's not sure. Best guess is the Peoples Republic of China, one of the big coastal cities, maybe even Beijing. Even though it's well inland, it has a big river route. Stoic thinks Rath is planning something huge. Hitting the most populous country in the world, and a sophisticated nuclear power at that, is likeliest in his view.

"What about the Muslims?"

"The Muslim population in China is nominal. It's a non-issue in Stoic's view. He thinks the Chinese are fearful enough that if attacked they would probably lash out at the West in general. They would see India and Pakistan as western targets. Stoic figures their strategy would be to knock out those nuclear powers first." Ted stopped and looked at Richard.

Audrey linked Richard, expecting more. *And...?*

Before Richard could pass it on, Ted resumed, "I told Stoic that if China is the target, he'd be wise to check where its leadership is at the moment. He told me he'd thought of that and had learned about an economic conference being held in Yantai within the next week. The provincial governors were all invited. It's especially interesting because Premier Han Duc Yin's chief rival in the government,

Provincial Governor General Fan Too will be there. Stoic's trying to get an agent in place before they meet."

"Whew! Sounds like Beijing. What an affront! Insult the highly sensitive Chinese culture but don't cut off its head and then leave it many directions to respond." Richard said.

"Plant the seeds to reap a quick harvest," Audrey acknowledged thoughtfully.

"It's dangerous," Ted said. "We need to get moving."

"The plan?" came from Richard.

"We get to headquarters as quickly as possible. We have to find the traitor now, but I need a couple hours of sleep first, we all do. We'll rest for three and rejuvenate, then leave at first light. The corporate office is heavily guarded at night. We don't need unwanted attention."

"What then?"

"If we're lucky, we'll get some of our missing information. Maybe we can save the situation."

"Audrey tells me they are on their way back with food."

"Good, we'll eat and tell Clarence what he needs to do. Then we get some rest."

"Right."

Knock at the door. Ted opened it. The two filed in silently carrying a tray of food.

"What's happening," Audrey said.

Ted outlined for Clarence their need to leave at first light, and told him what he needed to do to cover for the deaths of the household staff and its master. They ate quickly and made their way to their sleeping quarters.

Three hours later they got up and quickly made ready to leave. Clarence saw them to the garage. An older but beautiful Jaguar XJ6 sat there, bathed in the light Clarence had just turned on. Clarence twisted and grabbed a key off a rack by the door. He handed it to Ted.

"I kept it shining even after Mr. Nutting lost his eyes. You take care of it now."

"We will. If we can, we'll get it back to you."

"Thanks," Clarence said simply.

No speck of dust marred the glistening silver sheen. The white antelope glove-leather interior, all bumps and buttons with not an untoward scratch or dimple showing, greeted their eyes. The vehicle almost beckoned to them. Their gaze took in impeccably regular surface features; a surreal image of reflected light from the overhead bulb, the perfect alignment of doors and hood, all in a moment's time.

Ted moved around the front and made for the driver's side.

"What a beauty," Audrey breathed.

Richard opened the rear door and Audrey slid into the coolness of the seat. Her form sank into the leather and she reached for the lap belt, hesitated, and dropped it. Richard shut the door firmly. The latch made a soothingly secure click. He then climbed in with Ted. No one spoke. The car started quietly, smoothly. Audrey thought it a delicious extravagance in a world going crazy.

Clarence waved to them, turned on his heel and headed back to the communications room. Richard's repairs had gotten the house circuits back in operation and Clarence had control of the gates again.

Ted pressed the remote button on the visor and the door ground upward. He put it in reverse, backed out and made the turn onto the long gravel driveway. Driving slowly to anticipate Clarence's arrival at the grounds and gate controls, he timed it perfectly. The three watched the gate silently open. They drove through without slowing. Ted glanced at his watch. Ten minutes to six. The gate swung shut. No one looked back.

Audrey thought a silent "wish you well" to Clarence. His job of cleanup would now begin. She didn't envy him. Her last thoughts as they drove out of sight of the mansion reviewed all that had happened in this supposedly safe house in such an incredibly short time. She shook her head.

Clarence watched as the old Jaguar passed through the gate. His mind held grief and anger, but at the moment he felt curiously calm, the same uneasy calm he often sensed before a summer storm. This time it came tinged with regret. He knew he had to stay here, but couldn't help wishing he'd been invited to go along. Cleaning up the mess didn't appeal to him. One thing for certain, though, he did what he was told once Ted had impressed his authority on him.

"Whatever they're up to, it's gonna be worse for them than for me," he said, talking to the now silent rooms. "Mr. Nutting's gone. I don't have much stomach for this anymore. Believe I'll stay a few days and take care of matters. But then I'm gonna disappear, Alabama, Louisiana, someplace down south, I think. Time for a change."

He'd bury the dead and close up shop until Stoic decided to do something with the place. The place was solitary. Only company Wendell Nutting invited came when we called, he thought, and none due till next week. He'd been warned not to attempt to call Stoic, delicate business ahead, they said. Ted said he'd make arrangements. Didn't figure on Clarence lighting out, but it wouldn't matter in the long run.

Clarence sat heavily in a metal chair in the vault room and slowly lowered his big head into his hands. He stayed that way for a long time. Then, with a sigh and a grunt, he went upstairs to his former boss's bedroom.

45

Little was said for the first hour as the Jaguar purred its silent way along the bay into the D.C. area. By seven they'd picked up the Beltway heading northwest. Already congested, Ted fought high-speed traffic on the multiple-lane highway until they picked up Interstate 270 to Frederick. Traffic remained heavy but not frantic, most of it heading toward the Capitol.

Ted drove easily now, keeping a steady seventy. "Another hour," he said to his companions.

"I'm comfortable," Audrey said.

Richard nodded. "Take your time, Ted."

"I want to arrive there just after eight. It's the time most vendors try to get in and sell the company on whatever they sell. It'll be a good time to begin your quest."

They went back to their private thoughts. Every now and then Audrey would send Richard a curled message promptly returned. Even so, the three were vigilant. They kept an eye on their surroundings, noting that this far from the disaster on the Jersey shore, it appeared business as usual. The hype, as they expected, was all over the radio. They felt a heightened awareness in the local people they came across, and an element of sadness for those who had lost much, but no suspicion. Many reminded Audrey of people who give lip service to any disaster, while under their breath thanking their lucky stars it wasn't them. Who wouldn't, she thought?

About twenty minutes before they entered Frederick, Ted said, "You've familiarized yourselves with the plans to the complex?"

"Yes."

Audrey, my love, in a few short minutes we will start our search. How is your wrongness aura working?

Just fine, big boy. Actually, I'm getting longer distance impressions, like the ability is deepening.

Might have something to do with the healing?

No, I think it's like my mind is more in sync with the implant's focusing ability. The fuzziness I felt initially, when I was so surprised to find something added to the linking ability, is disappearing. If it keeps improving, I'm going to wonder what else I've got. Incidentally, what about your electronic "surveillance" thing?

Unchanged. Well, maybe a bit more...what...discernable?

Ted interrupted. "We're fifteen minutes away. Mind your accent, Audrey. You slipped a couple of times lately."

"Okay, Ted."

Richard, let me know if I slip. You're doing fine.

Sure.

Silence resumed. Richard put an arm around her neck and drew Audrey to him. She looked up and he kissed her gently. In the glove leather luxury of the racing automobile, their hearts melded briefly and their minds linked in connected ecstasy.

Ted glanced at them, almost jealous of what he surmised they had, suspecting that much was being withheld. He didn't like it, but they were right. He realized he'd created them and now, like a mother seeing her children drawing away, he felt those pangs. He knew what he must do.

"We'll stop at a rental car place near the facility. I want to leave you two to rent a car and approach Security that way. You have the letter?"

Audrey said, "It's in my purse."

"That'll get you into the main administration building and as far as Laura Baumert. Remember to watch for her reaction."

"We're ready, Ted."

"Sorry, Audrey, we're almost at cusp and it gets critical from here."

"We're as ready as we're going to be!"

"Yes, I know. Just antsy."

"You're entitled."

Ted subsided. Four minutes later they entered the outskirts of Frederick and turned at the third light, immediately pulling into the Hertz lot. Ted parked far down the row, not very near the rental office and stopped in a parking place, heading in. He turned in his seat to face them.

"As soon as you enter the building, I'm gone. I'll find a place to hole up for four hours; Frederick has a nice park not far from InFab. I'm expected back from assignment at noon and I'd best play it that way. The other four will have means of knowing of my arrival. Nothing needs to tie me to you two or even intimate a connection."

"Got you," Richard replied.

Ted reached over and shook Richard's hand, then put his arm across the divider and took Audrey's briefly with a firm squeeze. "Good luck."

I hate this part, Audrey thought.

Me too. So few days have passed since we met, but seems like years, and so much water over the dam. Let's go. No time like now to get things done.

There it is again. Why is that saying so important to me? Deep down she knew why. Dad had brought her up on it. A feeling of loss threatened to engulf her.

"Thanks, Ted. Who was the guy who said, "It ain't over 'til it's over?"

"Yogi Berra."

"Yeah, him. We'll make this happen and we'll be back together before you know it. Bye, Ted."

Ted smiled, but he wondered.

Richard got out. He opened the rear door for Audrey, who got out quickly. Ted popped the trunk. The two grabbed matching brown leather briefcases embossed in gold with the initials, A.P. and R.P. The dummied up, state-of-the-art computer interfaces were not very heavy, but they were all they would need to carry out their assignment. Briefcases in hand and sharply dressed in dark, Euro-cut tailored business suits, subtly pinstriped, an attractively packaged English couple strode purposefully into the rental office. They didn't look back.

A thin, balding man in a white shirt with rolled up sleeves looked up briefly from filing a contract he'd just written for an older man who left as they entered.

"Good morning."

"Good morning," Richard said, a marvelous English accent flowing expertly from his tongue. "We've a need for an auto for the week."

Richard placed a platinum Visa card on the counter.

The man glanced at it and said with a small smile, "Certainly. Will you be returning to this location?

"Yes, bit of sales work in your neighborhood."

"Fine, sir." The clerk deftly pulled out the rental form and began marking here and there, then handed it to Richard. "Please fill out parts one, two, and four, sir."

"Good-oh," Richard replied.

Oh, please, Audrey linked.

Richard smiled but said nothing.

The counter man seemed not to notice the accent, or not care. Audrey stood silent, not contributing more than her natural beauty, the breath of her perfume, and a smile that she kept gently across her face.

Richard completed the form and handed it to the man who asked for Richard's license. Richard pulled an International Driver's License from his wallet and put it on the counter. The clerk picked it up, wrote the numbers down and handed it back.

"You indicated you'll want a Ford Taurus."

Richard nodded.

"I'm sorry, our last Taurus went out a moment ago. Will you accept an upgrade at the Taurus rate?"

"That will be fine," Richard said. They completed their business and Richard took the proffered key, noting that they now had a current year Crown Victoria.

"The fuel mileage isn't quite as good. I hope you're on an expense account." The man laughed shortly.

Richard smiled. "Yes, we are."

"You won't have trouble with the left hand drive or traffic circles, will you?" the man offered.

"No problem, mate. This is our third trip over the pond. We're used to you Yankees wrong-headed driving."

The clerk laughed. "Have a good stay, sir."

"Good day." The counter man pointed out the location of the vehicle and they proceeded to the car. Richard put his briefcase in the back seat. Audrey held onto hers.

Audrey linked, *Deep honey beige. Not bad, honey.*

Play on words, pet?

Nah, not this time. I do like the interior.

"Well, off we go, my dear," Richard said.

"Right and left at the third light. My map shows it's about five miles outside of the center on Route 278."

"Right, navigator." He started the car and put it in drive and discovered its quiet competence. Ten minutes of eight. Time to get a move. He pulled out slowly and soon had the feel of the big automobile. Their right turn put them back on Main Street. Soon the Route 278 sign appeared and they turned again, heading southwest now. They discovered a smooth road filled with morning commuters.

They traveled with traffic, which ran about ten miles per hour over the speed limit. In ten minutes the sign for International Fabrications pointed to a wide secondary road. A grouping of signs on a post reminiscent of an old cast iron light standard pointed the way to the administrative offices, Shipping/Receiving, Power House Road and Warehouse Lane. The young operatives were suitably impressed with the size of the facility.

First time to the home office, love.

First time for everything, Audrey replied.

A hundred feet inside they came to a guard station, noting the wide, electronically controlled entrance and an eight foot Anchor fence that rolled away in the distance on both sides.

Richard stopped at the gate and a smartly dressed guard came out. He wore a sidearm in a police holster.

"Good morning. May I help you?"

"Yes. This letter will assist you."

The guard took the letter and looked at it and handed it back. "Follow the roadway to the left. That's the administration building in the distance. Give this to the receptionist and she will direct you. Have a good day, sir."

Richard drove off.

My, aren't they all so polite.

Seems so.

Audrey, recalled that eighty percent of the organization was recruited on the outside and worked from smaller headquarters. The cell structure of the covert side of the organization had been so exquisitely handled that the large majority of operatives never needed to know where the home office was. Stoic had created the plan and executed it with considerable cunning.

Ted had said that the three thousand employees who worked in this large complex were, for the most part, not part of the covert side of Stoics operation. Ted wouldn't give numbers, but implied that covert people were a small minority, tough, sure and dangerous, but minor. Yet they were movers and shakers, leading, altering, occasionally becoming a force within pressure points in a world full of people who hadn't a clue they existed.

Richard drove smoothly to Administration and found a parking spot marked "visitor." He and Audrey got out and walked into the company's modern offices. Automatic plate glass doors opened smoothly. The space beyond the seven-foot doorway opened out into a huge, pillared room very like a hotel lobby. Maroon marble shot with white abounded. Strategically placed tropical plants uplifted the stark coldness of the interior and mellowed it. attention to decorating created a nice ambience. In the center of the large room sat a large circular marble desk. On the front facing the doorway, a small, brass lettered block sign announced "Receptionist."

Audrey and Richard strolled up to the young woman behind the desk and Richard informed the lady that they were there to see Mr. Rettick. Her brows arched slightly and in her clear English accent, she said, "He only sees people by appointment."

Richard handed her the letter. She glanced quickly at it and said, "Just a moment, please."

A small brass oval pinned above her left breast purported her name to be Heather. She picked up the phone and punched in a four-digit code, announced the names of the visitors, waited for a moment and said, "Very well."

She hung up and smiled at them. "You may go up the stairs to the second floor. Directly ahead you will see an office. You may go in there. Have a pleasant day."

"Thank you," Richard said. They turned and walked fifty feet to the wide marble staircase and mounted it. It curved upward to the left, ending at a landing twenty feet above. They faced a door that said "Manson Rettick" in gold lettering.

Richard grasped the handle and the door moved silently inward. At a desk within, a thirty something woman in a pleasantly fitted dark business suit greeted them. An understated brass plate in a polished wooden holder told them she was Laura Baumert, Secretary to the president. She stood up.

"Mr. and Mrs. Penwarton. I'm glad you're here. Mr. Rettick isn't in his office at the moment, but he isn't far and he should be returning shortly. Will you have a seat?" She indicated two leather-bound chairs nearby.

"Thank you."

They sat primly near the front aspect of the furniture as if waiting to jump up at a moments notice. Audrey glanced around, eyes only, taking in her surroundings.

There is nothing here that peaks my aural sense. And downstairs I didn't get any vibes either. So far so good. Laura Baumert is okay.

Good. I like her. Just a feeling. I've been entertaining my covert electronic sense and I'm getting vibes all over the place. I find it a bit much and it's making it hard for me to concentrate.

That's not good. See if you can attenuate the feeling by focusing on some other thing.

Hmm...that helps. How did you know?

I didn't, but it stands to reason that you should have ultimate control over this ability. The implant is only a highly sophisticated amplifier, I think.

Yeah, but it seems to work in strange ways, Audrey.

What do you mean?

Well, you have developed something that seems to absorb a negative intent and your brain interprets it as a color, right?

Sort of, but I see where you're going with this. Our genetic backgrounds may be the determinant factor, rather than our sex. That what you mean?

Not altogether. Our gender is also is a factor in the whole package. Were I a female with my genetic background, I wonder what other facility I'd be dealing with now, if any at all? It's interesting. Are you developing any other features through this implant yet?

Audrey glanced at the president's secretary, apparently involved in her deskwork. She hesitated and appeared to look inward.

Not that I can tell. I thought I had something more coming yesterday, but instead my aural sense cleared up. Maybe we only get two major features and that's it!

Dunno. Anyway, I'm real glad you've got yours and I got mine and we got ours. Especially the mind link.

I know what you mean. Audrey sent him a curled love note.

Hey, stop that. You want me to melt all over this chair?

You're probably right. We'd better pay attention…hey someone's coming and my aura is up!

Just then the door opened and a medium height, slightly portly man entered. He wore an expensive business suit and as he looked over at the two of them Audrey saw that he had cold, malevolent brown eyes. Audrey sent a quick and startled message to Richard.

If this is Rettick, we got trouble!

Richard looked at the man, studying him for a brief moment. He felt his body tense, and he willed himself to not let it show.

The man's gaze shifted to the woman behind the desk.

She spoke. "Mr. Rettick, the computer specialists that were recommended to us are here. Let me introduce Audrey and Richard Penwarton." There was no guile in Baumert's eyes and her demeanor remained candid and easy. She didn't know! It also meant she had to be brought into this somehow. Ted had to become aware, and quickly.

Audrey had trouble holding back. The man had been subverted and it had to have happened within the past week! Ted had assured them that he was a player only as to the functioning of the company. Bad luck and a serious problem!

All top brass in any organization become good politicians. They have to, to remain on top. They are smart or they wouldn't stay there. Manson Rettick turned back to the duo and smiled a politician's smile, extending his hand first to Richard and then to Audrey.

"Well, happy that you are here."

"Pleased to meet you, sir."

"Come in, come in." The head of the company ushered them into his office and invited them to sit down. His well appointed office featured beige carpeted flooring and walnut bookshelves along its sides. A mammoth walnut desk sat near the large tinted glass window, giving him a spectacular view of rolling hills beyond the complex. Rettick went behind the desk and sat.

The man cleared his throat. "I have been advised that we have a knotty programming problem and I'm told that you can fix it quick. Think you can?"

Richard jumped in with his prepared remarks. "Yes, we should be able to assist you. Audrey and I teamed and wrote the original program your company is using."

"Well, that's just fine. What do you need to get started?"

"As much space and access as you can grant, sir. We don't want to step on any corporate toes, but because of firewalls and partitions and the security we wrote into the entire program, it will be necessary to undo the problem on a PC basis, unit to unit, and then tackle the servers and finally the mainframe. It will be like putting out all the small fires before tackling the major forest fire. We have to push it back and make it swallow itself."

Rettick smiled. "I see. I'm sure I can arrange that."

"That would be good, Mr. Rettick. Soon as you can get us clearance, we'll get started. We're ready."

"Fine. I'll issue a directive to all department heads right away."

He pushed a button on his desk and said into the air, "Laura, come in here a moment." They heard a "Yes, sir" and she arrived immediately.

"Where do you wish to start?" He looked at both.

Time for me, my man, Audrey linked.

Go for it, darlin'

"All PC's have been linked directly to your five major departments," Audrey began. "We can eliminate the slave PC's by disconnecting them from the network temporarily. They'll be down not more than thirty minutes, likely much less. We can deal directly with the master PC's at department level. Likely the problem emanates from one of them. Once we find it we can circumvent all others, isolate the offending one and wrap it up quickly."

Richard added, "We planned a week away, in case. You are a valuable customer. That's worst case. More likely we'll hit on it today and can wrap up by tomorrow."

"Well," Rettick said, "I will assign Laura to take you around to the various departments and get you started."

"Thank you."

The president stood. The interview was over. They stood and moved toward the door. Laura Baumert led them out into the anteroom, her office, and grabbed a pen and small pad.

"Let's go, Mr. and Mrs. Penwarton."

"Thank you."

Richard, we have a mighty big problem. We have to convince Laura that Manson Rettick has been compromised and she will have to get to Ted soon.

I'll think on it. Ahh, Rettick has picked up the phone and he's calling somebody. We'd better be very careful from this point. I think we've been made!

Laura walked out with them, heading for Finance.

46

The phone rang. Nick picked it up. "What!"

"Ray, Nick. It's Stretch."

"Okay. Put him on."

After a short pause, Stretch came on. "Boss, I'm on my way home."

"Where are you?"

"Laid over in East Islip. I'm on the motel phone."

"Which one?"

"Sea Horse Inn."

"Got anything?"

"No, boss. I gave it a good try, but that tidal wave messed everything."

"Yeah, don't worry, I got feelers out and maybe I'll have something else for you when you get back."

"Yeah?"

"Yeah. Get back here."

"Okay, Nick." Stretch heard the hang-up click before he could get the phone away from his ear. No prob so far, he thought. Least he's not pissed at me.

On the long drive back to the mansion Stretch had a lot of time to think. He'd never had doubts before about his abilities or his desire to be big in the rackets. The streak of meanness he'd enjoyed in killing Tommie Geacali and in other "projects" he'd completed looked different to him since his date with Barbara. He thought of her now and a strange feeling quirked the corners of his mouth. Some dame! Never met a pure one before. Powerful! Made him itch in his loins, but not like other women, not like the whores. Some of them made him itch, all right.

"Better get straight in my head before I get back," he mused, "Nick'd see the difference for sure. Don't try to jack that guy up!"

But he went right on planning his next junket to Great South Bay. About a month, he thought. I'd better get it straight what I done for Nick first. My chance to come up a bit. Freedom, umm, sounds good. Then it hit him. I get back and tell Nick while I was nosin' around I got a few vibes about some business he might want to approach in the near future. Yeah, that's it. He'll go for something that'll put shekels in his pocket. Gotta think about that.

Wonder what he's got goin' now?

The thought submerged suddenly. Stretch jammed on his brakes to avoid a car ahead that swerved to miss a bouncing basketball that came into the road from an adjacent driveway. A little kid too small to be wielding such a big ball ran out and tried to retrieve it before it left the sidewalk. The running six-year-old was brought up with a snap on hearing his Mom's screech, "JOHNNY!" The old invisible tether, Stretch thought as he narrowly avoided rear-ending the car ahead. The mom ran from her porch to retrieve her son. The driver in front barely stopped in time to avoid little Johnny's following the ball under the car. The driver got out, a little shaken and said, "The child all right?"

Mom answered, "Yes."

The man leaned down to look and discovered the ball had wedged under the middle of the vehicle. He got back in and slowly drove off the ball. Mom, now with a firm grip on her thoughtless child retrieved the ball and thanked the driver, who tipped his hat and drove on. Stretch watched with amusement, conscious of failing to get immensely irritated as he usually did in any traffic situation designed to hold him up. Not a man with patience, with Barbara on his mind it didn't bother him. He realized that thinking about what he might tell Nick had transferred to the pedal. He had been going too fast for the neighborhood and too close behind the driver ahead.

Damn! Nick'd have my ass if I crash his company car.

Soon enough he passed through the rest of the Hamlet of Bardot and cleared the last and only traffic light. He slowed down and checked his map. Another two and a half hours! The closer he got, the less he wanted to be there, but like a moth to a flame...

Stretch pulled onto the Sunrise Highway. With light traffic and a smooth highway, he kicked it up a couple of notches and the Ford ate up the miles. By nine-thirty he'd crossed Shinnecock Canal and soon after ran out of parkway. Going remained pretty fast on that less traveled road. By eleven he'd cleared Amagansett and was almost home. Stretch drove into the estate shortly after, turned the car in and gave up the keys. He talked with Finnegan at the guard station for a couple of minutes and then headed for the mansion. Nothing brewing he could figure.

Stretch decided it best to see Nick right away before going to his room to clean up from the long ride.

He knocked on the door to Nick's study.

"Come in."

"Just back, Nick," said Stretch as he entered. Nick looked up from his desk.

"Stretch, sit down. Got some interesting info ten minutes ago and I'm going to want you to follow it up. You'll be taking Quinn, Matatolis and Schaffer with you."

Stretch settled into an office chair.

"You'll head the kill team. I got the location of the girl and her partners. I'll have Rocco fly you four into JFK. Get a plane to Friendship Airport and rent a car. You're going to Frederick, Maryland."

"Rocco couldn't fly us the whole way?"

"No, bad idea. Do it the way I said."

"Sure. How'd you do it boss?" Trafalgar's tone excited the Weasel. Something he could gnaw on.

"Don't ask."

"You get it done, Boss."

"Don't forget it, either." The hit man stayed silent.

"You're going to leave tomorrow. I want to meet with you and the others. Look 'em up and tell 'em I'll see you all at two o'clock in the soldier's room."

"Right, boss. Can you hint what we got?"
"I'll tell you when I don't have to repeat myself."
"Sure. Yeah, I'll round them up."
"Get out of here!" Stretch left hurriedly.

47

"Mr. Limbertaire, I'd like to introduce you to Mr. and Mrs. Richard Penwarton. They are here from England to fix your computer problems." Laura turned and introduced a man of average height, bald except for tufts of hair neatly cut and currycombed at the sides. He wore a white shirt, a conservative two-color tie and light designer corduroy pants. "This is Norman Limbertaire, head of the Accounting Department."

"About time!" Limbertaire said, not quite ignoring the operatives and sounding very frustrated. "Manson finally got somebody in."

"Yes, sir. They are the team who created the original program. It has run flawlessly for two years. Don't blame them, but if anybody can fix it, it's these two."

"I shouldn't gripe," the accounting man said, now looking at the two with real interest. "Sorry, Mr. and Mrs. Penwarton, it's just frustrating, when everything has worked smoothly for so long."

"We understand, Mr. Limbertaire. We'll fix you up. There is an answer," Richard said.

He's clean, Richard.

Good. Still have to go through this.

I know.

"All right. What do you need from me?"

"We were given a general idea, but more than one problem may infect the servers to Finance and those to the rest of the complex. Tell me your indications."

"All right. Standard inputs using the calculation features for the last quarter yield aberrant numbers. When our operators try to refresh the data, we get a lot of weird garbage, meaningless stuff. It looks like programming language, but it's not. Two days now we're basically out of business, and I can't afford the time. They've tried to re-input fresh, and it always turns around at second level. They've tried the sysdoc without success."

"Can you run some numbers right now and show me?" Richard asked.

"Certainly. Here, watch." Limbertaire sat at the console in his office and rapidly punched in a series of numbers, entered and went immediately to second level. When he hit enter a second time the screen filled with odd characters.

Richard moved away from the network PC and turned his back. He started gesturing into the air like he was drawing some kind of circuit out in front of him. He pondered it for a few moments, rubbing his chin.

Richard turned to Audrey and said, "Audrey, I haven't seen this before, but it reminds me of QB-6. What do you think?"

"Yes, it does, but with a twist. Why don't we try the AL-23 Zip?"

"Um...good place to start. Right. You explain to Mr. Limbertaire what it is we need to do. I want to unearth my interface and get hooked in. You can hook up in a couple of minutes."

"Okay, love."

The accounting man stood by. Audrey began, "If it's a variation on what we have seen before, we have a program that will set it to rights, Mr. Limbertaire. If not, it should point us in the right direction."

"I don't know how you people figure these things out."

"We don't understand accounting, either, sir.

"Yes, of course."

"This could take a couple of hours or more, I'd guess. No point in your standing around for the duration. Oh, and we'll need to take everything down from the server input and disconnect your network, but only for a few minutes while we effect the fix. We'll let you know."

Limbertaire nodded.

Audrey linked, *The things we do to offer legitimacy to this sham.*

Got to do it, my love. Wouldn't do for them to find us out. Actually, not ever.

True.

Okay, love; let's get cracking. Pip, pip! Richard bent to his brief case and removed his dummy spec-op interface. Actually a sophisticated laptop, it also had a few odd bumps and lumps carefully molded into the body, giving it a distinctly unconventional appearance.

"What is that?" Limbertaire asked, eyebrows raised.

"Special equipment," was all Richard would say. "We'll work on this now. Try to get you back to speed as quickly as possible. Would you excuse us?"

"Oh, sure, Mr. Penwarton. Laura, I will call you when the team is finished."

"Thank you, Mr. Limbertaire," she said, and left.

"Believe I'll go out on the floor for awhile," he said to Audrey and Richard.

"No problem, sir. We work better alone. We'll be fine," Audrey said. Limbertaire left.

We'll spend about an hour here and then take a break to "discuss" our solution, then another hour for the fix. Appropriate downtime for the department, of course. Meantime, I'll try to get a coded packet to Stoic. He's definitely watching us. Only problem, not sure if our other problem is also watching.

Ted said Stoic was a master of disguise. Can you program a message that will alert him, with an encrypt key he can divine from the wrapper?

I think so. We should still try to get to Laura Baumert. She must have had a more certain access for a long time, at least to Ted. And we should get this to Ted. Laura probably doesn't even know about Stoic.

Agree. You think on that while I putz around in the computer system, looking intelligent.

Audrey casually removed the keyboard interface from her case and began running leads from her machine to Richards. Richard completed his connections to the Master PC and nodded to Audrey, who booted up. In a couple of minutes her screen filled with odd programming language. She thought to herself that it wouldn't be good if someone who really had a handle on computer programming walked in and started asking questions. Richard was good, but his partner was a total outsider and she'd have to bull her way through any searching discourse. Oddly, it made her smile.

For the unseen audience they worked, checking features and even hardware. They would have fooled all but the brilliantly astute.

Good enough for me, love.

Oops, didn't think I was projecting.

You slipped a little. Don't give it a thought.

I'm glad I can only slip in your direction.

Me too.

Richard worked over the interface for a time, took a few moments appearing to think about it and then went back to his system checks. When he'd been at it for a bit over two hours, he inserted an innocuous CD into the "D" drive, one of many he had tried, and hit "enter." For a moment nothing happened, and then a message came across the screen. It said, "Reboot now." Richard casually looked over at Audrey, encompassing the room as he did so. He brought the system down and immediately restarted it.

All there is to it, my dear.

Oh my brave and handsome man! Audrey exclaimed.

Two minutes later the system came up and it ran perfectly. The operatives re-hooked the slave PC's to the system, got up and went to Limbertaire's plate glass door. They saw him down near the end of the large office and waved at him. He smiled and started back.

Moments later, Richard spoke loudly enough for the Accounting Director and several within earshot to hear. "Bloody difficult, but it's solved. Your mates can get back to work, or whatever it is they do," and he smiled.

Limbertaire laughed in relief. "That's great. What was wrong?"

"After we checked the hardware and all profiles were nominal, we figured it must be a Trojan. Bloody clever one, too. When we located it, it came apart in pieces. Someone didn't want us to discover how it was constructed, but we'll find out just the same. We'll analyze the pieces we could save and reconstruct it. Then we'll decide what needs to be done to protect your system in the future, but you're good to go for right now."

"Thank you. I appreciate all you've done.

"Happy to help. Perhaps you could ring up Ms. Laura Baumert and tell her that we have energy enough to try another Master PC."

The Finance man laughed again, clearly delighted to do anything he could for these two geniuses who had repaired his system. "Absolutely!" He went to his phone and dialed a four-digit number. They heard him speak to Rettick's secretary.

"Laura, you were right. Couldn't help being skeptical, but they did it. Can you come down and take them to," he looked at them and Richard shrugged, "wherever they want to go?"

Guess what? Richard projected.

What?

I heard the entire conversation. I think Ted activated us too early. My stuff is still developing. I think the healing is having a major impact, more than we thought.

Could be. So, what happened?

It was like I could hear the two people as I stood between them. Almost came out of my gourd. I'm catching background conversations now, too.

Better practice dimming that stuff out or pretty soon you won't be able to hear yourself think.

Ha-ha, love.

I mean it.

I'll get a handle on it. Focus seems to be a big thing to the implants.

I'm sure you're right, but it looks like we're just going to have to grow with these abilities.

You're right, of course. Now smile, pardner!

Oh, you!

In a few minutes Laura returned and whisked them away to the Sales Department. There they met Leon Whitiker. Amber's aura sense told the two that he was clean, also. There they went through the same investigative process, but did so after lunch, as the noon hour had crept up on them as they were setting up. Mr. Whitiker offered to have lunch brought to them. They agreed and he ordered it from the cafeteria. The British team elected to take an hour off to eat and discuss innocuous topics, while linking their real thoughts.

Nothing yet, Richard linked, *but I have an idea how we can get to Ted.*

How?

I'm going to burn a CD and encrypt it, using "sextant" as a password. I can create a message within a message with the shell giving a hint of the sextant shape. I'll hand it off to Laura if we can get out of sight of prying eyes. The electronics are pervasive as far as I can "see." Ted should be able to figure it out quickly. Message will be "The main man isn't the man we seek, but he's dangerous now, evidently corrupted. Be watchful. Take steps if you can."

Ted will probably find a way to communicate with us.

I'd bet on it.

They finished setup after lunch and discovered, they told Whitiker, a different problem, very knotty. Richard said he thought it seemed related to the first problem they found, but it didn't act in the same way. They worked on it for four hours, stopping for tea at precisely three-fifteen for fifteen minutes, then finishing their system checks, reprogramming their fix as the general office personnel began to leave for the day promptly at five.

Audrey, this would be a perfect time to catch the flavor of the place and a perfect way to get the disk to Laura. Let's get a tour. I want to put to eye what I have in my head from the maps and plans I've read.

Good idea. I think if Manson Rettick has alerted the traitor, and I believe he has, then we might expect him to show his hand. Might work to our favor. Let's talk to Laura. She'll be easier to access between buildings, and easier to convince that her boss has gone bad. Actually, we may not need to say anything to Laura. Just palm it to her and tell her to get it to her real boss right away.

Agree.

They told Laura they were finished for the day and would like a tour and could she meet them.

"Yes, I'm free this evening. I'd like to. I need to finish up some things here, first. Can you wait a few minutes?"

"Sure." Three to go.

"Great. I'll meet you in my office."

"We'll walk on up there."

"All right." The two picked up their cases and shaking the hand of the Sales Director to his profuse thanks, left Whitiker's office. They walked through the complex, arriving at Laura's office as she closed and locked her desk drawer. Manson Rettick remained sequestered in his office. Richard got vibes from a phone conversation. He began to focus on it, but Rettick hung up and Richard withdrew his focus.

"Perfect timing. Where would you like to go?"

"Why don't we walk the grounds and get an idea of where the other facilities are so you won't have to take time from your schedule?" Richard suggested.

"Certainly, but I don't mind. Matter of fact, Mr. Rettick specifically asked me to keep your location known to him all the time."

Don't like the sound of that.

Might mean nothing, but I suspect you are right again, love, Richard linked.

They quietly followed her down the wide marble stairway and out through Reception. She stopped at the desk to tell the duty person she was leaving for the day but she'd be on premises for a while. The woman made a note on her computer, smiled, and they headed for the exit.

"You pay much attention to security, Laura," said Audrey.

Yes, Mrs. Penwarton. There is much to steal or otherwise damage within the complex."

"I see. Well, we feel quite secure, thank you."

Baumert laughed. "You don't get to be a multi-billion dollar company in our business without watching everything pretty closely."

"Quite so." Audrey returned.

"What kind of schedule do you plan for tomorrow?"

Richard answered, "We should be able to isolate and eliminate this devilish problem by tomorrow night, I would think. Then we'll get out of your hair, as you Yankees say."

Laura smiled.

Now we'll find out what this complex has. Your electronic sense will help immensely, Audrey linked.

They walked through the big plate glass doors and into the afternoon sunshine. The late day sun, too bright to look at directly, hung over the guard station in front and highlighted the heavy fencing that surrounded the facility. It reminded Audrey of prison fencing in the low security facilities in the North. It would keep out all but the most determined. She didn't think there would be any problem of infiltration in this assignment, but it always paid to know your ground.

Agree.

Damn! You listening again?

Better get used to it. My reading link with you is getting better all the time.

How about I want some privacy, big guy?

I think you'll have to believe that we're joined at the hip, from now on. But don't worry about me. I don't tell.

Oh, you beast!

Not really. Hey, we agreed to become experimental guinea pigs for this, didn't we?

Sure, but I'd like to be private sometimes.

Just say the word and I'll block you out, okay? Just transmit, "Privacy." That work for you? Same for me, right?

Sure, Richard. It's not that I don't want you to hear my thoughts, it's just...well, it's unexpected and takes a little getting used to. Besides, I'm not hearing yours. How come?

I don't know. The units are the same, I think. Must be a cortical difference. Physiology shouldn't matter, should it?

I haven't a clue, Richard. I feel like I'm on a roller coaster and I don't know when I'll be allowed to get off.

Might not happen, honey. Don't despair, Richard is there.

My hero! Audrey sent him a little love ding.

Oh, honey!

Laura walked alongside the two, oblivious to the spirited conversation going on beside her. They passed along the front of the building and Laura looked up. In the window of the second floor Executive office they could see Manson Rettick on his phone, his chair turned toward the outside scene. He stared at them. Laura waved and after a moment, Rettick smiled and waved back. But it seemed to Audrey that he gave himself away in that instant. His aura swelled, just for a second.

The man is scary, Richard.

Gotta believe it. Wouldn't do to sell him short. One more element in the continuing saga of the world's most secret operative team, huh?

How can you joke...?

Easy, just did. Wanna try one?

No, and pay attention. Tune in any exterior electronics you sense. Let's find out where they are.

Sorry. There are none, not that I can tell right now. Keep you posted.

That surprises me.

Well, there's plenty of guard presence. Maybe they feel that's enough.

They came around the north side of the Administration building on a well-paved cement walkway. It appeared in prime condition—everything did—wending its way toward an enormous, blue-sided building with a white painted roof that canted on a slight angle to the position of Administration. As they cleared the end of the building they noticed the walkway split midway behind Administration, one part angling to the right toward another enormous blue building, an obvious twin of the first. Laura explained it all as they came into view.

"Shipping and Receiving are to the left and our warehouse storage is on the right. Behind that we keep Security and a conference center. You can see the corner of the building beyond the warehouse."

Richard said, "I'm really impressed with the size of the complex."

"Yes," Laura replied. "It is huge, but comfortably laid out to promote efficiencies."

This Laura is no dummy.

No.

Other splits could be seen in the distance. Along the way, green-painted ornamental iron benches appeared occasionally, and they even noticed picnic tables near each of the large buildings they could see. Evidently Rettick, maybe Stoic, too, believed in productiveness as a function of morale, and promoted pleasant surroundings for the workers.

Richard, did you notice before we came around to the back of Administration that the woody area isn't all that far from the edge of the fence?

Yes, I did, but security seems pretty straightforward and there appears to be plenty of it, he gestured toward two uniformed security people he saw in the distance, walking near the fence line. *I imagine security is stepped up at night, too.*

Well, maybe.

Besides, you know electronics can be compromised.

So can people.

Touché! Audrey glanced around casually, noting other security people going about business with self-assurance and purpose.

Which brings to my mind a problem. If Manson Rettick has been compromised by our traitor, and think about it, he might only be an evil man not connected to the plot, then we have to watch out for the guards, too. Maybe everyone else. What about that? My sense seems to pick up on evil intent, but whose evil? Is Rettick part of it? I can't know.

Great! Never thought about it. That was narrow-minded. I mean, focused is one thing, but to overlook something that should be obvious...

Don't blame yourself, Richard, I just thought of it myself, and as you say, these abilities are new and unique. Mine is still clarifying, a little, anyway.

Laura interrupted their silent conversation. They had come to the main roadway, a wide, double lane highway. A big tandem tractor-trailer labored past. The huge oval label on the red side of the trailer said Hemmington Lines. They waited until the rumble faded.

"We'll cross here and visit Security and Conferencing. Then I'll walk you over to the Power station." They crossed quickly, as another trailer came pounding up the slight incline toward the guard station. "Those truckers will drive all night. Wouldn't want to be one. Tough job."

"True, but the trucks these days are pretty awesome," Audrey replied. She liked Laura. Girl with a head on her shoulders, assistant and secretary to the President. Had a lot going for her. And her other connection, the one with Ted's organization. Yes, bright and capable.

"No question, sleeping quarters, the whole nine yards. But to live on the road? Not for me."

"I have to agree there." But Audrey thought about how many days and nights she had been on assignment and the strange places she'd been. She felt an affinity to long distance truckers. Richard caught her thought but wisely did not acknowledge his eavesdropping.

"Shipping/Receiving and the warehousemen leave around six. Admin goes home at five, Sales stays until six," Laura said comfortably as they continued their walk, "and the rest of the place is perking 24/7."

"Three shifts?" Richard asked.

"Yes."

Richard, any exterior electronics yet?

No.

I still find that strange.

As the tree approached the Security building, Richard suddenly thought, *Lots going on here.*

Might not mean anything. It is the Security hub after all.

Keep me in the loop.

Could I not?

The threesome entered the building. The anteroom had two doors. In between them a uniformed security person sat at a small desk.

"Hi, Tanga." Laura greeted the young woman. "Anything doing?"

"Hey, Laura. Nope, nuttin' here. Slow night." The young black girl smiled at Laura.

"Do you know if Mr. Diglatori will be in, in the morning?"

"He's here now. Wanna talk to him?"

"I'd like to have him meet our computer repair team if he's in. They'll be here early tomorrow to work on your PC system."

"I'll see if he's available." She pressed a contact on her small console. "Mr. Diglatori, Ms. Baumert is here with some people she'd like you to meet."

"I'm busy now. I'm going to be some time. Can they wait, or can I see them tomorrow?"

"I'll ask, sir." She turned to her guests. "I can't disturb him. Do you want to wait?"

Laura looked at her two charges and said, "Can you wait?"

Audrey linked, *Let's not. I'm getting a creepy feeling. Bet he's not here in the morning, either.*

"No. We'll go on," Richard said.

The young woman passed the message to the man.

"Okay. Oh, is Shika Marver still in the building?" Laura asked Tanga.

"No, she's long gone, Laura."

"Ms. Marver is in charge of our Conference Center, just down the hall."

Laura said good night to Tanga. The two operatives nodded and they left.

What is it? Richard asked Audrey.

I got multiple aural displays, I guess you'd call them. Something's going on in there, that's certain.

Okay, let's go on and make this a later stopping place.

Okay.

"Laura," Audrey said to their guide, "let's go to the Power Station and check it out. Then we're going to quit for the night. It's been a long day."

Laura looked at Audrey sympathetically and nodded. "Sure."

They cut cross-lots, walking the now deserted road to the power plant, the only part of the complex that didn't have walkways leading to and from it. It was more isolated and any access to the plant would reasonably be by road.

They spent only a few minutes there. Fred Dodd, the plant manager had gone for the day and Audrey linked to Richard that they might have hit on it at Security. They needed to go somewhere and think it through. That was enough for Richard.

One more odd thing happened as the two walked back to the Administration parking lot to Laura's Green VW New Beetle. Audrey suddenly got a long distance vibe. She stopped abruptly! The other two stopped in confusion.

48

The old Rockwell Commander dipped and swayed in light turbulence at seventeen thousand feet. Rocco handled it expertly. Quinn complained and at one point said miserably to Rocco, "You got a barf bag?"

"Hang on, Johnny," the pilot said with a laugh, "we're almost through this stuff.

In a couple of minutes the plane straightened out and they cut smooth air again. Quinn looked a little green, but he calmed down and said nothing after that. The others evidently didn't get airsick. At least none of the other three said anything.

"What you boys up to?" Rocco asked into the air.

Stretch answered, "Just a quick job, Rocco. No thang."

"Yeah." The pilot paid attention to his flying, but he wondered. Nick rarely sent four soldiers out on a mission. His style was singles. Must be big. "Well, you guys, another twenty minutes and we'll be landing."

"That's good news," came from Quinn in the second row of seats. His stomach was still rolling.

"You gotta chuck, don' do on me, you little fuck!" said Lenny Matatolis, a sour faced man who usually went by the name "Greek." He laughed at his little rhyme. A burly barrel-chested guy with spindly legs, strong enough but out of place on his body, he was known for quiet presence and a crushing grip. And body odor. Nick used him as a destroyer. He seemed to like to tear things apart. Quinn didn't feel good enough to throw out one of his scathing Irish retorts.

Donny "Diddle" Schaffer sat looking out the window, an average looking man except for the arresting narrowness of his beady, feral-like eyes. It gave the rest of his face a fat look, though it wasn't fat. He had scrunched up features kind of like Johnny Quinn, but with a different effect. Disappearing lips and knife-edge nose completed the picture. He seemed bored, like maybe a good game of five-card stud might be on his mind.

All four wore good casual clothes, only remarkable because of the dark, rather plain shirts in varied colors, open at the neck. Black Chinos were also the order of the day. Stretch had little to say. He thought of Barbara a lot now. Funny how one broad could screw up his mind like that, but fact, she did and he liked it. Stretch reflected on his meeting with Nick. The four had listened to the boss intently. Nick's gaze went from one to the other and back, never stopping. It made them all nervous.

When he was through, he said, "You guys should make quick work of it, but ya never know, right? Lotta security in that place. No Fort Knox, but if you're gonna jump in, be careful."

"Yeah, right, Nick," came the mumbled replies.

"Stretch, you got a map of that place in your head?" The map of the complex Nick had obtained through Rathmanizzar's inside person. Nothing for a department head to fax a map to Nick's company line and nobody knows.

"Yeah, Nick, I'm five-by."

"Good."

The Boss had outlined the targets, but he only had two of them and Stretch had said there were three. Somebody evidently got to stay out of sight and nobody knew who.

"You soldiers go pack. Rocco'll be here to pick you up in an hour. Be ready!"

The four were waiting when the car picked them up to take them to Rocco's little airstrip.

Now in the plane and nearing JFK, Stretch patted his pocket. In his wallet he carried a fake ID like the rest, nothing that could lead back to Nick.

Twenty minutes later Rocco banked the heavy plane while talking on the cockpit radio. He was directed into a landing pattern and soon the party of five was on the ground, taxiing toward the commercial hangers. A few minutes after that they'd deplaned with their luggage, one small suitcase each. The four tramped in, got through the terminal and caught a cab over to United Airlines. They carried no weapons. Stretch figured they'd make a buy in Maryland. Nick wouldn't let them take any firepower.

The trip in the 737 took an hour and once again they landed, now hundreds of miles from their starting point. Stretch didn't have a clue what the others were thinking, but he marveled at how a guy could be in one place and hours later so far away. He smiled to think that he might still have a little of the kid he used to be in him. Thoughts of his mission and what a big man he'd be in the organization after this job soon crowded those notions out of his head.

"Let's move, you guys," Stretch said to assert leadership. People like those three didn't like to listen to somebody they considered an equal. Quinn would be easiest. They glanced at Stretch and said nothing, but moved along with him toward Baggage Claim and retrieved their suitcases easily enough in the bustle of the busy terminal. They rented a car from Dollar Days Rental for a week, unlimited mileage.

"Johnny, you drive. I'll take shotgun."

"Sure, Stretch. Feelin' good now."

"Figgered."

Stretch handed him the key and marched out. The others sauntered after. They found the late model Caprice and got in. The standout red of the car glared at them, but Stretch didn't care what color a car was, made no difference. The others could have cared less. Johnny started the car and checked the dash.

"Tank's full," Quinn announced unnecessarily.

Nobody said a word. He muttered under his breath and put the vehicle in gear. While Quinn backed out of the space, Stretch pulled out his map. He studied it for a while.

"Johnny, look for a Sears mall."

Quinn looked at him.

"Knives, man."

"Yeah, right." Quinn headed out. Near the edge of town, predictably, they found a Sears. Stretch sent the Greek in for the buy. He came back in twenty with a shopping bag.

"No trouble?" Stretch asked. The big man shook his head.

"Okay, Johnny, head out." The little man turned right for the I-270 beltway and Frederick.

Late afternoon traffic zipped along. Quinn kept pace. They entered the target area and Stretch directed them to and past Infab.

"You clowns take a good look at the outside, fencing, access, everything. High ground with trees over there. Maybe we'll jump the fence there. Don't look much."

Matatolis said, "Don't see nuttin' on the far side. Big field, no place to hide."

"Nuttin' to that, 'cept as a culvert on the far side's a possible. That'd take dynamite. No good. We gotta get past the place and double back, take a walk in those woods," Stretch said.

Grunts from the back.

"I think we'll stop on the other side of the ridge up there and I'll go in alone. Anybody hails me; I'll say I'm just hikin'. Looks deserted anyway."

They cleared the rise. Quinn said, "There're some big houses over this side. Watch out for dogs."

"Yeah."

Diddle spoke up. "I wanna go."

"No. I'll handle this one."

"Who you, Weasel?"

"Nick put me in charge of this. You do like I tell you alla way. Kapisch?"

"Bored, man, wanna do somethin'."

"Soon, Diddle. You'll get your fill." The other hit man subsided. Stretch made a mental note to watch him. He wasn't reliable. It surprised him that Nick assigned Schaffer to this hit. Boss must know something Stretch didn't. Maybe Nick was testing *him*. He'd have to be up for it.

Johnny noticed a pull-off up ahead and stopped.

As Stretch got out, he said to Quinn, "Don't want people lookin' at some strange car in these parts and wonderin'. You head out and pick me up in one hour. That's all it should take. Six o'clock now."

"Sure, Stretch. We'll get a coffee or a beer or something down the road."

"No prob, but stay sharp. Don't none of us want to queer this for the boss."

"Yeah."

Stretch Monaghal slammed the door, turned and marched into the near woods. He felt relieved to be out and about. The car seat confined him, stuffed in with the three others, especially that monster Matatolis. He knew none of them liked him much. Who cares, he thought. It's the job. Screw 'em all and what they like. Just do what I tell them, all I want.

The view of the parking area disappeared amongst the trees. Soon the going got tough. Brambles and other things reached for him. Branches whipped at him. Stretch got hung up on berry barbs several times. He had to disentangle gently to avoid tearing his pants and shirtsleeves. He didn't want to get bloodied here.

He cursed over and over, but not loud. "Damn briars."

He had to make numerous detours before the forest thinned enough to make the going easier. The sun slumped slowly in the west. It gave him good light, shining straight through the trees, but it cast strange shadows. Up ahead he saw the edge of the fence. He approached cautiously, stooping in the brushy cover.

The tree line stopped at a cleared area he judged to be fifteen feet across before the fence rose starkly, looking more impenetrable close up than from the road. He stayed back from the edge, as far into the brush as gave him a clear view. His eyes minutely searched the top of the fence for either razor wire or telltale sensors. Nothing! It surprised him.

"Eight foot fence. That's all? Yeah, that's all," he breathed.

He started to turn to leave. Suddenly his eye caught movement. From the edge of one of the huge buildings nearest his position a guard approached the perimeter fence holding with difficulty the largest German Shepherd he'd ever seen. The guard looked competent and so did the dog, in spades! Then he noticed the path worn in the grass about ten feet inside the fence. Perimeter guards, night only, probably. Just about time for the first run.

Security, and plenty of it, like Nick said! This required a change in plan. They'd need to neutralize any guards and dogs they found while inside the compound. Stretch's mind went into high gear. As he crouched there, three people came out of a building—a power station (the place evidently had it's own power plant)—in the distance. They headed his way. He watched for a minute and his excitement grew. A man, a big muscle-bound looking guy and two women. And the one in the middle—he was sure of it—was the woman Nick wanted wiped! Bingo! He waited until he could see her clearly. No doubt of it!

Suddenly the woman stopped and stared straight at him. Could she see him? Couldn't! Nah, not possible! He eased further back into the sparse underbrush all the same. The group stopped, but after a moment they resumed their walk. The other woman, the blond, seemed concerned for a moment but the auburn haired lady waved her off with a shrug and a few words. They continued walking back toward the multi-windowed building at the front of the complex, the one the plans showed as Administration. The woman never glanced his way again.

He'd seen enough. He backed quietly and made his way carefully up and over the hill. Stretch arrived at the parking area where he'd gotten out, two minutes before Johnny Quinn cruised slowly down the road from the opposite direction.

"Good timing," Stretch said as he climbed back into the front seat.

"What you find out?" Lenny Matatolis said.

"Got a good gander at the place. We can get in, but they got dogs and guards. We'll talk about it tonight."

"Why wait?" Diddle spoke up.

"I'm callin' Nick tonight. Guards, dogs, maybe we can get a piece and a potato."

"You want a piece and a silencer now?" Diddle said. "Why?"

"The place is crawlin' with security...but guess what I saw up there?"

"What?"

"The bitch, I saw her. She's there, and the big guy she's with. This is gonna be fun." Stretch took out his recently acquired buck knife, opened it and ran his finger carefully along the ultra-sharp edge. He smiled.

The symbolic gesture was just what they needed. The evil in each man reached out and grasped the Weasel's powerful thought. For the first time, the four became a real team, a kill team. And Stretch became their leader.

49

Richard, she linked, *don't turn your head. I'm getting a deep hue beyond the fence. Here's a picture.*

She sent him an image of the high Anchor fence. Beyond it Richard saw a nebulous blob. A figure crouching at the edge of the woods?

That's too odd to be nothing. And it's too coincidental with our arrival. This is getting dangerous from all sides. What could that mean?

It means we've been found out, Audrey. I'd bet dollars to donuts it's one of Nick's boys. Looks like the war just took on another front.

Laura looked at Audrey. "Anything wrong?" She seemed upset.

Audrey thought so fast she almost forgot her accent. "No, Laura, got a sudden pain in my left lung area. Gas bubble, probably. Okay now."

Laura looked searchingly at Audrey. "Do you want to go to the infirmary?"

"No. I'm all right, really." They resumed their walk. *She's so sweet, Richard.*

Yeah, she is. I was about to hand her the CD for Ted, but I'll wait 'til we get to her car.

Good idea. The person up there has faded into the brush and disappeared. I'm convinced whoever it was noticed me looking.

Gives you a range for this thing, anyway, Richard linked.

Yes, that's good, about thirty yards?

Around there.

They continued up the slight grade and around the administration building to the parking lot. They were parked only a couple of cars down from Baumerts car and Laura, like a good hostess, walked them to it. She extended her hand and as she did, Richard palmed her the CD. She hid her surprise well.

Richard said seriously, "Get this to you know who. It's highly important."

The CD disappeared into a side pocket of her business suit. She smiled brightly and said, "You have a nice evening. We'll see you in the morning."

"Thanks, see you then."

They laid their briefcases in the back seat, got into their rented car and left. On the way to their hotel, Audrey commented once again on Laura. *Sweet and smart, Richard. Hope all this comes out well for her.*

Yeah, she'll be all right.

50

Recognizing that he had the gang in his corner, Stretch started to think in command mode. His eyes narrowed and he faced front while considering what had just happened. Like a light bulb turning on, it came to him. His decisions now meant something to the others. He turned back to the others so they could all see him and smiled thinly. The glint did not leave his eyes.

"You guys, look. I think the two I saw will have to be leaving there sometime soon, you know, put up for the night. The plans I saw didn't have a bunkhouse. There's a lot of open space along the road up this way. We're gonna park out of the way," he looked around and pointed at a curve in the road that would effectively mask their vehicle, "and ambush 'em. Four of us, no chance for them, right?"

"Yeah, sweet!" Diddle liked that picture.

Johnny Quinn had no problem looking up to the Weasel; he'd worked with him before, right? "How we stop 'em, Stretch?"

Stretch thought awhile and then said, "Easy! You guys in back skunch down in the seats. There's enough room back there, even for the Greek. I'll lean over here. Johnny, you make like you're having an attack of some kind and stray across the centerline, kind of slow like. They'll slow down and then you'll go off into the dirt and block their lane. They'll stop, maybe get out and look. We jump out and get 'em quick. Lenny, you punched a few windows in your day, right?"

"Yeah, and I got 'knucks in my pocket. Easy shit."

"Your thinkin'! Cool."

The rest of them hunkered down. Johnny drove down to the place Stretch pointed out and turned around, heading in the direction of a gentle incline leading to International Fabrications entrance road. They could see the end of the road without being obvious.

"What if they turn the other way?" Johnny asked.

"Way you're headin', we can chase after them easy," Stretch said, "but why would they? No hotels that way."

"Yeah."

They settled in to wait.

51

Audrey sat silently smiling, wondering what would happen next. As Richard headed toward town he noticed a large red car a thousand feet ahead weaving on the road. It wasn't going fast and it looked like the driver was in trouble. There were no homes nearby, just trees and a lot of scrub brush and no cars in either direction. Richard drove on but slowed and watched intently.

Suddenly, a hundred feet away, Audrey linked sharply, *Richard, I'm getting deep aura. That's the guy I felt before, and there are more of them. Try to swing around and get out of here!*

You got it, honey! Watch my smoke.

Richard continued to slow. He felt the automatic gear down. The red Chevy, a late model Caprice Classic arched across the road, blocking his lane and part of the opposing lane. It stopped. He could see the driver. Where were the others?

They're there, Richard.

Not doubting, honey.

He stopped twenty feet away. On signal, the four doors of the other car sprang open and out boiled four mean looking characters. Before they could clear the doors, Richard floored the pedal and whipped his Fairlane Vic hard to the left! The rear wheels spun on the macadam and the back end slewed around. Sand and small stones peppered the roadway behind them, causing the attackers to put their hands over their eyes and duck. Richard then palmed the steering ring and spun the wheel. With a banshee screech the Ford accelerated into the empty oncoming lane just as they heard a hard whack on the passengers window. The vehicle switched back and forth as the left wheels dug into the soft shoulder. Richard fought to regain control.

"That wasn't a bullet, Richard," Audrey said, with relief.

"No," he spoke now, "that, if I caught the glint right, was a big old buck knife. Got some frustrated fellas back there!"

"How nice!" Audrey said, a little gleefully.

A smell of burning rubber found a way into their car.

Richard looked in his rear view mirror, *Mad as hornets, my dear. And here I am, feeling exceedingly good. Imagine!*

There were four of them, Richard.

Nick is definitely onto us, and I think our traitor is the key.

Makes sense! It surprises me that the traitor felt it necessary to enlist help from outside, though. Maybe he is feeling a little pinch, right about now.

Not sure. We'll keep our options open.

You're right, as usual.

Not all the time. Why, once a few years back...

Oh, stop!

Honey, they aren't pursuing us, at least not yet.

That's a plus. Wonder what evil old Nick Trafalgar is going to think of next.

I'm sure we'll be surprised.

Probably.

Let's head for a place to stay. They are way behind.

Okay.

"Oops, here they come again," Richard said out loud.

"Damn!"

"All in a days work, I say. What do you say we drive to the nearest Police Station?"

"That ought to cool their jets," Audrey said.

I don't want to take a chance on the one we are registered at tonight.

Good thought.

We'll lose them later. It's a game we can play, too.

Lead on, McDuff.

How'd you know my real name was McDuff?

Ha, ha, Richard.

There goes my titillating wit again.

Well, half of it. Audrey sent him a smirk.

Funny.

They came to the outskirts of the city before Nick's boys caught up to them. They hung back, unsure.

Gets safer from here.

Yeah. We'll stop at the P. D. anyway?

Sure.

They kept an eye on their pursuers. At the police station they turned in. The enemy car drove slowly by. Richard briefly caught the white of four faces looking his way in his rear view. Richard pulled into the handicapped spot next to the front door. Then he waited.

After a while, Richard said, "They're gone, love. Gave up for tonight, unless they are far more clever than I think, and how could they be more clever than us two super-operatives, huh?"

"I think we'd better change cars tonight, too."

"Good idea, my dear. We'll drop this in town somewhere and disappear on foot."

"Good old spy stuff. It's worked before."

"Let's try to find a place with a computer link. Maybe I can get a message to Ted."

I dunno. Audrey lapsed into mindspeak. It got easier all the time. *Might be best we disappear until tomorrow and then surface at the facility and watch faces while I work my aura.*

Maybe so. Richard looked thoughtful.

Anyway, I'm really tired, so let's do something.

Sure, hon.

Richard parked the car in a busy downtown area. He did a visual and Audrey did an aural search. Negative. They got out, locked and left the car at the curb. They walked a while in a crowd of evening shoppers. They found a coffee shop where Richard ordered them ham and cheese croissants. Audrey located a nearby phone and found an in-city hotel about ten blocks from where they'd left the car.

That'll give us a margin of safety for the night.

The hotel was over on Clark Street, a Hempline Inn, four star. She booked a room.

Got us a place.

Good. Let's eat and go before the crowds thin out.

Yeah. Audrey joined Richard at a table with a view of both doors to the little eatery. They enjoyed a quick meal and took to the sidewalk after a wary look around.

We're clear around here for thirty yards or so, Audrey linked. They walked briskly.

Good. The buildings would bring Nick's boys close enough to sense, but I think they've decided to lay low for the night and try again tomorrow. They'd have to be aware that we will be there again.

Danger inside and out. Just our speed, hey matey?

Living on the edge is a great way to conduct a life! Think of all those endorphins. Not to mention stomach acid.

Yeah. Audrey stopped projecting and walked along, shielding as best she could. After Richard's announcement that he could pick up on her thoughts even though she couldn't hear his, they both accepted the need for privacy. It didn't take long for Audrey to learn how to mask her thoughts effectively.

"What you thinking, love?" Richard spoke in a low conversational tone.

She linked, *Trying to create a privacy shield. How am I doing? Well.*

Out loud, she said, "Nothing much. Looking forward to settling in."

They found the Hempline Inn halfway down a pleasantly treed street replete with numerous old brownstone buildings. Most had porticos in an aging but carefully tended state. The designers made the buildings' exterior blend with the neighborhood. It looked very nice on the outside. Inside it was luxurious and not old looking at all.

"Lovely," Audrey exclaimed.

They carried their briefcases casually to the desk. Richard asked for a room with a Jacuzzi. The desk clerk was more than helpful, and soon they were on their way to Room 321. Richard inserted the card-key. As they entered, Richard closed and locked the door, being careful to hook over the mechanical privacy lock immediately.

Believe we'll be fine here tonight.
I think so. Tired. Wanna go to bed! Audrey said.
Big day tomorrow.
Yeah, c'mon, love, let's crawl in.
Umm...

.

52

On the sleazy north side of Frederick, a mean looking, barrel-chested man in a stained tee shirt opened a door in a non-descript place with the unlikely name, Cherry Blossom Motel and Suites. An old tannery sat a few doors down, silent now, but odiferous. His turned down mouth barely more than a thin line, he breathed deeply of the acidic early morning air, grimaced and snorted, coughed and spit.

"What the fuck?" he exploded. He pulled back in and slammed the door. No one noticed, least of all his fellows. His brand of anger was common in this part of town. He turned on a tall guy in the room. "Weasel, you pick this lousy place for stay over. You fuckin' crazy?"

"Lenny, shut your face. This is the best place we could be. Nobody asks no questions. Nobody looks at nobody. Good place," Stretch answered.

Matatolis snorted again and went into the bathroom, leaving the door open. Stretch had to listen to Matatolis clearing his bowels. He lay back on his bed and hefted the heavy bolt-cutters he'd stopped for at a late running hardware store the night before, ignoring the protests of his three henchmen, who wanted to hit a local bar a few doors down from the motel.

"How often do we get to Mary-land?" the Greek said.

Diddle followed with, "C'mon Weasel, it's party time."

Johnny Quinn, who stayed as far as he could from the other two—he told Stretch when he caught him alone for a few seconds that they both had serious bad body odor—had nothing to say…at the moment.

"Need these," Stretch held them up and said of the bolt-cutters, "I'll tell you my plan when we settle in for the night."

They had driven back to the motel. He'd told the guys to go to the joint.

"I'll catch up. Wanna talk to Nick."

Matatolis made a rude gesture. Stretch ignored him.

"And don't make no trouble. We don't need cops."

He had found a pay phone in the motel lobby, got a bunch of change and dialed the mansion on Long Island.

Tony answered the phone. "Stretch! Nick was wondering about you."

"Yeah, Tony. Is he around?"

"Yeah, hang."

After a few moments the gruff voice of Nick Trafalgar had come on the line. "Stretch. Gimme an update."

"Yeah, Nick. Here safe and sound. Cased the place. Easy break-in. Bought some bolt-cutters that'll go through that fence easy enough and found a place we can get in where we're not likely to be discovered."

"Matatolis listening to you?"

"Yeah, everything's cool."

"Good. Thought he might give you some trouble."

"Nah, he's okay. Anyway, Nick, I saw the bitch. Matches the description to a 'T' and the big gorilla is with her. Couldn't be anyone else."

"Told you she'd be there. But outside, hey, that's good."

"Figgered they was gettin' a tour. Pretty, auburn-haired lady."

"Yeah. Oh, my contact says they'll be there tomorrow, too. Can't figure what they're up to, but they'll be moving from building to building. That might help."

"Good. We need to catch them outside, as I figger it."

"Okay, what else?"

"I need a piece and I need a silencer."

"Why?"

"Place is crawlin' with security durin' the day and security with big dogs at night. Biggest German Shepard's I ever seen! Have to do this in the daytime after the dogs go off. Better chance."

"Yeah, yeah, whatever. Why you need a piece? I don't like it."

"Might have to clear an area, is all."

"No, Stretch, I don't like it. What you using for weapons?"

"We all picked up six-inch bucks."

"You're the best with a knife. Stick with that. Swift, silent, that's best."

"Can't convince you?"

"No. You do the slick and easy. Anything else?"

Stretch thought about telling Nick about their abortive attempt outside of the complex, but decided that Nick wouldn't be pleased with any botched job, no matter how it happened.

"Ah, no, Nick. We're all set. We'll get it done."

"You do that. Call me tomorrow night."

"Yeah, Nick, sure." The phone clicked in his ear. After that he joined his group, more to keep them out of trouble than anything. Johnny would get roarin' if Stretch didn't tone him down. They sat at a booth in the mostly dark, slightly reeking, noise filled, smoke swirling room. After eleven, Stretch looked at his watch and told them they had to go back to their rooms and talk about his plan for tomorrow.

About then Johnny had started a fight with one of the locals. Stretch grabbed him by the collar and hauled him back to the table. The local hothead wanted to go anyway, but the Greek got out of his seat and the other guy decided maybe he should go home instead. They waited twenty minutes and left. Luckily, no one was waiting for them.

They talked in Stretch's room until one a.m. The Weasel laid his scenario on the three men, getting little flak from them, although Diddle Schaeffer kept interjecting until Stretch told him to shut the hell up or he'd cut him a new asshole. After that he told them to hit the sack; he wanted them bright-eyed and ready in the morning. Johnny and Diddle went to their adjoining room.

While Matatolis took a leak, Stretch lay down on top of his clean but heavily stained and faded covers, hands behind his neck, thinking of Barbara. At the moment it irritated him. What did that frail mean by jumpin' into his shit?

Eventually his eyelids grew heavy and sleep came unbroken by any interruption from his roommate. The slam of the door brought Stretch back. As he lay there listening to Lenny rummage around, he realized that the big day had come.

53

In the morning, Audrey turned over, looked at her Richard. She tousled his hair and his eyes popped open.

"Big day, my love," he said.

"Maybe the biggest, pardner."

"We takes 'em as they comes."

Audrey mind-blew a curled love message across the thin space between them. Richard closed the space. *What's another twenty minutes?*

An eternity with you, Richard.

Shared eternity, nice concept.

Hush...

They made love gently at first. The mood deepened and they moved with increasing frenzy until beads of sweat made their writhing bodies glisten.

Now, Richard, now! They sank into sweet oblivion together, a moment held within, filled with shooting stars and images of happiness. Richard held still for a long moment, aware that their implants had enlarged the experience almost beyond their ability to handle it.

Finally he broke the connection.

Wow!

Double wow!

They lay on their backs, naked, drained, covers askew, sheets soaked, tossing each other image after silent image. Another ten minutes passed before Audrey, always practical before Richard, announced that they had a traitor to catch and wasn't it about time they got going?

Don't you want to save the world?

Nope!

Nope?

Breakfast first! Save the world later.

I could do that.

Audrey got out of bed and stretched mightily. Hands over her head, back arched, she reminded Richard of a cat.

"Audrey, don't do that or I'll jump out of bed and drag you back," Richard said.

"No, you won't. I couldn't handle you twice in one morning and still have enough energy to face our day."

"Yeah, guess so. Well, 'damn anyway' are my sentiments."

"Mine too, love. Now let's get cracking."

Richard grumbled but rose and started his daily exercise routine. He stopped and laughed. "Like I need these now!"

"Gives me time for the bathroom." Audrey disappeared.

Later, Richard and Audrey had breakfast in the hotel restaurant, checked out and left with the two briefcases and the one small suitcase they shared for this assignment. They took a cab back into town ten blocks to where they'd left their rented car. It sat undisturbed.

Good, Richard linked, *we'll turn it in and take a different car, different color. Think our friends will try to waylay us again?*

Not really. Best to believe that they are smart enough to figure out we'd be stupid to try the same route again after what they pulled last night.

I agree. The cabby pulled over and they paid him. They watched the cab until it turned the corner.

Clear. They got in and drove to the rental office. They picked a blue Mazda 626.

As they arrived at InFab's main gate and were let through, Audrey linked, *We were right. Wonder what Nick's boys have in mind for this gorgeous day.*

My guess is they will try to scale the fence near the power plant. It's the remotest part of the complex. We have to go there anyway, to check out...what was his name?

Fred Dodd, I think Laura said.

That sounds right.

Unfortunately, we can't alert the Security people, so we'll have to rely on your aural sense.

It's come through before. We'll be okay.

There are four of them, though. Also, I'm kind of hoping Ted will show up somewhere today and we can alert him about last night.

Yeah, I know. Best handle this as if we are alone.

Guess...

Might as well check out the Power man first and get it over with.

Okay. Let's go see Laura. They parked in the Administration lot as before and, now familiar with the internal process, approached the front desk and requested Manson Rettick's secretary. Laura answered promptly and invited them up.

"Good morning," she said brightly.

"Good morning to you, Laura," Audrey replied. Richard nodded congenially.

"Where do you want to go this morning?"

"Well, if Mr. Dodd is in, we'd like to start there. Don't believe any problems he might have will amount to much," Richard said.

"That's fine. Mr. Rettick has given me the time to finish bringing you around, so I'm all yours. I'm actually looking forward to it. It's such a nice day."

"Yes, it is," Audrey replied.

Laura led the two out of her office, down the hall and took a back stairway instead of going through the lobby. The door to outside pointed directly at the Power Station. A short sidewalk met the long walkway they'd used the day before.

Part way down the cement path, Laura, without looking at either of the computer people, started talking. Her lips didn't seem to move at all. This impressed Audrey. She casually looked at Laura and then away. She gave no name, but evidently she had had contact with Ted. The operative's ears perked up.

"The one you spoke of last night said to tell you that he is near and will be watching. He said time is very short. He's expecting something big to happen within the next two or three days. He suspects, but needs to know exactly where. He's worried. He asked me to tell you, you need to bring your part to a conclusion today. Doesn't think there is more time."

Audrey pointed at some flowering shrubs and said offhandedly, "We'll do our best."

Another minute later, after conferring with Richard, Audrey said quietly to the woman, "There is another problem, Laura. We were attacked last night on the road to Frederick."

Laura glanced at her quickly.

"There were four of them. We're certain they are hitters from a piece of unfinished business we left in New York. Richard and I have every reason to believe that these men are here, somewhere. We are the target!"

Laura absorbed the news without outward expression. "Glad you told me. Now we are three."

"What do you mean?"

"I mean that I am as highly trained as you are. I'll turn up the dials from this point. Being a Secretary is boring, anyway."

"Excellent. Welcome aboard."

I think I love this woman, Richard.

Richard smiled at Audrey and linked, *I don't want to share you, but I know what you mean.*

Not to worry, you won't share me, not after this morning. She tossed him a love note.

Nothing outward changed about their guide, but the two felt rather than saw their companions' energy level go up.

They needed to cross the road, catching the sidewalk on the other side. From there they could walk to where it branched off and went to Security. They walked along the roadside from there to Power. A short sidewalk and a few cement steps led to a door—the big one was closed—and they entered.

Richard looked around at the small area that passed for an office and beyond toward the noise and hum of big generators.

"I didn't think we'd find him that easily. Probably down in back." Laura walked through to the back of the office and out the open door.

Heads up, Richard, I'm getting a reading.

Right, Audrey. How do we let Laura know?

I'll figure it out.

The three entered a huge area in which sat the two massive power generators that served the complex. A third, smaller, but glistening with mechanical care, sat idle. Laura stopped and pointed to it. "Emergency backup only. Powers the security grid, phones, guard station and floodlights."

"Ah," Richard said unnecessarily.

Audrey concentrated on the aural image blobs she could read. There were three. Where was the fourth? She sensed two behind the first generator and a third crouched behind some unused panels leaning against a wall twenty feet ahead.

Richard, move to your right a little. Richard complied. *We can't afford to hesitate. When Laura gets to the front edge of those panels there, you sprint around the right end of Generator #1. You should be able to take the two behind it by surprise. They don't have a clue what we've got. I'll yank Laura back and go for the one behind the panels. I'll try to startle him with a yell. That should startle all of them. Laura will pick up on it right away, I think. Let's go!*

When you're ready. Richard moved further to the right.

NOW! Richard sprinted quietly on his sneakered feet, cleared the right side of the power generator and dived for the first of the thugs. It turned out to be Diddle Schaeffer. Before Diddle could react, Richard's fist went full into the side of his face. He crumpled like a rag doll. Stretch turned violently, knife ready, only a bare second to react. Richard twisted in mid air and tried to plant a foot into Stretch's upper body. He missed! Now the Weasel had turned and his big buck knife slashed at Richard's passing leg.

Richard felt searing pain drive up his leg and he cried out in agony. Worse, his mind projected his pain and amplified it!

Audrey had tackled Lenny Matatolis, thinking to gain purchase for a nerve pinch. The big man grabbed her wrist and yanked her to him.

"Pretty lady gonna die!" he yelled over the noise of the generators.

She tried to kick, but couldn't get the angle. Lenny held her with one arm while the Greeks big buck knife came up in slow motion, moving within inches of Audrey's throat.

Just then, as Richard cried out, Audrey froze. The sheer volume of the projection stopped her cold. The Greek was far stronger and she was losing. The knife came closer, almost touching Audrey's neck. In the eternity of the moment she realized that the man was pushing against her strength slowly, savoring the moment. Her eyes wide, Audrey could see a rare but malevolent smile on Matatolis' face.

Then from behind Audrey's left ear a small black business shoe with a pointed toe lashed out and caught Lenny in the throat. He made a gurgling sound and fell back. The knife clattered to the floor. Laura reached down, deftly snatched the knife from the floor and drove it deep into Matatolis' neck. Lenny's eyes bugged out and he slumped dead.

Audrey sat, completely dazed. Laura glanced at her to be sure she wasn't bleeding and immediately rounded the generator on the left. She saw Richard full out on the greasy floor and a tall, thin man starting to swing his knife again toward Richard's chest. Without thought, Laura flung her body at the arm and the knife. She caught his elbow and held on. Her momentum carried her across Stretch Monaghal, taking his arm with her and away from Richard. She grappled for the knife, but Stretch was stronger and quicker. He arched and twisted and suddenly Laura lay on the floor. She cried, "Audrey!"

Richard, who knew Audrey was all right, but in shock, sent her a strong message, *Audrey, help Laura, she needs you.*

The message jerked Audrey out of her state and she galvanized into action. She closed on the two writhing on the floor. Stretch had begun an arc that would bury the six-inch buck knife into Laura's chest. Laura tried wildly to catch his arm as it descended. The only chance Audrey saw to save their new friend required a quick swing of her acrobat's foot. She got beyond Stretch's arc and buried her blunt-toed foot into his temple. With a groan, Stretch lost consciousness.

With the directed inertia gone, Laura writhed away from the downward plunging knife. It clattered to the floor an inch from her right breast.

Meanwhile, Richard, bleeding profusely from his slashed leg but still operating on adrenalin, pushed himself past Laura to check on Stretch.

He winced in agony, but said to Laura, "He'll be out for awhile. The other guy with him is dead. Great work, Laura! What's the status of the other guy?"

"Dead! Big bruiser of a guy. Reminded me of Luca Brazzi in "The Godfather." Don't want to meet two of him in a lifetime," Audrey said.

Audrey, you okay?

Yes.

Where's the other, number four?

Don't know...wait...I'm getting a reading now. From the back of the place!

The aura came closer, but there was something wrong with it. It still had the pinkish red quality to it, but it also had a touch of green. Just then, a familiar voice called out.

"Hey, you guys, it's me. I heard the ruckus. All okay?"

Around the corner from one of the delivery bays came Ted, escorting Johnny Quinn, at gunpoint. Quinn looked beaten, and when he saw his three partners on the floor, not moving, he started to shake.

"Ted," Audrey said without thinking, "Richard is bleeding badly. He needs immediate attention."

Ted glanced at her as she bit her lip, and he saw the pain she tried to hold back. He handed his gun to Laura, who motioned the little hit man to sit on a nearby chair.

"Move and you die," she said to their prisoner. He sat, still shaking, head bowed.

Richard held his right leg now at the major pressure points, trying to slow the blood flow. Blood pooled below his leg, a dark red patch, growing too rapidly. Ted knelt down and looked the wound over. He instantly decided that Richard didn't need his pants anymore.

"Audrey, bring me up to date on what happened here."

While Audrey explained, Ted ripped Richard's pants around to the back, then took one of the captured buck knives and finished the job. He inspected the depth of the cut, twisted the pant leg into a long ropelike piece and wrapped it around the upper leg. He found a short piece of metal pipe, tied it on the pants loosely and began to twist-tighten the tourniquet. Pretty soon the blood flow slowed measurably.

Richard, barely keeping from going into shock, took hold of the pipe length and said, "What now, Ted?" Their cover was blown, not that it ultimately mattered, he thought.

To Audrey, Richard linked, *Audrey, I'm all right. Take a lot more than a little scratch to put me away.*

Stop it, Richard. It's bad and you know it. Hurtfulness and pain came into her projection. *And I froze! I can't believe it! I'm so sorry! Where was I when you needed me?*

Stop it, Audrey. There was nothing you could do. It's an unwelcome aspect of the implants. They overpowered you. I couldn't help it. Took me by surprise. Took both of us by surprise.

I love you, Richard. We knew this morning what the implants could do. We'll have to guard against this big downside.

Amen, love.

Ted had been studying the leg and now he put his mind to the major situation. In a moment, he started talking.

"Laura, great job. After this, I think we'll use you elsewhere. Now, for the three of us, you need to know that Fred Dodd is dead. This guy," he pointed at Johnny Quinn, "I caught dragging Dodd behind some barrels to hide him. He told me the other three had seen you coming toward the Powerhouse and didn't want to wait outside, so they left the little guy to finish up. He's Johnny Quinn, one of Nick's boys."

That's why only three!

"I am relatively certain that no one outside of our little group of eight here, have an inkling that anything is out of the ordinary. Not much goes on down here unless there's a power failure. The generators are noisy. No shots have been fired and security normally doesn't come into the power building. I think we should keep it that way."

"We're going to need to make some changes in our situation," Audrey said.

Ted agreed, knowing what Audrey referred to. "Yes, a couple of changes, actually. Audrey, you and Laura find the bathroom and make yourselves as presentable as you can. There is someone you need to find. You can still pretend to use the computer fix cover, and Laura will assist you. Make up some kind of story as to why Richard can't join you this morning. Richard, you are out of commission for as short a time as I can manage, but it'll be hours, at least."

"Ted, I need to speak to you privately." Audrey had just finished a long link with Richard.

"Sure, what is it?" He led her toward the front office out of earshot.

"Ted, we don't need the entire ruse. I have a special ability Richard and I didn't tell you about, deliberately, to protect us all. I can sense, well, essentially, I can sense evil intent. It's like foreseeing a bad thing about to happen, only not exactly. It's hard to explain."

Ted nodded. "I knew you had something else, but I had no clue. What will you do?"

"All I need is to get into close proximity with evil intent and we'll have our man...or woman, whichever. I'll carry my case and Richards, and Laura can get me intro's with the rest of the management staff here. Once I identify the traitor, I'll make an excuse to call you. Let's see, I'll call you Richard and ask after a certain program I need that isn't in the bag. I'll say who I'm with and you'll know who the traitor is. Work for you?"

"That'll work. Call me at 7549, the Powerhouse office phone."

"Right."

"Let's get back. We'll have to dispose of all of them, hide them in the Powerhouse until we finish our prime job and then turn them over to Security."

"I've had some doubts about Security already, and I haven't met the Conference Center lady, either."

"I'd bet Franco is okay, and Shika Marver is a sweety. But, you never know."

"If it's not one of them, we'll have to search the lower echelons, and that could be exceedingly time consuming. And what about Manson?"

"Stoic swears Manson is okay, but admits he has larceny in his soul. Stoic has a lot on the man and has watched him for years. He won't be the traitor. Let's get going."

They walked back to Laura and the fallen thugs. Richard was still on the floor in obvious pain. Ted took a silencer out of his pocket, took the pistol from Laura and installed it on his .32 Special. Johnny Quinn looked at Ted and finally broke his silence.

"What's with that, mister?"

"End of the line," Ted said to him, and shot him in the head. He slumped without a sound. Laura looked shocked, but said nothing. Ted put a bullet in Stretch's ear and did the same for Diddle Schaeffer. He checked Matatolis body, disconnected and put away the silencer and his gun.

"Laura, it's in our training and we have to be up for it, but just so you'll know, I hate it," Ted told her.

"I believe you. What's next?"

"Go with Audrey. She'll fill you in."

"Okay." Laura walked away woodenly. Audrey spoke to her in low tones.

"Hated to do that," Ted said to Richard, "but we have no time and big problems to solve *now*."

"I know, Ted. Did I mention I'm glad you're here?"

"You sit tight for a few, while I drag this mess out of sight. I'll stack them up over there, behind the generators. Then you need some serious stitching."

'Don't mind if I wait over here, then, do you?" Richard gave Ted his lopsided grin and Ted smiled.

By the time Ted finished moving the bodies, the two women had returned, looking quite fresh, for all that had happened.

"We came to say goodbye. Laura knows what we're up to. We'll call later."

"Good hunting."

They left. Ted went to the phone and called the company doctor. "Got a man needs stitches at the power plant. Bring needle and thread."

Richard couldn't hear the response at the other end, but shortly Ted broke the connection and came back to him.

"The company doctor is trustworthy. He'll be here shortly."

Ted thought for a moment and decided to call Franco Dilatori. The security man picked up the phone immediately. "Franco, we have a problem at the Powerhouse. You know who's calling, right?"

Richard couldn't hear the reply. Ted went on. "Bring a windowless van and two of your most close-mouthed security men over and park behind the station. Don't come now. I have a sensitive situation and it must resolve before you get here. Meantime, business as usual, but keep everyone away from the Powerhouse until I call you again. Got some garbage for you to pick up and dispose of quietly. Got it?"

Ted heard his reply and hung up.

A nondescript late model Ford Taurus made its way to the Powerhouse and parked outside the building. As the doctor alighted, a security man walked over to inquire if he needed help. Lying with a straight face, he said, "I won't need you to hold Fred's hand for this one, George."

"Okay, doc. See you around." The man smiled and started to walk around the building. Just then his cell phone rang. He answered and then headed directly for the security building.

Doc Simmons grabbed his bag and entered the power building. Ted met him at the door, just out of sight from outside. He took him to Richard while informing him that everything he saw from now on was totally confidential. The doctor nodded.

Doc Simmons spoke to Richard.

"Well, young fella, you're going to be glad I grabbed a pint of blood as I left the Admin building. You're also lucky your friend here," referring to Ted, "gave me your type. Knows you pretty well, doesn't he?"

"You could say that," Richard said amiably. After that he shut up, while the doc dropped a lot of Novocain into various parts of his leg.

"I should be using a canvass needle, I think." It took an hour, but a hundred eighty stitches closed the wound.

"Thanks, Doc," Ted said, as the doctor finished tightly gauze wrapping Richard's upper right leg from knee to crotch."

Doc Simmons ignored him. "Take these over the next ten days, young man." He handed Richard a small plastic bottle of pills. "Make sure the dressing gets changed in five days. You'll be all right 'til then. Don't get it wet. That's an order."

"I'll be good, I promise. Thanks Doc."

"You're welcome. Oh, and if you insist on moving around, lace a leather legging tie-patch around the middle of that wound to keep it together." He looked at Ted. "See me to the door."

They left. Richard's leg felt like a wooden log. The doctor had done the sewing right on the floor, on his knees, like a medic in a war. How apt! As he watched the process, he realized that Doc Simmons qualified as an artist in his field.

"I don't need to tell you that cut is nasty and deep," Doc Simmons started when they were out of earshot, "and he shouldn't be going anywhere."

"No choice, Doc," Ted replied.

"I thought not, but understand, he is to avoid strenuous activity, period."

"We'll take up the slack, Doc. Have to."

Doc Simmons nodded curtly at the door and went down the outside stair. Ted looked after him while thinking what bad luck Richard's injury made for their team.

Ted returned. "Got to help you up. You're going to have to hobble, and we have to get out of here. Doc Simmons told me you'll have to be careful for the next week and a half that you don't break out of those stitches. We don't have that kind of time and you've got to go with us, wherever this takes us, for Audrey's sake."

"And we gonna save the world," Richard muttered.

"Try not to impress me right now, Richard."

Both helping, they got Richard standing on one good leg and a wooden one.

"Your humor will save the world someday," Ted said levelly, "but not today. Change subject. Are you in touch with Audrey?"

"Sure."

"What's your range?"

"Haven't reached it yet on the mindlink, but the aural thing seems to fade at about ninety to a hundred feet."

"Hmm..." Ted thought for a while. "Got to wait for that call. I get a sense that time is against us."

"Doing what we can."

Just then the office phone rang.

54

Ted heard Audrey clearly. "Richard, I'm here with the Conference Director, Ms. Marver. I need program Q-56, and I can't find it."

Ted said, "I moved it into the side pocket of my coat yesterday. I'll send it down with someone."

"Fine. How long?"

"Only about five minutes."

"Okay, I'll be here." He could hear Audrey telling the Conference woman that the program was on its way. He casually brushed his pocket to check the location of the syringe.

"Richard, you might as well stay here. Now that we know we can trust Franco, I'm making use of his Security Department. First, I've got to inject our traitor before she can use any kind of post-hypnotic suggestion to kill herself. Shika Marver, hard to believe. Anyway, after that, we'll get what we need, if she has the information. I'll run over there and hand Audrey the CD. Audrey already knows to distract the traitor so I can get it done. I'll send someone for you as soon as I can."

"Good luck, Ted."

The Moonlight Man left quietly. Richard leaned against a file cabinet in the office and began waiting. He silently cursed being taken out of the game. His leg throbbed through the pain pills and numbness.

In the Conference Director's office, Audrey stared at a series of symbols on her monitor. She ran a few test patterns, generally make-work preparation, she said, for the new program that was on its way. Shortly, the outer door opened quietly and in walked Ted.

"Shika, hello! I was up in Administration with that other computer fellow and he asked if anyone could take a computer disk down here. I told him I would. How have you been? We haven't caught up to one another for a while."

The woman smiled her slight smile and acknowledged Ted. "Yes, it has been a long time, hasn't it?"

Ted reached over and handed Audrey the disk. "Here you are, Mrs. Penwarton."

"Thank you."

She took the CD and inserted into the drive unit. Shika Marver kept her eye on Ted, as if some suspicion clouded her mind. After a moment, though, Audrey called to her.

"Look, Ms. Marver, we're up and running, finally. I thought that would do it."

Momentarily distracted, Marver looked over at the display and watched it work as it should. At the same moment, Ted, slightly behind the woman, pulled the syringe out of his pocket and drove it and its contents into her left shoulder. Shika turned in amazement and collapsed, her eyes filled with the pain of the needle stick, but in her eyes Ted saw something much deeper.

"Okay, ladies, here's our traitor. We'll need to use special facilities I have in my office. We need to transport her there, but no one is to see her. We don't need any questions. I'm on the lower level. I think we can manage it with your help and I don't think I'll get Franco involved after all. Laura, we'll take Shika's car. Put her in the front seat. You drive. We'll get in back." Ted stopped. "No, I want Richard there, too. You go with Audrey. I'll take another car and bring Richard. It's mid-morning. Little traffic. Good time to go."

"Got it." Marver's keys were on her desk. Laura grabbed them and they manhandled the slight woman out a side door without passing the receptionist in front, who quietly sat perusing her copy of Ebony. In her mind it was as dull a day as they came.

With calm efficiency, Audrey and Laura drove Shika Marver to the back of the Admin building. Ted arrived shortly after they did, unseen, and helped get Marver into his office. Their luck held and in a few minutes he brought Marver to, but hooked to an IV drip that prevented her from exercising her will to commit suicide.

Richard stayed in the car until Shika Marver had been neutralized and then Ted came out and brought him into his small laboratory.

Before Ted began working on the traitor, Richard's electronics sense noticed a small regular signal coming from inside her.

"Ted," Richard said urgently, "she has some kind of implant, too, a signaling device, I think."

"Another ability, Richard?"

"Yes."

"Where?"

"Within her left breast, down low."

"Wired?"

"I think maybe a homing device."

"Rath would do that. Bet he can trace all his top people. Have to think about this."

Ted took a minute and then shrugged. "No matter what, we've got to go on."

"Yeah," Richard said.

"First, I need to call Franco." Ted dialed the security chief's private number again.

"Franco, thanks for taking up the slack for me over there. We can't get the local police involved in this one. You'll find four dead men behind the secondary generator. They need to disappear without a trace. You can handle?" After a moment Ted said thanks into the receiver and hung up.

"One more loose end tied up." He went over to the traitor and looked down at her, emotionless.

The interrogation began. Gradually over the next two hours, with the help of the drugged IV, Ted battered down the woman's resistance. The three were quite surprised that she could fight the drug at all, but she did. Finally Ted hit the key, and Shika broke. She told them all why she had become a traitor against the United States and her own organization. Loved ones in Sri Lanka, she said, had been kidnapped and were being held on threat of death to keep her in line. It went against her training, but once she had crossed the line, she couldn't turn back.

In the end it became easy to justify in her mind that what she did was what anyone would do. Not long after that, she told them Beijing was the target. She had no more useful information. All she could say about the timing was it would happen soon, days, hours, she didn't know. Ted asked her a final question.

"What is that implant for?"

Shika, under the drug unable to do anything but answer woodenly, said, "The leader installed it to monitor our location."

Ted said nothing. With that, he turned up the IV drip. Shika Marver went to sleep forever.

"That's it, guys," Ted said, "Let's talk, and then we're gone. First Stoic needs to know." Ted lifted the phone and dialed a number. His conversation was brief.

While waiting, Audrey raised an eyebrow to Richard's projected message, *I'm not going to be much help.*

Don't worry about it. You'll do fine. But she felt his pain and did her best to block it out.

They made plans. They would go through the French, who, if not soft on the Chinese Communist nation, saw advantage in playing ugly neighbor against the United States and actually enjoyed playing one against the other. They conducted numerous flights to and from China. The trip would take thirty-eight hours including several stops along the way, but with no unanticipated waiting. It couldn't be helped.

"Ted," Richard called suddenly, "her implant has stopped."

"That's bad news!"

Ted asked Laura to make a call from his office phone to the French Airline and set up a schedule. He outlined what was needed. She got busy. It took fifteen minutes.

Ted then contacted a source in France. If they took the one p.m. Air France flight from Dulles, they would arrive at DeGaulle International in about seven and a half hours. By swallowing the sun, the day would wing by, arriving in Paris about seven-thirty p.m. The earliest flight to Tashkent left De Gaulle at 6:15 a.m. the following day and would take ten hours. Another six to Dhaka, capitol of Bangladesh, then on to Beijing, seven more. Ted groaned inwardly. They wouldn't arrive in the Chinese capitol until four p.m. the day after tomorrow.

Ted couldn't alert the Fed. He said he and Stoic agreed on that. Time, time, did he have time? Laura would stay at Infab and monitor the Middle East for any helpful information. Ted gave her a special link to his cell-phone. If it bothered her to be left behind after making a connection to this dynamic group, she didn't show it. She had plenty to do.

Audrey and the badly damaged Richard would fly with Ted. They would pose as Interpol agents, gaining a measure of freedom of movement in the Chinese capital, at least with the Chinese Police. Audrey would be point.

They caught their flight to Paris. Ted laid out the plan for his two operatives.

If any of them found solace in prayer, they would pray for a successful execution of the plan and no hitches!

They would be wrong.

55

"The ship cleared Tianjin authority three hours ago, Master, as part of a flotilla of six Chinese junks." Ahmed Al Salud knelt in front of Rathmanizzar and waited.

"That is good, Ahmed. There was no trouble?"

"No, master."

"The parts that complete the bomb will be in the Chinese Capitol by tomorrow night, if all goes well?"

"Yes, master."

"And all cells have been advised of the start of the new order for the day following?"

"It is so, master."

"Good, Ahmed, good." The Word of the Book studied his disciple for a moment, and then said, "I will retire now. Awaken me if anything of import occurs."

"Yes, master." Ahmed bowed low and retreated beyond the tent flap.

Absently, Rathmanizzar drank from the urn by his side. He reviewed what had been accomplished in the two weeks past. The parts for the bomb had come from four countries. Russia had been helpful in providing the vehicle, but would not sell him fissionable materials. Much of the inner workings of the bomb he had obtained through the French, ostensibly micro-switches and shunts.

The North Koreans had sold him weapons grade uranium. They were desperate for money and unhappy with much of the world. That materiel had left the port at Haiju south of Pyongyang and made its way through Hong Kong to Shanghai. It was a delicate job getting the heavily protected fissionable material to the central collection point in Shanghai. Rathmanizzar had insisted the fleet of junks sail from a Chinese port to allay the more thorough inspections given foreign ships. Wang Ho had been instrumental there.

Black thoughts momentarily crossed his mind. He wished a curse on Amber Pierce for disrupting the acquisition of uranium from U.S. Atomics. Had he managed that coup, he could have moved the date back. The North Koreans had come through. It was as well.

Because of the border dispute between India and Pakistan in Kashmir, Rathmanizzar's operatives had managed to spirit away necessary timing devices through Pakistan. The leader's scientists had done well. Allah would be pleased.

The fleet had left Shanghai a week and a half before, sailed around the horn of the Shantung peninsula and entered Bo Hai, the gulf of Chihli. Ahmed now reported the second to last obstacle eliminated. Only Beijing authority remained to clear some innocuous boxes of "machinery." The parts would be delivered to Wang Ho's Beijing City home. Wealthy and well connected, Wang Ho actually knew the Chairman personally. His house, strategically located near the outskirts of the business district, provided a perfect place for Rathmanizzar's purpose.

Because he had cultivated Wang Ho, the Chinese businessman owed much of his wealth to the Lobala leader. He gladly offered his Beijing house to Rathmanizzar. Afterwards, the cell he commanded would swoop into the ruined city and begin agitating for extreme action by the Chinese government.

In the meantime, General Fan Too, provincial governor of Shandonc Province would be hosting a special, high-level conference on agriculture in Yantai, three hundred miles south and east of Beijing. The Chairman had been invited to address the conference. This would keep the Heads of State safe, but in a perfect position to quickly respond at the outrage to Beijing, Flower of the Orient.

Years of planning and work. Fruition! The leader savored the thought. The world would know of the explosion instantly.

Seismometers in most countries would announce it first. Conflicting and inflammatory information would be leaked to the world media. Demonstrations would further confuse the Chinese into belief of a world conspiracy against their nation. Without sufficient thought, China would loose its nuclear arsenal against all the nations it could reach with its weapons of mass destruction and war would follow.

Rathmanizzar, suddenly weary, lay back into the folds of his lounging mats. In the nature of the little religious dictator, he searched his beliefs at every cusp. Surely the mightiest cusp now approached, rushing at insane speed to alter the world forever. Why did he not feel exultation for the coming moment? Instead, he felt brain weary. It should not be. It bothered him in a most fundamental way.

The ships had sailed, no turning back. All that he had set in motion must reach its proper conclusion. Nothing could stop it now! Yet elation eluded him, as did that special feeling of oneness he felt with Allah.

The leader fell into a restless sleep and soon began to dream. In his dream the mosaic backdrop of his vision lost the white shine of purity and began to take on the character of dried blood. An odor of putrescence stirred in his nostrils. The hands...the white hands were closer yet, almost touching his neck. Worst of all, he stared at his inner self, and saw him looking back accusingly.

With a snap and jerk he pulled willfully out of his dream. Rathmanizzar's body lay drenched in sweat. Not as it should be...not as it should be! He sat up and looked around wildly. He was alone.

The Word of the Book breathed slowly against the will of his body and gradually regained his calm. Within, he felt his vision turning against him. And the hands, closer yet! A shiver found its way through his body. Should he call Ahmed and speak to him of the change in his dream?

No, he must remain leader, always.

Rathmanizzar rolled off his sleep pad and began to pace. The dream, he must reinterpret it. Now his tent, large enough for a gathering of all of his advisors and disciples seemed small, confining. He reviewed his original vision for the thousandth time. In it he saw glory for Islam in the name of Allah, his God, the only God. In it his followers had been ready when the bomb went off and the

383

world fell apart and into his hands. In it he had been standard-bearer for Islam. With flag in one hand and sword in the other, he had overcome the remnants of civilization and begun its conversion to the true religion.

Now his changed, troubled vision seemed wrong. Had he made some mistake, had he become unworthy? No, it could not be! He had followed his vision to the letter. He had made no mistake! Lobala, with Rathmanizzar at its head would march to victory. Had he not seen it?

He decided to stay in his tent lest his face accidentally communicate inner distress to any of his disciples. He must be the rock, the foundation of the new order. He lay down again, still weary, and fell into a fitful sleep. From time to time Ahmed, not far beyond the tent flap, heard his leader cry out, muttering words, but he could not make sense of them. He worried about the master.

From the corner of his eye he caught movement. Ahmed al Salud turned to see a messenger from the communications tent racing toward him. Finel Ben Ghira stopped respectfully in front of Ahmed and in an urgent whisper, said, "Important message for the leader, Ahmed."

"Give it to me. I will wake him." The messenger handed it over to Rathmanizzar's chief disciple, bowed and returned the way he had come. Ahmed glanced at the contents and immediately entered the leader's tent.

The Word of the Book came awake instantly with Ahmed's call. "What is it, Ahmed?"

"A matter of import, master." He handed the thin printout to his leader.

Rathmanizzar scanned it and then looked at the words again, as if in disbelief. "We have lost contact with Shika Marver? That is not good. It would appear she has been neutralized."

"That is my thought, master."

The leader stood silent for a time, thinking. Nothing could change what he had set in motion. "You will send a communiqué to Beijing and alert the staff. Watch for any unusual movement of people, either groups of men, soldiers or not, or lack of normal foot and vehicular traffic, anything abnormal. Tell the scientists to be ready the moment the bomb parts arrive to begin assembly. Perhaps they can be ready two or three hours earlier than planned. Go now!"

"Yes, master." Ahmed went off at a run.

56

A young female with straight black hair and of vaguely oriental appearance sat alone at the window of an Air France Aerobus bound for Paris. Her skin was pale and slightly yellow. She wore half-glasses and it would have taken a focused sidelong look to note that this woman wore black tinted contacts to cover her arresting blue eyes.

She sat in row 16E and appeared to be reading the French magazine Elle. Several rows toward the tail sat two men dressed in business suits. They were in two of the outside tiers of seats. They seemed relatively nondescript, but the one on the outside aisle, a good sized man, perhaps a wrestler, people might have thought, had stuck his right leg out beyond the edge of the seat and he didn't offer to move it when people walked down the aisle to the rear lavatory. They took one look at his stone-etched face and said nothing.

The other man, of average height, had an intent look about him. No one thought once, let alone twice about speaking to him. The three hundred people on Flight 1159 seemed unaware beyond the boredom of yet another transatlantic flight.

Composed and distant except to her partner, Audrey read in French—not well, not badly. I'm a bit rusty, she thought as she struggled through the text, but it'll come back. She glanced at her nine thousand-dollar Rolex watch. Another three hours before touchdown. In dress she appeared something of royalty and the documents she carried lent credence to her role. She'd found it easier to slip into the French than into the stolid old English typecast. Odd!

How are you doing up there, Madame Butterfly?

Richard, that's Japanese, not Chinese.

Whatever happened to that English girl I'd grown so fond of?

She's either gone entirely, or on temporary sabbatical. Haven't decided yet. Kind of got used to her, though.

Mmm...me, too.

Oh, so you don't like the Amber I used to be?

Oops!

Don't worry your head none, matey. Just keeping you off balance is all.

Doing a good job of it, my little sparrow.

Watch it, you don't know who I might become at a moment's notice.

If the stakes weren't so high, I'd brand this conversation a bit silly..

Yeah. Audrey became silent for a few, tied up with her own thoughts. Richard left her alone. Finally, he linked, *Couple more hours and we'll change planes. What's the itinerary, again?*

Uzbekistan, Bangladesh and then direct to Beijing.

Seems like a long way around.

Ted is considerably worried about the timing.

I know. The problem is, if we got faster transportation, we'd have to level with the Fed and that would most likely immerse us in the red tape we all know and love.

And cause even more delay. Besides, the Fed might not see it our way and think, why not? China's not exactly a friend, right? And wouldn't the Fed really like to know who we are!

Yup, all that.

No other choice, then.

Guess not, but we're all sweating it.

Yeah. The link went silent again. They renewed conversation from time to time. Finally, the pilot announced in English that they were almost there, gave flight information and weather for Paris and was silent. In a few minutes, the seatbelt sign came on followed by an announcement in both English and French to fasten seatbelts and put up trays.

As they descended, the flight staff made a last run through the passenger compartment, gathering cups and pre-packaged food containers. Moments before landing, they sat and strapped in. The cosmopolitan passengers paid no attention.

With a screech of tires, the usual shuddering, out of control feeling one always gets on landing, the massive jet touched down. They put their timepieces ahead six hours to gain Paris Time. It was now seven a.m. again. They disembarked and met their prearranged contact in the terminal coffee shop. He produced French passports and Interpol ID's. Soon thereafter, they were seated on an Air France jet bound for Uzbekistan. The three operatives had two days, maybe less, to avoid a nuclear catastrophe. More than twenty hours remained before they would set down in Beijing, barring problems.

Ted sat stiffly, lost in private thoughts.

Sure hope Ted is wrong. Four hours to meet with the police, convince them of the deadly danger, and search out the terrorists. Impossible!

I know, Richard, but if it's all the time we have, then that's what we have to work with.

I don't fancy becoming part of a radioactive cloud, missy.

Neither do I, but you know what they say about people who insist on racing into harm's way.

They're not smart?

Probably that, too.

What were you thinking?

I was thinking that courage is forcing action past fear. There's nothing in that one about sitting around.

Yeah, I feel this one pretty deep, too. I'm scared.

Me too, but we'll get through it or die trying.

It's the second part that makes me nervous.

Yeah. They fell silent again.

They landed at Tashkent Airport without incident. All passengers disembarked and went into the holding area while the Aerobus refueled. Forty passengers left, disappearing into the concourse, past security and presumably back to their homes. Fifteen passengers sat waiting to board, bound for Dhaka or points beyond, dark Muslim men in business suits with a suspicious eye for all foreigners, their somber carry-on held firmly in hand.

The Aerobus refueled and all the through passengers re-boarded. They waited third in line for take-off instructions. Audrey felt glad they were out of there. The place had such a morose air. She felt relieved when they were airborne again. She said nothing to Richard.

In Tashkent, they got off to eat in the concourse restaurant and use the rest facilities. The food had an odd taste, evidently local spices, but it felt good to get away from the plane's seating, even for a single hour. Finally they got the call to re-embark, and they got back to their assigned seats quickly. A surprising number of passengers left the jet in Tashkent. The three wondered about that. About half full, they went on. Next stop Dhaka, Bangladesh, another hot place.

Halfway to their destination they hit rough weather and dipped and swayed and bumped through it. A few minutes later the Captain came on and told the passengers that they were having engine trouble. All was well, but it would be necessary to take the Aerobus out of service in Dhaka. They would be required to change planes for the final leg of the journey to Beijing. He offered that there should be little delay, as he had called ahead and there was an idle Air France jet at the airport that should be ready when they arrived.

Should? Audrey linked

That's what the man said.

I feel like I'm on a tightrope again.

Join the crowd.

Ted leaned over and spoke softly to Richard. "I've been doing some thinking on how to speed things up at Beijing International. We'll have to go through the terminal in Dhaka because of the plane change. I'm going to call Stoic and suggest he have an escort meet us at the terminal. He'll have to let on certain information and we'll have to rely on our contact at Interpol not to foul up his end, but it should save us a couple of hours. We'll end up in police custody, but hopefully some of our ground work will be done."

Richard sounded grateful. "Anything to shave a few sounds good to me."

"Problem, I don't think I should use this phone until we get on the ground. Too many people around us."

"Okay, Ted."

Ted went back to his thoughts. Richard alerted Audrey.

The jet landed on the main runway and was diverted to a holding facility for Air France. The passengers disembarked. Once free of security, Ted made for a terminal phone enclosure, looking like most Far East businessmen. Rather than use the equipment, he hunched over his secured cell phone and when he came back, he nodded briefly to Richard. At that moment they heard boarding instructions for replacement Air France flight 456 direct to Beijing. Ted let his operatives know that he figured they had a half-day left, if that.

As the jet descended toward Beijing airport, Richard breathed a sigh of relief, but he kept his fingers crossed. Audrey caressed his mind in a way she knew, and kept her fears to herself. That kind of intimate giving helped Audrey keep her mind off the near future. They deplaned at four p.m., Beijing time.

57

Ted and Richard left the Air France jet in business suits, dark glasses and a constant alertness that an observer would take to be the watchfulness of a trained individual. A woman of evident Chinese and Western mix followed them, discreetly three passengers behind. The woman made her way to the terminal with the crowd. The two Interpol agents headed for a Chinese police car parked on the runway, two officers looking intently for their contacts.

Audrey disappeared with the departing passengers. Ted and Richard spoke briefly with the second man and handed him some papers. The man took and studied them for a minute, nodded, returned them and gestured them into the car. They were whisked off to Airport Security. Colonel Tao, in charge of the Beijing Police Authority, met them. The man spoke perfect French and English.

Ted and Richard briefly showed him their papers. Ted presented as a Frenchman by the name of Theodorus Muneau, working in England with his partner. He told him in good French that Richard originally came from the United States and to please conduct all conversation in English, as Richard would need to gather all information, too.

He noted that this was the famous Richard Penwarton, whom they had tapped for this very sensitive assignment as the genius behind the demise of the Indo-American Death cartel, which involved radioactives—perhaps he had heard of it—although it was still considered top secret amongst law enforcement in the West.

"No, it has not been reported to me, Mr. Muneau," said Colonel Tao, "but you have been cleared for immediate release by our highest authority. How may I assist you?"

"What do you know, Colonel?"

"There is a plot by a Mid-Eastern nation to set off an atomic explosion in or near the city. That makes it my business. Again I ask, what do you need?"

"We need a map of the city. Our best guesses indicate that the bomb will likely be planted close to its heart to cause maximum damage, panic and disruption. Can you access a list of Chinese businessmen who have ties to Mid-Eastern countries?"

"Yes, we keep records on many of our business people."

"Good! Let us begin."

Colonel Tao looked Richard over and said, "Mr. Penwarton does not look well."

Richard answered, "Leg injury, last assignment. Colonel, we don't have time to talk. We have an imperative, and perhaps only hours of time. Let us proceed."

The colonel said nothing for a second. "Yes, my car is this way."

They left the building. Colonel Tao was well known and feared. Airport security gave way before him. Soon they sat in an expensive Mercedes. Colonel Tao sat in the rear seat with his two guests. The driver, who looked very capable, drove away at the Colonel's nod. They entered the stream of traffic. The Colonel reached for his radiophone and after listening for a moment, made some rapid-fire demands.

Twenty minutes later they were at the headquarters building and Colonel Tao had impressive maps of the city pulled down and a computer generated list of local businessmen in his hand.

The Colonel knew the whereabouts of a large number of his suspects. By process of elimination, Ted and Richard disposed of all but seven possible sites—interpreted as most likely—for the bomb. With his link, Richard advised Audrey and she, having cleared airport authority without incident, found a taxi with an English-speaking driver and regally demanded she be taken to the area of Beijing City close to the suspected bomb's location.

She arrived in the Hung-Chien district at the same time Colonel Tao ordered his elite squad into action. They closed surreptitiously on the ten-block neighborhood. Audrey, only five minutes ahead of the massive movement of police, eliminated three of the suspect locations and had proceeded to the fourth when her aural vibes began to color her walk. She made a report to Richard, who frowned and suggested that he had an intuitive feeling. He asks the Colonel for information on Wang Ho, a colorful character and local entrepreneur. From his records, they determined him to be a very rich merchant with known connections to the Mid-East, specifically to Northern Africa.

"Colonel Tao," Richard suggested, "let's look up this man."

"He is connected to the Chairman, Mr. Penwarton. You had better be right."

"This man's name is on a short list I obtained through other sources. It is too coincidental. We have little time to debate this. Can your men make certain that there is no interruption in the flow of traffic? In this type of operation, they will certainly have watchers."

"Yes, Mr. Penwarton, my men are well trained." The Police Chief gave an order on his cell phone and disconnected. His special force shifted gears and homed in on the estate of Wang Ho. The Chinese infiltrated the neighborhood in a matter of moments. No strangers to covert operations, his field agents produced a map of the house and grounds and studied it.

Eighty strong and out of sight, one pretended to be a deliveryman for the local bakery. He was told there were to be no deliveries that day. The man screamed and shouted. He finally convinced an unknowing house staff member that he must make his delivery or he would lose face with his manager. The staff man looked back at the house and evidently got a go-ahead, because he let the deliveryman in with his tray of breads to the man's energetic thanks.

The agent entered the property alone and made his delivery to the kitchen. With eyes low and respectful, the agent nonetheless noted all activity in the area, counted men with guns hidden in their clothing and noted a general tenseness in the house staff. He also saw two turbaned men. He reported this to his leader as he left in a happily singing voice. Before the gate in the high-walled compound could be locked again, eighty Chinese special police bolted through the opening and ran into the kitchen.

A fusillade of shots rang out into the street. The Chinese overcame the few watchers on the first floor easily. In four groups, the task force moved through the building to designated areas, finally breaking into the lower level laboratory. Like Chinese berserkers, they rushed the defenders and killed them all. They lost twenty men.

One man in a lab coat who had been working on a large device near the center of the room turned in the commotion and managed to flip a timer switch before being gunned down. Moment's later control of the house went to the Chinese police.

Lieutenant Lao Tay, in charge of the raid, got on his cell phone immediately after inspecting the equipment.

"Colonel, we have secured the building, but the device has been armed. The running clock indicates that the bomb will detonate at dusk. The owner is not in the building. What are your orders?"

"Hold, Lieutenant." Colonel briefed Richard and Ted on the problem.

Ted said, "That gives us four hours. How quickly can you get us to Wang Ho's house?"

"Ten minutes."

"Let's go. Richard and I are bomb experts. If it can be disarmed, we can do it."

Great, Audrey, now I'm a bomb expert!

Good going, matey.

They left hurriedly, siren blaring. Cars and rickshaws scattered at the sound. Foot policemen stopped crossing traffic. The Colonel's driver deftly wove in and out as traffic scattered. They arrived at Wang Ho's city home in the projected ten minutes. The task force leader escorted Richard and Ted into the laboratory. They looked over the equipment. Ted spoke in low tones. Richard picked up Ted's lead. They started at both ends of the massive unit and met in the middle.

"No can do," Ted murmured and Richard nodded.

"Agree."

Ted spoke to Colonel Tao. "The bomb can't be disarmed. It will explode if tampered with internally. However, we can't see any motion sensors and I believe it could be moved without detonation.

If you can get some heavy equipment in here and pull the bomb carefully through to the outside, you could truck it out of the city limits before time runs out."

"The area is heavily populated," the Colonel said. "Four hours in any direction would still mean devastation of a large area, and the radioactivity would make an even larger area unlivable. It is not a good solution."

Richard spoke up. "The unit weighs about a ton. I didn't see any aneroid capability. Did you, Ted?"

"No, and that's a good idea. Do you have a fast jet that could carry this in its hold?"

The Colonel brightened. "Yes, if it can be carried by air without detonation, I believe I have a solution."

He turned to his Lieutenant and gave him orders. The Lieutenant left immediately. Then he pulled out his cell-phone and dialed a number. Colonel Tao spoke quickly into the receiver, listened for a short time, spoke some more and waited again. Within a minute, the Chairman came on the line. The Colonel spoke rapidly and urgently to the man. He stopped and waited, listening. Finally, with a curt nod and a final word, he hung up.

Turning to the waiting Interpol agents, he said, "The Chairman will cut through all of what Americans call red tape—an apt description—and we will have our fast plane. And I have another thought. Do you know who is responsible for this?"

"Yes, we do. He is a middle-eastern religious dictator with the name Rathmanizzar. We have his location and when I make a call, Interpol will descend on him."

The Colonel smiled. "Do not make your call, Mr. Muneau. Do you have his coordinates?"

"Yes, of course." Ted looked quizzical.

"May I have them?"

Ted put a strange look on his face and hesitated briefly, but gave Colonel Tao the coordinates for Tubela-ha.

"I propose to send him greetings from the Chinese Peoples Republic."

The Interpol agents feigned a look of horror. Then Ted said, "What would you do?"

"This little man and his people need to be excised from our world. Do you not think that a fair solution?"

"Yes," said Ted, "I do. But I cannot condone such an act. I would have to protest."

"As would I," Richard said, again following Ted's lead, although not completely understanding.

"Perhaps if I detained you two until the situation resolved itself, then you would have no say in what the Chinese government did to right such an egregious wrong."

Ted looked thoughtful. "No...we couldn't..."

He let the thought dangle. The Chinese Colonel felt he had sized up the men correctly. Let the Chinese mete out justice to this Rathmanizzar. Interpol would come away with its hands clean.

Perfect.

"Consider yourselves under house arrest. Sergeant," the Colonel motioned to a Chinese in civilian clothes, "take charge of these men. They are to be treated well, but don't let them out of your sight. They may stay with me. I don't consider them dangerous."

"Yes, sir."

Shortly, a small forklift truck appeared outside. It broke through the exterior wall of the large home and into the laboratory room. Competent Chinese workmen shimmed under the bomb and the forklift picked it up gingerly. Everyone held his breath during the operation. Delicately they extricated the bomb. It went into a waiting truck.

Colonel Tao rapped out new orders. The truck with the bomb disappeared into the morning sunlight.

"The truck, barring mishap," the Colonel told his waiting guests, "will arrive at the military air base at Dongba in fifty minutes. A MIG 27 will take the parcel and head for Qinghai Province. The aircraft will have less than two hours to arrive over the deep escarpments at the start of the Tibetan range. The pilot has been ordered to sacrifice himself to make certain that the plane crashes with its cargo in a very deep trench in the inner mountains. The area is remote and unpopulated. Radioactive debris should be kept to a minimum."

"You have thought it through," Ted said.

"On short notice, it would seem the best plan." The Colonel sighed. "It is a pity there is not time to deliver their own bomb to them. It would be such irony as to make a Chinese philosopher smile."

Ted and Richard both smiled at that.

"However, a small, long range ICBM will be dispatched in a coordinated move with the blast in the Tibetan mountains, and the middle-east terrorist will disappear at the moment our pilot dies. It is fitting."

The pseudo-Interpol men nodded.

"Come, my men will clean up here. Wang-Ho has been found and is under arrest. He will have many interesting things to tell us."

"We will have many cells to mop up after the head has been removed," Richard offered.

"I will detain you long enough to lend credence to your inability to alter China's resolve to destroy the terrorist. You will be free to go thereafter. The Chairman will make announcements to all major governments relative to this crisis to coincide with the bomb blasts. There will be much political fallout from this, but my concern is radioactive fallout. The Chairman can deal with all else."

"You have handled this with efficiency and dispatch." Ted said.

Audrey, have you been catching all of this? Where are you now? Richard linked Audrey.

Yes, I've got it. I'm in a taxi on my way to the airport. I'll arrange tickets for us. Tokyo?

Yes. Ted won't object to that and we can get an international flight to LA soonest from there.

How soon do you think you can break away?

Tentatively, because we don't know what direction the aftermath of this will take, around mid-afternoon.

Gotcha. I'll be ready.

Good job, Audrey.

All in a day's work for the super-team! How's your leg?

Hurts like hell, but the stitches are holding.

Good enough. Bear up, bucko.

Not much else I can do, love.

Audrey sent him a curled love message with salve on it.

Thanks. What do I do without you?

Not as much. Welcome playfulness continued silently, covering the overstressed reality. Finally Audrey announced that she had arrived and had better pay attention for a while, foreign country and all.

Richard sent her a big smile.

Colonel Tao looked the two in the eyes and said, "Although we cannot announce it, the government is grateful for your intercession in this delicate matter."

"Our job," Ted said shortly.

"No, there is more here than you have revealed. Be content to know that I will release you without interrogation as my gift to you."

Ted said nothing. Richard pretended to be otherwise occupied. He projected the conversation.

One smart man, that Colonel, Audrey linked.

Umm...

The Colonel resumed, "Is it not a matter of intelligence, rather than skin tone or philosophy that sets us apart from most in this world, Mr. Muneau, Mr. Penwarton?"

Ted nodded and bowed his respect to the Colonel. Richard nodded briefly.

"Enough said. Let us play this out," the Colonel offered.

58

Darkness had come hours before and Nick figured it must be around ten. Nick sat stiffly in his oversized leather chair. He felt so weary he wouldn't even glance at his watch. A barely noticeable nervous twitch jumped spasmodically around his left eye. It had been many hours since Monaghal last reported, or from Rathmanizzar, for that matter. Stretch promised to call as soon as the job was done. The silence worried him, but he kept it inside. Then he laughed harshly. Stone Goggins looked up from the printout he'd been studying.

"Nick?"

"Shit going down I haven't told you yet, Stone."

"When you're ready." Goggins knew better than to push the boss.

Nick sat, tapping his fingers on the big mahogany desk. Stone glanced at him again, said nothing.

"Want me get you something?"

"Nah, you know I don't drink except at parties."

"Somethin's eatin' you. Might help."

"Yeah, maybe." Nick made no move to get up. Stone went over to the bar and poured two shots of Hennessey into a wide glass from a decanter at the small bar opposite the book wall. He brought it over to Nick who took it automatically; too distracted to consider what he was doing. After a minute, he looked at the glass in his hand, made a quick decision and downed it. He continued to sit, staring at nothing for a long time. Finally he looked over at Stone and said, "Thanks."

"No prob, Nick."

Like he had just become aware of Stone, although the man had been in the office for six hours, Nick said, "Why don't you take off. We'll do this again in the morning."

"Okay, Nick, goodnight."

Nick stared ahead, unseeing. Stone let himself out quietly.

Alone for the first time in much of the day, Nick gave himself back to bad thoughts. Everything was going good; too good. Maybe now the hammer is coming down. He reviewed his support for Rathmanizzar's cause. He re-assessed his plan on how he would pull great wealth from the disaster that followed the bomb blast. All those things worked for him. They were good. They *worked*.

He smiled, a short, brittle, nearly lipless smile as he thought of the Chinese girl he'd fallen for so many years ago and he briefly wondered what she would have thought of all this. Nick was over her and any others who had come his way, present wife included. He grew up, went away and into a life he chose. He'd almost forgotten the exquisite little Chinese girl, and he focused on it. A few dulled memories passed in his mind. He pushed them aside. Learn from the past; don't live there. He laughed again. This time, no one heard him.

He got up, went to the bar and poured himself another double shot of cognac. He threw it over ice this time. Although late, as Nick's mind still waded through thoughts of the day, his concern for Stretch and his boys grew.

Where the hell are they? He looked at the clock on the far wall. Two a.m.

59

Rathmanizzar rose from his sleep pad. With a small shock, he realized he had finally slept. Night had flown and day showed through the tent material as a dirty white brightening circle. An uncommon thrill coursed through his body. This was the day...*the day*...the end of all the evil in the world and the beginning of a new order. Under a banner carried by Rathmanizzar, the world would change. It would become a place for the devout, the believers in Allah, the God, the one God... the only God. He stretched. He felt wonderful!

After a few moments he began to reflect. His last memory had been of the vision, the dream, a dream that had begun to take on characteristics of a nightmare. This day was new. He would allow nothing to interrupt his pure vision. Within the vision was victory.

The Word of the Book called out for his attendant. Ahmed al Salud parted the tent opening and entered.

"Ahmed, you are up early."

"For the master, the disciple never sleeps."

"Yet you appear well rested, Ahmed."

"The Word of the Book has known his disciple for many years. Does the master doubt the power he has invested in his servant?"

"No, Ahmed. Approach. Victory and the new way are upon us."

"Yes, master," Ahmed knelt before the leader, who laid his hand briefly on Ahmed al Salud's shoulder.

Despite the nagging black spots in the vision, Rathmanizzar would not bring himself to question over-riding purpose coupled with mighty desire, the drumbeat to which he moved and the same drumbeat his followers would give their lives for.

After the benediction, Ahmed rose and backed out of the tent. Rathmanizzar looked after his disciple. Casually he went over to his eating tray.

At three-thirty p.m., Lobala time, Rathmanizzar and Ahmed went to his communications tent. A desert storm blew southward, only kilometers outside the little city. It would not interfere with transmission at their satellite antenna, camouflaged under netting that passed microwaves but appeared invisible to the spy satellites in high orbit.

As Rathmanizzar entered the specially constructed and sealed tent, duty personnel bowed and moved aside for him. The man in charge of communications quickly brought a chair over for the leader. He placed it in full view of the tracking equipment and the plot board.

"Word of the Book," he said, "All goes according to plan."

"Good, Mahmeth."

"In one half hour a mighty explosion in the capitol city of the Chinese Peoples Republic will signal the beginning of the new era. You can all feel pride in this monumental achievement," Rathmanizzar said to his devout.

A half hour passed.

60

Ted, Richard and Audrey were at 41,000 feet on their flight to Tokyo and just beginning to cross the Korea Straight north of the tip of Cheju-do Island when two atomic bombs went off simultaneously in different parts of the world.

Instant furor blanketed the world. The Captain piped the Chairman's address into the jet's passenger cabin in Chinese. Simultaneous interpreters available for Japanese, French, English and Indian passengers aboard translated. Ted, Audrey and Richard turned to the English channel. Businessmen and a very few women also accessed their laptops and read the news, instantly available on all the wire services. They viewed it in shock and disbelief. After the first silence, sound rose in babble, seat by seat.

You getting the same messages I am? Audrey linked.

Yes. The Chairman is smooth. I'll bet he notified all the major nuclear powers only a few minutes beforehand by Red phone. Bet he asked all heads of state to sit on the information lest anyone in their governments alert anyone who could get to Rathmanizzar. Bet he asked them to delay when those countries with spy satellites caught the ICBM launch.

Bet he did.

The Chinese have studied the psychology of the human mind for thousands of years. They are masters at both spoken and unspoken word.

Read that somewhere.

I want to listen.

Okay, big fella. Audrey subsided.

"...and on excellent information from agents of Interpol, the Chinese Government was able to put an end to a plot by the Lobala Liberation Front to destroy China's national capitol, Beijing. No active hostilities will follow. Peoples of the world, a threat to world peace has been abated. There is no further cause for alarm. As I speak, remnants of the terrorist group are being rounded up and will be brought to justice."

Audrey smiled inwardly. Bet Interpol knows it wasn't them. They'll be happy to take the credit. They'll also know somebody else is out there. Her attention flashed back to the broadcast.

"I am joined in this quest by the President of the United States, the Premier of Canada and the rulers of the European states, Russia and Asia. All smaller nations are invited to partake in the search for the evil issue of the terrorist Rathmanizzar. You all must be alerted! The Evil One is dead! His organization, what is left of it, is in shambles and will soon disappear.

"There will be heightened security in all ports of call, and there may be delays, but you should welcome them, because they represent your governments' working to eliminate the threat posed by remnants of the Evil One's armies."

Ted sat silently listening, an inexpensive shipboard phone stuck in an ear. He stared stonily ahead. His mind, like all but two on Earth, captured in a solitary inability to really know any other, relied on the external world's sights and sounds for meaning. He alone, among all others, knew that a charged conversation took place in seats rows apart, and he tried not to think about how much he wanted to be part of it.

Wonder what Ted is thinking right now, Richard projected.

Probably our next move.

Probably how to keep our cover, maybe how to disappear when we land.

Dunno, maybe he's wondering how it would be to mind link.

Could be. He only says what he needs to.

Yes.

Change subject. The only way to get back quicker would be with an Air Force jet over the pole.

No can do.

We have just foiled the most dangerous plot the world has ever seen and we have to stay hidden. Pity!

Bad people don't stop being bad.

I know, but wouldn't it be nice... Richard projected a map of the world and highlighted a point north of Rio, *if we could take a long vacation, right there, and forget about...everything...for a while?*

After we take care of Nick and his boys, maybe we can. Really want to?

Sure. Time off sounds good to me.

Me, too.

Have you discussed with Ted how we're going to confront Nick Trafalgar?

Briefly. He says he has some ideas on how to handle it, but wanted to think it through some. Wasn't anything to share, or I'd have passed it on, partner.

I know you would. Now, the ability! I sense mine has reached maximum. How about you?

Nothing new here. I really have to be careful to block out the electronics I can read. I catch conversations. They are weird in foreign languages. Sometimes I want to laugh, but people would think I'm loony.

You are.

Ha, ha. We'll keep that our secret, okay, Audrey?

They landed at Tokyo and changed planes. A Northwest Airlines 747 took them to L.A. They went through customs without incident, although slowly, as the world rebounded from the news.

Imagine, Audrey, the Chinese are the second peoples of the world to use nuclear weapons! Who would have thought it?

We are so lucky it worked out the way it did.

Upgraded security blanketed the nation. Still, traffic appeared normal over the skies of the U.S. and they arrived at JFK at 8:53 p.m. Eastern Daylight Savings Time.

Through Ted's special link to the Infab computer, he passed on some instructions and assured himself that Nick and Company hadn't moved from their spot. Supreme confidence or supreme paranoia? Didn't matter. Ted told the others he hoped it would make their job easier.

"You ready to share your plan, yet, Ted?" Audrey asked.

"Yes."

61

On entering the Lodge, Ted moved the ashtray the requisite quarter of an inch. The wall panel opposite slid silently away. They entered. Ted went immediately to the interior door and pressed a special code. The duty people inside, who were aware of the intruders, went back to work, but monitored them on non-visual sensors.

"Just to let them know we are who they are expecting."

"Right," Richard said.

"Richard, you stay here. You are out of this part of the operation. We've already given your leg too much of a workout."

Richard grumbled, but returned to a comfortable lodge chair. The panel door closed. Audrey and Ted accessed the cavern passage and made their way to the first ladder.

Audrey tried to keep it light as they made their way down to the sea level entrance to the Eastern Depot. "This looks familiar."

"Doesn't it?"

Ted led the way. The damp rock persuaded them to watch every footfall. Even with knowledge of the conditions, the trek wasn't easy. Audrey again got that heart flutter as they walked rapidly across the deadly drop-down floor. The muted roar of tons of water passing under her feet each second daunted her as it had the first time. Understanding the mechanism of the trap didn't make her any less antsy.

When they had traveled far enough beyond the roar for normal conversation, Ted said to her, "That might have been a serious problem to my plan, but it has been provided for..."

"What do you mean?" Audrey asked.

"The nylon rope ladder used in construction of the trap is still there."

"Ah-hah."

They finally ducked under the last, low overhang and straightened up on the other side. The cavern opened out before them. Stepping through, they stopped, blinked and stood quietly, adjusting to the brighter light. They followed the natural passage until once more the depot building met them, silent and waiting.

Ted now went to the door and punched in another set of numbers. He received a silent blink of acknowledgement from the watchers within.

Outside the doorway, neatly piled, lay two sets of wet gear, suits, tanks and special body hugging overalls designed to carry plastic explosives and firearms. The overalls had a special bib made of a rough but supple plastic material that carried over the top of the tanks, obviously for protection against damaging tanks or valves.

"Nice stuff," Audrey offered.

"Top of the line, invented by one of ours," Ted said. "The sausage shaped, ganged, very thin tanks are set on rotatable universals. Will allow us to get past tight places. They can be disconnected and float free if necessary."

He bent over one set of equipment. "This is your intro to these units, Audrey. To save air and give us several hours of use, this valve," he pointed, "flips down to shut off the flow..."

Ted went over the equipment piece by piece. Audrey watched carefully, bending for hands on as needed.

Got it, Audrey?

Yup.

"What's next?" Audrey said, as Ted stopped and stood.

"We're rested enough. Let's bring down Nick Trafalgar's house of cards."

"Good metaphor."

They grabbed their gear and awkwardly walked it to a large opening from which icy water poured rapidly.

"This is the place, Audrey."

Donning suits and overalls, they carefully attached the equipment and checked each others connections. Ted gave the signal to submerge. They held their facemasks and fell backward into a deep cleft cut by the running channel. Water pressure at the outflow pushed them toward the middle of the underground lake. Ted motioned Audrey to follow him.

Wow, this is cold! Audrey linked.

Sure is. You'll get used to it quick enough, Richard replied. *Churn that water, baby.*

Yes, dear. Oh, boy!

Ted headed toward the far side of the outflow region and Audrey noticed that the pressure abated quickly. He disappeared into the moving blackness and Audrey followed. Dome lights in their wet suits showed the way ahead. Audrey mentioned how ethereal it felt to Richard on the link and then to Ted on the suit radio.

I haven't done a lot of this, but enough so I can relate, Richard linked.

Ted's electronic voice came to her clearly. "I never quite get used to it."

They pulled themselves deeper and deeper into the low, cavernous waterway. Audrey soon realized that she was actually warm in the wetsuit and the only drag she felt came from water pressure against the outer suit. Ted had mentioned that rocky outcroppings would appear at the right times as handholds, and sure enough, she found plenty of gripping surface.

Grateful for their gloved grip-surfaces, they made good time. A half-hour in, the way became suddenly steeper. Ted waved at Audrey and pointed with his light to a heavy nylon rope ladder casually affixed to the rough bottom of the subterranean river, metal pegs driven into rock every five feet. The fairly wide channel narrowed abruptly and water pressure increased sharply.

"Best hook your arm over each center rope and pull yourself along. You'll have to fight the current. It'll be awkward, but you don't want to get yanked back and have to start over," Ted said via radio.

"No wonder you said anyone who tripped the trap above had no chance," Audrey replied.

"Right. I struggled with it when I went through here last time, but it's doable. Just hang on tight."

"Oh, I will, I will," Audrey said. Her voice was unnaturally loud in Ted's earpiece. The roar around her made it natural to raise her voice, but the radio's were good.

"Ten minutes and we'll be past this."

"Good to hear. Let's go."

"Right."

Here the river had carved out a flume. Its appearance was starkly circular, like a long tube. It reminded Audrey of lava tubes she'd seen years before in Hawaii. Her light bounced off the water worn smoothness and flickered rapidly in a surreal, dreamlike way. She paid attention to her every move. As she removed one arm from each rung of the ladder, the pressure of the moving water pushed her free arm backwards. She found it tiring, but thanked her lucky stars she was in top physical shape and uninjured. There were plenty of places she could have been hurt before. She closed her eyes for a moment and sent a picture of the scene to Richard.

Wow! Hang on tight, my dear.

Funny you should say that. Just what I'm doing!

Want you back in one piece.

Me, too, Audrey projected fervently.

She could hear Ted's effort through the earphone. No breath for conversation. It seemed much longer than ten minutes and Audrey was about to lightly ask Ted if her underwater watch went slower in a subterranean river when he came on the radio again.

"Here we are, Audrey. Another few feet and the pressure eases."

"Be right there." Another minute of struggle put her up next to Ted. The river had suddenly widened into a massive cavern. The water, not quite still in the large area, clearly funneled into the flume. She saw no other outlet. Ted confirmed her query.

"Where was that trap?" Audrey asked.

"Doesn't surprise me you were too busy to look. It's about twenty-five feet back, in that last smooth section."

The cavern stretched to about twenty yards wide and proceeded upriver beyond the ability of Audrey's light to reach. Above her the low ceiling grew with distance, and thin stalactites hung from the ceiling, all of them cut off in a kind of water-worn, flat nub on the bottom.

"Soluble rock worn away during flood times, right?"

"Yes," Ted replied, "It's stuff most people never see. I find it interesting."

"Me, too. Why are the stalactites so thin?"

"A dearth of lime in the area is my guess."

"Makes sense."

Ted changed the subject. "It will be much easier going now for another three quarters of a mile. That's as far as I got last time. Evidently the water in this cave never rises six inches higher than it is right now, if you can believe the stalactites. Makes it easy to move, anyway. We should be able to walk upright in a little bit, and you can turn off your air for now. It's dank, but breathable."

Audrey turned the air valve off and took a breath of the underground air. Like Ted said, it was dank, heavy. It felt almost grainy in her lungs.

"Not like the air back home, Ted."

Richard! Can you see anything on GPS?

Your last hour puts you nearly a half mile in. I lost you from the start, but I didn't want to say anything. GPS doesn't work through rock.

"Ted, Richard says we're about a half mile west of our original position, but he lost the signal at the start."

"That's what we could expect with four hundred feet of rock over top of us."

Audrey let the conversation run through her to Richard, so he linked Audrey, *Tell Ted we have a better system than GPS.*

I think he knows that. Audrey sent him a Cheshire grin.

Ted said into the phone, "How's your connection?"

"Great! Rock doesn't seem to make a difference."

"Didn't think it would."

The two felt their way over the smooth bottom. By pushing their knees against the water they made very good time. The water remained at knee depth for nearly a quarter of a mile. Then the bottom got rougher and the cave narrowed again. They started to rise in steppes. More than once they slipped on unseen rocks and once Ted disappeared altogether when he stepped into a pothole.

He surfaced quickly. Audrey grabbed his hands and pulled him back to her level. They stopped and shined their lights upward. A vertical tunnel three feet across above them rose out of sight. No water flowed from it.

"Must have been an access from the surface. The geology changed and it stopped running. Didn't hit that last time. Glad it was just a pothole."

"Know what you mean." Audrey shuddered to think of her Moonlight Man suddenly sucked down and away to who knew where, held under by the pressure. Could she have saved him? Who knew?

"I certainly would have seen a whirlpool or felt dragging pressure before I got that far, I'm sure," Ted said, but he sounded relieved.

Audrey wasn't so sure, but said nothing. They made their way around the pothole and shined their lights up every now and then to check the ceiling. Another half-hour passed.

"Ah, here it is." Ted stopped and shined his light on a piton pin he had left in a cleft of rock above the water line. It shined with moisture and showed almost no rust.

"This is where I stopped."

Audrey looked ahead. Several thousand tons of granite ceiling had fallen. Water cascaded out of numerous orifices, all of them too small to crawl through.

"By myself, I couldn't pass this, but I had an idea that a little C-4 properly applied might break out enough of this so we could get past it."

"You're going to blast?" Audrey said incredulously.

"A little risky, but not much. I checked over the character of the granite walls and maybe a major quake could bring it all down on us, but not a shaped charge."

"Is there anything you don't know how to do?"

"Lots of things."

Richard, who sensed that Audrey needed to concentrate on what she was doing, finally projected, *I remain in awe of that man.*

What about me?

Awe doesn't do it for you!

"You say the nicest things."

"You just get through this and get back to me, you hear"

Aw, Richard, you are there when I need you. Don't worry about it.

Right! I sit up here in the easy life, antlers and leather for company, enjoying a rich man's pastime, while my wife is taking a chance with her life! Mine, too, by the way.

What do you mean?

I love you, Audrey. I can't make it any clearer.

Audrey remained silent for a couple of minutes. The danger, the risk, the totally surreal, impossible adventure they were in at the moment, the mission, it all came together and she stopped, confused.

Audrey?

"Audrey?"

She broke out, present reality running at her like an old steam train...out of control! "Yes, Ted."

"Help me with the charge wires." He indicated, "Over there."

"Right."

Get back to you, honey. Duty calls.

Sorry, Audrey. My mistake. I just realized I put a guilt trip on you. Don't let anything get in the way, okay?

I won't.

Audrey grasped the wires and a tiny circuit maker that Ted held out for her and began to move back into the stream slowly, as he fed them out.

"Hold it there." The tinny voice stopped her fifty feet downstream.

Ted bent over his project and then stuffed it carefully into a crevice.

"The wall behind will hold and the blast should knock out enough rock to let us through." He paused and said, "I hope."

Ted slowly made his way to Audrey's position. Then he directed her to the side and behind a smooth hollowed curve in the river's course.

"This is good enough. Cover your ears." He took the igniter from her, flipped up a safety and pressed the contact. A deafening boom sounded in the confined space and the walls reverberated. A wall of water several inches high went past them. It calmed quickly. From their vantage point, they saw no other change.

415

"It's safe now. Let's go." Ted led Audrey back to the blockage. Most of it remained, but now a large hole in one side of the mass boiled with water. The other jumbled exits diminished noticeably.

"Looks like success." Ted grasped a huge piece of granite at the side of the new flow and pulled hard on it. It didn't move. He moved to the other side and pulled on another big piece. Water streamed with considerable pressure through the opening between them. Ted's extra pressure on the piece caused it to move suddenly and pinion toward him. He tried to get away but the water slowed his movement. He let out a cry.

"Audrey, my foot is caught. I can't move!"

"Are you cut or bleeding?"

Silence for a moment. "No, but I'm caught."

Audrey closed the few feet of distance between them and grasped the top of the boulder. She pulled hard and it moved a little.

Ted pulled his left leg. "No good."

"Hang on."

Richard, Ted is caught. Any suggestions?

Yes, I caught my foot in a rockslide when I was a boy. Look above the point where the rock is wedged and see what's near it. Be careful not to dislodge anything onto Ted, of course, but more important, make sure anything you do above him doesn't make the rock that has him trapped move until you're ready. It's like the old game of Pick Up Sticks. Anything you can clear out that will give you a handle to use your body as a fulcrum, that's what you want.

Got you. Hang one. She relayed her conversation to Ted.

"Okay," he said. He looked above the mass as far as he could. "Be careful."

"I will."

"First..." She put her hands into the crevasses near Ted and felt for pivot points. Then she moved beyond where Ted remained trapped and started climbing the rubble. The piece that had him she estimated weighed half a ton, but a small area at the bottom held most of the weight. Could she use that to advantage? Her acrobatic skills, how to arch, how to move, how to gain a weight advantage, they could help. The wet suit and overalls hampered her.

"What are you doing, Audrey?" Ted said.

As she removed her overalls and her wet suit, she thought, I'd better get this done quick, this water is frickin' cold!

You sure about this, Audrey?

Yes, Richard. Only Houdini could work in all this stuff.

Be careful, love.

I've got to free Ted. I see no other choice.

All right. But Richard sounded skeptical.

"I can't work in this, Ted. Trust me," she said into the radio as she pulled off her wet cap. Now she worked alone.

Ted stared at his operative as she shed her protections, leaving them in a pile she could find later. He didn't say anything more. Now free to move in all directions unencumbered, Audrey disappeared from Ted's view. Nimble and nearly naked, she scaled the mountain of loose rock. Picking smaller pieces near larger ones, she heaved them off to a side, leaving only pieces that might cause other rocks to move. Finally she'd worked her way to within two feet of Ted's head.

Without her radio, she couldn't talk to Ted, and Richard kept out of her head while she concentrated. She reached the top of the piece holding Ted. It was about five feet long and relatively narrow. Carefully she felt down to her arms limit to assess the character of the rock. Good! Now to get her powerful legs against the rock and her back against anything substantial. Got it! A small, sharp protrusion gnawed at her back as she prepared to give it her all. She ignored it.

She saw Ted looking at her. She motioned for him to lean as far to the right as he could. He caught on and moved right.

NOW!

Audrey pushed with all her strength. Slowly, the rock swung out like a pendulum. Below her Ted felt the movement, grasped his leg and pulled it free. He moved quickly out of the way of the massive piece of granite as it turned and tumbled away. He followed it downstream a few yards in case anything else dislodged behind him.

Sensing movement behind her, Audrey lost no time leaving her perch. She made an arching dive away from the pile into what she remembered as a four-foot deep gouge in the subterranean floor. She landed on her belly, got her footing and immediately looked at the rock pile. Nothing else moved now. She carefully retrieved her suit and gear.

Success, Richard.

Bless you, baby. You're the best.

You say that to all the women.

Used to, but I'm reformed.

You wait...

She dressed quickly. Ted made his way over to Audrey and helped her suit up. With her adrenalin gone the cold river had begun to slow her down. No longer a stranger to this underworld, Audrey moved inside the suit and soon warmed.

When she'd reconnected her radio, Ted said, "You were wonderful. Thank you."

"Didn't like the idea of being alone in here. Not as much fun, you know."

"I'll bet! Anyway, thank you."

"Can't let anything happen to my Moonlight Man."

Ted was silent for some moments. Audrey had made light fare of what clearly could have been tragedy. Highlights of their adventures came to him, reaffirming his great pick. Finally he said, "We'd better get moving."

"Our date with Nick."

"Right."

Richard, we're on the move again.

I know.

We're climbing the rubble. Seems stable now. There's an opening large enough for us to get through. Lot of water coming through and not much to hold onto, but I have an idea.

"Ted, pay out some of that thin nylon rope and hang onto it. I'm thinner. You can push me through the stricture and I can pull you through after I'm on the other side."

"Works for me."

Ted got his hands against Audrey's feet and pushed as she scrambled into the opening. Audrey couldn't see a thing and water pelting the top of her head made it hard to think. She pulled against anything that stayed still. A couple of brain-busters got loose and headed back toward Ted, but he didn't give up the pressure on her feet.

"Throwing rocks at me?" Ted tried to make it seem light.

"Sorry."

"Kidding. No damage."

An occasional grunt said worlds about the effort he made that kept her moving forward. Otherwise he had nothing to say. Finally she passed the lip of the stricture and moved down the other side. The pressure abated abruptly.

"Through."

"Good. How's it look over there?"

"Low ceiling on one side, higher to my right as I face you. My light, hold on...shows clear sailing for some ways."

"Okay. I'm coming through." Audrey pulled on the line Ted had attached to his belt and took up slack quickly as it eased in her hands. Soon Ted's powerful arms brought him through the opening.

"Pretty turbulent," Ted said. "Glad you could help me through that."

"What are fiends...I mean friends for?" Audrey said demurely.

"Funny. Let's get moving." He moved ahead of Audrey and went on.

Richard, can you see us on your equipment?

Truthfully, no change from the start. However, I sense your radios electronically. I can't actually triangulate, but it gives me some idea of where you are. Next best thing.

Don't take anything away from what you've got. Didn't have it before.

Right you are, my dear. We see more clearly that anyone else in the world, and here I am complaining. See, what did I tell you about being idle. Nice place, but I hate it up here.

Don't give up, matey.

No fear of that, but I feel helpless.

Do you a world of good.

Did I need to hear that?

Humpf!

Humpf?

Please don't repeat. Okay, gotta pay attention.

Ted and Audrey had reached another wide, low place. They had to go on bottled air again.

"What do you think, Ted?" Audrey asked through the radio.

"Plenty of water coming down here. Not much fear of running out of river. If we can get through, I think we have another three miles to go."

"That far?"

"Yes, all of that. Remember, I scoped this out on geodesic maps of the countryside before we started this operation."

"Yeah, I remember."

"The going isn't tough yet."

"You think what we went through in the 'flume' and this last passage wasn't tough?"

"Not what I meant. It could get much narrower. We have no idea. We might run into an impassable cave and have to backtrack, maybe a long way. We might get lost down here in the twists and turns. Fortunately, we haven't run into a split in the tunnel yet."

Audrey shined her light ahead. "Oh, yes we have."

62

Nick sat at his huge desk with his big head in his hands. Got to keep what's happened out there from my people, he thought, but I got trouble. Time for damage control. He picked up the phone and asked Ray where everyone was.

"Most of the guys are in the card room, boss. Everybody's sticking kinda close after the news."

Damn, they know about it, he thought. Hell, why not? Somebody's got a radio, and it's all over the TV.

"Call a general meeting in the soldier's room. Everybody! Now! I'm going to make an announcement. Call the gate and tell 'em to lock it up. One man stays on lookout, the rest come in."

"Sure thing, boss." Silently worried, Ray broke the connection.

Nick got his thoughts in order. Best not to show worry. Leadership required stength. The boys would want to know what he thought, and he knew his life and his organization depended on them. But he had a lot of enemies, too, and more than one of them would be looking to see what they could carve out of Nick Trafalgar. Worse, some of Rathmanizzar's organization—some of it must have survived—might know of his connection and try to get in touch and that would be the worst thing that could happen! I can handle what comes, he thought. He smiled and got up.

The last stragglers were filing in as he arrived in the soldier's room below the mansion. He felt the tension in the packed assembly. They know, all right.

He got right to it. "Boys, you know about the atomic bombs, one in Tibet and the other in North Africa."

An uncomfortable rustle and a few coughs told Nick they did.

"The one in Tibet was supposed to go off in China. Sumptin' went wrong."

He stared out at the crowd, his eyes searching yet unseeing. Just his presence made his audience blanch, but behind the eyes, questions began to rise. They waited.

"The other one wiped out a, ah...business associate. Won't be long before all hell's going to break loose and I can only guess the direction it'll come from. Right now I think we're safe, but we have some enemies out there who know the score, and they'll be coming for us.

"I'm turning this place into a camp. I've got my army and when I chose this location for my operations, I planned it carefully. When I say the word, the mansion becomes a fortress. I'm sayin' it now. I want you soldiers to start earning your pay. Grab weapons! Get out to the perimeter and keep an eye out. I'm havin' a top level meeting with the short group immediately and they will be assigned other responsibilities. Now get goin'!"

Chairs shifted and babble swelled as the soldiers filed out. They went to their rooms, picked out their favorite firepower and made for the six-foot wall that surrounded the estate. Uneasy to a man but so inextricably tied to the boss that they didn't question his orders, the men sat...and waited...and waited. A lot of them thought black thoughts. Some were scared but everyone held in their feelings. A few thought about deserting, but didn't have the guts to run. They knew Nick. He'd have them shot in the back.

Not a few of them thought about the Weasel, and Bernie Homenio and the kid, Mikey. Not a few of them noticed how things had begun to unravel. It didn't feel the same anymore. Shifty-eyed glances flew.

They did as they were told.

Back in the meeting room, Nick addressed his elite staff. "You know I never miss a trick. We got trouble, not from the government, but from the New York families. Fazio's been on special assignment. He tells me the Tarizzio and Montebello families held some secret meetings last week and I figure they're going to try to pick our plum.

"There's another organization out there that may be even more dangerous to us. I don't know where they are, but their front organization is International Fabrications. Yeah, it's the one I sent Stretch, Lenny, Johnny and that fuck-up Diddle Schaeffer to, to wipe out that bitch no one in my organization seems to be able to touch. They haven't reported back. I'm guessin' they're dead.

There was a rustling in the small group. They gave Nick their full attention.

"That's the background. You guys are my lieutenants. Your regular duties are suspended. We got a war and we're gonna conduct it right here, sink or swim. You all with me?"

Murmurs from his audience, "Yeah, Nick, one for all and all for one."

"We're not the three fuckin' musketeers. We'll get through it. Okay, here are your assignments." He handed out a copy of the soldier's list. "You get ten men apiece. I'll figure the logistics and the defense plan. You'll get it in ten minutes. You carry it out. Kapisch?"

Nods of all heads.

"Dismissed! Get crackin'" The audience dissolved. He stayed long after everyone had left, thinking and weighing options. Tight-lipped, he noticed that his hands hurt. He looked down and willed them to release the edges of the podium. They were unnatural pink and white from the pressure. He hung them by his sides, not looking at them, but aware when they finally began to feel normal. Then he shook them, looked around silently and purposefully strode from the room.

Back in his office he turned on his office TV. The local news didn't reveal anything. He flipped channels, looking for something he might recognize, any hint. Nothing!

"Am I being paranoid?" He answered the question immediately. His intuition worked full time now. He could sense something but he couldn't see it clearly. Danger, but from where?

Nick sat still for a time, but his nerves required him to move around. He called Ray at the phone exchange. "Anything doing?"

"All quiet, Nick."

"Keep on top of things."

"I will, Nick."

Nick left his office and paid a rare visit to his wife on the third floor, off-limits place for all staff, the luxurious prison Hermona Trafalgar voluntarily lived in. She knew that many things her husband did were not right, but he was powerful and fearsome and he scared her to death. In his own way he loved her and she knew that, too. Tonight she didn't expect him and it surprised her. She smiled a little smile as he walked into her huge apartment and her guard went up, as always.

"Nick!"

"Hello, Hermona. Just wanted to know if you're comfortable?"

"Comfortable, yes. Lonely, yes. What brings you up tonight?"

"Got the mansion locked down. Expecting trouble. Nothing we can't handle."

Fear blazed in Hermona's eyes. A hand went to her mouth. "What...?"

"Some business went bad. Don't you worry none about it. It'll be okay." Nick's hand went out and stroked his wife's hair. She closed her eyes and the shivers he felt coursing through her pale body calmed under his ministrations.

"Yeah," he said, "not to worry."

Nick reached over and took his wife's face in his big hands and he kissed her. Then he uncharacteristically laid his head in her lap. "Not to worry."

But she did worry, a lot. Her mind was on fire. Nick's behavior, his gentleness...she didn't understand. Hermona searched her memory for any time when she'd felt this combination of bad news and her husband's gentle touch. She couldn't and it scared her out of her wits.

"Oh, Nick," was all she could say. Her fingers now ran through his graying hair. The scent of him called back sweeter memories. After a few moments, Nick raised up, kissed her again and then straightened.

"Got to go."

"Stay, Nick. I'm scared." The gruffness she normally heard came back into his voice.

"Got to go," he repeated, and pulled away. He stood over her, regarding her as if she were a china doll, then turned on his heel and left as quickly as he had appeared. Hermona looked after him, wordless, fear aching in her heart.

63

Ted gazed at the split water source. "Had to happen sometime."
"What now?"
"What would you do?"

Audrey looked carefully at the outflows. They were remarkably even. They were narrow and high and separated by a wall ten feet wide. She tried to create an Arial picture the lie of the land above their heads. Judgment call.

"I'd stick to the right."
"Let's go."

Audrey moved into the high but narrow tunnel in front of her. Cold water poured at her with great force. Ted saw the problem, came up behind her and pushed her along. With Ted's added strength, she grabbed an out-jut and a cupped area, hand holds that helped her through the stricture. Beyond, once again the pressure diminished and she reported to Ted that the going got much better past that point. That could end in a second, but it helped her. Ted began to recount some spelunking adventures.

"Okay," Audrey replied and wondered if Ted was talking just to hear himself. To Audrey, they seemed spurious, not to the point.

She projected to Richard, *Ted's a little strange since his problem back there away. Should I say something?*

Negative. Let him work it out. None of us can go full tilt all the time. He'll normalize soon, is my guess.

427

I'm sure you're right. Okay, I'll say nothing.

But she did, along different lines. "Ted," she asked into the radio, "How much air do we have left?"

Audrey knew, but wanted to engage him in conversation.

"Check your gages. We should be about even on air. You might have a bit more, based on your heroic efforts on my behalf a little while ago, if you remembered to turn off your air."

"Given."

"Of course."

Audrey was silent for a time. Ted broke her reverie. "I'm okay, Audrey. Pretty seldom for me to get a case of nerves, but I suspect you noticed."

"Who, me?"

"It's past. Let's move along."

"Right."

Ted now took the lead. They found the tunnel they'd entered continued to be narrow, but it didn't hamper them much, except for the all-pervading pressure. There were plenty of handholds. The underground stream twisted and turned; scooped out areas and potholes provided. Audrey wondered out loud on how underground rivers could go in so many directions and still get there.

Ted didn't respond.

Very funny, Audrey.

Oh, you again.

Want me to exit?

No, no, but you do seem to burst in when I'm thinking.

What can I say; you're always thinking!

All right, Richard! Guess I'm really lucky to be cared for by two guys. Kinda unique for this girl.

Wait a minute. Who's the other guy?

As if you didn't know!

Oh, that guy. Can't blame me for asking.

Yes, I can.

A guy can never win with them females.

We'll keep you on your toes.

Just then the two underground river rats came on another split, where the water poured out in equal measure.

"Your guess, Ted."

"The one on the right seems to lead in the direction we want. Who knows? At least we're making progress."

"What's you're guess?"

"Two and a half miles."

"And how much further?"

"Not sure, but I don't think over a half mile more."

"I like the sound of that. I mean, this underground stuff is terrific and all, but I'm really starting to appreciate the old outdoors. The rats can have this place!"

"I doubt you'll find any rats in this place," Ted offered.

"See, even the rats wouldn't want to be here."

Ted smiled.

Careful, Audrey, your hysteria level is going up, Richard linked. *You come down here and do this!*

I know what you are feeling, my dear, I really do. But the way back is a lot longer than the way forward. Think of it like that. You're catching claustrophobia. Don't let it get you.

She stopped and considered. *Yeah, I believe you're right, Richard, old bean. I don't think spelunking is my kind of adventure. Give me a high-wire any day. All that free space up and down...*

It's the unknown, too, right?

Yup, pardner! Sure glad I've got you on the other end. I'd feel foolish explaining to Ted that I've suddenly got a case of nerves about millions of tons of rock over my head. Silly me!

Now, now! Think about how extraordinary it is that you just came up with that feeling and not two miles ago. Feel privileged.

Right, Audrey thought, as sarcastically as she could.

Ooo...

Got that, matey?

Ted and Audrey made their way carefully forward, ever forward. Audrey gulped and subsided. She refocused on the plan and tried to put the narrow walls beyond her peripheral vision. She stared straight-ahead and only worried about the next step, the next turn, and watching Ted's back. It seemed to work.

Working against the cold water tired her out, but neither she nor Ted wanted to stop to rest, not here. A few hundred feet further they discovered another split, this time going in the opposite direction. Here the water pressure in the subterranean tunnel lessened and the ceiling lowered again, but the way ahead expanded horizontally until neither of the two could shine a light to its end.

"Aha!" Ted said.

Richard, the river reconnects here. Really good thing. Getting seriously tired.

I hears yuh, honey.

"Let's take a break." Ted stopped. He was breathing hard and Audrey suddenly felt ashamed for the way she'd carried on with Richard. Ted had led the way and most of the time while Audrey drafted behind him. His body had cut away some of the pressure she had lived with, it seemed forever.

They settled down, squatting, the ceiling now not more than a couple of inches over Ted's head. Audrey recalled that Ted was a man in his late forties or better. In top shape, yes, but this kind of labor wore on him and she could see it. She felt compassion, yet knowing the man as she did, but she didn't feel right to say anything.

After a couple of minutes he signaled her to move on, and they started forward again. Now they crawled.

"I hope the ceiling doesn't get any lower," Ted told Audrey in their radiophone.

"Me, too."

After another half-hour nearly crawling, Ted noted a deeper channel that moved off to their left.

"Looks like our only option. I can barely move here."

"Lead on."

Ted slithered into the channel and began to follow it, Audrey in tow. At the far wall the ceiling met the level of the water and Ted felt low down, his hands searching for the sides of an opening. Here water welled up from an underwater source.

"Let me try this, Audrey. You stay here." Ted handed her a thin nylon rope, hooked into his air supply again and submerged. Audrey paid out line freely while over the radio she could hear sounds of Ted working against the water pressure. She didn't expect him to talk. Finally, about five minutes later, he reported.

"I'm okay and I'm on the other side of this. Looks okay. Take a good hold and I'll pull you through."

"How gallant, monsieur. Hang until I hook."

She knotted the line to the top of her harness and said, "Okay."

Ted tugged on the rope and Audrey allowed herself to be dragged into the small flume. She kept her light shining ahead. Finally, Ted said, "I see your light. You're almost here."

Audrey came level with Ted. He grabbed her hands and pulled her up.

"What next, my leader."

"Keep going." They went on. The broad, flat, ceiling sank and stalactites became numerous again.

Twenty minutes later Ted said, "Do you smell something?"

"Yes. Smells like...like lime, I think."

"That's what I thought. There's something up ahead." They crawled carefully upstream, following the smell. It got stronger. There, ahead of them, a dry tunnel branched off to their right. It led upward on a gentle slope.

"Do we dare hope?" Audrey breathed.

You found it? Richard sounded excited.

Maybe. Give us a few.

Okay.

"This looks promising," Ted said. He stepped out of the cold stream and gave Audrey a hand. They entered a tunnel tall enough to accommodate people of good stature. Ted and Audrey shined their lights around. A few feet up the tunnel they discovered a deep pit with no outlet and a heavy smell of lime.

"We're here. Got to be pretty near under Nick's mansion, and whaddya know," Ted remarked, "he's got a working lime pit. Nice way to dispose of bodies."

Audrey shuddered, but remained elated at being out of the water.

Richard, we've found his entrance. Great guess on Ted's part. I'm looking forward to what comes next, and I'll get out of these damned water caves.

Great! Standing by for instructions.

Ted started to move along the natural tunnel. Soon it showed signs of men, pick marks and blasting holes. Then they came upon the door! It filled the tunnel, end-to-end, top to bottom. The door showed rust on the river's side, but not deep rust. Ted looked the heavy steel door over and noted it had been used recently. It would swing toward them on massive hinges. Ted remarked that there'd be no telling what was on the other side of it, but they didn't come this far to be stymied by a door.

Audrey smiled at that and agreed. "Beyond that, I don't hanker to go back the way we came, either."

"I got the impression you were a bit antsy about all that underground."

"Putting it mildly."

Ted got out his torch and a canister of acetylene, fired up and began to gnaw at the big lock. He cut it out altogether. Using a light pry bar, he tested it, but it wouldn't open.

"Have to go for the hinges. Didn't want that."

Audrey stood mute, letting Ted sort it out.

The torch cut slowly and deeply. First the bottom hinge gave way and then he worked on the top. The door stood. Ted used his short pry bar again. Audrey stood back ten feet, gun drawn, ready for anything.

Finally, with one hard twist, the door moved and began to fall outward, toward Ted. Audrey saw blackness on the other side. Ted went with the door, trying to keep it from thundering to the rock floor of the tunnel. At the last moment he jumped free and the door crashed down its last two feet. It made a loud noise, but not as loud, Audrey knew, as it would have without Ted's taking much of the weight to himself.

"Heavy!"

"I'll take your word for it, Ted," Audrey replied. She shined her light inside. It was a room, outfitted with a porous mattress, no chairs, but a steel cabinet with a Master Lock. The four sides of the room were of unadorned cement. Around the base of the floor deep grooves ran to a drain. Opposite them stood another steel door, looking very proficient. Sprinklers ringed the top of the room.

"Looks like Nick's killing room," Ted said softly.

"I'm beginning to dislike that man some."

"He's smart, and totally without conscience."

"Let's go get him."

64

Nick Trafalgar opened the door to his office and entered, glad to be alone. His inspection tour of the perimeter through the captain's glass on the mansion's cupola assured him that his soldiers and lieutenants were doing their jobs well enough. He noted a couple of weak areas on the north and east, and it looked like the hitters watching from the south end of the peninsula were too casual; they seemed to think that lounging on the sand represented keeping a good lookout.

He sat at his desk, reviewed the brief session he'd had earlier with his wife and thought about how scared she was. Bit of a rabbit, he thought, not really cut out for tribulation. Then he put her out of his mind and called Ray.

"Ray, security is lax already. I want you to call Strango, Nikko and Thaddeus."

Ray waited.

"Tell them to get on the stick. Their boys are fuckin' up! I told them to keep an eye out. Does Mack and Charlie playing cards by the fence sound like keeping watch? Strango's in charge. Does Switch need to stretch out on the ground behind the big Elm? Let Nikko straighten him out. Tad, does he know his guys are lounging on the grass yakking? Next thing you know, they'll decide to go swimming! Tell the three of them I'll hold them responsible for any breach, *any* breach, got it?"

433

"Got it, Nick. I'll get right on it."

"Yeah!" Nick slammed the phone down.

Nick was unusually antsy, like he might be losing his grip. He knew he'd felt that way in the past when something important or dangerous loomed, but the feeling he had now came up like bright lights in his brain and it overshadowed his thinking. Before, he had time and got through it. No one noticed then, he was sure. Different now.

"I'm going down," he murmured to a small statute on his desk, a replica of the Madonna, a gift from an old boss. He'd had it many years. Roberto Neethmoos, long dead and dust had given it to him. Nick didn't feel religious, but he sometimes looked at the icon and asked for things. Sometimes they worked out and he'd thank the statute. Always aware that a porcelain figurine couldn't be expected to produce anything Nick couldn't cause to happen, he still held onto it, because he didn't want to take a chance he might be wrong. The statue stared, unseeing. It gave no answer.

Nick sat slouched in his chair, motionless, deep in thought.

He heard a soft click behind the book-wall.

65

Audrey approached the steel door on the other side of the room and tried it. Locked as expected.

What did you think?

Quiet, Richard.

"Too easy," she said.

"We'll cut the lock out. I kind of doubt anyone is on the other side of that. The noise I made dropping the other door should have brought plenty of company. Maybe they're waiting on the other side, but I don't think that's the way Nick and his boy's work."

"Agree. I'll keep you covered."

"Okay." Ted went to work on the second door. It didn't take long. He cut a large circle around the lock, crisscrossed it, knocked out the innards, drilled a hole in the lock bolt and grasped it with a screwdriver. The door opened obediently.

"Nice work," Audrey said, lowering her weapon. They faced a long narrow stairway that moved away from them into darkness.

"Ready?" Ted said.

"As I'll ever be."

Ted smiled. He led the way, stopping after thirty-five steps. "Look, Audrey, the strata changes here. And here we see where the house was set into the bedrock. We should set some C-4 charges at this level, right on the wall. I think that would cause maximum damage to a majority of the structure.

They went about creating their first line of death. Four minutes later they were on their way again. Treading softly on the cement steps, they finally reached the top. Another wall faced them, and in the wall they discovered a sliding panel. Ted gingerly slid it aside and looked into Nick Trafalgar's inner office.

The big man sat in his leather chair, slumped but not sleeping. Audrey had been looking around and pointed to a button that could only be an access button.

"Ready?" Ted said.

"Yes." Audrey pushed the button. The door opened.

66

At first it didn't register, a sound from the book wall? Silently the wall swung inward and Nick saw himself staring into the bores of two .38 caliber automatics, silencers fixed. His face went up and he saw death in the eyes of the holders.

Nick came out of his trance and reached under the desk.

"Don't or die!"

Nick stopped moving.

"You're still alive. Don't test it!"

"You'll never get out of here alive. How'd you get here?" Nick seemed confused.

"Never mind. Where are your 'employees'?" Ted asked.

"About to take you out."

"Pity," Ted said, "You'll be the first."

"Who are you?"

Audrey stepped aside and Nick got his first good view of her. "You!"

"Amber Pierce, in the flesh."

"How'd you get here? Those steps lead down to the underground river." Nick's eyes got wide. "No!"

"Yes."

"There's a way through. I never suspected!"

"Now you know," Audrey, now Amber again, said.

"Enough chit-chat," Ted said, "We're here to do a job. I want to know where all your soldiers are, as well as the household staff."

"Go scratch!"

"Guess we'll have to do it the easy way." Ted pulled a strange looking gun from an inner pocket of his wet suit's oversuit and shot Nick with it. The ampoule of specially formulated drug similar to Pentothal, but infinitely more autosuggestible, took hold in a few seconds. Nick slumped onto his desk.

Makes you do things you don't want to do, Richard's mind link provided.

Hush, Richard.

"We can rouse him in five or six minutes. Get out of your suit. Let's look around." Ted went to the door and locked it. Then he climbed out of his wet suit. He stashed his and Amber's behind the door to the underground river. "Let's hope nobody knocks or tries to barge in for a few."

Amber looked at Ted quizzically. He seemed to be molding the situation to fit the facts.

"I'll explain in a couple."

They systematically went through the office, locating everything. Nick had a loaded, 9mm Beretta under the desk in a special compartment.

"Must be what he was going for," Audrey murmured. She checked it out and pocketed it. They couldn't find alarm devices.

"Arrogance or confidence?" Audrey asked.

"Arrogance. No thug can ever feel completely safe, even in the heart of his own empire..." Ted's voice trailed off as he picked up a small metal box. Only a couple of inches, square, it was incredibly heavy.

"No markings, but feels like lead. A minute sample of uranium or plutonium, I'll bet. Now why would Nick have this, here?"

"Might suggest his interest in radioactive materials from a business standpoint," Audrey offered.

"No doubt," Ted replied, "but Stoic didn't brief me on this, so it may be one of the aspects of Nick's businesses he didn't know about."

"Maybe."

Richard linked, *Likely.*

Why do you say that?

Ted told us a long time ago that Nick's empire was far flung. Stoic's got most of it pegged, but who knows?

Speaking of that, what do you suppose Stoic is doing right this instant?

Simple. He's put out the word to plug all the gaps out there and pick up Nick's people, and he's on his way here.

Here?

That's what I'd bet.

Why?

Makes sense. You can't take out an organization like Nick's, unless you want to start a worldwide search for the group that got to him. Stoic wants to remain invisible to the world and the world's intelligence agencies. I figure he has arranged for an invasion by local and state police and maybe even the National Guard to come in and clean house. My guess is he'll be somewhere in the neighborhood.

Really?

My feeling. Look at it this way. He's got the entire household of Nick's thugs on the fence and trigger-happy. My take on Stoic is he wants to end this totally, right now, so this blight on the coast of Long Island will disappear permanently and not just filter into the prison system. Some of them might even get off and disappear into the landscape.

I've often thought that Stoic was an unforgiving soul.

Seems so to me. I'm sure he has his reasons.

I'll talk to Ted about it after he gets what he wants from Nick.

A few minutes later Ted shook Nick awake. His eyes popped open but remained vacant. "You can hear me, Nick?"

"Yeah."

"The drug I put in your system will allow you to answer my questions truthfully and without reservation."

"You can do that?"

"Of course."

"Who are you?"

"To borrow a line, I am your worst nightmare. Now, how many of your people are on site?"

Nick tried to hesitate, but found he couldn't. "A hundred-fifteen including the house staff and my wife."

"How many soldiers?"

"Eighty-five."

"How many in your inner group?"

"Ten."

"That include Malfo?"

"Yeah."

"Where are they placed?" The questions went on and on. After ten minutes of intensive questioning there was a knock on the door.

"Ask who it is and tell them you're thinking and it's a bad time. Tell them to come back in a half hour."

Nick did this, as easily as if he had wanted to. He seemed surprised, but unable to do anything about it. It was Stone, wanting to make sure the boss was okay.

"Yeah, Stone, I'm thinkin'. Come back in half an hour."

"Sure, Nick."

"Tell him to tell your communications man to hold all calls." Nick did this, too. Faint footfalls told Ted that Stone had left the area.

The questioning resumed. Finally, Ted looked at his watch and told Nick he'd said enough. From a side pocket, Ted pulled some narrow material similar to duct tape.

He told Nick to hold his hands out in front of him and bound him tightly.

"You will have nothing to say until I tell you," Ted told Nick.

Nick sat silently, like an automaton on standby.

"Amber, the drug will wear off in an hour. Until then we have total control over him. We're going to get a visit from the National Guard in about a half-hour. I want to arrange for the entire population of this den of thieves to be completely subdued when they get here. I don't want any bloodshed. I wasn't sure until now, but the air conditioning system in the house will help us.

"Nick has a special hall, low down in the mansion where he gives orders to his soldiers. According to Nick, only Stone and Ray, his communications man, and his wife are in the building. Her name is Hermona and she's up on the third floor. The rest are watching the periphery for an expected invasion. No need for us to bother the wife and no reason she has to get a look at us. She's been sheltered from Nick's operations and doesn't deserve to be part of this."

"Okay."

Ted turned to Nick. "Call Ray and tell him to order all your people into the soldiers room right away. Tell him there's a change in plan and you got a way out of the mess. You'll tell them all at the meeting. Tell him to leave two sharp-eyed soldiers on the walls with cell phones to Ray, in case of a surprise. Do it now."

Nick reached for the phone. "Ray..." he began.

They looked out of Nick's windows on the mansion's second floor. Soldiers and house staff made their way slowly into the lower part of the building. Some had pistols, most had long range hunting rifles slung over their shoulders. Even the house staff was armed.

"Okay, Amber, tell Richard to head for the main gate."

Richard, what's going on?

Ted and I had a talk when you were in the bathroom back here, before you two went swimming. It was a secondary plan, if it could be worked out. Now, from what I hear, it's our best option. Ted said not to let on, as he felt you had enough to deal with crawling through that subterranean river.

YOU could have said something.

No, Ted's the boss and he knows what he's doing. I apologize for holding anything back, but I think he was right. I'm on my way. I'll be your transportation out of there. Should be at the front gate in fifteen minutes, about ten minutes ahead of the National Guard.

Well... Amber sounded hurt.

Look, my love, do you remember Ted telling you how we were to exit the mansion after we blew it up?

No.

Do you remember having Ted tell you that part of the operation was fluid and you couldn't get him to tell you more?

Yes.

Well, you were going back the way you came, okay?

NO!

Yes, and that, our esteemed leader felt was more than you needed to know.

Amber gulped. The thought of retracing their steps and swimming back nearly five miles to the hidden depot didn't appeal to her at all.

Richard, he was right.

Be there soon.

You can drive with a bum leg like that?

An automatic? Sure. Can't wait to see you.

Me, too. C'mon along, darlin'

Having trouble with these bells...

Ha, ha.

Girl, you've got fifteen minutes to finish your job. Better get crackin'.

"Richard's on his way."

"Good."

He turned to Nick and told him to get up and follow them. They left by the office door. Once outside, Ted told Nick to take the lead and walk to the soldier's room. Ted handed Amber two small, round, transparent glass vials.

"Take these and break them into the air intake of the room as soon as Nick walks in. Put this," he handed her a pad that looked like a thick chamois, "over your nose. Breath through it."

The pad had a strap that went around the head. Amber did as she was told. When Nick walked into the soldier's room through his special, small door onto his podium, Amber broke the glass vials against the metal frame. Some kind of vapor immediately entered the room and spread out innocuously.

Ted sped down the outside hallway toward the rear entrance, placing a similar pad over his nose and head. He got to the rear doors and slammed them simultaneously. No one in the hallway. Good! He dropped his silenced gun onto the floor beneath him and held on to the curved handles.

Men in the front of the room were wilting already. A few in the back sensed something wrong and tried to get out, but the doors opened inward and panic is a great way to prevent people from leaving a room.

Fifteen seconds later, resistance ceased and the last of Nick's soldiers fell to the floor. Ted held the doors another ten seconds. He then released them. Job done!

He went back to get Amber.

"There are two on the outside and Ray. We needn't worry about him. We'll have to neutralize the ones outside. Richard should be arriving at the gate in three minutes. Let's take care of this last chore."

"The people inside, unconscious?"

"No, Amber, sorry."

"They're dead?" she asked incredulously.

"Yes."

"Why should it shock me?" she asked.

"Because you have a good heart, and when it stops mattering to you, you are done," Ted said simply.

Amber didn't answer, but instead projected to Richard.

Did you know?

No, Amber, but I suspected.

Amber remained silent, but at some level she realized that Audrey had gone. She wondered if forever. Strangely, Richard remained Richard.

The two left the building and headed for the positions of the two remaining lookouts.

Richard O. Benton

67

The mansion grounds were spotted with trees, with huge open areas of green. Close cut grass reminded Amber of a well-groomed fairway. They knew the relative positions of the two watchers and it didn't take much to follow the sparse line of trees, using each obstruction to gain ground without being seen. Ted believed the watchers would be looking outward for signs of an invasion, but it only took a moment to glance back for no good reason. He wanted to be in range for a single shot from each to end it. He wanted it clean.

Amber took cover behind a forsythia bush. She spied her man ten yards ahead. She looked over toward Ted. He moved stealthily but at the moment he was in the open, blocked from his man but in sight of Amber's. Just then the man turned. He didn't recognize Ted and he let out a shout.

Amber stepped from behind the bush and made two quick shots. The man fell and didn't move. Alerted, Ted's trigger-happy target turned and blazed away. Ted, hit hard, fell to the ground. Amber, aghast, kept a tight rein on her feelings, took careful aim and brought the second man down.

She raced toward Ted and past him, made certain the second man was incapacitated and then ran to Ted. He was bleeding from three holes, two in his right leg and the third from his chest. Amber saw he had trouble breathing. The bullet to the chest had pierced the lower lobe of his left lung. It hurt Amber to do it, but she turned him and found an exit wound. The bullet had gone clear through.

Richard, come a-running! Ted's down.

Be there in thirty seconds.

Amber heard the sound of a car and suddenly it broke through the gate at high speed. The iron spearhead gate slammed on its hinges and left them. The ruined gate flew through the air and crumpled to the ground. The pieces skidded thirty feet and came to rest. Richard's car stood, smoking and steaming, going nowhere. Gasoline began to drip from the front end.

Richard, are you all right? No sound, no thought. *Richard, RICHARD! GET OUT OF THERE QUICK!*

Vapor rose from the hot engine where the gas touched it. Amber looked on in horror. Flame blossomed under the wrecked front of the car. It started small but grew rapidly.

Amber? Richard's thought, but disoriented. *Amber?*

"Ted," Amber agonized. " I gotta go, Ted. Hang on."

Ted groaned, but nodded and Amber raced away to the driver's side of Richard's car.

Richard! Hang on. Amber pulled a knife from a side pocket as she ran. The car was engulfed in flame now. Without thought she grabbed the door handle and wrenched it open. Thank God it wasn't jammed, she thought. The hot metal burned her hands. She reached over Richard and cut the seatbelt quickly. With a superhuman effort, she dragged Richard's unresponsive body out of the car and kept going until her strength gave out.

She lay on the grass next to Richard thirty feet from the burning vehicle. With a whoosh and a bang, the gas tank blew. Hot embers and car parts flew past them. She buried her face in the grass. In a moment it was over.

Amber, are we okay?

She sent Richard love and a smile. *Made it, bucko.*

Good, leg hurts. Where's Ted?

Back over there, Amber linked.

He's hurt?

Bad.

Go tend him. I'm all right here.

All right, Richard. Amber got up and moved away, back to Ted.

"Ted, what can I do?"

"Need doctor, got to get out of here." He lay in a pool of blood. His voice was too weak!

"First we have to stop the bleeding from your leg. I'll make a tourniquet." She took her knife and cut the leg off the trousers of the nearest of Nick's soldiers. She tore it into strips and tied them around Ted's leg. Using the knife as a stick she turned it until the blood slowed to a trickle, then she tied it to itself.

"Got to find a car."

Ted coughed and Amber looked at him worriedly. Blood seeped from the corner of his mouth.

"Go," he said.

Amber ran to the guard shack, looked over the keys on the rack and chose one. She hunted out the car, another Taurus, started it and drove onto the lawn next to Ted.

"You're going in the back seat, Ted." Amber pulled and lifted. Ted did his best to help. Between them he managed to get into the back of the Taurus.

"Now for Richard."

On my way, darlin'.

Amber turned and looked. Richard was on his feet, dragging his bum leg ever closer to the Taurus.

"Richard," she cried. She ran to him and got her weight under him.

"Thanks, honey. That helps."

She guided Richard into the front seat. Engine still running, she put the car in gear and drove out of the main gate.

From the rear seat, Ted said with strain in his voice, "We've got to disappear before we get stopped by the authorities. Be here any time."

They heard a gurgle from the back and silence. Amber looked fearfully in the rear mirror.

With great effort, Ted said, "Plan B. Drive to the main road and turn left. Two miles on the left, big house, beige stucco, long drive, doctor. One of us."

"Right, Ted." He didn't answer. Unconscious.

Amber drove like the wind. She straightened the road out everyplace she could.

Behind her, the muted sound of wailing sirens came to her ears.

68

"Feeling better, Ted?" Amber looked at her boss in the big bed, white sheets surrounding his brown body.

"Much."

"Great."

"How are your hands?"

"Took the skin off, but I'll survive."

"How's Richard?"

"The activity opened up his leg again. Doctor Fareed says he'll be all right. Insists he stay off it for at least a week."

"That'll be tough for the big guy."

"I'll make sure he does what he's told."

"I'm sure you will." Ted smiled at Amber.

"He's messed up that pretty face some, but the doctor says plastic surgery will fix him up."

"Considering all the times we could have been killed or otherwise, I guess we got through it pretty much all right."

"Good way to look at it."

"You two could handle some vacation time," Ted said.

"So could you."

"Can't. Been away too long already."

"No you don't. What makes you so special?"

Ted hesitated for a long time, eyes closed and Amber thought he'd gone to sleep. But then his eyes opened and he said simply, "I'm Stoic."

Amber's eyes went wide with shock. "No, you can't be!"

"'Fraid so."

"No!" Amber repeated.

"And there's one more tidbit of information I've been holding back on you. Amber, you are my daughter."

More shock! Tears welled up in Amber's eyes. "Father? Dad?"

"Not a very good one, I fear." Amber reached for him and buried her head in his chest. He said "Oof!" and Amber tried to raise her head, but Stoic's hands went up and held her there. They stayed that way for several minutes. Finally, Stoic pushed Amber gently away from her and began to talk.

"I'm sorry for the charade, Amber, but it was necessary. When I was a prisoner in the Middle East I learned a lot about a malevolent society on the east African coast run by one Rathmanizzar in the little country of Lobala. What I picked up on was that this man's vision could destroy civilization as we know it. It wasn't politics as usual. He wanted it all to come tumbling down, and without some breaks we got along the way he might have succeeded.

"Years ago when I escaped, I made my way back to America. A lot of rotten things had happened and I knew about some of it, so I tried to reenter the system carefully. I found I'd been burned—written off by our government. Essentially I didn't exist. Right then I made a conscious decision to form an anti-terrorist organization and keep all knowledge of it from the agencies of the world. I succeeded there, too, perhaps my greatest success. I've been going after Rathmanizzar and his crew for fifteen years. That's not all, but he..." He stopped for a few seconds.

"Much of what had to be done, I did myself. The fewer people involved, the less likely a leak and the disaster that would, no doubt, follow. I've been lucky. I have excellent, key people overall, and I keep tabs on every aspect of the front business and the behind the scenes business.

"When I recruited you, it wasn't a fluke. I'd been following your career for years and I even steered you toward acrobatics. Your mother knew, but I had to swear her to secrecy. She never made a mistake or a slip until the day she died. A piece of me died that day, but I was so deep under cover that I had to go on, and I did."

"Mom knew?"

"Yes." Stoic breathed softly for a time and then began again. "When Rathmanizzar managed to get his fissionable materials and the parts to make the bomb, I knew it was time to get you into the inner organization. You, and Rolph—he can stay Richard if you like, up to him—were a matched pair for what I needed. I was not wrong in that."

Richard, you hearing all this?

From behind her, lounging in the doorway to Stoic's room, Richard said, "Yes, love, every word. Somehow none of this surprises me at all."

Amber turned slowly. "You big lug!"

"Me?"

"Yeah, you."

"So, you see, you two," Ted resumed, "I have to get back to the nerve center and count my ducks again—so to speak. I'll be ready to go in another two days, Fareed says. It's what I want to do. You two are going to take that vacation, on me, of course. Where do you want to go?"

Amber spoke up brightly. "Rio!"

"Rio it is."

Richard came into the room and stood beside Stoic's bed. He gently took Amber's hand. Amber grasped his firmly.

"I'm so glad you love each other," the Moonlight Man said.

"That part of your plan, too?" Amber countered.

"Not a part I ever had any control over, but very glad anyway."

"So are we." Amber sent Richard a curled love message. Richard returned it with interest. They gazed into each other's eyes.

"Now get out of here. Get in touch when you're tired of relaxing or playing. There's plenty of work to do."

If you enjoyed

Moonlight Man
by Richard O. Benton

.....you won't want to miss

The Mission

A story of Apocalypse and rebirth of humanity
with a shocking twist.

(See prologue on the next page)

Available in paperback from

STORYCRAFT PUBLISHING
in 2010

The Mission
by
Richard O. Benton

Prologue

The world had changed beyond the ability of any mind to comprehend. It had gone through a cleansing process, but the few people who lived called it apocalypse and wondered for what reason had they been spared. They felt desolate and hopeless, and terribly alone.

For those with a deep faith in God, it was a calamity of greatest proportion. For those without, simple calamity sufficed. In the end, the faithful retained their faith out of habit because they couldn't conceive of an alternative. The nonbelievers shook their heads and held their tongues.

Twelve years before, the world had spun on its axis into chaos. Earth became in one horrifying day and one lethal night a smoking ruin. Four hundred and ninety seven thermonuclear explosions flashed and thundered across the planet. Of the thousands of missiles that remained in caches around the world, it only took four hundred and ninety-seven to destroy civilization. The bomb that wiped out San Francisco set off earthquakes along the North American and Pacific tectonic plates, as did the bomb that hit Tokyo along the Japan Trench. All of Earth's major cities died immediately. Everything else died slowly.

The bombs that hit Europe eradicated political boundaries. How can there be politics without people? In Asia, the vastness of Russia and China became instant wasteland. Some ICBM guidance systems failed and bombs exploded in every ocean Man had named.

Tidal waves destroyed millions. They avoided the slow death. How lucky!

Dormant volcanoes along the Aleutian trench reactivated, adding their noxious gasses and dust to the poisoned atmosphere. Oahu died in a cataclysmic blast. The shock wave fractured the Mona Loa and Mona Kea lava shields. Both erupted simultaneously and covered the Big Island with molten lava. There were no people to see it.

Exactly four hundred and ninety seven multi-megaton hydrogen bombs had wiped out civilization. Teeming billions died. It took only a small step to believe that the animals and insects and fish followed them into oblivion.

Malevolent forces brought all the world's nations and peoples to their knees on that day, first in lightning war and then in suicide. Apocalypse. The end. Nighttime for humanity!

But it wasn't the end of all. By some fluke, one hundred survived. Deep inside a mountain in the Canadian Rockies in a completely self-contained biosphere, one hundred scientists and technicians stood in shock and horror and waited and listened to their one radio as the world died. They were appalled, disgusted, afraid, but they were not stupid. They realized immediately that the murder of more than six billion souls along with countless trillions of other life on Earth had indefinitely extended their underground experiment.

They had to live for as long as it took in cramped surroundings designed for a two-year stay on bottled and chemically recycled air and water. They grew what they lived on. Additional plantings took up every otherwise unused space deep within the mountain. Thus they lived on the thin edge for twelve long, almost impossible years, fifty men and fifty women. A pitiful number.

They who had deliberately and willingly allowed themselves to be buried under the mountain faced their uncertain future. In a cave filled with bright souls, men and women with specialties in refrigeration, atomics and atmospheric reprocessing, and the agronomists and chemists amongst them went to work. They learned how to extend their resources well beyond the biosphere's planned timeframe. They developed the means to recycle air and water indefinitely. Plants and animals helped one another in a thankless symbiotic exchange of oxygen and carbon dioxide.

They had animals, five cows and a bull, five sheep and a ram, a male and two female goats, several dogs and cats, and a few rabbits. They carefully husbanded their animals and the population grew slowly. As they expanded their living area for plantings, they tinkered with the walls of their prison, exploring and widening small cracks here and there. In the sixth year it paid off. They unearthed the caves.

With relief they discovered that their tight surroundings had expanded. At first they feared greatly, but quickly discovered that the caves were also closed off to the surface. Nothing of the radioactivity above could leech into their environment to poison them. They made a decision to grow into the caves.

In the sixth year they ended their moratorium on children. With ample space they began to think about repopulation as a necessary feature of re-growing the race. Some resisted it, thinking that perhaps the Earth ought to spin along empty; that humanity had had its chance and blew it. Hot debate ensued. There existed surprising support for letting the race die, but in the end, they decided they owed it to themselves to try again and to do it better this time. The will to live ran strong.

Chemical inhibitors designed for recreational sex were removed and the resultant couplings began to produce children. They renamed Biosphere I and their home became New Beginnings, a hopeful name.

Chapter 1
Out of the Caves

Arthur Mavis, Chief Scientist and oldest resident, now sixty-seven and a kind of grandfather to them all asked the hundred to meet. Recruited in their early twenties, all but Arthur were now in their mid thirties. They and forty children ranging in age from one to five congregated in the large, strongly stone-pillared main hall.

Arthur addressed them. "The world remains a dangerous place, my friends, the southern latitudes especially, but my instruments tell me that radioactivity levels above us have diminished to a point where we can safely tunnel to the surface and breath the world's air again."

His next words were torn away by shouts and tumult. He stood, mouth open, wondering if these were the same people who had moved quietly about their tasks with hardly a smile for twelve long years . . .

Breinigsville, PA USA
06 October 2009
225309BV00001B/2/P